TRANSFORMED

THE LIGHTBEARER CHRONICLES BOOK TWO

DAN KENNER

AKEWNON BOOKS

CONTENTS

First published by Akewnon Books 2021 Copyright © 2021 by Dan Kenner

This novel is entirely a work of fiction. The names, characters and incidents portrayed in it are the work of the author's imagination. Any resemblance to actual persons, living or dead, events or localities is entirely coincidental.

First edition

Editing by Rachel Harris

❀ Created with Vellum

For Samuel, and the love you've found for reading.

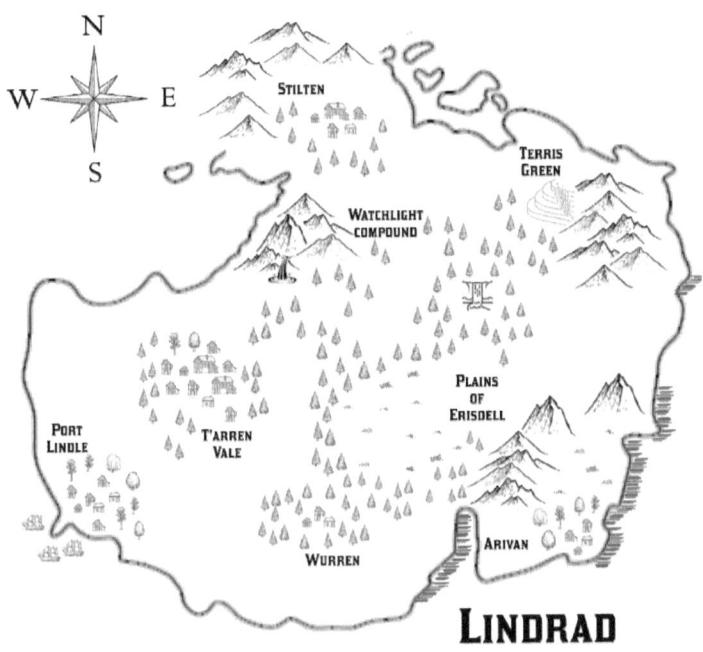

STILTEN

TERRIS
GREEN

WATCHLIGHT
COMPOUND

PLAINS
OF
ERISDELL

PORT
LINDLE

T'ARREN
VALE

WURREN

ARIVAN

LINDRAD

PROLOGUE

◇

Fire crackled in the corner-set fireplace of the lodge room. Among the tables and chairs, people milled about in a spirit of merriment. Women in colorful dresses roamed with trays of spirits and other fine foods, stopping to allow the people to eat and drink as they pleased. It was hot and dry, the air devoid of moisture due to the roaring fire. Nearly a hundred conversations caused a loud hum to thrum in the ears of those in attendance.

Luden sat in his high-backed leather chair, staring at the corner and the fire there. His hair was bright blond, curly beyond normalcy, and cropped close to his scalp. He hated growing it out to any degree, for it sprung about like an unruly pet, tickling his ears and making him look like a cherubic baby. He was of average build and had green eyes the color of the Veruvian sea.

His men never understood why he liked to face the corner. They assumed it opened him up to assassination and showed weakness that would make him vulnerable.

Luden knew better than they did.

There weren't many people in the world that would dare attack him. He found that money had given him an incredible immunity from any who might seek his demise. That, and anonymity. As of now, there were few who knew the numbers of his men, the locations of his warehouses, or even what his intentions were. The fact that he was rich allowed him to keep all these things secret and still maintain his followers, who didn't necessarily *trust* him, but obeyed him all the same.

The power of money is unnervingly effective in this world, he thought to himself.

His thoughts immediately shifted to when he'd first hired Janis to kill the boy, Marric. She was one of the best, and money controlled her easily. Unfortunately, this no longer seemed to be the case.

Now the deadly woman is likely brainwashed by the lot of them, Luden thought, seething.

Footsteps sounded behind him, barely audible above the loudness of the room. In fact, by the time he'd heard them approaching, they were nearly behind his chair.

"Master, I gots news of the wench," a burly voice said.

Luden didn't answer immediately. He wasn't in the mood to hear about Janis and the happenings of the boy named Marric.

Sighing heavily, he tore his eyes from the flickering flames and spoke in a lazy voice.

"Oh joy, share with me the news of your failure *again,*" Luden said, displeasure thick in his tone.

"We still 'aven't 'ad any luck findin'em. They were righ' slippery, they was."

Luden growled inside his throat, displaying his frustration on his face. He stood up sharply and spun on the man.

"Why in Lanser's name are you wasting my time? I gave you one job, Triliv, and you obviously are incapable of following directions. Remind me, why did I hire you in the first place?" he hissed at the tall man before him.

Triliv stood there, a look of resignation on his face. He failed to answer, which was probably better in this instance, anyway. Luden felt his anger starting to spiral out of control, the veins protruding out of his neck. He eyed Triliv, noticing how each of the man's arms was as thick as Luden's neck. His size didn't help his looks, for his eyes were beady and small, as was his nose. The only aspect of his face that seemed to match the size of his body was his mouth, which hung open most of the time.

Luden rolled his eyes and crossed his arms before him.

"Oh yes, you are impossibly large and practically unkillable."

Triliv smiled at the explanation, as if it pleased him to hear Luden saying the words. The man wasn't clever, but he sure could take a beating. In times when money and words would do you no good, brute force was often the only other way. Suddenly, the large man's pleased look melted away in an instant.

"Uhh, boss. There's a mite bit more yeh oughtta know," Triliv stated.

Taking in a deep breath, Luden steeled himself for the news. "What is it, then?" he snapped at the large oaf.

"Uhh, well. The woman killer, the assassin lady . . . uhh," the man paused.

"Triliv, will you get to the point, please?" Luden yelled.

The sound of Luden's raised voice made the man jump, but he spoke quickly.

"Th' gal, Janis, she became one of 'em—tha's what the informants 'ave said, a' leas'.

Energy sprang through Luden's whole body at hearing the news.

"Lanser's might, you can't be serious," Luden said.

Triliv just nodded. "Was a nasty one at tha', hurt lots a people."

Why in Lanser's name did the Seer not See that? Luden thought.

When the Seer had Seen Marric awakening, Luden immediately thought of hiring Janis to take him out. Normally, he and his men preferred to track down and kill Lightbearers on their own, but this one seemed different. The Seer had Seen relatively nothing about the awakening, and they were without a timeline for it. Consequently, Luden needed a discreet individual as opposed to a large group to protect his cover. Janis had seemed the obvious solution, with her minimal fee and surefire methods. There had also been the added benefit of her not knowing about Lightbearing or the risks associated with the job.

This time, though, hiring Janis hadn't been a risk worth taking. Luden offered her more than the normal bounty for the boy, but someone had intervened. His men were found dead after he sent them to Arivan to give her the job. By the time his operatives had gotten to Wurren, there were others already escorting the boy out of the town.

And one of them is a blasted Lightbearer, Luden thought, anger building inside.

He hated them all. If he could, he would eliminate them in one go. Unfortunately, he wasn't in a place to do that quite yet. He was getting closer, though. For now, he settled for little victories here and there. He'd tracked down and killed them for years, though with some effort. Meeting the Seer six months ago had changed that. Now his men could get to Lightbearers before they awakened, solving the problems before they started. In some cases, they were too late and the awakening had already happened. It complicated their elimination, but didn't make it impossible.

That is, if his men got there first. Luden knew that there were others gathering Lightbearers. They sometimes beat him to the awakenings, sweeping the targets away before his men could take them out. Working with a Seer made his success possible, but Luden had learned that Seers weren't always reliable. He assumed that, at least. It was the only explanation for why his men got to the target first sometimes, and other times they didn't.

Luden relaxed as best as he could into the chair before the fireplace. As he slumped down into the padded seat, he raised his hand in the air and wiggled his fingers. Just as expected, a servant woman appeared and bowed deeply.

"What can I git fer yeh, sir?" she said, her thick accent showing her lack of education.

"Please, the strongest thing you have."

Nodding, she turned and shuffled through the crowd of people.

A memory of his family struck a tone in his chest, sorrow building there until the woman appeared with a drink. Without too much of a pause, he grabbed it and held his other hand out, palm facing the woman, asking her to wait. He drank the contents in four swallows and put the empty flagon on the tray before asking for another.

The woman stared at him, shocked, but nodded and rushed away.

As he felt the effects of the spirits, Luden stared into the fire bitterly.

Dead—my whole family is dead, and for what? My sister's 'blessing' of Light-bearing?

The memory flashed in his mind of his sister doubled over in pain, his parents consoling her before they were blasted to pieces before his eyes. He'd lived for years in his grief, until he finally discovered the reality of Lightbearing and its plague on the world.

His throat burned from the strength of the drink. He could feel it in his stomach. It wasn't comfortable, but it wasn't painful, either.

"You called, sir?" a voice suddenly spoke behind him.

Luden's stomach clenched and he turned to see him—the Seer—standing behind the chair. Hair long and dark, he kept it tied back in a pony-tail that stuck out straight from his head. Eyes green and brooding, they topped a slender nose and a tight, sharp mouth. One wouldn't know that he was a skilled fighter with practically any blade until they found it in their stomach. That, coupled with his Lightbearing power, was enough to keep Luden's anger in check.

"Ah yes, here he is, the man of the hour. Care for a drink?" Luden said, miming holding up a glass.

"You know I don't take drinks from anyone unless I've seen how they are prepared," the man said flatly. "You may be drunk, but you are not stupid—this I know. Why have you asked for me?"

Luden grunted at the man's brusqueness, but internally, he appreciated it.

"While your service has been helpful, *Seer*, you know I could kill you at any moment."

A pause.

"You know I'd See that long before it happened, and simply kill you first."

Luden's stomach twisted at the comment.

"You fogging *fool*. Was that a threat?" Luden shouted, standing up and facing the man.

"Threat—no. Reminder—yes. Now, what is it you wanted from me?"

"Have you Seen the boy? Have you Seen any awakenings? Ugglyn's back-side, have you Seen anything at all?"

The Seer's face didn't change, other than a pointed stare and some exaggerated blinks.

"I cannot See Marric's location or where they are going. I *do* know that he's with a man named Avryn, and Janis, the assassin you wasted your funds on."

Luden's anger rose again, building like a wild sea in a hurricane. Still, he held it in reserve to avoid death from the man before him. He was faster than Luden, that was sure.

"Keep your opinions to yourself, Seer."

"I don't believe you hired me just to keep my opinions to myself. If I did keep my opinions in check, I imagine that you and your men would have been killed long before now."

The crackling of the fire behind Luden seemed to get louder as the anger continued to rise in him. As much as he hated to admit it, the man was right. When he'd first paid the Seer, he didn't have any idea how invaluable he would become. He was not only useful with his gifts, but with his intellect as well. Though the Seer didn't disclose much of his past, Luden knew that he had combat experience from his profession, though what it had been, Luden couldn't be sure. The Seer was unnervingly clever, and understood the general rules of engagement. Luden, against his better judgement, had taken the man's advice on numerous occasions, only to find that it was spot on.

Even so, Luden didn't have to like it. The fact that he employed any Lightbearers at all felt like a betrayal to his parents and his sister.

Pushing away the thoughts, he focused once more on the Seer.

"You may have been right in the past, but you are only here for one reason, and you seem to be failing at that right now."

The Seer smiled, clearly not threatened or concerned by Luden's tone.

"And *you* are well aware that I am only here for the substantial pay. If I found any other jobs as lucrative, I'd have left ages ago," the man said, a slight smile on face. He looked perfectly comfortable standing in front of the fuming Luden, which infuriated Luden even more.

"Let me remind you *again* that I cannot control when I See awakenings. I don't control when they happen. If I did, you wouldn't be wasting so much time fattening up your subordinates." As he said the words, he shoved his thumb over this shoulder. The party around them was unexpected, but Luden couldn't have his men leaving and betraying him. If he treated them right, he was likely to keep them. Hiring greedy men and women was to his advantage, considering his unlimited access to money. Just then, one of his men laughed loudly and fell to his backside, where he giggled, half-conscious. It was clear that he had drunk far too much for even his own body weight. Cheeks red, he quickly fell into a drunken slumber.

Luden stared at him, unimpressed. A part of him thought to discipline the man for being so ridiculous and foolish, but he thought better of it. He *had* told them to have fun, to live it up and not worry about tomorrow. He couldn't take that back now, not without being loathed.

Some men got their power from their strength, some from fear, some from being smarter than those around them. Luden wasn't in a place to use any of those. His power came from something he was just born into: money.

Lanser help me if they realize I'm little more than that, Luden thought.

Luden looked back at the Seer and was about to say something when the man's eyes began to glow violent red, shining brightly, small beams shooting forward, spreading out and disappearing into the air.

Breathing heavily, Luden stood there, counting the seconds before the red glow softened and the man's eyes returned to normal.

"Well, wasn't that timing just right? There is an awakening right here in Stilten. I think we got lucky with this one—I don't See any interruptions from the others in the chase for this Lightbearer."

Luden bared his teeth, pleased at the news.

"Are you absolutely sure of this?" Luden asked.

The Seer looked at him, bored at the question.

"I can check again, if you like. I am sure, however, that I Saw enough before and after to know that this will be an easy target. The only thing we need to watch out for is that he'll be a Mover. Can't be too close to him when he awakens. That is, if we let him awaken at all. We could just kill him before he even gains his powers—"

Luden held up his hand, interrupting the Seer.

"No, I am very eager to try this new ... serum of yours."

Pride showed on the Seer's face when he spoke.

"I am confident that it will work. The instructions were very clear when they were given to me."

Luden nodded.

"Yes, yes. I haven't had the chance to give it a try. Perhaps now is the right time?"

Pulling out a short dagger from his belt, Luden used it to pop the cork off a slightly glowing silvery poison. Oddly, it smelled of nothing. One would have thought the vial housed only water with such a lack of scent. The sight of it amended that impression quickly.

Taking care to not touch it, Luden stepped up to the man that had just fallen down. Crouching low, he tipped the vial into his mouth until a few drops fell in.

In his sleep, the man giggled at the feel of the liquid in his mouth and he gulped it down hungrily, likely expecting it to be more spirits. After a few beats, his eyes shot open and he screamed.

"The fog is 'appenin'?" he shouted, grasping desperately at the shirt over his stomach.

As the man pulled his shirt up, lines of silver streaked outward on his skin. They grew quickly, twisting around his back and down his legs.

The man tried to speak again but only gurgling came from his mouth. He bled from his mouth and nose, but only for a moment. The blood was consumed by the same silver liquid before turning to smoke as well. His eyes rolled back in his head and he collapsed, dead.

Luden stared at him, a bit nervous at the strength of what he'd just seen. Luden corked the vial immediately, afraid of any bits of the poison getting loose. Knowing that he needed to explain himself, he stood straight and announced loudly to the room, which had gone deathly quiet at the scene, "He was a traitor! I found him sharing secrets to our enemies! This is what happens to those who betray me."

It was a lie, of course, but Luden couldn't let them think he'd just killed a man for no reason. Money might not keep their loyalty through something like that.

A few people stared at the man's corpse, but most turned back to their tables and drinks, continuing as before.

By now his anger had faded, and instead he felt a joy that should have made him feel more self conscious, guilty even. Instead, he knew they had discovered something that could turn the tide against the blasted Lightbearers. For years, he'd tried to hunt them with little success, trying to best them one at a time. Unfortunately for him, fighting them without powers of his own proved too costly.

That is, until he'd met the Seer. He'd almost killed the man on sight, but when he had explained to Luden how he could help him, how they could get to Lightbearers *before* they got their powers . . . that had changed things.

And now we have something that will help us take them out even after they awaken.

The pleasure burned in his chest. Luden chuckled at the feeling.

"What of the boy's father? Have you found him?" Luden asked.

The Seer dipped his head in affirmation. "Yes, he's traveling north, though I am unsure where. It took me time to See him, but your description provided enough detail."

Luden smiled wickedly.

"I presume some other Seers, perhaps the boy himself, will soon locate the old man. Make sure our men know exactly when and where they can expect to run into the Lightbearers coming for him. I think a true test of this poison is in order," Luden said.

Lifting his hand, he looked at the vial and turned to the fire. He viewed the contents with the flickering light of the fire behind it. The liquid, almost black, but slightly silver and glowing, sloshed around the bit of empty space at the top as he moved it side to side.

It's time for me to eradicate every Lightbearer from Lindrad, Luden thought darkly.

1

Janis sat in a stone chair, opening and closing her hand repeatedly. Her other hand held her favorite dagger, straight and slim, as long as her forearm. She wasn't looking at the dagger, however, but instead at the hand she was flexing. The stone walls around her were gray and made from the same material as the chair she sat in, which seemed comical to her as it caused the chairs and tables to blend into their background. She wondered if this was intended by Evenir or if it was a design oversight.

As she opened her hand again, Light flashed in her palm and a second dagger appeared there, this one made of blue Light. She squinted at the intensity of the burst of Light, but it was only a reflex. Despite the Light being piercing and bright, her eyes were unaffected by it. In fact, she could stare directly into it without any trouble at all. This only added to how unnatural it felt. As intended, it was an exact replica of the real steel dagger in her other hand.

Lightbearing is much more complex than I imagined, she thought to herself.

It had been two weeks since the incident at the hidden cave where she had nearly been killed—twice. She recalled bleeding profusely while Prost stood before her, ready to deliver the final blow. If Avryn had not shown up, she most certainly would have died right then and there, but he had. After

Evenir operatives had come to help, the battle with Watchlight had turned for the better. Janis remembered engaging with Prost, his speed and battle prowess matching her own. Around them flashed blue and red Light repeatedly from the Lightbearing on both sides as they fought.

As if in rebellion to the thought, the Light-created dagger snuffed out, the blue Light disappearing into nothing. However, after only a moment, the Conjured dagger flashed back into existence in her hand.

Janis stared at her hand as she summoned and dismissed the blade a few more times before she gripped the blue-Light hilt of the dagger more tightly and raised both blades to compare them. She inspected the two different-but-same blades and found them to be virtually identical. There was a small nick in the metal blade of the real dagger. The same nick could be seen in the Light-made dagger, in exactly the same place.

In a rapid motion, Janis struck the two blades together and the familiar metal-on-metal clash rang through the cavern. The blade of Light held strong, as if it was made of the same material as the steel one. She placed the two blades together again and rubbed them, observing the sound that it made. It indeed was the sound of two metal daggers rubbing together, which still astounded her.

Her mind wandered back to the day of the battle. She remembered staring Prost down, bleeding from the new wound he'd given her after Evenir joined the battle. She wasn't panicked, she was merely taking her time to analyze the situation as she paused momentarily. Then it had happened.

Janis remembered the pain more than anything. It was by far the worst pain she had experienced at any moment in her life. That was saying a lot, considering her profession as an assassin. At any rate, the pain had started in her stomach, as if she'd eaten something bad and it was just getting to her. Unfortunately, it wasn't something that benign. Pain had rapidly spread through her chest, limbs, and even to her head. Her vision blacked out and she felt like she became a ball of pain, her mind losing access to all her other senses and thoughts.

Then she'd seen some pretty strange things; things that both made sense and not at all.

Janis shook her head slightly at that thought. She had analyzed and remembered what she'd seen multiple times, but didn't feel that now was the time to do so again. Instead, she thought about waking up on the bed of furs next to Marric, his youthful face full of concern for her. She had been relieved to see that he survived. What stood out more from that memory were his next words.

"Janis . . . you just awakened."

Her mind reeled at the words and she still could not believe them, even as she sat there now, holding a dagger made completely out of Light. She tightened her grip on the handle of the real dagger and felt her gut twist slightly. Lightbearing had always felt unfamiliar, and it *still* felt that way, even now. Janis felt tainted, though she couldn't describe why.

She let the Light dagger fall from her hand and it snuffed into nothingness.

Where is Marric, anyway? she thought.

Since the boy had Awakened, he'd been passionately training and learning about his new abilities. Janis could scarcely keep track of where he was at any moment, but it was clear that he was quite thrilled about his newfound powers. After all, he was somewhat of an anomaly, even for a Lightbearer. The people here at Evenir definitely treated him so as well. They called him *Iridar,* which to Janis meant absolutely nothing, since she didn't speak any of the old language. Avryn had said it meant thrice-powered.

Marric had awakened with three full powers of Lightbearing. Those who awakened normally only had one greater and one lesser power, thus making him an anomaly. Even more than regular combat skills, the people of Evenir gave the greatest weight to Lightbearing prowess. It was for this reason that Janis felt somewhat dismissed by Evenir at large, despite her considerable non-lightbearing abilities. Many simply saw her as "Iridar's scary companion," which showed their fear of her, but not their respect.

Janis had always appreciated being labeled as scary, but she didn't appreciate being underestimated. It was almost as if since she'd awakened, her poor Lightbearing had somewhat negated her other skills in the eyes of many in Evenir. Maybe they were right, to an extent. Something about being awakened had made her lose confidence.

She only stayed at Terris Green because she wasn't confident she'd be able to resume her assassin duties now that she had this plague of Light-bearing. An assassin thrived in the shadows, hiding either literally or figuratively from their mark, but more importantly from those that protected the quarry. What if she was in the shadows, about to eliminate the target, when a burst of Light exploded from her unintentionally?

Janis blanched at the thought. *So much for subtlety at that point.*

As much as she hated to admit it, Evenir knew about Lightbearing, and she knew absolutely nothing. It seemed in her best interest to stay for some time, to listen and learn. She *had* tried to train with some of their teachers, but she was no good. No one knew what to make of her. She had awakened, but to what, not a soul knew. As far as she could tell, she had minuscule abilities in each of the classes, each one so weak that it seemed as if she didn't have a class at all. They had tried her with all seven of the classes, but in each trial, she only displayed weak renditions of the powers. It was as if she had no real power whatsoever.

This only frustrated her more. She apparently had drawn the short end of the stick. When she'd first tried to come to terms with the fact that she had these powers, she thought she might at least be able to make use of them, but no. Instead, she had this inconvenient Light that just got in the way, and no added abilities to show for it.

That is, except for the strange things that happened every once in a while. It was actually because of one of these strange things that they'd given up on her. Yesterday, as she was failing to produce destroying orbs on command, she'd somehow exploded the whole cavern and caused the ceiling to come down, almost killing herself and the instructor. Fraltan, the Destroyer instructor, said it was one of the most impressive displays of Destroying he'd seen in a newly awakened Lightbearer. However, after the incident, she'd shown only weak Destroying abilities. Before that, she'd accidentally chopped down a supporting pillar with a summoned sword and the ceiling almost gave in. Before that, well . . . lots of unfortunate instances.

With each odd manifestation of extreme power, her Lightbearing had only been weak and unhelpful afterward, so many began to see her as some type of useless anomaly. She had heard the word 'broken' at one point. The speaker later found his belt cut by someone in the middle of the eating area, his pants sliding to his ankles.

Janis chuckled darkly. No one called her broken and got away with it.

With each incident, she'd spent time in the in-between, analyzing what happened to try to make sense of it. Not once had she gotten any answers. If anything, the in-between just made it all more confusing.

A shuffling sound to her left interrupted her thoughts. She stood to face the oncoming noise, stiffly gripping her real dagger. She relaxed slightly when she saw that it was just Avryn coming down the hall. He wasn't the quietest person when he walked, which surprised her, considering his fighting skill.

"What are you working on, here?" he asked, seeming genuinely curious.

"I'm merely reflecting on the irony of my situation," she said, looking past him to make sure there wasn't anything amiss.

He raised his eyebrow at the comment, clearly not understanding.

"I am not the least bit surprised that you don't understand, Avryn. You, who walk as loud as a donkey. Stealth used to be my main asset, but with my new *skills*—" the word dripped with sarcasm, "—well, I can kiss it goodbye."

Avryn just stared at her, opting to not say anything. Instead, his mouth turned up at the side.

Janis sighed in frustration and opened her empty hand. A flash of blue Light announced the arrival of the dagger, shining with brilliance. Taking the opportunity to not only prove her point, but get rid of some frustration, she shouted and jabbed the dagger into the wall, where it clanged off, not even putting a scratch there. She let it fall and disappear.

"Lightbearing is useless to me. I've managed to learn nothing in the past few weeks, and what I *have* learned about, my powers aren't capable of handling. At this point, Prost is more useful when up against Lightbearing."

The man's face looked thoughtful.

"Yes, being immune to Lightbearing has its advantages, save for the Fixing immunity."

Janis stared at him flatly, anger growing in her eyes and posture. Avryn's face flushed.

"But that doesn't help you. I'm sorry. I—"

"*What do you want?*" Janis said through gritted teeth.

"Hmm?" Avryn responded. It took a moment for him to realize that she didn't want to discuss the matter further. "Oh—yes, Magness would like to see us all in the war room."

Janis didn't feel in the mood to talk to that woman, or to anyone else for that matter, but it was better than sitting here wasting away and doing nothing. She stood and stalked down the hallway where Avryn had just come. Avryn followed without a word, which didn't bother her one bit.

Perhaps it isn't in my best interest to stay. I am getting nothing from these people, nor they from me, she thought.

But then there was Marric.

The boy had proven very adept at his powers since his awakening. Unlike herself, Marric clearly had a class. Well, *classes.* Before the incident at the safe house where she'd awakened, Marric had shown some skill with his Seeing powers. Though it unsettled her to no end, Seeing had proven very helpful. Considering the dangerous situations they were in while Marric used it, his Seeing had saved their lives a few times. Janis was impressed by Marric's quick development of his abilities, perhaps even proud. Though, she didn't relish the fact that he'd become the talk of Evenir while she'd become the liability.

Part of Janis was proud of his accomplishment, and part of her loathed him for it. The only thing that kept her going was knowing that she was still quite good at fighting and her speed was unmatched.

She and Avryn entered the last chamber before the war room, which was a type of library, just before the beautiful dark-wood doors with the carving of the tree. A man was sitting to their left, reading a book and starting to doze off. Each time he started to nod off, the hovering blue orbs Lighting the room would start to flicker and fade, causing him to wake up. For a moment, the two watched him, Avryn looking amused.

Avryn walked up to the desk where the man sat, and slammed his hand down loudly. The poor man threw himself backwards at the sound, his chair toppling over. As he fell, the Lights in the room flashed intensely, causing the other people in the room to grumble and cover their eyes. Janis knew that the effect had not only occurred here, but in the whole compound for the thousands of others in these caves.

"You need to stay awake, Ulig. We can't have this place going dark all of a sudden." There was a bit of sternness in Avryn's voice, but he smiled, clearly amused.

Ulig blushed and shuffled to his feet. He grabbed the book, which he'd thrown in his surprise, and positioned himself behind the desk.

"Uh . . . sorry, sir. Won' 'appen again, eh? Oi jus' ain't been able t'sleep, see?" the little man said sheepishly.

The short man was completely bald, and about a head shorter than Janis. His build was strong, clearly having worked physically hard in his life, yet his height made him seem like a child, much younger than his face actually showed him to be.

"Perhaps discuss the Lighting rotation with Narinda. See if you can't get time to capture some extra sleep."

"Aye, S'ren. Oi'll do jus' tha'. Sorry."

The little man sat back in his chair and resumed reading his book. Avryn, seeing this, walked over to one of the others in the room sitting on a couch, studying a book as well. He said something to the man, then gestured at Janis to follow him. This she did with curiosity, wondering what he said to the lounger. True to his nature, Avryn didn't wait a moment before telling her.

"I don't think that Ulig will be able to stay awake for much longer, so I asked Tralist to keep an eye on him and poke him awake if needed." Avryn was amused, that was clear.

How in Lanser's name does he remember all these people's names? Janis thought. She'd only met a few dozen whose names she could remember, but the fact that Avryn seemed to know everyone at Terris Green was fascinating.

Janis nodded at his assessment, but said nothing. Instead, she trained her eyes on the carving in the wood of the double doors just before them. It was an exquisite artwork, indeed. Each small branch of the winding tree had many smaller twigs breaking off into many different directions, and she wondered how long such a thing could have taken to make. Images appeared among the branches, most of them seeming random. Symbols here and there were carved and housed by circles to make them distinguishable. They were in the old language, so what they meant, Janis couldn't know. But they were quite fascinating, and somewhat familiar. Her eyes landed on one of the faces that was carved of a beautiful woman.

She really does look like Marric here.

Evenir's current leader, Magness, was sister to Talatha, the woman in the carving. Magness had intimated to Janis that Talatha was Marric's mother, who had since passed on. How she died hadn't been discussed, but Janis got the feeling it wasn't something that would be easy to get out of Magness.

It was obvious that the face was carved in a way to stand out, and it did that very well.

"It is quite a scene, isn't it?" Avryn followed her gaze. "The skill and time that had to have been required for this beautiful work of art is something that I can't fathom."

Janis grunted in response.

"Are you finished examining it, then? I didn't want to open it until you were done."

The assassin realized that they'd been standing just before the door for some time and hadn't moved to enter. Avryn apparently had seen her inspecting the door and didn't want to interrupt.

Janis tried to act casual about her interest.

"Fine artwork, however fine it may be, isn't worth an assassin's time unless it plays a part in their undercover role."

Then she unceremoniously pushed the doors open herself.

"I'll take that as a yes, you are done," Avryn said, raising his eyebrows at her statement.

Inside the room stood a medium-sized round table covered with an intricate map of Lindrad. Magness stood bent over the map, pointing at a spot that Janis couldn't see. With her were three others. One was a woman with long blonde hair down to her waist. Her features were sharp and petite, yet she was very tall, as tall as Magness herself. They both stood almost a handspan taller than Janis was. To her right stood a man of middle age with pure white hair. He wasn't balding in any place, so his hair seemed to stand out. He had a bushy white mustache which he twirled in his fingers, looking thoughtful. Finally, another woman, this one dark-skinned with deep black hair, sat brooding in one of the chairs that ringed the outside of the room.

Her hair spun in tight ringlets, making her head appear much larger than it actually was.

A head popped out behind Magness and smiled broadly. Marric was almost fully covered by the leader's stature and height. He waved at Janis and Avryn and gestured for them to join the group.

"—we must not give up our search, it would really give us a tactical advantage over Watchlight if we could just locate their lair," Magness said.

"But General, we've 'ad no success findin' it," the mustached man said. "Even if'n we 'ad more people, which we don', Oi fear tha' we just don' 'ave wha' we need t'locate it. They 'ave Shielders prolly working overtoim, 'cause our Seers 'ave found no luck. Even Marric ain't Seen nuttin'."

Marric stiffened at the comment.

"I have been trying, ma'am, I hope you know that," Marric said, blushing deeply.

Magness merely waved her hand dismissively.

"You need not worry about that, Marric. I fear this has nothing to do with your newly developing powers. Our most skilled Seers are having trouble as well."

Janis noticed that when she said this, the tall blonde woman looked both embarrassed and offended.

"If there were some way to extract the information from Marric's subconscious, then we would have more success," Avryn said, causing the whole group to turn.

"Tha' is only a dream. Ain't nobody seen a thing such loike an' Oi don' think it be worth bringin' up again," the tall blonde woman said, apparently annoyed.

Avryn shrugged, unaffected by the tone of the woman.

"You know, I've said this before," Janis said, nonchalance lacing her words, "but I followed Prost when he abducted Marric at the falls. If I go there, I think that I could trace my steps back to where their lair is. I've done this hundreds of times, and I know I can find them."

"We've been over this, Janis," Magness said, "that place is not safe. Watchlight is inevitably there with an ambush. It's not safe for you or any of us to go there at this time."

The blonde woman scoffed loudly.

"Not t'mention tha' t'was dark when yeh followed 'em, no? Oi've Seen it. Can' see a Foggin' thing in yer past. No useful Seein' fer us at all."

"The darkness comes with the profession, which you'd know if you were more than a simpleton," Janis said condescendingly while giving the woman a simpering look.

The blonde woman's body stiffened at the comment, and she balled her fists at her side.

"For Lanser's sake, would you two please stop? We don't have time for this banter," Magness plowed ahead, "our scouting parties will continue to make their rounds. Based on what we've gathered from all of you, we feel that their lair is somewhere in this area."

She pointed to a spot on the table that Janis was still too far away to see. Even if she could, she wasn't confident she would know what it all meant. She could read maps to some degree, but only when there were major cities or landmarks; she hadn't learned to read coordinates yet. Then again, she'd never needed to.

"I could easily find my way there, this is a waste of time," Janis said under her breath.

Magness ignored her comment, continuing.

"It would be too risky for our soldiers to go back to the falls. Watchlight is most definitely watching the area, as *previously* mentioned."

Janis shrugged before doggedly arguing, "So we bring a bigger group than them. I could at least pick off a bunch before I went down, anyway. I see no other option."

Magness smiled, though not joyfully, more like she appreciated the sentiment.

"Though your commitment is refreshing, Janis, I do believe that isn't the best plan of action. At least, not yet."

The dark-skinned woman piped up suddenly at that.

"I agree with the assassin, we can't sit on this much longer. Each moment we wait is an opportunity for Watchlight to find Terris Green and ambush us. The faster we find them—" she paused, moving her hands toward the table where a few figurines suddenly glowed blue and were thrown off the table as if some invisible force and shoved them.

Janis tensed at the event and trained her eyes on the dark-skinned woman, reassessing.

Magness noticed Janis's reaction and looked at her curiously. The look lasted only a moment before Magness spoke.

"Oh—silly me, I failed to introduce you to my other generals, Janis."

Magness gestured to the dark-skinned woman first. "Alsry is a Mover, as you can tell, and she heads up companies six through ten. She also oversees the training of all Movers here at Evenir. As you have seen, she is quite skilled in the ability."

Alsry glanced again at Janis.

My kind of person, Janis thought, inclining her head in acknowledgement.

"Turrin, here," Magness said, pointing to the burly man with the mustache, "is a Conjurer, and heads up companies sixteen through twenty-one. Likewise, he trains and oversees all Conjurers here."

Turrin smiled brightly and walked over to them, extending his hand out.

"Pleased t'meet yeh, Janis. Heard a roit bunch about yeh an' 'ave been eager t'see yeh in person."

Janis looked at him, then down at his hand, then back at his face, not moving her own at all.

The burly man only chuckled and walked back to the table, shaking his head. Magness, observing the whole exchange, raised an eyebrow at Janis as if irritated by her reaction.

She shouldn't be surprised, Janis thought, *I'm not one for shaking hands unless I'm undercover.*

Clearing her throat, Magness continued on with the introductions.

"This is Rivelen," the Evenir leader said, gesturing to the unnaturally tall blonde woman. "She's our most accomplished Seer and leader of companies one through five."

Rivelen stood up a bit taller at the introduction and stuck her nose into the air as if she was the highest authority in the room. She did not, however, say anything else. Janis stared at her flatly, even more annoyed than before. It was clear by her comments that the woman had an ego, making Janis inclined to contradict everything that she said. Janis loved pushing audacious people to their limits.

"Could never afford an education, then?" Janis replied.

Rivelen's face turned red and she huffed out loud.

"Fog it, wench, 'ow dare yous attack me such loik? Oi ain't dun nuttin' t'ya, eh? T'ain't moi fault yous chose a roit man-loik job an' became a brute."

She was shaking her fist at Janis, much like an old crone would to a group of troublesome youngsters.

Janis smoothly whipped out her long dagger and held it aloft.

The blonde woman's eyes widened and she backed away, hands now in the air in surrender.

"Janis, stop that right now!" Magness said, stepping between the two.

Grunting, Janis put the dagger away and folded her arms.

"Sorry, it's just a habit when I see a towering urchin coming at me."

Rivelen's face seemed to take on a deeper shade of red, but she said nothing else.

"Are you two quite done with your spat?" Magness snapped at them both. "We don't have the luxury of time for any infighting. Either get over it, or get out."

That struck Janis. Technically, she could walk out at any time and move on with her life. Unfortunately, the blasted Light was preventing her from doing that, even if she wanted to. She had to learn some control over her powers.

Magness swept over to the table smoothly and resumed speaking.

"Of course, you've met Avryn, my second. With his unique abilities and excellent leadership, we are lucky to have him. With the rest of the generals and companies out scouring for the lair, we can't afford to let any more leave Terris Green. On the off-chance that Watchlight is able to track us down, we need to be prepared for an assault."

She gripped the table hard, her knuckles turning white as she did so. After a lengthy silence, she sighed.

"For now, the best we can do is pray to Lanser that the other companies find something," she paused and looked at Marric, "and continue training Marric. Perhaps there is something that he can glean from his past using his Seeing."

Everyone in the room looked at Marric and he blushed.

The boy turns red so easily, someone might think it's really his natural color, Janis thought.

As he always did, Avryn took the liberty to speak up and ease the tension of the conversation.

"And how is that training going then, Mar?"

The long-haired man had adopted Marric's nickname that he'd had since he was a boy. Janis thought it far too mushy and odd to use, so she continued calling him by his real name. Marric, however, appeared to like it —his expression lit up every time Avryn used it.

"It's going very well, as far I can tell," he said modestly.

"Why don't you show the generals your progress, Marric?" Magness asked kindly.

Making a show of it, Marric held out his hand and Conjured a bow, much like the one he'd carried on their journey from Wurren, seemingly ages ago. The bow was simple, but looked perfect for his size. In his other hand, an arrow of pure blue Light flashed into existence. Calmly, yet quickly, he nocked the arrow and drew it back in a clearly practiced fashion. With an exhale, he let the arrow fly. It zipped through the air with a swish and connected with the wall, a loud crack echoing in the stone room.

Janis narrowed her eyes as she saw that the arrow had pierced the stone wall easily, causing web-like cracks and chipping bits off here and there. The whole group nodded in approval. Marric smiled and let the arrow fall, causing it to disappear to nothing.

Turrin chuckled loudly.

"Well, Oi'll be. Oi fink Oi picked the roit person t'train yeh, din't Oi?" he said, putting both hands on his belly as he said it.

Rivelen spoke up then.

"What of yer Seeing? A class tha' needs o' bit o' concentration and *skill*." She gave a hard stare at Turrin as she said it, provocation in her eyes.

Marric nodded and breathed in, closing his eyes. Not a moment later, he opened them, eyes aglow with blue Light.

"What do yeh see?"

Janis's skin crawled slightly at the sight of his eyes, but mostly because he had said the same words back to Rivelen at the same time, with the same accent.

"I See us here."

As if it was rehearsed, Rivelen and Marric spoke the same words at the same time, in exactly the same way.

"Impressive. Oi'm 'appy t'see the old crone ain't killed yeh wif all the meditatin'."

Rivelen smiled, obviously pleased with the display. All along, Marric's eyes glowed blue and he looked off in the distance. Suddenly, he gasped and dove to the side, Janis crouching down and pulling out her dagger almost simultaneously. As soon as he jumped to the side, a glass mug flew through the air right where he'd been standing a moment before. Wreathed in blue Light, it flew with a force much stronger and faster than a normal throw would be. Rather than hitting the ground, however, it stopped and redirected toward Marric again. Eyes still aglow, he dodged the mug as it soared at his face a second time. Finally, his eyes dimmed and he cupped his hands as if gripping something. The chair to his side glowed an intense blue and he raised the chair in front of him as the mug flew at him once more. It hit the makeshift shield, shattering into pieces.

"Very impressive," Alsry said, lightly clapping her hands. "I see that your Moving has improved as well."

Marric sat down heavily, gasping loudly from the quick exchange. Janis stared at him, surprised at his quick reactions and how versatile his powers seemed to have become. How he'd made so much progress in such a short amount of time, she couldn't understand. His body wasn't up to the physical task yet, as she could see, but his reaction times and ability to not freeze up like before were impressive.

Janis felt a pang of jealousy, knowing that her Moving had proven useless in her own attempts at training.

"I appreciate the progress you've all made teaching Marric, but next time, can you show me without destroying the war room?"

Alsry put her fist to the palm of her other hand and bowed to Magness.

"I am sorry, mistress, but a Mover must be prepared at all times. He can't fully show you his progress without somewhat realistic threats."

The leader waved her hand dismissively, as she seemed to do frequently, and looked at Turrin. She pointed to the wall where the Light arrow had put a hole and a large set of cracks.

Turrin shrugged and put on an innocent looking face.

"Oi din' tell 'im to do tha'. 'E chose tha' 'imself."

Magness sighed, eyes rolling up with a slight shake of her head.

"And I'm sure that your training has *nothing* to do with it. As I recall, part of a Conjurer's training is increasing the strength and solidness of their Conjures. I know that you pay Fixers to clean up the messes in your training hall, you can't fool me."

The burly man grinned annoyingly and shrugged again. He reminded Janis a lot of Harmel.

Her mind shifted to the silly man, their jovial companion on their journey from Wurren. Inside, she felt annoyed as she thought of his antics, but at the same time she felt fondness for him that she couldn't describe. She hadn't seen him since she'd woken up, because he'd left Terris Green with one of the companies.

Harmel had taken a hard blow to the head from a rock wall that had exploded during the scuffle at the safe house, and Janis had thought him dead. It wasn't until she woke a few days later that she heard of him getting Fixed and going along his merry way.

"Avryn, if you don't mind."

The man smiled warmly and moved to the wall. Placing his hand there, a blue and intense Light glowed from his palm and a cracking sound occurred as the wall knit itself together again, pieces and dust from the floor moving swiftly back into their place.

"Thank you, friend."

"It's my pleasure. I'm happy to make myself useful whenever I can."

After Fixing the wall, he set to work on the mug, the table, and the chair that had been Moved by the exchange.

"As I said, I am pleased to see progress being made, Marric. Remember, however, to not wear yourself out. I fear that at any moment, Watchlight could appear on our terraces, ready to fight. We need all Lightbearers and warriors alike to be ready for that at any moment."

Janis squeezed her daggers tightly at the comment. Part of her was itching for that to happen. She would be happy to dig her knife into Prost after their last exchange.

The door to the room suddenly burst open with a loud bang and Janis, clearly tightly wound from the conversation, crouched low and pulled her daggers into her hands aggressively.

Everyone in the room looked at her, a mixture of emotions on their faces from anger, to fear, to surprise.

The man who had entered stood there, frozen from seeing Janis move in such a combative way.

With a stern voice, Magness spoke loudly to the newcomer.

"What is it that would cause you to burst so suddenly into a war council, courier?"

He stood there shaking for a moment more, a bit of wetness on his trousers.

Janis noticed that his clothes reflected that he was a messenger. He was of medium height with long legs and of slender build. It was clear that he was not strong, but she had a suspicion that he was quite fast. Breathing loudly, he gasped for air again before turning to Janis and backing away as if she would jump out at him.

Without looking away from Janis, he spoke.

"Companies eleven and twelve have returned. They've taken a heavy hit from Watchlight."

2

Prost sat on the edge of his bed, massaging his forearm, frustrated at the feeling of pain that still lingered slightly from the battle with Janis. The red Light seemed to tease him as it hovered near the low ceiling of the cave in which he slept. Normally he'd have already risen from bed and begun making his rounds in the Watchlight compound, but this morning he hadn't felt up to it. A slight lance of pain ran up his arm as he opened his hand, and he growled at the feeling.

He had been hurt before, that wasn't the problem. The problem was that the injuries he'd sustained from the engagement with Janis weren't from normal hand-to-hand combat. Prost considered all of his wounds and scars —save those on his face—as a lesson. It was an indication of something he had since learned from.

This was different.

Prost closed his eyes and thought back to the fight. He saw the fire in the woman's eyes as she clutched her blade tightly, her knuckles white. Blood poured from a wound on her arm where he had struck her. He remembered the slight sting on his face where she had cut him and almost laughed at its insignificance to the pain he felt now.

Confidence, that is all he remembered feeling. It was ironic, because he could see that she felt the same, though he couldn't know why.

Had she known that she'd awaken? he thought, even more annoyed now.

She couldn't have known. The look on her face when it happened betrayed her. He could see it all written there.

Prost remembered they had both begun to lunge at each other when something changed. Janis's face contorted in pain and she stumbled. It didn't feel right, but he lunged anyway, ready to take her life at her mistake, her blunder.

He was blinded then.

Blue Light, intense and fierce, burst from Janis and he couldn't see anything. He remembered the feeling of it, hard and strong, shoving his body with so much force that he got vertigo from flipping through the air. Before he had even been hit, there was pain. Prost hated the feeling. Not so much the feeling of the broken bones from the force—he'd broken bones before. It was something else.

Helplessness. The lack of any control.

His insides twisted at the memory—having zero control over his motion, over his circumstances. Before he had blacked out, he felt panic. This panic was something he couldn't remember feeling before. Even when he spoke with Riln, who both frightened and intimidated him, he didn't feel helpless; his master's powers were useless on him. Prost technically had the strength and skill to end Riln's life at any time. But if he were to exercise his strength over Riln, Prost knew a ripple effect of consequences would follow that he knew he wasn't prepared for. He couldn't see Watchlight responding well if he were to murder their beloved leader. Prost couldn't understand why everyone loved and trusted such a person with their lives.

Prost's mind flipped back to the scene of Janis's awakening, and he was angry again. Janis was now a Lightbearer, that much was obvious. What was *not* obvious and which bothered him most was that the Light had worked on him. Up until then, Prost had been immune. No Lightbearing ever, from anyone—however powerful—could affect him. Even Seers couldn't see situations with him there. But it was unmistakable. Janis had a power that could hurt him, that made him feel useless, like any other man against a *Tar'n*.

The scars on his face seemed to itch as he remembered when he'd gotten them. Ancient fear blossomed in him again as he thought of Riln. He was, after all, the man who awarded Prost with the scars.

Prost shook his head forcefully, shoving the memory out of his brain. It was a memory that he didn't like to relive, yet it still gave Riln some semblance of power over him. Instead, Prost thought back to when he'd woken from the blast. His left arm was limp, pain being the only feeling there. He felt warmth on his face and sharp pain from his nose. Broken, bleeding. He was fortunate that his legs hadn't gotten anything but bruises. Janis was gone. The Evenir warriors—gone as well.

He remembered the Fixers trying to work on him, but their powers did nothing. This was both a comfort and a frustration to him.

Doubt filled Prost's insides and writhed there, like an angry monster wanting to take control. When he'd gotten back to the lair, he'd yelled at Movers to try to throw him, Conjurers to cut him with their Conjures, even Destroyers to try to blow him up. Each time, Prost expected to feel the Light, to feel the power cut into him or push him, to make him lose control. Each time, the Light failed. That should have given him confidence, proven to him that he wasn't broken, but the feeling still lingered.

Footsteps clacked on the stone of the hall leading to his room. The curtain prevented him from seeing who was there, but he didn't have to wait long to find out. A hand reached in and moved the cloth that blocked the doorway to his chambers. One of their runners poked her head in, her small round face looking nervous.

"Riln wants to see you," she said, voice squeaky and high.

"Now?" Prost said, intentionally lacing the question with anger to assert his power over her.

The woman jumped at his tone and nodded furiously. "Y—yes, he said that it's important."

Making a show of it, he stood up quickly and forcefully, causing the woman to yelp and rush down the hallway, feet hitting the stone floor loudly.

Prost needed that. It was probably unnecessary, but keeping the fear alive that everyone seemed to have for him was in his best interest. It didn't fix the situation, or even what happened, but it did help him feel more powerful, less bothered by what had happened before. Fear is what kept him ahead. Riln may have wished differently, but Prost was his second— despite the leader's fondness for Jord, the insufferable Destroyer.

He wasn't in the mood to discuss anything with his master at this very moment, but he had little choice. Riln had to have his way, and Prost had to give it. The *bond* between them, though he would never call it just that, was an odd one. Riln had all seven Lightbearing powers, and Prost had none, while also being immune to Riln's. It was poetic, in its own way. Annoying, yet poetic.

Prost steeled himself as he rounded the corner and entered the throne room, tall stone pillars lining each side of the center, creating almost a hallway with their design. A single red orb glowed from the ceiling high above them, casting eerie shadows in the corners and behind each of the pillars. Without hesitation, Prost stalked to the center of the room and turned to his right. As expected, Riln stood in the darkness of the pillars' shadows, staring at him.

"You called, Riln?"

"What do you make of my army, Prost? Is it enough?"

He said nothing, choosing only to stand still and stare at his master. The small white-skinned man had chosen a pure and bright white set of robes, full and flowing all the way to the ground. Prost knew it was a show of power, but he personally used other methods, specifically intimidation, for his own displays. It was an odd choice in both style and color, for Riln's skin was sickly white, as was his hair. A robe of that color washed him out more since he was all one color—save his eyes, which shone with bright blue irises. The whiteness of his clothes and person soaked in the red Light from above, making him seem even more eerie to look at.

Riln spoke again.

"We have almost a thousand Lightbearers, and even more normal soldiers at our behest. More are flocking to us as we find them day to day, and yet I still ask, is it enough?"

Riln doesn't actually want an answer, just someone to talk to or yell at, possibly even—

Just as Prost thought this, Riln roared loudly and lobbed a ball of red Light directly at him. The Light collided with him and exploded on his arm with a loud crack, blowing the sleeve of his cloak to bits as it connected. Prost didn't even flinch.

So that's it. He just needs to blow off anger, then, Prost thought, unaffected.

It had taken some time to get used to the aggression from Riln and his Lightbearing. Before, the Conjures used to make him flinch as they hit him, and the Destroying used to make him cry out in fear. No more. This was a common meeting of theirs. Once Riln had gotten over the fact that his powers did nothing to Prost, he had turned Prost into little more than a training dummy to relieve his anger.

"Our armies are *nothing*, Prost! If we can't find those Evenir idiots, then we can't do anything. Numbers are pointless if they can just hide away for eternity, likewise gathering strength. I have trained them, trained *you,* and for what? Nothing! Two weeks it has been since your failure in the foothills and we have made no discoveries and gained no advantage. Meanwhile, you are lying about, sniveling at your broken body."

Prost tightened his jaw at the comment. He was frustrated enough about how hurt he'd been, at how great a loss he'd sustained, yet Riln continued to bring it up at every possible moment.

Riln opened his hand and a dagger appeared there. Roaring again, he ran toward Prost and stabbed the dagger through his head, then through his chest, arms, and legs before stopping and panting. As expected, each time the dagger came in contact with Prost, it had no effect. Instead, it passed through Prost as if it were made of nothing.

"I will find them, sir," Prost said, jaw still tight. "I am ready to leave now, just give me men and I will find the boy."

The red-lit man chuckled darkly, without amusement.

"The *boy?* This isn't about the boy anymore!" Riln shouted, "This is about more than that! You failed with him already. By now, he's already loyal to them, lost to their brainwashing and weak ideals. Not only that, but they have Mert and inevitably more of our soldiers. We are lucky they didn't take more of our Lightbearers."

Prost always hated being called a failure. Yet that's what he was, especially now as he stood there having accomplished nothing for his master, pain still lacing his body.

"No, this is about Evenir—about their insufferable *leader*—" Riln continued, speaking of her with contempt, "they struck hard, but they have provoked me. I will strike harder."

Riln stood there for a moment, fists clenched tightly. Without warning, he growled loudly and slapped Prost in the face, causing his head to turn away from the force, pain causing the area to ache slightly. Amusement filled Prost as he felt how weak the slap was compared to his own punches. A man that could fill him with so much dread, cause fear among thousands, had less strength than himself. He had known that his leader had become dependent on his Lightbearing for a long time, but he hadn't realized it was this bad.

"What will you have me do, master?" Prost said, leaving his head to the side where it had landed after the slap.

A wicked smile spread across Riln's face—joyless and menacing. Shivers found their way up Prost's back as he turned to see the smile, meaning so much more than he could say. Scars tingled on his face at the sight of the smile, and his stomach dropped slightly.

"Find them, and kill them all," Riln said.

Prost nodded, then turned to leave.

"Wait."

The tall man stopped and waited for Riln to speak again.

"We may not know where they are yet, but I have faith that you can extract the knowledge we require from some of our new guests."

Guests? Prost thought.

"Jord returned a few hours ago with prisoners—some Lightbearers. I believe they are from Evenir, though none have been forthcoming with any information of the sort. Do what you do best, dud."

Prost's chest burned with anger at the term. Ever since Riln had publicly used 'dud' in reference to him, many more had followed suit. Prost wanted nothing more than to kill anyone who called him that. Yet he knew that it wouldn't help. Riln detested him, and Prost felt the same way about the leader. Without another word from either man, Prost stalked off quickly and drew his knives.

I may not be able to act on my anger against Riln, but that doesn't mean I can't use it elsewhere. How about we put this anger to good use? he thought to himself.

3

Marric felt like he didn't belong as he followed the group out of the war room. He was the youngest person there; at least, as far as he could tell. He didn't really know each of the generals very well. Coincidentally, all three of the ones that were in the room were the leaders in the Lightbearing classes he was a part of. Each had attended at least some of his training and coached him here and there. It struck him now, as the courier mentioned the returning companies, that it was likely his fault that Turrin, Alsry, and Rivelen had stayed at Terris Green while the others went scouting. He felt suddenly guilty at this realization.

The group's shuffling footsteps echoed off the hallway's stone walls. The network of tunnels and caverns was somewhere deep inside of a mountain that Marric only barely remembered from the outside. He had not emerged from the mountain many times, and when he had, it was only to high terraces that were only accessible by huffing and puffing up tall stone stairways. Normally the thought of all-stone rooms and hallways deep in a mountain would be eerie and depressing. Fortunately, the Lighters kept the place very well-lit.

Glancing up at the top of the wall, Marric saw the large orbs of blue Light, about the size of his head, hovering just a handspan from the top of the ceiling and spaced about his body length apart. He marveled at how one person could produce and maintain that many orbs of Light and hold them for hours on end.

Avryn *had* said that Lighters ought not to be underestimated, and that it was indeed a great power in and of itself.

Without much notice, Magness took a sharp left at the end of the hallway. Marric, lost in his thoughts, continued forward and tripped on Rivelen's foot, causing him to pitch forward onto his hands. Rivelen cursed loudly and said something in an unfamiliar language.

"Roit, y'need t'pay attention, lad, afore yous kill us all!"

Marric blushed at her tone and got up quickly. He rushed to catch up to Magness and the others who had continued on without him, almost not noticing that he had tripped at all. Movement over his right shoulder made him look to see Janis shadowing him as she usually did. It was somewhat of a comfort to know that she was always there, keeping an eye on him.

"Don't mind her. She's just bitter that she isn't getting all the attention," Janis said, smirking.

He blinked at her comment, taking a bit to understand it was Rivelen Janis was referring to. When he did, he chuckled to himself. Rivelen was definitely a hard woman, but not in the way that Janis was. Janis was hardened in all ways, likely from her being an assassin for so many years.

Rivelen is so grumpy. I wonder if she's ever happy, Marric cocked his head as he thought this.

He realized that he didn't really know much about Janis and her past.

In only a few minutes, the whole group emerged into a cavern. The room was large; the ceiling at least fifteen times his own height, and perhaps fifty in width. Unlike the main cavern, this room did not have spiraling terraces up and down on all sides. Instead, all the walls were smoothed and shaped nicely. Marric marveled at the size of the room, but mostly wondered what its purpose was. It must have taken so long to carve out such a large space that was so rarely used.

A group was already present. Men and women were sitting or lying on the ground. There weren't any halls to this room other than the one they came through, so Marric figured there must be a door to the outside from here. All in all, there appeared to be just over a hundred people in the room.

Many of them looked fairly roughed up, like they'd rolled in dirt. Their clothing was ripped, dirtied, and worn.

One woman, short and somewhat stout, stood up and saluted Magness firmly before standing in position. Her brown hair was very short, kept like a man's. However, her voluptuous chest gave her away as a woman.

"We 'ad a rough one ou' there, Magness. While we was scoutin' aroun' the area of Arrant Falls, we was ambushed by Watchloit. They 'ad at leas' as many men as us—a fogload of Destroyers. Blasted brutes flung their evil Loit and shattered our ranks to bits. Fortunately, Oi've trained ma Shielders well and we stood our groun' a while."

"How many were lost?" Magness said hastily.

"Ummm, more than we loik t'—"

"*How many, Trease?*" Magness urged, voice sharp.

The woman flinched at her tone.

"At las' count, seven'y-one."

Magness sucked in a sharp breath at hearing the news. Marric's stomach dropped. He did not know many people here at Evenir, but he knew enough that losing that many was not something they could afford, especially if many were Lightbearers.

"We din' lose the battle though, m'dear. Oi'd be plum surproised if they 'adn't los' as many as we did.

"I appreciated the news, Trease, and am pleased to hear of all your companies' training and skill in battle, but any loss of life is no need to celebrate, Watchlight or not."

Magness turned sharply to Janis and said, "And *that* is why we can't send you and Marric to Arrant Falls. That could be you dead out there."

A vein popped in Janis's neck, but she said nothing.

Trease hung her head at the comment, but perked up slightly after a moment.

"We did manage t'take a few of 'em. Mos' got away, but we did get a couple."

Magness straightened up and immediately asked to be taken to the prisoners. The group was led by Trease toward the edge of the great cavern. Here, a couple men sat with their arms and legs bound, gags in their mouths. One of the men was very thin, and only of average height and build.

His head was bald, save for a thick black ponytail which was greasy. His eyes burned with anger. Marric stared at him, realizing that he had seen this man before. He gasped when his memory flashed and he saw him Moving swords in the air as Harmel and Shrell fought him.

The other man was slightly taller with short brown hair and round features. He was big, had brown eyes, a round face, and a round midsection. For some reason, he looked a bit comical to Marric.

"Before we take them to our holding facilities, we must check them. Rivelen, if you don't mind."

The long-haired man squinted his eyes as Rivelen approached, but he held still while she stood towering over him and his companion. With practiced hands and powers, Rivelen held out her arms and focused, breathing evenly but quietly for only a few seconds. In no time, her eyes began to glow brightly and she hummed to herself.

"Oi See tha' this one," she said, pointing to the greasy-haired man, "has both a temper *and* is a Mover. Seems 'e's picked Destroyin' as 'is second power. 'Is companion 'as no powers, bu' is quite skilled wif knoives."

Upon hearing this, Trease immediately produced a small metal dagger as well as a vial. Without hesitation, she opened the vial and dipped the point of the knife in, covering part of the blade with the green concoction. As she did, some Evenir men standing nearby glowed red and were Moved forcefully backward by the Mover man. Trease cursed, but moved to the side of the greasy-haired man and jabbed him lightly in his arm, drawing a small amount of blood. Almost instantly, the man's eyes rolled back in his head and he fell to the ground, unconscious.

The other man, seeing his companion collapse, jumped to his feet and in a whirl of motion, spun out of his captors' arms and darted to the hallway quickly. A flash announced a wall of blue Light sprouting out of nowhere in the cave opening. The unfortunate man, not expecting this, bounded directly into it and was thrown backwards, knocking him unconscious. Marric marveled and turned to see Trease holding out her hand toward the hallway, a look of concentration adorning her face.

Marric gaped at the situation, mouth slightly open.

"Noice one, Trease," Turrin said, a chuckle escaping his mouth.

Trease only grunted at the comment as men subdued the captive again before he could surprise them with anything else. Their worry was not well founded, for he was out cold. In moments, he had been given the same sleeping agent for extra measure, and laid next to the other Watchlight operative.

"Take them to the holding cells. *Don't* put them together, and make sure that we have at least a Shielder and two other combat Lightbearers guarding them. Ensure that a runner is available, should a Fixer be needed. If this one —" Magness said, pointing to the greasy-haired man, "—really is a Destroyer, even by second-birth, it might get ugly when he wakes. Once they do, interrogate them with a Shielder. Try to get whatever information we can out of them."

A few Evenir men nodded at her request and rushed off with the men.

"Let's relocate to the war room to continue this discussion, Trease," Magness said, turning to lead them out of the cavern.

THE GROUP HAD TAKEN a direct course back to the war room. Marric hadn't met Trease before now, though he'd heard some things about her from Alsry. She'd said she was fond of Trease for her strength. This was a bit perplexing to Marric, as Trease seemed like a comfortable and somewhat homely woman, not the type who would pose much of a threat to anyone.

Marric realized his mistake very quickly once they heard more of her tale. Trease and her company had determined to circle back to the waterfalls where Marric's awakening had occurred, despite Magness's warnings to stay away from there. Trease said she was tired of getting nowhere and said she would rather have a fight than nothing. They were ambushed by Watchlight almost immediately, and a battle had commenced.

Despite her appearance, the detail she went into for the battle was very graphic and unfiltered. It wasn't long before Marric felt sick from what he heard. It was at this point that Magness suggested Marric head off to practice his Lightbearing, which he happily obeyed.

Marric now stood in a small room somewhat secluded from the rest of the hallways. He closed his eyes and breathed in, concentrating. As he'd been taught by Turrin, he held out his hands and focused on an image of a man, slightly taller than him, toned and muscled, yet faceless. Behind his eyelids he saw a flash of Light and opened his eyes to see an image of a man exactly as he had pictured it. The faceless Light-being wore a standard tunic, pants, and cloak, and had short hair.

Holding out his left hand, he Conjured his bow, and a quiver of arrows flashed into existence on his back. Marric squeezed the shaft of his bow, still marveling at how real the Light-creation felt in his hands. He modeled it, as usual, after his own bow—the one he'd left Wurren with weeks ago—the one that he felt most familiar with. A small pang of regret ran through him as he remembered he'd lost it at Arrant Falls when he was taken by Watchlight.

In a quick and fluid motion, Marric snatched an arrow out of his quiver and nocked it. As he pulled it tight, aiming at the Light Conjure of the man, his stomach twisted.

It's not even a real man, calm down, he told himself.

The feeling didn't leave him. Instead, he turned the bow slightly to the left of the man's head and let the arrow zip just next to his right ear. With a crack, the arrow smacked into the wall, wedging there only slightly before falling to the ground and disappearing.

Turrin had said that a bow and arrow was not the finest choice of weapon for a Conjurer, but had finally agreed to let Marric start there when he'd insisted he had no experience with any other type of weapon.

Marric stared at the bow a bit sadly before letting the thing puff into the air, disappearing instantly. Focusing again, he Conjured a short sword. It was simple, with no adornments or designs at all. He wasn't familiar with many weapons, nor had he taken much time to inspect any of them, so his was plain by default.

Raising it above his head, he swung the blade back and forth to get a feel for how it moved in front of him. The Light sword swished as it moved. Marric decided to focus on the sound of it moving, to avoid feeling ridiculous. Closing his eyes, he thought through the motions that Turrin had taught him a few days ago.

Step, lunge, parry, swipe. . . .

He practiced a few sets repeatedly for some time, letting himself get lost in the motions of his practice. Turrin had only taught him a few sets, but he

said that the basics should be mastered before they got to the more complicated things. He said that if he taught Marric any more sets, Marric would
get distracted and not practice what he should. It seemed a logical approach,
since the lack of more advanced knowledge forced him to practice what he
already knew.

Swish, swish.

The sound of the sword was somewhat relaxing. His mind wandered to
what Trease was saying before he'd left. The woman had said that the
Watchlight group they'd run into had around the same numbers as they did,
but seemed a slight bit more Lightbearer heavy, which contributed to the
loss on their side.

Marric shuddered slightly as he remembered some of the gore that
Trease had described from the battle. Apparently, there were an oddly large
number of Destroyers on Watchlight's side, which led to some very quick
deaths before Trease could mobilize her Shield and the rest of the Shielders.
At one point, Trease mentioned something a Watchlight operative had
shouted at her, *"You know nothing, wench! You are a lost cause. We are
preparing for the new race to rule Lindrad."*

A chill ran through Marric at the thought. Knowing Riln, he assumed
that by 'new race', they meant Lightbearers. An image flashed in his mind
again—an eye shrouded in a beam of light. Marric had seen the tattoo on
Prost's hand, as well as on his step-mother Tins's arm.

Do they really think that Lightbearers are a race? Marric wondered.

Lost in thought, he swung the blade in his hand sideways, imagining
that he was fighting another Conjurer who had a sword of his own.
Suddenly he felt his sword hit something soft. Snapping back to reality, he
saw he'd struck the image of the Conjured man right in the arm. His
stomach twisted slightly, but as there was no blood, he didn't get sick. He let
go of the sword, but it stayed stuck in the Light-man's arm, sunk into the
Light-flesh. Marric knew that the Conjure wasn't real, but the feeling of the
blade entering the real-feeling flesh made him uncomfortable. The only
time he'd felt that was when he cleaned the flesh off of animals in preparation for a meal—firm, but soft.

"Yeh know we've been over this, yeh can't hurt 'em."

Turrin stalked confidently through the door to the cavern where Marric stood practicing. Startled, Marric swung his arms around and Conjured the first thing that came to mind. Unfortunately, it happened to be the bow that he was most familiar with. Without hesitation, he lobbed the bow at Turrin who caught it without any trouble at all.

"Good work," Turrin said, "yeh successfully distracted me wif a bow flyin' at me face. Oi mus' say, not me first choice fer a projectoile, but it could work inna pinch."

Marric flushed at the words. Turrin, seeing this, laughed heartily at the reaction.

"Now, now, no need t'be embarrassed. If anythin', Oi'm glad t'see that yer at leas' gettin' the reflexes that yeh'll need in a real foit. Last week Oi could've snuck up on yeh easily, and yeh wouldn't 'ave moved even a smidge."

He appreciated the jovial man's positive comment, but he still felt silly.

Why couldn't I have Conjured something more useful? Marric thought to himself.

"Is there anything else that I should know from what Trease had to say?" Marric asked Turrin.

"Oi believe," Turrin said, "that yeh left because her sayings were a bit too severe for yeh. Let's jus' say tha' th'rest of wha' she said was abou' the same." He commented with a wink.

This didn't make Marric feel any less silly about the whole situation, but Turrin was someone who was easy to get along with. The man reminded him of Harmel. The thought of Harmel made him sad. Shrell and Harmel had set out with one of the companies to continue the search for Watchlight's lair. They knew the approximate geographic area of their base, but had no way of knowing the lair's actual location due to careful Shielding. Marric secretly hoped that they wouldn't have any success because he feared his friends would not make it back alive if they were to run into Watchlight.

"Oi'm 'appy to see tha' yer practicin', an' it's good to see yeh making progress with yer Conjures."

The large man patted him on the shoulder, making him wince slightly at the force. He was quite strong, after all.

Marric watched as Turrin's face fell.

"There be somethin' else, though. Magness needs t'talk t'yeh back in the war room. She 'as some news that yeh'll want t'ear."

Marric's stomach clenched. The tone of his voice indicated that the news wasn't good. Something was off.

"What is it? Did something happen to Harmel? To Shrell? What is—"

"Now, now, don' question th'messenger. Oi was just sen' t'get yeh. News arrived not a few bits ago. It's best if we let'er talk it through with yeh."

The two left the room, Marric moving hastily. He normally had a bit of trouble finding his way around the caverns, but the one place he knew was the war room. Not only had he spent a significant amount of time there for the past couple of weeks, but the nervousness filling every part of his body and tingling his senses made his mind more aware. Each sense sharpened with the growing fear that something had gone horribly wrong.

In no time, the two burst back into the war room, Marric's eyes lingering like they usually did on the image of his mother carved into the door. A messenger, seeing them enter, nodded to Magness and darted out quickly.

Magness looked worried.

"What? What is it?" Marric asked.

"Oh Marric, I'm so sorry. We should have been more careful," Magness said, "we should not have left him without protection. . . . " she paused. Marric bristled at the silence.

"*Who are you talking about*?" he said through gritted teeth, trying to steel against the frustration he felt.

"Marric," she said slowly, "it's your father. We just had reports that your home has been burned. It's gone."

Marric's whole body went cold. Tears filled his eyes and he stood there, saying nothing.

"There's no sign of your father. We fear that he was taken in the fire."

A flashback filled his mind. Images he'd seen as he awakened that he didn't understand. He heard the strong and fierce waterfalls from that time, beating the rocks harshly. He had Seen his home in Wurren burning. It was a short vision, but he remembered Seeing it now. Only he hadn't understood it then.

Now he did.

4

Janis watched as Marric stood there, tears running down his face. The world wasn't a kind place, regardless of the age or feelings of the people in it. His body was limp, yet he didn't fall down. Magness rushed to him and embraced him, tears welling in her eyes as well. Avryn, seeing the exchange, walked over and put a hand on both of their shoulders as Marric sobbed.

It's been so long since I've felt such sadness, Janis thought as she watched.

Life had not been fair or easy for her. She had decided when she was about Marric's age that she couldn't expect life to treat her kindly. So, she had changed her path. She had spat on her old life and seized a new path, one where she had control. It had felt both wrong and right at the same time. She had let go, to become someone entirely different.

Shaking her head, she turned so as to not watch the display of emotion any longer. It appeared that Trease was done sharing what she needed to, for she had fallen asleep in the corner, immune and unaware to the current happenings. Seeing this, Janis slipped out the door and stalked down the hallway.

It wasn't long before she arrived at the main chamber, the large dome that stood high in the air. She marveled slightly at the size of the cavern and how it could have been carved. The large blue orbs of Light continued to hover, unwavering, scattered over the dome and the walls. If she cared about such things, she might have said that it was beautiful or a sight to see, but she didn't have the time to care.

The main cavern was abuzz, likely from the news that Trease and the company had returned and brought news of Watchlight. She dodged a woman hustling with a basket of bread stacked so high, it blocked her vision.

"Eh, sorry ma'am, Oi—" she turned to the side so that she could see whom she'd bumped into, and paused when she realized it was Janis. "Umm, roit. Oi'll be on me way," she said, then moved quickly away.

Janis chuckled darkly at the woman's reaction. The only acceptance she'd received since arriving was from Magness's seeming appreciation of her combat skills. That, and Turrin's odd humor, which wasn't reserved for anyone in particular. He was just liberal with his cheery mood.

It struck her that Turrin reminded her of Harmel. An odd sensation filled her breast and her gut. She balked at the feeling.

It was longing. She hated to admit it, but she missed the goon. He had been gone for over a week with one of the companies searching for Watchlight. Something about the man was intriguing. She definitely wouldn't say that she'd *liked* him at all, but there was something.

Janis pushed the thought from her head and moved on, quickly making her way through the cavern and all of the moving people. She caught snippets of conversations here and there. Every person seemed eager to hear the news that Trease had brought back. Rumors of spies and deaths filled their conversations. She chuckled at the ridiculousness of a few of the comments. She was in awe at how effective rumors and lies could be in posturing oneself. Janis herself had leveraged such strategies in her line of work numerous times.

As Janis walked, she thought back on how simple her life was before all of this mess. Now that she was caught up in it, she wished she could go back to the way it was. Working alone was always what she enjoyed.

But the Lightbearing. . . .

After rounding a corner that finally blocked her from view of the main cavern, she held out her hand. A small ball of blue Light burst into life, hovering just above her palm. Staring directly at the intense Light was uncomfortable, but she did so anyway. Perhaps she hoped that if she stared at it more, something would happen, or maybe she'd uncover some secret about how to unlock her powers that she hadn't seen before.

Unfortunately, no such revelation came. Gritting her teeth, she lobbed the ball at the wall where it snuffed out into nothing. This only made her more annoyed. Janis felt that the ball should have done *something*. Once again, the uselessness of her so-called awakening was brought to her attention.

"Did you hear of Trease?" a voice rang around the corner up ahead.

Janis stopped in her tracks just before she emerged into the opening. The voice had come from the left. She had planned on heading right, but paused to listen. Something about the comment made her pause. It was the way it sounded: condescending, angry. Not at all what a loving follower would sound like.

"Roit did. Oi finks she shoulda died out there. Woi did she bother even comin' back at all? Magness is gettin' soft. Shoulda replaced 'er roit away," another voice added.

"It seems our *fearless* leader isn't all that she's cracked up to be, no? Why do we even bother following her? She can't possibly care about us like she does the Lightbearers. We're just plain old people."

Both of the speakers were men, Janis figured. They were speaking quietly, but their timbres indicated male.

"What ya finks we should do?"

Silence.

"Put someone else in charge. That's what I'd do."

"Ya mean . . . replace 'er?" the second voice said, hesitation prevalent in the comment.

"If it takes that, then sure. There may be other ways to—"

Footsteps sounded in the hallway opposite of the two men. The conversation abruptly ended as she heard the shuffling of the mutineers' feet. Janis almost made to follow them and find out more, but she paused.

Why in Lanser's name would I get caught up in politics here? This is not my problem.

And it wasn't. She would make a point to let Magness know that there was some unrest. A leader at least had the right to know what was happening, but Janis was not going to ingratiate herself in the situation any further than she already was.

In time, the footsteps that interrupted the conversation increased in volume until Janis saw a robed man, hood up, walking casually down the stone hallway. He hummed silently to himself and seemed not to notice anything or anyone around him. When he got closer, she slunk into the shadows, watching to see where he'd end up moving. At the junction, he turned left into the hallway where Janis was hiding. Then she noticed it.

His eyes were closed. Nervousness filled her stomach as she realized that he had his eyes closed the whole time he'd been approaching. Suddenly, things felt eerie.

He paused right in front of her. Only then did she realize how odd it must be for her to be standing there, doing nothing.

Eyes still closed, he turned slowly and faced her.

"I may be blind, but I can still hear."

Blind. Could he be lying? Janis wondered.

"Excuse me, sir—I didn't mean to intrude. I was only watching because I am new here and I wondered if you needed any help," she lied. At least she could take advantage of the fact that he couldn't see her. He probably didn't know who she was and couldn't tell that she wore the garb of an assassin.

A smile spread across his face, causing creases to appear all over, indicating his advanced age. Or perhaps, it told about how strenuous his life had been if he happened to be young. Crows feet dug deep on the outsides of his eyes.

"I see. Well, I am quite capable on my own. I may not be able to see with my eyes, but I have Sight beyond your own. Though I appreciate the offer, albeit a lie, I am quite alright."

She stiffened internally at the comment.

His eyes flashed open and the chills ran through her body. They were completely blank white, no pupils or irises at all. After a beat, his pure white eyes began to glow the intense blue of a Seer.

"I am not sure where you are going or what you are up to, my dear, but do try to stay out of trouble. At least, stay out of the *wrong* kind of trouble. I don't really believe that you will stay out of trouble altogether. That seems to be your nature."

He turned at the comment and closed his eyes again, concentrating on the space in front of him. The odd man then slowly started moving down the hallway as if he had not spoken to her at all. Something in the way he walked seemed happy—jovial, even.

"Oh, and Janis, dear?"

She froze. Why she was surprised that he knew her name, she couldn't be sure. It just felt awkward that he did, as if he knew so much more about her from Seeing it and not mentioning any of it to her.

"I would definitely tell Magness what you heard if I were you. Unrest in our ranks would not do well for Evenir."

At that, the odd man slowly sauntered off, withdrawing into his own little world again, humming slightly to himself.

As quickly as possible, Janis turned down the hallway the man had just come from and moved at a quick pace. She felt an urgency to get as far from the man as possible, still feeling the chills slowly fading from the encounter. No matter what exposure she had to Lightbearing, it still unsettled her, whether it was used against her or not. Especially Seeing.

Given that she had displayed weak powers in all seven of the areas, the only positive was that she would likely not have to deal with her own eyes glowing strangely and losing herself to another place as often as Seers apparently did. She imagined the experience was somewhat similar to going into the in-between, as she had done many times. The difference being that she needed to be asleep for that, and she had more control over her ventures starting and ending than most Seers expressed they had in one of their odd visions.

Janis rounded another corner and dodged a messenger-boy that was hurrying on his way. She barely missed him, only because her reflexes were so quick.

He mumbled something as he walked, but paid no attention to her as she stood there. She didn't run into anyone again. At length, her thoughts wandered to the conversations that Trease and the others were having about Watchlight. She thought back to how she'd gotten into this mess by taking that job from Luden all those months ago. Immediately, a thought tugged at her insides.

Why did Luden want to kill a boy like Marric, anyway?

She knew about Marric's significance *now* of course, but how had *Luden* known that Marric would awaken? She'd been doing jobs for him for years, and never heard anything about Lightbearing.

Luden had hired her to kill Marric. Not moments after that, Watchlight had intervened. Quickly after, Evenir had scooped her up in this complicated power struggle between two groups with ideals that she frankly didn't care about. Yet here she was in this predicament. She'd thought about it for some time, and she still couldn't believe what had transpired since then. All these thoughts did was fill her with more questions. How had Luden known about Marric? Did he have any Lightbearer operatives? Why had he chosen her specifically for this job?

Janis didn't respect Luden for the people he hired in his entourage, but she respected him directly. She called him stupid time and time again, but that wasn't entirely true. For some reason, he just *hired* stupid people. He himself was quite resourceful. And his resourcefulness wasn't entirely monetary in nature, either.

At last, she arrived at the small opening to her quarters. There weren't any doors fastened on any of the sleeping rooms, only a thick curtain. Unfortunately, this meant that anyone could technically come in at any time. For that reason, she kept her knives close while she slept. She doubted it would be a problem, based on the fact that they all seemed scared of her.

Janis sat on the bed and held out her hand, willing a small ball of Light there. Inside, she still marveled slightly at the idea that she could create something like this out of nothing. Unfortunately, she knew that it likely didn't *do anything* either. In an effort to prove this to herself, she lobbed the ball of Light. Connecting with the stone wall, it made a loud crack before disappearing into nothingness. Once again, carrying out her intentions with her powers eluded her. Rather than an explosion, Janis was left with only a slight ringing in her ears from the sound.

Her thoughts wandered back to Luden as she absentmindedly summoned another ball of Light.

Is Luden a Seer himself? Janis thought, moving the ball from hand to hand as she considered this possibility.

For some reason, she doubted it. It wasn't necessarily impossible, but the ego of the man made it unlikely. If he really did wield a power like this, he would abuse it left and right, not to mention brag about it to everyone. She had worked with him enough to know that, at least. He was very rich, his money inherited from his family's business, and that made him unbearably arrogant. More than once, she *had* wanted to drive her long dagger into his eye socket, but that wouldn't have been a good career decision. She thought back to when she'd taken the job from Luden's men to kill Marric, and it gave her pause that the offered price had been higher than her usual rate from him. Luden *must* have known Marric was valuable. But how?

With a start, she realized that she had not re-watched the moment she met Luden's men from the in-between. When confusing events occurred, she normally preferred to re-watch them a few times to learn something. However, that particular experience had shaken her a bit too much and she suspected that was part of the reason she hadn't taken the time to re-watch the moment.

The ball of Light in her right hand floated higher in the air for a moment before everything around her began to spin. She gasped at the dizziness fogging her brain while the world blurred around her.

Suddenly, she was there on the roof of the bakery where she'd waited for Luden's men. The fog lingered heavily in the air as it usually did at that time. No one roamed the streets at this hour, though she did remember hearing someone shout in the distance, likely from an opened window. Movement to her left caused the air to catch in her lungs and she spun toward the source.

Her stomach dropped.

An image of herself crouched to her left, perched like a bird waiting for its prey. Her hair was down, coming almost to her shoulders as it usually did. She remembered choosing to leave it down to deceive those who came to see her from Luden. She recalled getting his message about the meeting from a bag of apples her contact had conveniently left near her in the market earlier that day.

How am I here? I don't remember going to sleep. How did I get to the in-between?

What was more, the in-between never worked this way. She normally could only see from her own eyes and feel through her own senses, re-living the experience as if it was happening all over again. This just felt wrong. The only other time this had happened was—

Riln.

Whipping around, Janis reached to her sides and pulled out her daggers, which had thankfully traveled with her to this strange pseudo-in-between place. She knew that he had to be here somewhere. He had to be behind all of this. She scanned the rooftops next to her, behind the bakery, and even in front.

Nothing. *I must be Seeing this*, she thought in a mixture of wonder and fear. Janis wondered if she'd finally entered a Seer vision.

A shuffling next to her pulled her attention back to—well—herself. Past Janis grinned menacingly as two men approached in the fog from the end of the road. They were talking about her, as she had remembered it.

"I don't see why we have to meet with the wench—don't we got better things to do tonight?"

"Luden said that he needed someone he could trust to bring this job to the assassin. I reckon that be more of a compliment than anythin', given our past history of job-doin'."

The two men talked exactly as they had months ago, when she'd first seen them. They were just as annoying to listen to now as they had been back then. Janis's skin crawled at the out-of-body experience and she tried to avoid looking at her own past self to minimize her disorientation.

She stopped listening, and instead took advantage of being separated from her own body. She knew that Prost and his men were hiding in the shadows and on the rooftops, and she intended to scout them out.

Just before she turned, she saw Past Janis in her peripheral vision leaping off of the roof to scare the men. She smiled slyly as she witnessed the result: Luden's alarmed oafs. Realizing that she didn't have much time to see what she came here to, Janis leapt from the roof to the house next door and continued leaping for a few houses. She stopped when she was roughly across from the roof that Prost had to be hiding on.

Her hands gripped her daggers strongly, eyes darting left and right. Riln hadn't been able to hurt her the last time he'd yanked her into the odd experience, but that didn't mean it couldn't be different now. Janis turned to look across the street, trying to make anything out in the fog.

Sure enough, she could just make out a dark shape on the door across from her.

How did I miss him standing there?

Janis figured that Prost must have known how she would scout around before she stood there waiting for Luden's men, and so he had only appeared after she'd made her rounds. Janis squinted down to the road, trying to make out anything behind her old self in the shadows. From where she was, she didn't have the vantage point to see enough.

She knew that she didn't have time to jump down and make it to Prost before—

SWISH.

The sound of the first bolt flinging from the crossbow reached her on the opposite roof. The body of one of Luden's men fell to the ground just as the other bolt flung through the air to strike the other man. Janis tensed and pulled out a small throwing dagger just in case Prost somehow could see her. Logically, she knew that he probably couldn't see her, but she didn't want to take any chances. She watched as Prost casually stalked to the edge of the roof and jumped off, landing lightly on the cobblestone road below.

He looked cocky then, and he still looks cocky now, she thought to herself.

Janis scanned the road below and could see figures moving in the shadows. There had to be at least ten of them.

She felt somewhat flattered. The fact that Prost had brought so many to surround and ambush her gave her a bit of pride. He even knew then that she wouldn't be taken down so easily. She laughed as she watched Prost address her down the road. She was out of earshot, but that didn't bother her, as she already knew what would happen. Janis turned to jump to the road, thinking to get behind Prost and assess the situation more. Before she could, however, she noticed movement on the roof from where Prost had just jumped.

There was a man there, though she couldn't make out his features just yet, she could tell it was a man. He was looking at her.

Janis tensed and adrenaline rushed through her body. She leapt back from the edge of the roof as a dagger flew by her head. In turn, she lobbed one of her daggers back at the shadow man, but he sidestepped it easily. His reflexes were as quick as her own. Part of her wasn't even sure that the dagger would have any effect on him, or his dagger on her own body, but the risk wasn't worth taking.

Pausing, she waited to see what he'd do next. He made no movement with his arms, so either he was out of daggers, or wasn't in the mood to try for a second shot.

For a moment, neither moved. The air felt cooler now as they stared at each other. The fog thickened almost as if in response to the stress of the situation.

Finally, after some time, the man slowly stalked to the edge of the roof. He gradually moved his hand upwards, probably knowing that sudden movements would award him with a knife in the chest. The man pulled back his hood, eyes glowing bright red with Light.

Janis froze. Her stomach felt sick inside. Emotions slammed into her with the force of a cannon ball.

Macks?

There he stood, face chiseled and sharp, tall and strong. He was lean, yet muscled. She could see through his tight shirt the muscles he'd developed as an assassin in those years before he'd left her. His hair was jet black, like her own, and held back in a small pony tail, his bangs swept to the left. Though she couldn't make them out exactly from this distance, she knew those eyes—green, full of wisdom. Dangerous.

Old feelings rushed through her and she growled in frustration. She stared at him, baring her teeth.

This can't be! He's dead, she thought.

As much as she wanted to believe what she was seeing, she knew that he was dead. Word had come only days after he'd abandoned her that his corpse had been claimed by the gangs in Stilten. Yet, there he was. Janis was frozen, her hand still gripping the dagger. Not once had memories been mixed like this. For years, she'd relived memories in the in-between, but they'd never been combined like this. Even if this was a Seer vision as she suspected it was, it still made no sense that she was seeing memories of two different times.

Once again, slowly but surely, he moved his other hand, the one hanging to his side, and put his finger to his lips, telling her to be quiet. With a wink, he disappeared to nothing. The world began to spin, and Janis gasped as she found herself sitting back on the edge of her bed. Startled at the sudden change in environment and what she had just witnessed, she threw her hand forward, letting a small blue ball of Light fly into the opposite wall. It collided with the wall like the first ball had, only this time the loud crack was joined with the sound of exploding rock. Dust and rock chips flew everywhere, pelting her as she fell backwards on her bed. A rumbling sound announced the ceiling cracking. Instinctually, Janis slid to the ground and pulled the wooden cot up to block the debris.

Then the ceiling fell in.

5

Prost left the room with the Evenir prisoners and turned toward the guards standing there. Each was very stiff, not looking at him. He got the sense that they were afraid of him.

Good, he thought, *fear helps me keep control of them.*

"I am done in there with this prisoner. Dispose of his remains."

One of the guards nodded curtly at the command, while the other just stood there, shivering slightly.Seeing this, Prost paused and turned to him. It was clear that the fear ran deep in this one.

"Did I not make myself clear, soldier?" Prost said, a bit more forcefully this time.

"No—yes, *sir.* We will take care of it, sir," he sputtered, still not making eye contact with Prost.

Prost nodded at the answer, opting to not say more, then moved down the hallway away from the room.

The prisoner had proven unhelpful. Prost figured that Evenir trained their operatives very well against torture and pain so that they wouldn't lose all their secrets to a blade. In the end, it hadn't mattered for that man. He wasn't a Lightbearer, so he didn't have anything going for him. When it had become apparent that he was not going to relinquish anything useful, Prost had just ended the conversation with his knife.

Prost paused as the red orbs of Light near the ceiling along the hallway started to flicker, one by one. The stone floor and walls in front of him plunged into darkness, and he cursed quietly to himself. He knew that this would only cost him a moment, but it still was a nuisance to have to wait for the Light to stabilize. As usual, it was only a few moments before the Lights began bursting back into life. A Lightbearer could only maintain the Light in the lair for so long before they needed to sleep. This was the changing of the Lightbearer, which happened twice a day.

Grateful to not have to sit in the dark for very long, Prost continued moving.

"Prost!" a voice called from behind.

He stopped and turned toward the woman who stood there.

"What, Alts?" his voice came out harsher than he intended. Given that he'd just failed to get information, he was in a foul mood.

"Hey, calm down, yeh grump. I was jus' wondrin' what yeh learned from 'im," Alts said, pointing over her shoulder. Her hair was tied back in a long, blonde ponytail. A streak of it had been turned purple, likely from a dye concocted from the flowers that grew just outside the mountainside. Her eyes were almond-shaped and dark brown. Her nose was small, which made her eyes seem large in comparison.

Fog it, she's beautiful, Prost thought. He had never entertained the thought of courting her, despite her beauty. He knew that he didn't have time for women. Plus, Alts had a thing for the idiot, Mert. A part of him was thankful that Mert had been taken by Evenir. Unfortunately for Prost, Evenir wouldn't kill any of their prisoners, so Mert was likely still alive. They had proven in times past that they refused to harm anyone unless it was out of defense. That had always been a mistake, in Prost's opinion.

"He gave me nothing, as I suspected. I am hoping to get more out of the woman."

Alts folded her arms.

"An' why is tha'? 'Cause she's a woman? I'd be careful wit' tha' one if I were yous," she replied.

Prost rolled his eyes.

"Don't get all preachy to me. I just need something to bring Riln, and she's all we have right now."

He turned and started walking toward the cell where the woman was held. As he walked, he could hear Alts following behind, quickly catching up. Prost didn't turn around to look at her, but instead just stalked onward, speeding up a bit.

"I hope yeh don' mind. I think I could 'elp, f'yeh need it."

"No."

A hand landed lightly on his shoulder and Prost tensed, resisting the urge to snag it and yank its owner over his shoulder.

"Look, yous don' have t'loik tha' me and Mert are lovers an' all tha', but don' be stupid 'bout all this. Let's get wha' we need and be done, eh?"

Gritting his teeth, he made a sound that indicated affirmation. It was a bit more of a grunt than anything, but Alts apparently had no trouble interpreting its meaning, for she stalked ahead and into the small room just in front of the cell. Three guards stood around the gate. Prost wondered why an extra was needed. One of the guards held a red longsword Conjured out of red Light. In her left hand sat a large and intricate shield, Conjured from the same power. The guard on the left was casually passing a ball of Light back and forth in his hands. The third stood unmoving, staring at the wall, completely ignoring the two newcomers. Each had the hoods of their standard black cloaks up so Prost couldn't see their faces.

"Ey, what'r' *yous* doin'ere? T'ain't no one s'posed t'see the prisoner t'day. Riln's orders." One female guard said, her voice annoyingly high and screechy.

Prost paused and stared at her flatly.

This one must be a Destroyer. They have a way of being unnecessarily cocky and egotistical; this woman is apparently no different. Mert and Alts act the same way, as Destroying is their secondborn power. That young fool Jord is also like this. Something about their powers makes them overconfident in themselves, Prost thought.

Without warning, Prost snatched the ball of red Light out of her hand, causing it to puff into nothing. He opened it to show his unharmed palm to the guard.

This had the reaction he intended. On instinct, the Destroyer had summoned and lobbed another small ball at his stomach. It collided as expected, and blew the front of his clothes to shreds. His stomach, now exposed to the air, showed no marks. At the same time, the Conjurer swung her sword at Prost's arm, but that also had no effect.

The two guards stopped and cursed loudly. The third, still unfazed by what happened, just glanced over at him.

"Riln does not dictate where I can and cannot go. He is my leader because *I* choose him to be. Despite this, he does know that I am here. Now *move aside*."

Each of them stepped to the side quickly, nodding their heads. Prost knew that those words would likely get back to Riln, probably making the man furious at him. At the moment, he didn't care. Prost's frustration was too high to care.

Though Riln would consider him as insubordinate, the comments were necessary. Prost didn't know every one of the people here at Watchlight, and he knew that they didn't all know him much either, but likely they'd heard of the *K'alek Tar'n*. The words meant, 'Opposer of Lightbearers' in the old language. He'd gained the term in his time here, and he felt it appropriate, given his unusual powers.

Sure as fog beats 'dud', he thought.

Grinning, he stepped through the guards, nodding to them like his loyal subjects. The bars of the cell were thick and made of iron. An archway of thick stones framed the bars. If the prisoner had been a Destroyer, even this cell wouldn't hold them for very long. In those cases, they either killed the Destroyer immediately, or drugged them to keep them asleep until they could bind their hands behind their back. Luckily, without their hands being free, Destroyers couldn't summon their powers.

To Prost, it mattered little what class of Lightbearer sat in the cell behind the bars. Her powers wouldn't do anything to him, anyway.

Making a show of it, Prost banged the bars heavily with his fists to make them ring loudly. The figure inside jumped at the sound. It was dark inside the cell, as was intended. The darkness was meant to intimidate those who were held there. Prost looked at the Conjurer to his right and gestured his head toward the gate.

"Light."

The woman produced a red ball of Light—small, yet piercing—and floated it into the room slowly. As it entered between the bars, the shadows flipped outward to cover his own face, revealing a young woman standing inside. She looked clean, strong, and completely unworried. Her hair was dark brown and woven into a twist down her back. Her face was covered in freckles, her cheeks bearing them so thickly that her skin looked darker there. Her eyes were light brown, complementing the brown of her hair.

"So are you here to torture me, then?" the woman said, unmoving.

Prost inspected the woman from head to toe, even more curious now. Her clothes look perfect. She wasn't wearing anything grandiose or beautiful —however, they all looked prim, clean, and immaculate.

"Let's get on with it then, I haven't got all day," she said, sounding bored.

Prost stood up straight, emphasizing his stature over her own.

"You aren't really in a place to antagonize the questioner, are you?"

The woman scoffed at the comment. "Don't act all high and mighty. Brutes like you have no place in this world."

Prost seethed inside at her impudence, but he held back, keeping his voice calm and measured.

"I must say, I am impressed with your bravery. Though you judge me to be someone you understand, you do not know who—or what—I really am," Prost said, eyes narrowing.

She smiled at the comment. It wasn't a happy smile, or an overly arrogant one, but it showed confidence.

"Say what you will—you will not get anything from me."

With that comment, she summoned a blade of blue Light and quickly jammed the blade into Prost's chest.

Prost could easily have parried the attack, but he made a point not to. It added to the effect.

Her eyes widened when she realized that the blade had done nothing. Quickly, she backed away to the far wall, pushing up against it.

"You."

A smile spread wide on Prost's face. He could feel the scars pulling tightly on either side of his face. He knew that it would make his smile even more imposing and scary, which is what he wanted.

"Yes, me," Prost said, sounding smug, "I am glad to hear that you know of me."

The woman glared at him even more.

"*K'alek Tar'n* or not, you still won't get anything from me today."

Pacing around the room, Prost began clicking his tongue in rhythm with his own steps. He pretended to be deep in thought, though he wasn't entirely. The only thought on his mind was how he could get the woman to break.

Slowly and surely, he slid one of his daggers from the sheath on his side. The dagger's metal on metal sound seemed even louder in the echoes of the cell walls.

"We shall see, then. Who are you, and where is Evenir located?" Prost figured that he might as well just get to the point.

"Bold, yet stupid. Why bother asking when you won't get anything?"

Without warning, Prost swung out with his blade and stabbed the woman through her right shoulder, the blade of the dagger clinking loudly against the stone behind her. The woman gasped loudly and gritted her teeth.

"Why not answer, when you know you'll die if you don't?"

Pulling the dagger out slowly, he felt the woman's hot breath on his face as he stayed close to her. She breathed out heavily, clearly not trying to give him the satisfaction of seeing her in pain.

"Pain means nothing to me," she said this as a bright blue Light appeared just over the wound on her shoulder. The Light grew brighter and brighter, until it flashed intensely. Where the wound had been, her shirt was unripped, unbloodied, and appeared brand new.

"Ahhhh," Prost said, now realizing why she looked so clean and perfect, "you know, this doesn't inspire much confidence for you. You would make yourself quite a nice target dummy now that I know you can Fix yourself. You will eventually tire, we both know that."

He did marvel internally at how she'd so quickly been able to Fix herself, even without putting her hand over the area. There were not too many Fixers so skilled at what they did that they didn't need any physical touch to use their powers.

Unexpectedly, she burst out laughing.

"That's a bit of an odd threat. Do all you want to me, I guarantee it won't work."

Challenge accepted, Prost thought.

With a loud growl, Prost ran forward and stabbed the woman in the chest, the knife sliding in easily. Just as before, she made no noise other than a grunt from the force in her chest. Once again pulling the knife free, he saw the blinding Light and the wound healing.

"Where is the boy?"

She smirked. "Safe. From *you.*"

Prost chopped off her thumb. This time, she screamed quietly at the pain and the shock of losing a finger. Light burst into life on the stub where her thumb was, and the flesh began knitting together again, her thumb growing back.

Before she could make much progress, he chopped off her other hand. This time, a panicked look came on her face. Light began glowing on the stub where her hand had been, the hand growing back. He kept ahead of her, intentionally pulling her attention to Fixing herself.

"Where is your base? Where can I find Magness?"

Over and over he asked a question, then promptly sliced her when she wouldn't answer. He injured her left and right, only to see more blue Light shining and Fixing everything. The woman focused, gritting her teeth.

"Where is Avryn? How many Lightbearers does Evenir have? What is your name?"

Question after question, Prost made cuts with each one. The woman continued to grit her teeth and Fix through it all. Despite the situation being very frustrating, Prost found it oddly therapeutic. After his run-in with Riln, he needed to exhaust some anger on something, *someone.* In a way, it felt like he was now Riln and she was now him. Riln periodically would take his anger out on Prost as a practice dummy. He now understood a bit why Riln used him this way.

"Where is Evenir hiding?"

He was yelling now, and she was starting to crack, he could tell. Sweat was beading on her brow from all the pain, and her energy was quickly waning. She might be able to Fix it all for now, but the stress from her body being injured in so many places was getting to her. It was only a matter of time before she would lose it. That, and a Fixer didn't have unlimited powers —eventually, she would get too worn out to continue.

Just when he thought he might be making progress, she smiled wickedly, staring over her shoulder.

"*Why are you smiling, you wench?* I *can* and *will* do this all day!"

In a flash, the woman threw her hand up between them. A flash of bright, intense, blue Light blinded Prost. He growled and jumped backwards, spots filling his vision. Another flash of blue Light flew right at his eyes, and he grunted at the brightness. His eyes burned and his head began to throb.

"*K'alek Tar'n* or not. Your eyes aren't immune to Light."

Anger boiled in Prost's chest. Growling loudly, he kept his eyes closed and ran toward the woman. Jamming his forearm into her neck, he pushed her against the wall. She gasped for air as he blocked her airway.

"I can see that you aren't going to oblige and help me out. Fine. Let's consider your work done. Thank you for helping me take out some of my anger. That's all you are good for, anyway."

Prost was impressed by the hard, confident look in the woman's eyes. She wasn't going to back down, and for that he commended her internally. In the end, it wouldn't matter. Taking his knife firmly in his hand, he slammed the blade into her eye socket and let her body fall to the ground.

As he turned, he paused to see Alts there, a look of disgust and fear on her face. A part of him regretted the look. He felt bad making her feel this way. The guards stood to either side of her, tense and equally full of fear. Prost squeezed his fist together, telling himself that actions like this were the only way to get the respect that he needed in this place. They all hated him and expected him to fail. Being impervious to their powers put him in a position of power that they didn't want to admit.

"What will you tell Riln?" Alts said.

"I will tell him what happened. Keeping her longer would have been a waste and a strain on resources. I made the diplomatic decision—he can deal with that."

Alts nodded, clearly not in agreement, but not willing to stand up against it. Up until this moment, Prost had been too subservient, too weak. He was realizing now that he could not serve Riln blindly any longer. He knew that he wasn't considered second in command, he was merely Riln's pet, his servant. Everything had to come to an end, and Prost was ready for this to be finished. By killing that powerful Lightbearer the way he had, by showing that their powers did nothing to him, he had postured himself well. Rumor of this moment would spread through their ranks, and perhaps he'd get the respect he deserved. At least, maybe from the others.

Never from Riln.

6

The Evenir caverns had never really seemed dank or dark to Marric, mainly because of the numerous spheres of blue Lights summoned by the Lightbearer on duty. Large rooms and stone hallways spread everywhere in a seemingly endless underground network below the green terraced fields. Marric had learned that these fields had been created naturally from a long-since dried up waterfall. Occasionally, drops of water leaked out of the walls and found their way down pathways here and there. Marric had even found a few hallways covered in threads of liquid color from leftover sediment dripping into the caves.

Today, none of that seemed beautiful anymore.

Marric felt empty, sad, and strangely alone despite the many people roaming the halls of the sanctuary. When Magness had told him of his house burning, everything changed. At the same time, Marric had remembered Seeing the event before. He hadn't thought much of it when he'd first Seen it, mainly because of the newness of his powers. He *should* have thought about it the moment he'd realized his awakening brought him the abilities of a Seer. Everything had happened so fast, and he'd gotten so caught up in training and feeling needed that he didn't even think too much about what had transpired up until this point.

After the news from Magness, Marric ran from the room not

moments after, and secluded himself in a hallway that he had found a few days ago. There was always a draw for him to be alone, to have time to himself. Other kids in Wurren had made fun of him for hiding away, but he didn't mind. Something about being alone and hidden made him feel safe, even when there wasn't anything to hide from.

A dripping sound echoed quietly from the ceiling a few paces away. It dripped fairly quickly and had been wearing a hole in the stone below for some time. When he'd first gotten here and seen some of the drips and the holes, he'd asked if they were worried about it getting too deep, or the ceiling falling in with rushes of water. He'd been simply reminded that they had sets of Fixers to clean up messes and to mend such problems on a regular basis.

It's a shame. All the work that was put into this hole, just to have it filled in an instant.

Marric didn't really care about the hole, nor did he have particular feelings or opinions about whether the hole was Fixed or not—he just didn't want to think about his father.

Sadness gripped his insides as his thoughts flashed to Narim's face, his humor, and the way he loved to joke with Marric and make him feel uncomfortable. Aside from losing his mother before he could remember, loss wasn't something that Marric was acquainted with, and his reaction now was proof of that.

Magness *had* said that they didn't find any remains of his father in the ashes, but that didn't mean that they weren't there before. Fires had a way of erasing everything—turning everything to ash. The thought caused Marric to just feel hopeless.

Here I am, weak and unhelpful just as I was before, he thought.

Before he'd awakened, Marric had felt like a burden to his father; worthless and unhelpful. He knew the only reason Avryn and the others hadn't left him behind was because he was the one who would awaken. Ever since he *had* awakened, he knew he could finally make a difference. Training had gone well, so far. Each of his trainers had seen him make progress and learn quickly. Having three of the seven powers when you awakened had already proven an advantage in his training. Avryn explained that awakenings like

Marric's own were rare, which was why Watchlight had been so intent on going after him.

Unfortunately, Marric didn't think it made a difference—especially as he sat there in his sadness, hiding from the world. No one had come to find him, but he suspected that they had tried. One of the first things he'd learned, even without being a Shielder, was how to put up his own Shield to keep watchful Seer's eyes away. Glancing to the side, he could see the slim, translucent-blue Shield that encased his whole body. As he'd learned before, he flexed the Shield outward slightly and saw the shape become almost invisible as it was stretched thin. The effect of the Shield weakened as it expanded. Pulling it back, he could see the Shield more clearly.

Inevitably, Magness had Seers looking for him. But with his Shield up, they probably couldn't locate him easily. Marric blushed. It wasn't *much* better knowing that they could see him crouching, hugging his knees with a tear-streaked face, but at least they couldn't find him to talk. He wasn't in the mood.

A thought came to him as he sat, and he welcomed the distraction. He didn't have to *trust* Avryn's word about trying to See someone with a Shield up—he could just do it himself. It was silly how he'd forgotten that he was a Seer himself.

Focusing as he'd been taught, he breathed deeply and let the Seeing take its hold on him. Through training, he'd realized that Seeing affected his whole body, not just his vision. He felt his body grow lighter and the air around him grew just a bit cooler. His eyes felt as if they expanded even wider, and the world around him changed.

He Saw Avryn sitting on a stone chair as he had his head turned to the side, talking. Marric focused the Sight and saw that he was with Trease and Alsry, both to his left. Attuning his ears, he started to make out what they were saying, though it was fuzzy and almost incomprehensible. Somehow, Marric knew that Avryn instinctually held up his weak Shield.

"Do we have any new recruits for your companies, yet?" he said.

A woman spoke, though Marric couldn't quite tell who.

"We dun' got a good 'un a few days back, Oi 'ear. Haven' met 'er yet, but Oi 'ear she's a roit good Shielder."

Avryn looked pleased by this news.

"It's good to hear that we are still having success with finding new Light-bearers. I had to remind Magness that we couldn't abandon all efforts there, despite her drive to find Watchlight. She's changed recently."

Marric could now tell that the third speaker was Alsry by her distinct lack of accent as she spoke.

"She should be careful. We can't afford to let any awakening *Tar'n* to fall through our grasp. Our purpose is still to protect our own. I guarantee that Watchlight hasn't forgotten. Numbers win wars."

The vision got a bit fuzzy and he had an even harder time hearing them. Marric tried to focus his Sight outside of the faces and immediate persons of Avryn and Trease, but he wasn't able to go far. Avryn's Shield was blocking him, making it all fuzzy and hard to comprehend.

So that's how it feels, he thought.

"'Ave yeh found the boy?" Trease asked suddenly.

Marric focused back on the conversation, his interest piqued.

Avryn sighed at the question, but shook his head.

"It seems he doesn't want to be found right now. Rivelen tried to See him and it was clear his Shield was up—"

As if an invisible force shoved at him, Marric lost Sight of the whole party and the conversation. Baffled, he nudged again with his Sight, only to find blackness. He focused on Trease and Alsry with the same disappointment.

Trease—he thought, *she's a full Shielder. She must have put hers up after his comment.*

Fascinated by his revelation, he shifted his Sight back to where he was. It was a strange sensation, as if his whole body was light and weightless. Of their own accord, his thoughts shifted to his father and he was suddenly zooming quickly over landscapes in a flash of greens and browns. Coming to a halt, Marric's insides burst with relief.

His father Narim sat on a log in the forest somewhere. Marric didn't recognize the exact place, but all he could think about was that his father was alive. The forest around Narim was wet, but more than just the morning dew. Dew alone would have evaporated with the sun already. Branches and leaves dripped with heavy drops, making pattering sounds around them. His father was soaking wet as well. Looking upward, Marric could see that the sky was gray and thickly clouded, the smell of rain and wet forest thick in his nostrils. He hadn't thought much about it, but he realized that he had no idea what the weather was like most of the time since they were shut up deep in Terris Green.

"Father! I'm so glad that you are alive!" Marric said, rushing to his father. When the man hadn't reacted to him or looked up at him, he remembered that this was a vision and that he wasn't really there, only Seeing events outside of his own body.

He paused when he noticed a bandage on Narim's left arm from the wrist to the middle of his upper arm. His father sucked air through his teeth sharply, making a hissing sound as he unraveled a piece up to the middle of his forearm. The skin was charred and red, severely burned by fire.

Marric's stomach roiled at the sight of the burned flesh. Now panicked, he looked around to try to understand when this was. He hadn't yet practiced enough to be able to know *when* things were occurring in his visions, and he wished he had spent more time on that. He'd have to ask Rivelen the next time they trained together so that he could learn.

He suddenly had an idea. It wasn't something anyone had ever said to him, but one thing that he had noticed was that Seers had a way of connecting to each other in their visions. Knowing he didn't really have much to lose in trying—he couldn't talk to his father right now, nor could he understand the timing on his own—he focused on Rivelen, and the world spun, causing everything to blur. Eventually, everything went black and an image of Rivelen appeared in the darkness. Slowly but surely, the world filled in around her and Marric saw that she was sitting at the round table in the war room, writing furiously.

"Rivelen!" Marric said to the sitting woman. Her long blonde hair cascaded over her ears and down her face as she stooped over the table, still writing hurriedly.

Grumbling, Marric realized that she couldn't hear him either. The theory *had* seemed a bit too grandiose, but he figured he had to try *something.*

As he watched, Rivelen sat up in her chair and started to focus on the wall in front of her. Her eyes began to glow bright, blue Light filling in her whole eyes, fading the pupils and the irises completely as it did when someone was Seeing. Marric jumped back slightly as a copy of Rivelen slid out from the sitting woman and began to disappear into the air, as if going to another time or place.

"Wait!" Marric shouted, desperate.

The image coalesced into Rivelen and she turned around.

"Marric?" The tall woman asked. "Wha' are ya doin'ere? Have yous been watchin' me?"

She sounded somewhat annoyed that he was there.

"Help—my father. I See him, or Saw him . . . I don't know! I need to know where he is!"

Rivelen knit her eyebrows and stalked over to him. Her annoyance at the boy seemed to disappear at the mention of his father. Holding out her hand, Rivelen nodded to him.

"Take me there."

Marric felt a bit awkward holding her hand—she was a woman after all, but he did as she said. He reached out and grabbed hold. When they touched, it felt strange. Their hands weren't physically touching, at least, it didn't feel like that. Instead, there was just the sensation of closeness, like one might get if they were within a finger span of someone, but still weren't touching. It was just the feeling that something was close.

Unsure of what to do to take them back, he let his thoughts wander to Narim. The world began to spin again, and it stopped back in the forest, though now it was nighttime, the darkness seeping into every corner and crevice of the trees, branches, and bushes. A fire blazed brightly in a small cleared area and Narim stoked the fire there.

"When I'd last come, it was day. I don't understand," Marric said.

"Seeing can be a mite bit tricky fer yeh new Seers. Oi took a roit long toim t'figure it out, meself. We'll do s'more of it later."

Marric just nodded, opting to get to the point as soon as possible.

"Where is he? *When* is this?" he asked, shaking from both excitement and fear about his father's safety.

Rivelen paused and closed her eyes briefly.

"This be las' noit. Jus' past Stellan. Yous can see Mallan's blue loit gettin' ready to shoin up above th'trees, there."

She pointed to the tops of the trees to Narim's left, and Marric could barely make out a bluish hint of light framing the tree's leaves.

"What about now? How can we see now?"

The tall woman clasped her hands in front of her and thought for a moment.

"Oi don' know this man, so i' moit be a bit tricky, but if Oi fink fer jus' a flick. . . . "

She closed her eyes while Marric watched quietly. Her eyes suddenly snapped open and she threw her hand out to him.

"Take me 'and. Now!"

Jumping at her tone, he rushed over and snatched her outstretched hand, once again feeling the odd sensation of them touching-yet-not at the same time. The world spun only briefly and landed once again on the now dying fire. Narim lay on his stomach, either sleeping or dead. His arm was exposed now, the flesh charred.

Marric's stomach clenched as he saw him. Moving quickly, he shifted to the side of the lying body and watched closely. The man's chest was still moving up and down slightly, so he was alive.

"We need to help him! I don't think he'll last long on his own."

Rivelen looked thoughtful for a moment, then nodded.

"Yes, Oi qui' agree. Oi will talk t'Magness roit away an' get some'un' out as soon as possible."

"But he needs help now! Can't you see him? He's barely alive and—"

Rivelen waved her hand over his father and the world around them melted until everything was black except for the two of them.

"Marric, we can' do nuttin roit now. Oi knows it all looks real, but t'ain't real, we's only Seein' 'im. Now, let's—"

A loud explosion sounded somewhere, and Marric felt his body fall backwards in shock from the sudden sound. The vision ended and he was back in the hallway where he had been physically hiding before the visions started. Unsure of what just happened, Marric heard shouts echoing loudly down several hallways and he instinctually jumped to his feet, running down the hallway as fast as he could. He couldn't describe what was happening—that had been the longest he'd ever spent Seeing, and he'd definitely never interacted with anyone else in a vision before.

Something about the urgency of the shouts made the air thick with nervousness and panic. Part of him was worried to find out what actually had happened, the other part of him was so immensely curious, that it got the better of him.

Stopping short, he had the thought that he could simply See the situation from afar.

But that wouldn't be the same.

Shaking his head, he bolted forward again as fast as he could. One of these days, he'd have to think further on what Seeing could do for him—how it might save him time. In this situation, he felt that being there in person might be more ideal.

Marric nearly tripped as he bounded around a corner and felt his feet skidding on the somewhat smooth stone floor of the hallway. The shouts were coming from the sleeping quarters where his room was.

Nervousness sprang up like an unwanted pet vying for his attention, yet he kept running.

As he rounded the last corner, he froze, not because he knew what was happening, but because he almost ran headlong into a woman who was standing in front of a huge crowd.

"EVERY ONE UH YOUS, MOVE!"

Marric jumped at the loud tone and turned to see Trease bustling forward, every bit of her seeming to bounce with the urgency of her movement.

"Oi 'eard crackin' rock! Do yous wanna be th'one t'die by fallin' rock t'day?"

That seemed to have the intended effect. The crowd crammed themselves against the walls of the tunnel, many looking up worriedly as if the ceiling would fall on them at any moment. Trease moved to the very back of the hallway and gestured a few others forward.

"Hold it fer yer life, got it?" she said to one of the women.

The woman, who Marric hadn't met before, knit her eyebrows together and held up her hands. In a flash of bright blue Light, a Shield extended outward like a dome and pushed on the ceiling immediately above her. After connecting with the rock, it expanded backward slightly down the hall, but mostly pushing forward.

Marric suddenly felt safer. He remembered only now that Trease had said it, but the sound that had snapped him out of the vision was exploding rock and the sound of a cave falling in.

Trease rushed forward with two others—these were men—and instructed them to put up their Shields, intersecting them over the previous Shielder's work. He saw that most of the people didn't dare step into the hallway, despite the Shields that were up. Realizing quickly that it wasn't a problem of safety, but of fear of Trease instead, he rushed forward to follow in her wake. This rushing awarded him with angry glances and looks from those that opted to stay out of the way, but he didn't mind.

At length, Trease stopped and threw her own hands up into the air. Her glimmering Light-Shield flew upwards and reinforced the last bit of hallway in front of a doorway with dust billowing outwards.

Marric felt sick as he realized the stone archway was Janis's. Hers was only just across the hall from his own. His eyes flashed there, but he saw no dust or rock chips flying out of his own room.

Janis? Lanser's feet, what happened? he thought, trying not to panic.

He must have made some sound, for Trease quickly spun around, a scolding look on her face for anyone that might get in her way. When she saw it was him, her face softened and she nodded to him.

"Bes' stay out the way, eh? Bu' Oi've no problem wit yous stayin' close."

She turned back to a couple of the spectators and yelled, "Stop standin'ere, and git th'Fixers!"

A few of the spectators broke off and ran backwards.

"I am a Fixer!" a small voice shouted from somewhere in the crowd.

Trease, hearing the voice, stopped and scanned the tight group for who had spoken. A small girl, perhaps only eleven or twelve, poked her head out of the crowd.

"An' who moit yous be, missy?" Trease said.

"Millcent, ma'am. I'm only just awakened, but I might be able to help."

The portly woman didn't look impressed at the sight, but she must have figured there weren't other options at the moment. The little girl wore only a simple dress with no embellishments. As it went, she was a fairly nondescript girl. Marric could see nervousness in her whole body. She was shaking from head to toe as she moved forward, shrinking her head down into her shoulders like she expected the ceiling to cave in on her.

Millcent moved just to the edge of the Shield, which Trease had extended downward from the ceiling so that it connected with the floor in front of them, blocking the doorway where the dust was still settling.

The young girl paused and stood there, turning around to look at Trease. It was obvious that she felt awkward at the situation.

"Ummm," Millcent said, embarrassed, "can I—get through, please?"

Huffing slightly at the sheepishness of the request, Trease lifted one of her hands slightly, and the Shield moved upward from the ground to just above the girl's head. As it did, some dust entered with them and Marric watched with fascination how the translucent Shield could block the dust.

Millcent shuffled forward quickly and put her hands on the broken doorway. Intense blue Light spewed out of her hands and ran along the archway, moving into the ceiling above. As it moved, the cracks mended themselves and became whole. Pieces that were missing, great and small, moved through the air around them and found their places back in the holes from which they came. Even particles of dust seemed to glow with the blue Light and shifted into the archway where they had originally come from.

Trease whistled softly at the scene. Marric merely gaped. The cracked and broken archway to the entrance was Fixed in mere moments, as if it hadn't been destroyed at all. The ceiling above them and immediately outside of the room was Fixed as well, so Trease allowed the other Shielders to drop their Shields, ordering them closer to the room.

After the Fixing of the archway and ceiling was complete, Millcent drooped slightly. The event itself must have taken some energy from the girl.

She is new, after all, Marric thought. Despite her awakening only days ago, the girl's Fixing was very potent.

Dust continued to billow out of the room as the Fixing had only taken effect on the outer archway and in the hallway. Trease extended her Shield into the doorway of the arch, and nodded the other Shielders forward. A few spectators started moving with her, and she commanded them to stop and back away. Marric understood why Magness had selected the woman as a general. She seemed like someone that no person would dare go against.

Fortunately, Trease allowed Marric to join them in the room. He coughed as the dust that had been allowed into the Shield hit his nose and mouth. The Shield otherwise kept the bulk of the dust out of their faces, pushing away from them as they moved. Instinctively, Marric ducked under the newly Fixed archway and gasped at the sight.

Destruction from a blast had snuffed out all candles, so Marric held out his hand and summoned a ball of blue Light to hover next to him. As he looked around, he saw that the other Shielders, including Trease, had done the same, each Light-ball very small, perhaps only the size of his thumbnail, but very bright, with the exception of one. One of the Shielders, the woman, had summoned a ball the size of her head.

Seeing that the small balls of Light wouldn't help them see the fullness of the destruction, Trease nodded to the woman with the larger Light-bearing orb.

Putting her hands together palm-to-palm, the woman extended her arms outward just under her large ball of Light, and then separated her hands. Immediately, the large orb of Light split into seven or eight others and they zoomed around, illuminating the area.

The room was a mess. Large boulders had fallen to the floor, destroying stone furniture and the table. There was hardly a spot in the room that wasn't covered with rocks and stones of all sizes. Marric's gut wrenched as he noticed that there was no sign of Janis anywhere. Part of him wanted to believe that she hadn't been in the room when this happened, but he knew better. He got the feeling that this was something she'd done, or at least it had something to do with her.

Millcent began working on an area of the broken room, causing rocks and boulders to begin flying in her direction, mending the wall and ceiling there. Before long, other Fixers reached the room and began Fixing things here and there, the air around them undulating with power as rocks and wood from furniture flew around, mending the room as quickly as they could.

"Over here!" a man said in a low and booming voice, "I see someone under the bed!"

Ignoring Trease's curses and comments, Marric rushed over to where the bed lay under a large boulder that had fallen from the ceiling. He could just make out a hand and a wrist poking out from under the bed.

It took three Fixers to get the large boulder put back in its place and mended. While they worked on that, Trease and the remaining Fixer had pulled Janis out from under the bed and were Fixing her back up so that she could regain consciousness.

Marric watched as the Fixer with the booming voice held his hand over Janis's head, his hand glowing so brightly that they had to shield their eyes.

Sputtering and coughing, Janis sat up quickly on the ground and looked around. Her hands flicked into her bodice and Marric knew she was going for knives there. Not wanting to cause any issues, Marric waved his hands in front of her face until she saw him.

"It's me—Marric. What *happened* here?" he asked.

Janis stared at him for a moment before pulling herself to her feet.

"Lanser's sake, I have no idea," Janis said, "I have a feeling that it was me."

"What do you mean? I thought that your powers—" Marric paused, realizing that he might offend her by suggesting her powers couldn't have done this.

Her jaw tightened, and he was glad he'd stopped when he did.

"Despite the truth of what you were going to say, something happened this time."

Janis paused and stared past Marric at the wall for just a moment before focusing on him again.

"I think I must speak with Magness. Do you know where she is?"

Marric shrugged. "I'm not sure, I've been . . . " Marric stopped, realizing he had been about to say that he was hiding in an abandoned hallway so he wouldn't have to talk to people.

" . . . exploring," he said finally. "There are so many places to go here, I am trying to learn my way around."

A slight smile tugged at her mouth, and he knew that Janis was aware of his lie. She probably wouldn't press him though, unless she thought that getting the truth would be important here. As usual, he blushed at the thought.

"Can you not just See her?" Janis asked.

Marric stared at her, blinking. He looked around for a moment and turned back to her, confused.

"No, I don't think she's here, I can't see her any—"

—Oh, she means for me to use my Seeing to find her.

Blushing even more deeply at his silly mistake, he nodded to her, then concentrated on the space behind his eyes. The familiar feeling of his eyes opening up wide started, and the world around him melted away to blackness. Focusing, the spinning slowed and then landed on Magness, rushing down a stone hallway with urgency. She appeared stressed and bothered by something. His Sight followed her as she moved around a corner to a hallway full of people, dust, and fuss.

Magness approached the stone archway and rushed through, almost colliding with a Fixer who was working on cracks in a wall there. His Sight turned to see Fixers all around, and then he saw—Janis.

"I guess there's no need for this," he felt his mouth say out loud, "she's here."

He saw himself kneeling in front of Janis, face upward, eyes glowing, so bright that you couldn't see his irises or pupils at all. For some reason, he saw that his hands were extended slightly outward. It was odd to See himself from this perspective, and it was a bit distracting.

Watching in awe, he saw Janis reach out to him and shake his shoulder slightly. It was odd to see her doing this from the outside and to feel it at the same time. She shook again, slightly harder this time, and he saw the world around him spin until it cleared and he was looking at Janis again.

Marric's vision took a moment to fully clear, and when it had, he felt slightly sick from all the visual motion.

"Uhhhnnn," he groaned, shaking his head to snap himself out of the feeling.

"I'm impressed. You made quick work of that, didn't you?" Janis said.

"What in the fog happened here?" Magness said. Her tone wasn't quite mad, but at the same time it felt laced with aggression, as if Janis had intentionally tried to bring down Terris Green on top of all of them.

Magness was looking at him, he realized, and he stumbled to say something.

"Uh, I—she . . . but—"

"It was me," Janis said frankly.

The normally beautiful leader of Evenir looked a bit severe as she stared with an incredulous look on her face.

"I beg your pardon? *You* did this? Why would you use explosives to—"

Janis held up her hand sharply to silence the woman, which didn't seem to make Magness's mood any better.

"First of all, the fact that you think I'd use explosives to sabotage you and the others here is simple lunacy. I'm an assassin, not a brute. Second, where would I even *find* explosives? I'm going to assume that you don't have any here since you have Destroyers to handle that work, correct?"

Magness paused at the comments. Her angry face melted away to a more thoughtful one and she nodded to herself.

"I suppose you are right. Unless you had carried explosives on you to begin with, you wouldn't find any here. If it wasn't explosives then what *happened*?"

With intention, Janis didn't immediately answer. Instead, she turned away from the Evenir leader and stepped to the wall where she'd thrown the small ball of blue Light.

"I was dozing, there on my bed," Janis said, idly gesturing to the bed behind her, which had already been Fixed at this point. "I was dreaming. It's not uncommon for someone like me to have dreams of the past, or even dreams of those who want revenge on me. Regardless, I remember defensively creating a small ball of blue Light—"

To iterate, she held out her left hand and a small but intense blue ball of Light blossomed there, hovering half a handspan above her palm.

"In my dream, I was surprised by someone behind me, and I remember my real arm moving with the dream, the blue ball of Light being flung through the air and into the wall, just here."

Janis pointed at the wall, presumably where she remembered the ball colliding and the explosion that followed. Marric wondered what she wasn't saying. Janis was adept at half-truths, but Marric was starting to get a sense of when she wasn't being totally truthful.

Perhaps it had been more than a dream? he wondered silently.

Raising an eyebrow, Magness looked at her pointedly. "Why do I have a hard time believing that?"

"Ugglyn's butt if I care what you believe or don't, that's what happened. I was *alone* in here. I clearly have no explosives. Who else could have broken the wall and ceiling?"

Janis seemed cool and calm about the whole situation, though Marric suspected she was burning and boiling at Magness's reaction. The room had been put back together very quickly. Marric was impressed at how quickly a team of Fixers could work. It had been quite a disaster from the explosion.

Magness set her jaw, dimples showing in her cheeks as she pressed her lips into a thin line. She was upset still, but she wouldn't say anything more. This wasn't the time to ask her to elaborate, and Marric knew it.

"The timing just seems too strange, too perfect."

"Hmm?" Janis said nonchalantly.

The tall woman clasped her hands together in front of herself and seemed to be considering her next words. After a few beats, she clapped her hands loudly and started shouting commands to the rest of the group around them.

"I need everyone gone! Leave! There are private matters that must be attended to between myself and Janis. Thank you, Fixers, for your fine work. Please return to your posts and let's hope there are no other incidents today that require your immediate attention."

Marric stood there awkwardly, not sure if he should be included in the group that should leave. He watched as the rest of the people filed out of the room quickly. He stared at Magness, who watched Janis and himself with a serious look on her face.

"Oh, bother, Trease has gone as well," Magness said.

Deciding that Magness had indicated wanting to speak with Janis alone, Marric turned to follow the others.

"Marric. Wait just a moment."

He paused and turned back to the two women.

"I believe that I will actually require your services for a minute. You are not a Shielder by nature, but you still have the ability. I was hoping that Janis might be able to leverage her undeveloped ability to Shield, but based on the current events, I fear asking her to use any part of her power."

Marric watched as Janis stiffened slightly at the comment and clenched her fists at her sides.

"Oh, Janis, I don't mean to offend, calm down."

Despite her words, Janis didn't relax at all—if anything, she seemed more annoyed. Marric had seen Avryn try to tell Janis to calm down before, and that had never gone well. Apparently, Magness was still learning the ways of working with Janis.

"Now, Marric. Please Shield us as best you can."

As instructed, he focused and felt a slight tug inside as a dome of blue Light flew out from him and covered the three of them. He wasn't sure how effective it could really be; he wasn't a Shielder after all, and he hadn't spent much time with any Shielder trainers given that all his time had been focused on his three powers.

Regardless, Magness looked satisfied with his shield, and nodded to him before speaking to the assassin.

"Janis. I'm going to be frank since I feel that it will help us save time in the end."

Janis narrowed her eyes at the comment. Marric detected, likely as Janis had, a bit of suspicion in the words.

And suddenly I feel even more uncomfortable being here, Marric thought.

"I've found that slipping around the issue is a waste of everyone's time as well. Please, say what you feel you have to," Janis replied, with her own frankness.

The air around them grew tense and palpable. A silence that in reality only lasted moments felt extremely long as the two stared each other down.

"Are you a spy?" Magness asked finally.

Marric's insides twisted at the question. Where had an idea like that come from? Janis couldn't have been a spy, that wouldn't explain anything. She'd fought too much for them. She had saved his life on so many occasions that Marric couldn't help but chuckle at the odd accusation. The mood didn't last long as he realized that Janis might not feel the same security he did in the question's silliness. He looked at her quickly, watching to see what she did.

She laughed.

It sounded so strange coming from her. Since they'd been together, never had he heard her laugh like this.

"Magness, please. I'm an *assassin*, not a spy. Sure, you shouldn't trust assassins fully unless you've paid them well, but I am sure as Mallan's light that I am *not* a spy," Janis spoke honestly, "though, I am very curious to know where this is coming from."

Sighing deeply, Magness stared at Janis. She looked to be considering something complex.

"Then why the fog did a woman come knocking on the door to Terris Green this morning looking for you?"

Marric's body chilled at the question.

"What are you talking about?" Janis said, "I work alone. How could you be sure that she was looking for me?"

Magness frowned.

"She asked for you by name. When she did, we took her away and locked her in a cell. As far as we can tell, she is alone, but she won't talk. She insists on only talking to you. I do not find it only coincidental that you managed to blow up your quarters only hours after a strange woman somehow found her way to our hidden sanctuary. What's more, we asked her how she found us, and all she told us was that she was drawn here by you. What for Lanser's sake does *that* mean?"

Janis just laughed again, though this time it was a bit more nervous.

"Magness, I have no idea what you are talking about. Need I remind you that I was *unconscious* for the entire trip here from the safe house? Even if I had wanted to instruct someone on finding us, I wouldn't have any idea how to get here."

The Evenir leader's eyes narrowed slightly before she continued, "Yes, that is true. I had already thought of that, but I had to be sure. We have tried to ask her other things, but she refuses to talk unless it's with you."

"Did she at least give you a name?" Janis asked.

"None. As I said before, she is uninterested in talking to anyone but you. We thought she might be amiable to at least some benign questions, but she has proven otherwise."

Marric thought it was odd that someone would be so resistant to answer anything. He figured that a person who came knocking on the secret sanctuary of a random group would normally be agreeable to those people.

Janis shrugged, not saying anything else. Magness shifted uncomfortably and bit her lip as she thought about something to herself. Silence engulfed the group. Marric disliked silence when he wasn't alone. He somehow felt like he had to fill the void with *something*. He absentmindedly started to tap his foot. The sound was small, but it echoed on the bare stone walls. It was a wonder to him how sound could travel so easily. Janis raised an eyebrow at him and his noise.

"There's more," Magness said finally.

"Well, we guessed that there was," Janis teased, "your body language said it all pretty clearly. I also don't make a habit of standing in a room with random people staring silently at them. What is it, then?"

"Well . . . " Magness paused again, "it seems that this woman might be immune to Lightbearing."

A pause.

"You mean like Prost?" Janis said, eyebrows knitting slightly at the revelation.

The Evenir leader nodded, pressing her lips into a thin line. As Marric watched, he realized that she was wearing small dangling earrings in each ear. They were each moons, but they were different ones. Her right ear held the earring that was red, a depiction of Stellan, the first moon, while the left held a blue moon, representing Mallan. It seemed ironic, yet at the same time, intentional.

Evenir Lightbearers have blue Light, while Watchlight has red, he thought.

He was sure that he wasn't the first to notice this.

"We can't be sure, because we don't want to alarm her by trying to Destroy her or cut her with a sword made of Light, but I *did* have Rivelen try to See her to find out where she came from. Rivelen told me that she Saw nothing. Just blackness. Even if you don't know a person, or you just know their face, you can See *something*. Their birth, a random scene from their childhood, something. There are only two times when you See nothing. When they are a Shielder, which she most definitely is not. Or . . . *Ka'lek Tar'n.*"

"Wait, what did you say?" Marric said, jumping in unexpectedly.

Magness chuckled quietly.

"Oh yes, I'm sorry. It's a term that some use for Prost. We aren't sure where it originated, but in the old language, it means—" Magness paused, "—well, the *literal meaning* is 'Opposer of Lightbearers'."

The familiar feeling of dread and fear came into Marric.

"Despite its brute name, it isn't common. Prost is one of a kind—or so we thought," Magness said, unabashed by the term. "We can't be sure, but the assumption is that people like Prost existed anciently as a way to assassinate or eliminate *Tar'n*, or Lightbearers. However, we don't have time for a history lesson—we need you to come now, Janis."

Shrugging again, Janis gestured grandly to the door behind Magness.

"Lead the way, my liege," Janis said with a slight bow, obviously sarcastic.

Rolling her eyes, Magness spun around quickly and rushed out the door. Janis followed suit. Realizing that he might not be able to keep up at that pace, Marric ran after them. As he moved through the door and around the bend, he almost ran headlong into Janis, who had paused there.

"I'm sorry, Marric, but your services aren't required anymore. I think it's best if you go train a bit more," Magness said.

His heart sunk as he realized what that meant. They didn't want him coming along. Part of him felt offended at this, but he didn't feel like arguing, nor did he have a good case as to why he should be included.

He looked up to see a twinkle in Janis's eye, and she slowly raised her hand to her face and pointed at her eyes. Her body was angled so that Magness wouldn't be able to see.

The gesture was subtle, but he got the message.

Just listen in with your Seeing.

Marric smiled at her, an unspoken message passing between them. Making a show of it, he slumped his shoulders and looked down.

"Okay. I guess I'll find something else to do."

Magness nodded at his comment and turned away again, rushing down the stone hall, footsteps echoing on the walls back to him.

Janis turned to follow, but with one last look, gave a wink.

7

Janis hadn't yet ventured into the prison ward of the sanctuary, and she soon discovered why. Not only was the passageway there boring and unassuming, but it was crowded full of guards. She recalled passing the hallway to the cells a few times, but determined that it wasn't worth convincing her way through the sets of guards standing every ten or so paces, blocking the way. It seemed odd to her for some reason. Evenir couldn't have *that* many prisoners, could they?

The guards hardly noticed them now, however, since Magness was leading the way. It was clear that she was well-revered and respected within their community.

After nearly a dozen sets of guards, they finally arrived at a bend with a doorway blocking the whole hallway, floor to ceiling. Three guards stood here. Two of them held weapons made of Light, indicating their status as Conjurers. However, the middle guard stood there grimly with her hands simply folded in front of her.

"Please, Adona, if you don't mind, we'd like to see the woman that came to Terris Green today."

Even as Magness said this, the woman in the middle didn't move. Instead, she spoke in a gravelly voice, oddly low for a woman.

"Do you want some company in there? I would be happy to join you if you need."

Magness smiled sweetly at her, but shook her head. After doing so, she glanced over her shoulder at Janis.

"I'm confident that I have the protection I need."

The comment was oddly placed, given that she hadn't shown even the smallest amount of approval for Janis since she'd arrived, other than a bit of respect at her nerve.

Magness turned back to the guard and nodded. "Let's get it open then, shall we?"

The gruff woman tilted her head obediently, turning to the doorway. It was then that Janis noticed a distinct lack of handle or hinges on the door. Instead, it was a solid piece of wood bracketed to the stone walls and ceiling with thick spikes pounded into the stone.

What? How are we supposed to—

Her thoughts were interrupted when the strange woman in the middle held her hand up to the wooden wall. The moment her hand touched the wall, a brilliant flash of blue Light appeared, quickly followed by the loud bang of an explosion and splintering wood.

Janis instinctively drew her dagger and jumped backwards at the event. She spoke quickly, anger leaking into her words more than she intended.

"What the fog was *that*? Don't you believe in doors these days?" Janis shouted, still holding a defensive position, knife raised.

Magness turned, huffing quietly.

"Oh, stop that. She didn't try to hurt *you*, did she? Now, put that knife away."

Magness sounded more annoyed than anything, which felt out of place considering a Lightbearer had just Destroyed a solid wooden door to bits. Magness made eye contact with the guard and stepped past her lightly, positioning her feet to not step on any pieces of wood or large splinters.

"Come now, Janis. Don't mind the mess—they will clean it up as soon as we are through."

It was curiosity more than anything that moved her forward. Janis stepped lightly, following Magness's lead, and slid into the room.

"Wait until we are well past the debris before you mend it all, if you please."

A man to the right of the strange woman looked at her and mumbled something along the lines of, 'yes, ma'am', though his head was down and his hood up, so Janis couldn't be sure.

The two women moved until they were twenty or so paces from the place where the spiked iron brackets had held the now-destroyed wooden door, and then stopped.

"Let's watch. I think you'll find this fascinating."

Magness turned back to the broken door and eyed the remnants of it on the floor.

"Now, it's alright."

Janis watched as the man, now to the left of the woman, held out his hands. They immediately began to glow bright blue. Wood fragments all along the floor began to glow blue before moving independently by an invisible force. The process was silent, which made it seem even more strange and eerie. Each piece appeared to know its place, zooming to the broken door and holding there. In mere moments, the door was reformed.

The assassin didn't normally like to gape, but this time, it felt appropriate. She did so easily, given the strangeness of it all.

Magness, sensing the question that Janis was about to ask, spoke first.

"We've found that doors don't do the job well enough when it comes to Lightbearers in captivity. So instead, we just use a solid wall that can only be opened and closed by a Destroyer and a Fixer. A bit barbaric, but it serves us well. In the infrequent case that we need to hold an enemy Lightbearer, they can't get out easily. Each guard pair has at least one Lightbearer and they are mixed in so that any person escaping can't be sure what they are up against. This all works especially well when we make a point to explain it to the prisoners as we go."

Janis listened without saying much. It did seem like a very logical approach to a prison ward, but it was also a bit over the top. Perhaps it seemed this way because she herself would not be able to break anyone out of this cell, let alone escape herself. An assassin's work didn't normally involve having to break anyone out, but she wouldn't say no for a good price. Immediately, she reminisced about past jobs of hers that required her to sneak *into* a prison to take someone out. Those were always a bit more fun, given the challenge they presented.

Magness moved more slowly now, as if she didn't really have anywhere to be. Why that was the case, Janis couldn't know, and it was even more odd given how fast they had rushed to the entrance—as if they were running from someone.

"I imagine Marric is busy practicing his Seeing right at this moment."

The woman didn't turn as she said it, but instead kept walking to a bend just before turning left down the hall. It didn't really surprise Janis that Magness knew exactly what Marric was doing.

"Did you expect anything less from him? You told him that he couldn't come *after* you asked him to stay and hear about this strange woman."

Magness turned her head so that she could peer slightly at Janis.

"Yes, that was actually intentional. It is merely another test to validate her immunity to Lightbearing. I anticipated his curiosity and hoped that he would try."

She paused briefly and looked up at the ceiling.

"Yes, Marric, we know you are listening, and that is fine. Please report later what occurs when we enter the room with this woman. In theory, no Seer can see us when we are near her."

It irked Janis a bit to see her speaking to Marric even though he was far away. Every time that she thought about or even considered how Seeing worked, it made her feel very exposed. Janis made a mental note to focus some attention on trying to develop her Shielding power. Privacy was her most important commodity, and she felt that it was just stripped from her with the knowledge of Seers and their powers.

Before long, Magness came to a halt outside of a tall stone archway full of bars in the middle. Two guards stood at attention on either side. Each nodded to their leader as they approached, but they held their position.

"Has she said or done anything since we last spoke with her?"

The guard on the left, a somewhat short and fat man, spoke out.

"None, ma'am. Oi finks she ain't got much t'say, given 'er circumstance. Tho' we din' roit try much, did we, Berl?"

The other man, one of medium build and quite a bit older, just shrugged.

Magness smiled at the comment and moved closer to them so that she could speak more quietly.

"Any attempt at escape?"

"None t'all, ma'am. S'far as prisoners go, she's roit borin', f'yeh ask me."

"Well, despite your sentiment, I believe that is for the better of every-one," Magness replied. "If you don't mind, Janis and I would like to talk to her alone."

"NO!" a voice from the darkness behind the cell spoke out.

Magness jumped at the sudden shout. Janis felt her skin crawl at the sound of the voice. It was high-pitched and a bit shrieky in nature.

"I want to talk to Janis *alone*," it said again.

Stepping closer, Janis peered in, allowing her eyes to adjust and pierce the darkness. With her training as an assassin, she had learned to focus on the right things in the dark, giving her an advantage over others.

"If that is what you wish, then fine."

Magness sounded offended, but Janis didn't care.

"Are you comfortable with this arrangement, Janis?"

Janis shrugged.

"If this woman really knows me and my reputation, I don't have much to worry about."

To emphasize this point, Janis reached to her sides and patted the slings where her daggers lay. Magness accepted this, then nodded to the guards to allow her in. The older guard Conjured a small key with specific cuts out of blue Light, and inserted it into a metal lock. Janis watched as he turned the lock so that it clicked, then let the key disappear into thin air.

"Why not just Conjure the cell doors?" Janis challenged.

Magness shook her head. "A Conjured door would have to be main-tained constantly. Changing guards would mean a moment of the door being let down. See, Custom locks with no actual keys for each cell are more secure. Real keys get stolen, Conjured keys cannot."

The Evenir leader gestured with both hands toward the cell, nodding at Janis.

Scowling slightly, Janis turned and entered the cell confidently, completely unworried about the situation. As she moved closer, the dark-ness adjusted even more and she could make out more of the imprisoned woman there. The woman was smaller, a few finger-widths shorter than Janis herself, and had mousy brown hair. It was wavy and tied back in a ponytail by a reed of some sort. Though she couldn't see an eye color, Janis could see that her eyes were large and her nose quite small, thus making her eyes appear even larger.

"Livella," the woman said suddenly.

"Excuse me, what?" Janis said.

The woman snorted.

"Well, I assumed that one of your next questions was going to be, 'what is your name?', so I figured I would save us time."

Ooh, I like her, Janis thought.

"Unfortunately, your assumption was wrong, though we would have gotten there eventually," Janis said out loud. "In reality, my first question is, are you here to kill me?"

This had an odd effect on the woman. She leaned back, face looking fearful.

"Wh—what? Why for Lindrad's sake would you ask *that*?"

"You'll find it's a very valid question from someone likely being hunted. I am a wanted assassin, after all."

The woman, Livella, shifted uncomfortably. "I see. That's what you are, then?"

"You don't know that already?"

Livella scoffed at the comment. "I have no blooming idea who you are. I just know that your name is Janis, and that I had to find you as soon as possible."

"What does that even mean?" Janis said, sounding nonchalant.

Livella eyed the cell door to their right, staring briefly at the guards and Magness standing there.

"Umm. I don't know how to explain."

Janis folded her arms and raised an eyebrow at her.

"Well you better try, or you won't be getting out of here anytime soon."

The woman squirmed a bit in her seat, uncomfortable with the comment that Janis made. She once again glanced over at the guards and Magness standing there. The group of three were speaking in hushed tones to each other, causing echoes to bounce around the cell all the way back to where she and Livella sat. Janis couldn't make out what they were saying. Not because she didn't have the ability, but because she was focused intently on the woman—how she sat, how she moved, what her face told. It was this part of the job that Janis enjoyed most. Testing her ability to understand a mark was always a fascinating thing. It had taken years for her to be able to get things right about a person.

Just another skill that I owe Macks for, Janis thought, a pang of sadness piercing her chest before she pushed it away.

What she saw about Livella was perplexing. She was young—perhaps about twenty, very innocent, and very weak in stature. She was, however, bullheaded, quick to speak, and crafty. This type of person is one that you'd find hiding in the shadows, avoiding confrontation and minding their own business. At the same time, this person was the one who would speak up when challenged, become brave in moments of defense, and was wildly intelligent, smarter than most people around them.

She's making a show of being confident and brave, but she's panicking on the inside, Janis thought.

This could potentially play into her advantage at some point, but it wouldn't be necessary now. Livella hardly seemed a threat to anyone.

"Now is the time where you talk, my dear."

Livella scowled at the term Janis used as she realized it was a negative reference to her youth.

"I'm not that much younger than you, I suspect," she said, her voice a bit hard.

There's the lion. Just have to poke at it a bit.

Janis raised an eyebrow at her, but said nothing more. The silence would eventually get her to talk.

As expected, the woman rolled her eyes but began talking in her high voice.

"I was minding my own business at my home in Arivan a few weeks back, when one night, the strangest thing happened. My father is a fisher merchant—he runs the majority of the local fish markets in Arivan."

Glancing down, Janis noted how it matched. Her clothes were a bit worn, but from travel, not from being poor. In fact, her clothes were of nice make and were well kept by someone, probably not herself. Her hands were too clean, no calluses. The fingernails were dirty and chipped in places, but those were recent. This girl was rich, indeed. She was also educated, as indicated by her speech. Her eyes flipped back up to Livella's face as the woman kept talking.

"Well . . . one night a few weeks back, I woke up from a dream. I don't really remember much about it, all I remember is seeing a woman; raven-black hair, dressed all in black, screaming in pain and surrounded by blue Light everywhere and—"

She paused, her own eyes scanning Janis's face. Janis squinted her eyes at the young woman, her brain trying to comprehend what she was saying.

"I mean, it was you, it seems. I couldn't have said it until now, but . . . I recognize you."

Janis made a mental note to see if she could search the in-between and relive her own awakening. Obviously, what the girl had described was that moment. Livella *had* said a few weeks ago, which likely landed around the same time.

"What do you know of Lightbearing?" Janis cut in.

The woman jumped at the interruption, clearly not used to it in any way.

"What? I don't understand what you just said."

Janis leaned in closer, eyes narrowing more.

"Lightbearing. What do you know?" she asked one more time.

Livella paled slightly at the sudden question and menacing feeling behind it. Janis intended for her to feel this way, after all.

"I—I don't have any idea what you mean. What is that?"

Janis looked for signs of deceit in Livella's face, body movement, or posture. None came. She was genuinely surprised and had no knowledge of Lightbearing.

What is happening right now? Janis thought, feeling uneasy.

"Fine, go on."

Livella gulped, but then continued.

"Ummm . . . yeah. After I woke up, I tried to continue life normally but I just couldn't. Every time I paused for a thought, every time I stared away for just a moment, I heard a whisper. It scared me to death—I thought I was going crazy."

Tears welled up in her eyes now, and she started having a harder time talking.

"My father thought I was insane. My mother called a doctor; he said I was insane. All the while I could just hear a whisper of the name 'Janis' and I could feel a force in my gut pulling me north. At night I would see a bright blue Light in this direction. After a few days, I couldn't take it anymore!"

She was crying now, sniffling loudly and hugging her arms around her chest. Janis was irked inside, unsure how to handle being so close to emotions like this. It wasn't that she was *surprised* to see the woman act this way; it was exactly what she expected. Janis hated it nonetheless.

"I noticed that when I moved in the direction of the Light, the whispers got quieter, and came less frequently. The Light was the direction of the market, see? When my mother wanted me to undergo treatment for my insanity, I got scared and just . . . ran. I ran toward the Light. I took one of my horses and rode as quickly as I could until I came to this place, and it all just stopped. I don't hear the name—*your* name, anymore."

Something ominous coalesced in the air. Janis felt her skin crawl at the story, not believing it, yet hanging on every word at the same time.

What in the world have I gotten into? she thought incredulously.

"What *are* those people?" Livella asked suddenly, pointing to the guards and Magness, "They have powers of some sort. I saw them *break a wall to pieces.*"

The last words were practically spit out at her.

Janis hummed loudly before settling into a chair nearby. "I don't know if I am the best person to explain that to you. I'm new here, myself."

The wily assassin opted to make the woman think that she was unassuming and weak. Her tight black clothing wouldn't help with this objective, but Livella might just overlook that.

"However, I can show you a bit," Janis said, not actually needing to pretend that she felt lost about Lightbearing.

She held her hand out toward Livella and summoned a small ball of Light. Once again, she had no idea what the ball could do. It could be a Destroying ball, or maybe just a Lightbearing ball, or even a Conjured marble for all she knew.

The Light flashed brightly in her hand and exposed Livella's face better. Janis quickly noted that the woman had been through quite a run to get here. Her face was very dirty, her hair ratted in places, and she had some cuts on her face that looked like they had come from running through tree branches at a rapid pace. Fear shone in her face as she saw the Light in Janis's hand. Livella had instinctively leaned away from the Light, but she was also pushing back on her feet as if she was trying to scoot away. Of course, the chair in which she sat was stone, so that didn't amount to much.

"It won't hurt you, it's just Light."

Janis hoped what she said was true. Knowing herself, the ball could very well hurt this woman. The last time Janis had created something like this, she had almost killed herself.

"But how?" Livella whispered, eyes wide.

Janis shrugged at the question, once again revealing how little she really knew about Lightbearing.

"All I know is that I have some of the power. It doesn't amount to much for me, though. What you see here is pretty much all I have."

Livella, eyes still wide, reached forward, looking to touch the Light. She thought better of it after only a few moments, and pulled her hand back.

"Perhaps I shouldn't touch it. Are you sure it can't hurt me?"

"Well, *can't* isn't necessarily true, but *won't* probably is. I wouldn't take any chances with me though; I don't know that I am doing it right, and if I don't do it right, it could hurt you, or anyone else, for that matter."

Unless you are truly immune, Janis thought.

For a moment, Janis thought to just ask her if she were immune, but then figured Livella likely had no idea. Based on her odd circumstances and an even stranger story of how she came here, Janis anticipated a non-answer from her. Unfortunately, Janis was a bit impatient.

Magness had said only moments before that *Ka'lek Tar'n* could not be affected by Lightbearing, so technically anything Janis did couldn't hurt her, in theory. Besides, there wasn't really a relationship between them other than the odd dream Livella had and the strange way that she knew Janis's name and what she looked like.

Janis held up her hand and made a face like she was about to sneeze. Finally, she feigned the sneeze and lobbed the ball of Light at the woman in front of her. The moment that the Light connected with Livella's shoulder, it snuffed out. Without even a beat of hesitation, Janis used the woman's shock to summon her small Light-created knife and jabbed her right in the chest. Having found evidence of Livella's immunity with the first test, Janis felt secure in doing a more drastic one. It was the one thing that she *did* have control over.

Livella gasped as the Light-knife went through her chest and to the other side. As it did so, however, Janis felt nothing. There was no familiar feeling of a solid knife hitting a solid object. There was no sound, no blood —nothing.

Livella jumped up and backed away. As she did so, the knife slid through her as if it didn't exist at all.

"Forgive me," Janis said, realizing that her innocent act was ruined now, "I was testing a theory that was brought up earlier."

The woman was crying again and pressed herself firmly against the wall as far from Janis as possible. Their commotion had caused Magness and the guards to halt their conversation and peer curiously into the cell.

Knowing that they were watching and listening, Janis spoke up.

"I think that you are right, Magness. She *is* immune, which means all of the high security details were for nothing," Janis said, smirking.

As she said it, Janis held a Conjured knife in her other hand and pressed the point lightly into her palm. Sure enough, she could feel it. It was a bit more blunt than she had intended when she had first Conjured it to life, but that was just evidence of her weak powers in all seven areas. Regardless, it did prove that the knife was a Conjure and had physical substance, yet it had no effect on Livella.

"Perhaps you could have chosen a more conventional way to test her than to stab her with a knife!" Magness said, quickly realizing what had happened.

The cell door opened and the Evenir leader entered, dress sweeping behind her with a light swishing sound. Janis found her garb extremely impractical, but she knew the woman's prowess with her sword after having seen her spar with her soldiers, so Janis didn't overtly question it any more.

Magness moved slowly, holding her hands out.

"Livella, please don't be alarmed. I apologize for Janis's act. It was merely a test to confirm you were someone we thought you were. I know this doesn't make sense, but I promise that you will not get hurt. We could be allies, not enemies."

"Then why did you throw me in prison the moment I got here? I just want to go home!" Livella yelled, voice shaking from fear.

"We did not know your intentions, dear, and you wouldn't speak to any of us. If you had merely spoken, told us the truth, we wouldn't have needed to," Magness said softly, trying to calm her down. "There is much you must know, but for now, know this. This is a sanctuary, a safe haven for people like Janis—and you.

The pause wasn't lost on Janis, but Livella apparently didn't put much stock in it. Livella wasn't like a Lightbearer; in fact, the person that she was *most* like gave Janis much more pause than it apparently gave Magness.

"We have enemies in this world, and we didn't want to put this place at risk by not knowing if you were one of them. It's clear that you are not, so please—try to calm down and let's just talk."

The guards began to close the cell door behind them, but Magness gestured for them to stop.

"I think a different venue for this conversation seems best. Livella means us no harm."

Magness gestured toward the door and stepped back slightly, making room for Livella to leave the cell. Livella's eyes flicked to Janis, then Magness. Janis didn't blame her for being still. She had just had a knife made out of blue Light shoved into her. Considering the circumstances, Janis could only imagine her own reaction if she was in the same situation: without any knowledge of Lightbearing whatsoever. In fact, she recalled how ready she was to run Avryn through when they had first run into each other in the woods.

It took a lot more coaxing and Janis leaving the cell completely before Livella would consider even leaving the cell herself. The three made their way back to the war room to continue the conversation. When they arrived back at the Fixed wooden wall, Livella closed her eyes when the Destroyer had broken through it.

The trip back to the war room was awkward and slow. Unfortunately for Janis, these were two kinds of travel that she very much disliked. Janis had to breathe evenly and slowly at many points just to avoid yelling her frustrations out loud. At one point, she had almost left the two of them and went on her own to the war room, opting to get there in at least semi-decent time.

Something kept her there, though she couldn't explain what. It was as if something inside was drawing her to Livella's side. As they walked, she tested the feeling. Despite the slowness of their pace, Janis would hang back slightly until she was a dozen or so paces behind the others. Magness would look back at her, brow raised as she noticed what the assassin was doing, but she wouldn't say anything.

When Janis had reached a certain distance from Livella, she could feel something. There was a slight tugging in her stomach toward the girl. It was subtle, yet easily noticeable to her. The tugging would get a bit stronger with distance, but it never became overwhelming. Given that she didn't have anything else to do on their slow trek back to the war room, it seemed relatively harmless to hang back and test it a few times.

The three women turned down the hallway that would lead them to the final stretch before their destination. Just as they did, something odd happened. Janis felt the tugging in her gut again, though this time it was stronger, as if an invisible rope was somehow tied to her organs inside her belly and was yanking forcefully forward.

Livella gasped and looked down, arms folding around her midsection.

What in the blazes is happening? Is she experiencing this too? Janis thought.

The strange woman looked back at her, eyes desperate as she too struggled against the urge to run forward. The feeling of pulling wasn't unpleasant, just an unnatural feeling. For some reason, it reminded Janis of when she was a slave with a rope tied around her midsection. She remembered being pulled behind a horse, trying to keep up as the rope bit into her skin. There wasn't pain with this pulling, though.

Moving quickly, she stood next to Livella, testing once again the proximity factor of the strange force.

"Magness," she said, "something's off—"

Magness turned just in time to see Livella yelp and begin running down a separate hallway just before the entryway to the library room. Janis felt the same pull and rushed after the mousy-haired woman. Without hesitation, she shoved her hand into Livella's and squeezed tight. This had the opposite effect of slowing them down; Janis felt the pull strengthen on her own midsection, yanking them both forward.

Lanser's might, what the—?

They were running hard now, barreling down the stone hallway, Magness shouting behind them.

Janis didn't have time to listen before the other woman's shouts were drowned out. Normally, holding hands would have made Janis uncomfortable, but she didn't have time for that. All she could do was focus on her feet and try not to trip with the speed that they were going.

Whispers in her ears distracted her further. She couldn't decipher what they were saying, but it felt as if there were a hundred people whispering quietly, the collective sound building until it was a loud sound swimming in the air around them.

"Do you hear that?" Janis yelled over their thumping footsteps echoing on the stone around them.

"Yes!" Livella said, fear in her eyes. "What is happening? What have you done to me?"

"What have *I* done to *you*? None of this strangeness started until *you* showed up here. Who the fog are you?"

Livella opened her mouth to answer, but was stopped by what they saw ahead. They had just turned down the last corner and could see that they were running toward a wall. This hallway was empty, except for a couple doors on the right of the hall.

Gasping, Livella squeezed Janis's hand tight as they realized they were moving quickly and would soon collide with the wall. Janis still felt the pull, but started to slow her pace, struggling against the force tugging in her gut. She was soon breathing hard trying to pull against it. Livella was of no help, as she seemed resigned to letting herself get pulled.

Desperate and realizing quickly that she didn't want her face colliding with a solid stone wall, Janis held out her open left hand and shot the first thing that came to mind. A half sphere of Light sprung from her hand and expanded into a Shield in front of them, the Light both translucent, yet piercingly blue. The moment the Light Shield came up, the force pulling on her gut ceased entirely, and she quickly slowed down. It must have done the same for Livella, for she slowed herself as well. The two women were a mere three paces from the solid wall, both breathing hard from the rapid and manic run they had just been forced into.

"Are you alright?" Janis said to the younger woman.

Livella was unable to speak from breathing so hard, but she nodded.

"Who are you really, Livella?" Janis said, angling herself so that she could pin Livella in against the dead-end of the hallway, should the girl make any sudden moves. "I said it before, but here we are again. This is yet another oddity that only began when you came here. It's odd in and of itself that you are here in the first place. Terris Green is hidden. It isn't recognized on any maps, and is only known to people of Evenir. How are we supposed to believe you were led here by a disembodied voice?"

Grimacing at the words, Livella started shaking her head.

"Can't you see I have no idea what's happening? I tried to tell you this before. If I had a choice, I'd go home right now, but I *can't*. I know that if I do, the whispering will start again, and I can't take it anymore! Do you know what it's like to be called crazy so many times that you feel like you are crazy yourself? Have you ever heard voices that won't leave you alone?"

She was yelling now with balled-up fists. Despite her reaction and how she was acting now, Janis didn't feel threatened. This girl was young and weak. For that reason, she really couldn't be anything other than what she claimed. It was obvious to Janis that the girl had no sense of self-defense by how she backed up to the wall, penning herself in.

"No, I have not admittedly heard any voices, except for just now. I definitely haven't felt that way though," Janis replied in an attempt at sympathy.

The moment Livella's back touched the wall at the end of the hallway, a loud whispering burst into Janis's head.

Tar'n Yiv'len videsk frinn K'alek Tar'n yrillnan grisk.

Janis whipped out her daggers quickly and spun around in circles, seeking the voice that she'd just heard.

"Until now, apparently," she said, heart racing.

Livella's eyes filled with a bit of hope at Janis's reaction.

"You—you heard that too?"

Janis nodded, waiting.

The voice came again, echoing on the walls around them.

Tarn' Yiv'len videsk frinn K'alek Tar'n yrillnan grisk.

The words made absolutely no sense to her, yet they felt familiar. It was as if she was hearing a lullaby—words that she'd only heard as an infant, yet couldn't comprehend, but were familiar from repetition.

"What does it mean?" Janis said aloud, speaking both to Livella and to the unseen speaker.

"I have no idea, but they're almost like something out of a forgotten memory."

Janis paused and looked at where Livella was leaning against the wall.

"They started whispering when you touched the wall."

Moving quickly, Janis positioned herself next to Livella and inspected the stone there. Livella was still breathing hard, but her face bore a bit of a smile. Janis could understand Livella's relief at not being the only one subject to the voice anymore, as much as she didn't want to. There had been times when she'd felt all alone, even insane in her isolation. Macks came to mind then. She had been alone for so long, either enslaved or homeless, and he had brought that peace back to her. Until he had abandoned her in turn.

She shook the thought from her mind, packing Macks away again. At some point, she'd have to go to the in-between and see if she could find him there. Instead, she held out her hand and hesitantly touched the stone wall.

The moment her hand made contact with the smooth stone, a burst of bright blue Light flashed directly in front of her, blinding her. She gasped and jumped back quickly, raising her daggers in front of her. Just then, movement behind her made her turn to see Magness with a few guards alongside. They all gaped at the Light that shone from the wall. As the Light grew less intense, Janis realized that she saw two odd symbols made from the Light:

The voice spoke again this time, though it wasn't a whisper.

"Tar'n Yiv'len videsk frinn K'alek Tar'n yrillnan grisk!"

8

Prost stalked heavily down the hallway, glaring at each person he passed. They all despised him, even those who weren't Lightbearers. For years he had just dealt with it, but he now realized that he didn't have to live this way.

As he walked, he made a point to stop and give a few orders to people here and there. His rank within Watchlight wasn't really defined, but at the same time it was inferred, based on his constant proximity to Riln and how his orders were received. Many called him Riln's lapdog. Though he disliked the term, it at least allowed him some connection to power.

Most gave him annoyed glances as he walked by, especially those whom he ordered about, but they all listened despite the looks.

"Sir," someone said behind him.

He turned to see Yanlin, squat and muscley, standing behind him.

"I may be wrong, but I don't know that ordering people about is in your best interest. Perhaps you should take a more gentle approach to your commands."

Prost snorted, "Fog it, Yanlin. You think that would actually work?" Prost shook his head derisively.

"It could, after some time. If you'd learn to be patient, it might turn out good for you in the end."

The scars on his face itched at the mention of being patient. He recalled the origin of the scars, and anger welled in his stomach.

"Patience has failed me time and time again, Yanlin. I choose to act, and those that can't keep up can either work harder, or get out."

Yanlin pressed his lips into a thin line as he stared at Prost. As of yet, Yanlin seemed to be one of the few at Watchlight who dared to speak up to him. Prost wondered how Yanlin had the gall to give Prost pointers on leadership. Yanlin *had* saved many people with his Fixing, especially during the time of both Marric's and then Janis's own awakening a few weeks back, giving him respect and weight among his peers. But the simple fact that Yanlin's Fixing didn't work on Prost made him inclined to be bitter and resentful. It wasn't Yanlin's fault, but Prost still couldn't let it go.

Yanlin pressed forward with his point, "Though I'm sure you have had some nasty experiences in the past, whatever they are, they don't merit you acting the way that you do. I suspect that the only reason Riln allows you to be this way is because he doesn't care—"

Prost didn't even let him finish. He rushed the man and snagged the front of his tunic, spinning swiftly and shoving him into the wall.

"Why Riln allows me to act the way I do has nothing to do with lack of care!" Prost shouted at him.

The crowd around them scattered at the sudden scuffle, and Prost was somewhat pleased at this. If he was to get the respect that he needed, fear would have to be the route. He had tried many things in his years here at Watchlight, and nothing had been successful. The one thing he did know was that people feared him. He had come to terms with that fact, and planned to keep using it to his advantage.

"Riln *trusts* me. He knows I get it done, and do it well. If you don't like my methods, feel free to *leave*."

A few of the people to his left cowered in fear; a part of him felt regret at the sight. But he knew it had to be done. It was time he started taking control of his destiny.

"Fog it, Prost! Who do you think you are? You don't own me. I answer to Riln and *only* to him."

Prost gritted his teeth at the comment. Words like these stole his power, making people pull away from him and respect him less. His mind reeled, slightly panicked at how he could take control over the situation. He decided to fall back on a simple truth that no one could deny.

"Riln is our leader, yes. I *am* taking into account his orders and following through with them. But need I remind you that I follow him out of respect, not necessity? I am fully capable of taking care of myself—even Riln's own Lightbearing is useless against me. I choose to not kill him, because I recognize him as our leader. If leadership was based on power alone, then I by default am second in command, regardless of who says what."

It was a lie, of course, but Yanlin didn't necessarily know enough to contest it. There was something much larger that kept Prost from stabbing Riln in the dark.

In the corner of his eye, Prost saw someone move suddenly. He glanced over to see a boy wearing the garb of a courier spin around and run in the direction of the throne room.

I suppose I should have expected this to get back to Riln. He may not be able to See me or anything around me, but he has eyes everywhere.

Prost found it somewhat ironic that he wasn't the least bit scared. He knew that Riln would probably take out more anger on him by Destroying Prost's clothing or stabbing him with Conjured weapons, but he didn't care. He found himself less and less scared of Riln. They had an inherent need for each other, contrary to Prost's preference. Persistent whispers in his mind reminded him as much.

Prost let Yanlin down slowly and purposefully so that he wouldn't get hurt. He didn't really want to let him down softly, but he felt that it was part of the power play. He may use fear and threatening to gain control, but Yanlin had a bit of a point—respect was solidified when mercy was shown.

"I don't want to hurt you, Yanlin, nor do I get any pleasure from it, but insubordination must be taken seriously here in Watchlight. If we are to prevail, to quell the threat of Evenir and truly control Lindrad as our own, we cannot be split in purpose and resolve. I demand your respect."

With a curt nod, he turned away and stomped toward the path leading to the throne room, and his inevitable punishment from Riln.

The people around him didn't run, nor did they look confident enough to face him. There were some, however, who nodded to him with looks of reverence on their face. Despite the unexpected nature of the encounter and

Yanlin's words about Prost lacking real authority, Prost felt that the situation had flipped in his favor.

As he walked, he dwelled on the past for a moment. He recalled how things had changed since he'd arrived ten years ago. There were parts of the past that still filled him with regret, and others that made him angry and hardened for his next move in the game of life.

The whispers had brought him here. That, and the odd dreams of a man with all white hair and pale white skin. Prost was younger then, training to be a soldier for Lindrad. Things had been going so well for him. He had been training for years to become a general, and he had proven skilled enough to achieve his goal.

Then everything had changed.

He thought back to those times when life had been more simple and full of purpose—when he'd had friends and something to work toward.

It's funny how life always seems to be progressing and moving in the right direction before it all gets ripped out from under you, Prost thought, shaking his head.

The whispers had started a few days before the new general would be named. It had started small, but each day they grew and grew—until he couldn't imagine anything else but to find the source and to make them stop. The other soldiers thought he was crazy. He finally chose to desert the militia out of an intense need to be free of the voices, despite his chance of making general. Only one person believed anything he said.

Avryn, Prost thought, *what would have happened if I had gotten to you before Evenir did?*

He pushed the thought from his mind and instead let the memory flow in, the one of his arrival at the Watchlight compound.

Prost felt wet. His boots and clothes were soaking and his patience was running thin. The pouring rain hadn't let up for days, and he wasn't sure how much more he could handle. Normally, he liked rain. The smell was generally pleasant, the sound soothing; even traveling in the rain hadn't been a problem for him until now.

A voice whispered in his ear and he growled in frustration.

Shut up, *he thought.*

He knew that it wouldn't do anything. For weeks, he had tried to push the voice away. No matter what he tried, it always continued, getting stronger with time until he couldn't focus on anything else.

Prost looked up at the height of the mountain he now climbed. At the top of the mountain, there shone a Light. It was a strange color shifting rapidly from blue to red, as if it didn't know what it wanted to be. He'd been able to see it ever since he had left the capital, and he assumed it was connected to the whispers he'd heard. They had started about the time he could see the Light from afar. Then the dreams had begun.

Prost pictured the man in his mind, hair pure white, skin even whiter, eyes so blue it seemed impossible. It was as if the color had been drained from him by some mystical force and left a plain canvas, ready to be painted.

He shivered, partially from the cold and partially from the sight of the man.

If this man is to blame for ruining my life, I'll kill him, *Prost thought, anger swelling inside.*

Days. That is all that had stood between him and finally being sworn in as a general of Lindrad. He knew that he would have moved up. Prost had already proven himself a good soldier and a leader. Becoming a general in the army would have been inevitable.

Glaring at the light above, he growled at the persistent whispers in his ear. Normally they were incomprehensible, but every so often he'd hear a word that he assumed was a name.

Riln.

It pushed at his mind again and again, only subsiding if he was actively moving in the direction of the Light that he saw above the mountain. He felt ridiculous, roaming the wilderness, hearing voices, following a Light that only he could see.

A pang of regret and appreciation filled him when he thought of Avryn, the only friend that believed him when he spoke of the voice. He knew that if he'd asked Avryn to come, the man would have. That is why he had to leave without notice. Prost was a fugitive now, a deserter, but it was better than being locked away for being insane, or causing his friend to suffer the same fate.

A flash of lightning high above blinded him for a moment just before a crack of thunder drowned out the whispers entirely. Sure, the sound hurt his ears a bit, but it was a nice short break from the annoyingly persistent voice.

Prost had no idea where he was going. The only thing he knew for sure was that he had to keep moving to keep the whispers quiet and somewhat at bay. So, he walked.

The slope of the mountain steepened as he continued, and he started to worry that this couldn't be right. Fields covered the mountain on every surface with wild-flowers of many colors filling in small patches between the greens of the tall grass. He thought that under different circumstances it would be beautiful, but not today.

His head was down, angled to avoid rain pelting him directly in the face. Because of this, he almost ran smack into a rock face that jutted out of the mountain randomly. Squinting, Prost looked up to inspect the rock that had appeared out of nowhere. For a moment, he thought to sit down and try to shield himself from the rain, but then a feeling pushed him forward to stand next to the stone.

The voice came back then. It instructed him to push on the rock. A mixture of confusion and wonder filled him and suddenly the coldness of the pouring rain seemed to disappear along with the flashes of lightning and the sound of the wind.

Feeling a bit ridiculous, but not knowing what else to do, he raised his hand and placed it on the rock just above eye level. He jumped as a portion of the wall opened inward, a switch of some kind, and the rock face cracked and moved, rumbling loudly. Prost felt uneasy, but curiosity got the better of him. Stepping into the cave, he cautiously pulled out his short sword from his belt.

Stairs cascaded downward sharply inside the opening. Just as he passed the threshold of the door, it rumbled closed behind him. He leapt backward to try to escape before he was shut in, but missed it for fear of being crushed.

The sound of the door closing was loud and foreboding, as if it announced his final fate.

Prost felt dread as he realized why the stairs all looked odd. Purple orbs of Light about the size of his head hovered near the top of the wall.

What in the name of Lanser are those? he thought, making a clawing motion with his hand, a religious symbol to ward off evil.

"HEY!" a voice shouted.

He looked down to see two men in black with their hoods up.

"Ow did yous get in 'ere?" one of them shouted.

Instinctively, Prost crouched into a defensive position. What happened next made no sense.

The other man, the one that didn't speak, held up his hand just before a flash of purple Light announced a sword made of the same Light appearing in his hand.

Prost's skin crawled at the sight.

Fog it! How—? he thought, just before the man lunged.

The Light sword swung directly at Prost, his attacker moving into a standard offensive move. Prost had trained in combat for years and had little trouble parrying the attack. The sword, however, passed through his own steel sword as if it was made of nothing.

Cursing, Prost tried to spin out of the line of the sword but was unsuccessful. The blade connected with his cheek and continued to pass through.

Gasping in fear, it took Prost a moment to realize he had felt nothing.

The man with the Light-sword cursed and swung again, yet with the same result. Seeing this, the other man summoned a ball of purple Light and lobbed it at Prost. Once again, instinctually, Prost dodged. Rather than hit him, it grazed his shirt and exploded, cracking loudly and shredding the arm of his tunic.

Prost grit his teeth and spun around, pointing his sword at the men. He felt nothing, but assumed that he'd broken something, that his arm was damaged somehow. Chancing a glance downward, he saw that his shirt had been destroyed completely from the arm down, but oddly his skin was clear, no wounds of any kind.

Hearing movement, he looked up to see the man with the sword charging again.

"Wait!" the other said, holding his hand up.

The man stopped his mad charge, but held his sword up.

Not understanding why his companion had ordered the halt, Prost looked over to see a hollow pipe protruding from the man's lips. Prost's eyes widened as he realized what it was. He felt the sharp pain of the dart going into his chest and cursed.

Then everything went black.

Later, Prost woke up feeling dizzy. The world around him was dull purple and gray, nothing else. As he came to, he realized that he was staring at a stone ceiling and stone walls. It took a moment for the fuzz to lift from his mind and for him to remember what had taken place beforehand.

"I must know," a voice echoed on the walls around him, "how did you find us?"

Prost didn't answer. Actually, in reality, he couldn't answer. His senses had come back, but the poison was still affecting his ability to think.

"*Normally when I ask a question, I expect an* answer. *In your case, staying silent will not serve you well.*"

Frustration rooted in Prost's chest as he knew that he must say something. He sat up slowly and looked around, jumping when he realized that there were men surrounding him on all sides.

"Can't . . . speak," he said, coughing slightly.

A pause.

"*Yes, the poison will inevitably take some time to get out of your system.*"

The voice was high and masculine, but sounded inhuman given that it came from someone he couldn't see. At that moment, he realized that what he saw around him wasn't men, but pillars.

Taking in more information mentally, he realized that this was some sort of throne room. To confirm his suspicion, he turned his head and followed the columns stacked in two rows to the end of the room where a throne made of the same stone sat regally. It was, however, empty.

"*Right now I only care about one thing, which I have already asked, and I would be loath to have to repeat myself.*"

Fear twisted in Prost's stomach and he remembered the question.

"I have no foggin' idea how I found it," Prost said through gritted teeth. There were momentary pauses between the words, but he was gaining control again. "I followed a voice, and a Light that hovered above the mountain."

"*LIAR!*" the voice roared. Despite the echo, he realized now that it was coming from his left, in the shadows of the pillars there.

"What makes you think I'm lying?" Prost asked, feeling annoyed. There was still fear, but when someone hid in the shadows like this, it normally indicated insecurities.

"*Hmmm, confident, I see. I commend you for that. It will not, however, serve you well here.*"

Out of nowhere, a flash of bright purple Light blinded Prost. His head turned to the place from where it came and he flinched as a ball of purple Light flew from the shadows and collided with his chest. Just as the Light touched his chest, his clothes exploded there, accompanied by a loud crack like before.

He closed his eyes tight and braced for the pain, fear gripping him again at this strange sorcery. Yet when he opened his eyes, his skin was unscathed.

"What I need to know, even more than how you found me, is why the poison had to be used in the first place."

Another flash of Light revealed a dagger, bright and menacing, intricate, but seemingly made of Light. Prost stared, mouth slightly opened at the sight. He could see nothing else from the darkness except the dagger and a place where the Light was interrupted on the handle, indicating a hand clutching it there. His mind couldn't comprehend what he was seeing. It had to be a dream.

Slowly, the wielder of the strange magic knife stalked out of the shadows, the purple Light revealing his face. Prost only realized now why it was so dark. A lone purple sphere of Light, like the ones he'd seen when he first entered, hovered near the tall ceiling, causing shadows from the pillars lining the hall. The moment he saw the face, Prost froze.

"Riln."

The man stopped, eyes narrowing at him. Prost saw that his skin and hair shone purple, the same color of the Light above. Though he couldn't see, Prost knew that it was the whiteness that was soaking in the purple, bleeding into his coloring more so than the Light above colored Prost's own skin.

"How . . ." Riln said, eyes widening now. "Who are you? Answer me!"

Prost flinched, but launched into an explanation of who he was, what had happened, and how he got here. Before he'd made it too far, Riln held up a hand and stopped him. Saying nothing, Riln focused on the wall and his eyes filled with purple Light. His eyes had already been reflecting the Light from the orb above, but this was different. They now glowed with their own Light, small beams leaking out of his sockets.

"I can't See you," the man said. "How can this be?"

He growled and threw the knife at Prost suddenly, the dagger's blade sliding into Prost's stomach with a well-placed throw. The oddity of it froze Prost in place. Once the dagger had gone through him with no effect, he jumped to his feet and reached for his own weapons, cursing when he realized it was silly to have even checked. They would have disarmed him first thing when they knocked him out.

"Now that you've had the chance to ask your questions," Prost said, seething inside. "Let me ask a few of my own. What is this power that you use? Are you a servant of Ugglyn?"

Prost had only heard rumors of magics of the anti-god, Ugglyn. He marveled inside that he'd never heard of or seen power such as this before.

Oddly, the man laughed at the question.

"Lightbearing is not derived from the anti-god Ugglyn. This power is far more ancient and powerful than anything else. It may be fairly new to me, but it isn't to the world."

Prost cocked his head, not understanding what the words meant. He then balled his fists and held them up, prepared for another fight.

"Nothing you say makes sense. Why do you bother speaking in gibberish and stories when you have nothing to gain from me? I gave you my answers. If you choose to ignore them, that is your problem," Prost spat out.

Riln's features softened at Prost's words and he put his own hands down, clasping them in front of him.

"I apologize for my quick reactions," Riln said, voice calm now. "You see, this location is secure from all those except our own. We both know that you are not our own, so it vexes me so to know how you found the location. You speak of voices, of Light—yet I hear none and see none."

"You—" Prost cut in, not wanting to lose his own footing, "—use powers unknown to me and speak as if they are some known force in the world. What is it you want from me?"

Prost sounded far braver than he felt—weaponless, confused, buried deep underground in a place he did not know.

A silence followed that made Prost uncomfortable. Riln continued to stare at him, something in his eyes. It wasn't anger, it wasn't kindness, but it was something else. Rather than try to interpret the look, Prost just stared back, eyes narrow. He focused on his other senses so as to prepare for an ambush from behind if it came. Prost heard nothing, nor did he feel any subtle vibrations in the stone beneath his feet that might give away someone behind him.

"For me," Riln said at last, "I merely care how this—"

White hand opening upward, Riln summoned a purple ball of Light and lobbed it at one of the pillars. The moment it struck, a loud cracking sound rang through the cavern and bits of rock exploded everywhere, stinging Prost in the face.

"—doesn't affect you even one bit."

Prost gaped, his hands loosening and his focus broken. Never in his life had he seen something like that before. The cavern shook from the explosion, making Prost quake even more at the sight.

"How...?" Prost couldn't even finish his sentence.

Riln smiled, but not sweetly. It was the kind of smile that a child might wear just before he pulled the legs off of an insect he'd captured. Mischievous, evil.

"Through the same power by which I can do this," Riln said.

He shuffled quickly to the pillar that was broken and held his hand out, touching the surface. The dust was still settling, and Prost felt his stomach churn from the odd encounter. The sound had been loud enough already, but he had yet to see the damage of the power. The pillar was shattered completely through the center, the top half hanging from the ceiling like a stalactite, the bottom like a stalagmite, reaching to its companion up above. Purple Light glowed intensely from Riln's outstretched hand.

Movement around Prost caused him to tense and he spun to see who was there. Shocked, he saw that it wasn't anyone, but instead the bits of dust and shards of rock all glowing with purple and moving like they had a will of their own. Each flew quickly to Riln's hand. Eyes wide, Prost watched as the pillar formed back into its shape, restored as if nothing had happened before.

Envy. Somehow, jealousy sprung inside Prost at the unknown power he'd just witnessed. Before seeing this power, all that he'd sought was becoming a general, high up in the army of Lindrad, but this changed everything.

"I awakened only weeks ago, yet my power has grown stronger with time," Riln said. "I can teach you the meaning of Lightbearing, but only few are chosen."

Riln eyed Prost standing there, relaxed now that he was distracted by the display of power. He quickly tensed, however, when Riln started to walk slowly toward him.

"You are the first I've seen that is immune to such power. I have been here for a long time. I used to be powerless, like you. But even now I am subject to my superiors, full of the power of Light. How do you withstand such power?"

Prost stepped back, flexing his muscles in preparation for a fight. Riln was now within a few paces of him. He casually held up his hand and summoned a sword. The Light was a mixture of blue and red, creating a type of purple. Riln looked up at Prost and stepped closer.

"Be calm, I cannot hurt you," Riln whispered.

Prost's skin crawled. The white-skinned man dropped the blade of Light into Prost's hands, but it fell through.

"Be patient, and I will teach you all that you need to know."

Prost relaxed and let his hands down, staring at the floor where the Light blade had fallen, making a clunking sound like that of a normal one.

"I do, however, need to assert my power over you."

Hearing the words, Prost felt confusion. He looked up quickly to see twin short-bladed daggers clutched in Riln's hands. His eyes widened as Riln growled loudly and slashed forward with both hands, blades cutting into Prost's face. He felt the ripping of his flesh from nose to ear, pain taking a few moments to blossom and burn there. Prost screamed and threw his hands to his face.

"You may be immune to my Light, but you will never be immune to my power."

These were the last words Prost heard before he blacked out from the pain.

PROST WAS ANGRY NOW. He'd served Riln out of fear for too many years. It wasn't necessarily fear of Riln, though that was a small part of it. Prost feared the unknown.

I can't upset the balance; who knows what problems that would cause, Prost thought to himself, seething inside that he felt so stuck.

Words flowed into his mind that he'd recited many times since he'd been here, since the day he'd met Riln. *Tarn' Yiv'len videsk frinn K'alek Tar'n yrillnan grisk.*

As if whispering from the depths of the ground below him, Prost heard the words loud and clear in his ears. Nostalgia filled his whole being at the sound of them. He had memorized the words almost instantly, the experience burning into his mind. Something felt different this time, though he couldn't explain what. The words came to his mind again, pressing there intensely.

He spun around, looking for signs of Light symbols on the walls around him. The last time he'd experienced hearing the ancient words in his mind, he'd been with Riln. Now he was alone, and it didn't feel the same. An urgency filled his being and he rushed to the throne room, feet slapping the ground loudly as he abandoned all his usual stealth and replaced it with sheer speed.

Something inside felt different about the words today. It was when he realized that he wasn't thinking the words to himself as he usually did, but instead the whispers were actually echoing in his mind, that he understood why they felt different.

Making the final turn into the throne room, he heard the words again:

Tarn' Yiv'len videsk frinn K'alek Tar'n yrillnan grisk!

They pierced his mind like an unwelcome thought, interrupting all else.

"Riln!" he shouted, frantically searching for his leader.

"Yes, I hear them," the high-pitched voice echoed from the shadows.

"What does it mean? What is this?"

Riln sat on the throne at the front of the long room. His face was hard, as if he'd just received terrible news.

Resisting the urge to shudder, Prost stared at him, heart racing from the rapid pace he'd just adopted as well as from the sight of Riln glaring at him.

When he didn't get an answer immediately, Prost spoke again, frustration leaking into his voice.

"What is *happening*?" he asked, gritting his teeth.

Riln's eyes narrowed at him, clearly deep in thought.

"Patience, my friend. I am considering the situation as we speak."

Prost flinched at the words. He disliked the sudden use of 'friend' when referring to himself. It all felt like a lie. Riln gave him false respect, paid him false kindness, then undermined him by addressing him as 'dud' or other derogatory terms in public. In reality, Riln treated him like a slave or dirt, yet taunted him by ironically using terms like 'friend' and 'dear'.

Riln's eyes filled with red Light, and he focused on the wall behind Prost.

"I cannot See her, or the boy. However, I See something. I See her future. Something has changed, dear Prost. I believe the message we are both so very familiar with was not meant for us this time."

Prost stepped back at the words, hearing them, but not fully understanding what they meant. Flashes of more memories came to his mind. He saw the silver and blue glowing ancient symbols on the stone wall, and the secret passageway that opened only to Riln and himself for a moment in time. He heard the words again, though this time they were only in his memory,

Tar'n Yiv'len videsk frinn K'alek Tar'n yrillnan grisk!

He remembered the odd familiarity of them and how he was somehow able to understand their meaning: *The Prime Lightbearer and the Voidbearer must balance!* Prost thought.

Prost looked up at Riln, seething inside again. The white-skinned man was the *Tar'n Yiv'len*, the all-powered, and Prost, the *K'alek Tar'n*. Oh, how the power dynamic could change by giving a man unprecedented powers. Prost was superior in combat, strength, and likely will, but by law of nature, he was subject to Riln.

Balance, Prost thought, *that's the only purpose I serve here.*

Riln's eyes stopped glowing and he peered at Prost before speaking. "I believe the world has been changed in a way that we couldn't have anticipated. You described the awakening of Janis yourself, and for that reason alone, I believe you. I have observed her awakening from the small Sightvision I had, and I agree that it was unusual. Add the fact that she is twenty-five years of age, far later than normal awakenings *and* that she survived, like me."

Prost's eyes snapped to his master's face.

Like his awakening? Am I understanding him correctly? Prost thought, mind reeling.

"We are not alone anymore, my friend. I believe a new Seal has been created. Janis is a newly awakened *Tar'n Yiv'len*, and you, dear Prost, are no longer the only *K'alek Tar'n* in the world."

Prost's world shifted at the words. Nothing had physically changed in the room, but the knowledge rocked Prost more than words alone ever could.

Alone. He'd been alone for years and years, an anomaly to the Lightbearing world. Now he wasn't. There might be another man out there who could be called a dud and could share the burden of being hated by normal people and Lightbearers alike, yet feeling powerless to do anything about it.

"If the situation is anything like our own many years ago, I'd wager that the *K'alek Tar'n* joined with Evenir only just recently. Never, since this all began, had I thought of a new Seal being created. This brings a whole new meaning to it all. I fear that our lives are only to become more complicated. We must stand together in this if we are to come out on top."

Prost heard the words and hated them instantly. All he wanted now was exactly the opposite. He imagined a life without Riln, without the oppression from a man weaker than himself. He knew, however, that the balance must remain.

Wearing a false smile, Prost nodded.

"Yes, Riln. Together."

9

Squinting, Janis covered her eyes with her hands, peeking only through the slits between a few of her fingers. Blue and silver Light emanated from the walls, blinding both her and Livella. She turned slightly to see if Magness was seeing the same thing, and found the woman frozen—eyes wide but making no other movements or sounds. Wind began rushing through the hallways as a loud rumbling announced rock sliding against rock.

The once dead-end wall that stood before them now split down the center, both sides moving inward somehow. Janis turned again to see Magness still frozen with a look of surprise on her face. Part of Janis wanted to move toward the leader to see if everything was alright, but she feared looking away from the mystical door, lest something horrible emerge. That would prove potentially deadly if her back were turned, or if she left Livella there alone.

Peering to the side, she could see that Livella was panting, face white from fear at what was happening.

"Get behind me!" Janis yelled to her, trying to project her voice over the wind and the rock grinding.

It took a few more moments and a couple more shouts before Livella finally fell out of her trance and moved behind Janis, shaking like a leaf.

Janis whipped out her daggers as the two parts of the wall reached halfway to the insides of the intersecting wall. The sound of the grinding rock suddenly stopped and all was still. All sound stopped, leaving them in eerie silence.

Breathing hard, Janis felt adrenaline rushing through her body, urging her to spring into action. She was ready for any attack that might come from inside the room. Blessedly, nothing came from the new opening in the wall. The silence was piercing after the loud voice screaming in her ear and the grinding of the rock door.

"What is this?" Janis said quietly, really asking no one, but half expecting someone to answer.

No one did.

"What do we do now?" Livella asked, still cowering behind her.

"Well, lass, we need to get you some combat training," Janis said lightly.

Livella huffed behind her, but kept hiding as if she was a little child hiding from her parents after breaking a piece of fine pottery.

Once Janis determined that nothing menacing was coming out of the new opening, she stepped backward with one foot.

"Move slowly," Janis said. "Something is off. Magness appears to be frozen back there."

Livella started at the comment and turned around fully, exposing her back to the new door with only Janis between. This caused Janis to roll her eyes.

She really would die so easily. I can't imagine she's anything more than a spoiled, rich, merchant's daughter, Janis thought.

"Move slowly, now."

The two inched their way back to Magness as quickly as they could, still tense as if something might surprise them at any moment. Once they reached Magness, Livella squeaked and backed away.

"What happened to her?" she said, sounding desperate.

Janis squinted at the cavern opening, now fairly far away. Nothing seemed to be coming, so she tuned her ears to any sound other than their own breathing. Once again, there was no indication of foul play or surprise.

Finally, she turned her head and observed Magness. The woman was frozen in place, like a life-like statue, eyes wide as she stared past Janis to the wall where the symbols of Light still pulsed on the two halves of the wall. They were half-hidden, of course, now that each part of the wall had receded into the stone walls they intersected. Janis waved her hand over Magness's eyes, but there was no reaction. Moving more closely, she put her ear to the woman's chest. A chill ran through her body as she heard nothing. No breathing, no heartbeat.

By Lanser's might, what is happening? she thought, wheeling around to look back at the symbols. Janis had heard Magness behind them just as the symbols appeared. There must be some type of magic in them that had caused this to happen to her. Pausing for a moment to take in the situation, she tried to work out a solution.

A thought came to her that seemed driven by something else, by some other force entering her thoughts. She felt partially uncomfortable with the idea of some external force in her mind, but at the same time, it didn't feel malicious.

This is only for our eyes, she thought.

"I think we're meant to go in there," Janis said bluntly.

"Wh—*what?*" Livella stammered, "I mean, I felt it too, but you can't be serious? What if we die in there?"

"If we were to die, we probably would have already."

Janis was unafraid, though she couldn't explain why. She still felt her muscles tense and ready, knowing that she could always change her position in a quick movement, so she stalked forward confidently.

She stopped when Livella didn't follow her.

"I believe that it's for both of us," she said, not turning, "meaning I should probably—by Mallan—I probably *can't* get in there without you."

Janis turned back to look at Livella when she heard no answer.

"What are you talking about? What do you even know of all of this?" Livella asked, incredulous, "What if this is some trick for you to take me in there and kill me?"

Forcing herself to not lose patience, Janis breathed deeply for a few moments.

"Livella, I'll go ahead and point out that if I wanted you dead, I would have already killed you."

Livella's eyes shifted down to Janis's knives and back up to her face.

Addressing her gaze, Janis spoke. "Oh, yes. I did fail to emphasize that I am an experienced assassin. I carry many knives wherever I go. Fortunately for you, my dear, they are not intended to hurt you. Self protection, that is all."

The woman still didn't move, and Janis resisted the urge to rush over there and drag her by whatever she could take hold of.

"I know this seems odd," Janis said, feeling an odd sense of security, "but this feels familiar. I'm following my gut, here, which is often right. If that weren't the case, I'd be dead."

Livella did not seem overly comforted by this. Janis figured she'd try another route.

"I think that this is like the voice and the Light you followed to find us."

The mousy-haired young woman perked up at that, but narrowed her eyes slightly.

"How experienced are you?" was all she asked.

Janis pointed to the stone wall twenty paces away. "See that notch there?" she asked.

Livella furrowed her brows, but nodded.

Janis fluidly flicked her dagger. It spun in the air before slamming directly into the notch.

Livella was beside herself.

"How *did* you—?" No more words came out of her except other partial sentences and sputters.

Smirking, Janis just eyed her with an amused look.

"Let's just say that whatever lies in that tunnel, they have more reason to fear us than we them," she said. "Now, I suspect we better get a move on. I have a feeling that Magness will stay frozen like that if we don't go in."

Janis didn't really know how she knew this—it just felt logical. The voice that Livella had apparently heard now pressed into Janis's mind, but only after the mousy haired woman had come here. Likewise, Janis had been here dozens of times without any doorways opening, so it was obvious that Livella was the different variable.

Livella shrunk back when Janis mentioned going in, but she nodded and moved closer to her.

"Just stay behind me and keep an eye out. Shout if you see anything strange."

The two women proceeded forward at a normal but cautious pace until they reached the opening that had appeared out of nowhere. Blue Light from the pulsing symbols on the left and silver light from those on the right caused shadows to extend out behind them. Curious, Janis reached out and touched one of the symbols. Nothing changed, but she thought that she could feel a slight buzzing in her fingers, as if there was some power inside that longed to be set free.

Janis turned and started walking in. She paused when she didn't feel the presence of Livella behind her.

"It's so dark, can't we do something about that? I don't feel comfortable just walking in without being able to see anything at all."

Janis cocked her head at the comment. Years of training had allowed her to be comfortable in the dark. In fact, darkness was the preferred state of the world for an assassin. Though hiding in plain sight had its own advantages *and* thrill, Janis understood Livella's reservation about walking into the dark and potentially dangerous tunnel.

Determined, Janis sheathed one of her daggers and raised her hand up, a small ball of blue Light blossoming into life there. Livella's breath caught in her throat when she saw it. It took a few moments for Janis to realize that the woman wasn't looking at her hand, but instead over her shoulder.

Panicked, Janis spun around, fully expecting someone to be approaching, readying for an attack. Oddly, she noted an instinct to throw the ball of Light that she held in her right hand.

Where had that come from? Janis thought, *I think this ball must be a Destroying one—why else would I feel the urge to throw it?*

Janis opted to store that experience for later recollection and analysis. Instead, she focused on the reason the mousy-haired woman had gasped earlier. It seemed that summoning the ball of Light had triggered some type of response in the tunnel, for blue symbols like the ones around the opening had sprung up on the wall in a line down the wall at about her eye level. She noted that the tunnel took a gradual turn to the left until the Light symbols disappeared around the slight bend.

"I suppose that takes care of the light problem, doesn't it?" Janis said, even more curious now.

Janis let the ball of Light fall to the ground, where it promptly went away. The moment the ball of Light snuffed out, however, the Lights on the wall disappeared, plunging the hallway into darkness again.

Face scrunched at the chain reaction, she held her hand up again and summoned another blue Light. Sure enough, the moment her Light illuminated the area around her, the same symbols appeared next to her and down the hall. It was as if a fire had been started, and the flames were running down the rope line.

Janis noted that the symbols looked to be a pattern of the same seven symbols she had seen when she awakened, and they were arranged in repeating order. Fortunately, she had a mind that could remember seeing anything. Details were lost over time, but in this case, the symbols had only just gone and come back, so she was reasonably sure that the pattern was the same.

"I suppose I will just have to keep this going, then. Wouldn't want the Light to fail us when we get too far."

She had said it as a joke, but Livella was less than impressed. The woman scowled, but moved in to stand next to her.

"How do you think it works?" Livella said, staring at the string of blue symbols.

Shrugging, Janis said, "This whole Lightbearing thing is new to me. I can't say I have much of an idea on how to answer that, but it seems to be connected to my power somehow."

Livella nodded, face distant as she followed the symbols slowly down the wall with her gaze.

"Why do you think they are only on one wall? Don't you think—" Livella paused, moving to the dark stone wall opposite the one full of Light-symbols. A new set of Light symbols—a dull silvery color rather than blue, sprouted on the wall the moment her hand touched it. They extended quickly, and like wildfire, moving down the hall to mirror those on the other side. Once again, the hallway proved to turn slightly left as the symbols disappeared around the bend ahead.

Different, however, was the sound that followed. A loud grinding sound echoed off the stone walls, washing over the two women. Janis tensed at the sound and once again felt the reflex to lob the ball of Light as far as she could down the hallway. Thinking better of it as she remembered the disastrous events in her quarters, she raised her other hand with the dagger.

"That didn't sound good," Janis said.

Livella's face paled and she gulped in agreement.

It took only a few moments for the grinding sound to finish, leaving the hallway lit and still again. Quiet engulfed them as they stood there, taking it all in.

"I think that was another door," Janis said, putting it together.

The symbols on either side continued to pulse, different, yet the same. Each set was made of Light, each symbol about the size of her head, but the text wasn't the same. That, and the pulsing silver color was not like any Lightbearing Janis had seen before. Janis had dabbled in other languages as she traveled in and out of Lindrad, so had some understanding of their concepts. It was quite obvious that whatever each side of the walls said, they weren't the same.

Curious, Janis let her orb of blue Light disappear. This time, the Light symbols persisted on the wall to her right, as did the symbols that Livella had somehow triggered on the left wall.

"Any chance you are hiding any Lightbearing powers?" Janis said, raising an eyebrow at Livella.

The woman scowled at her, clearly disliking being accused of such a thing.

"I think I would know by now if I possessed odd Light powers."

"You'd be surprised," Janis answered, remembering the strange circumstances of her own awakening and how she didn't feel any different after waking up in Terris Green.

"Regardless, your involvement with Lightbearing has been made even more clear now. Something tells me that it isn't coincidental that it's you and me in here, and that each of us caused these to appear." Janis gestured at the wall to her right, then nodded to the wall on the left.

"And that sound definitely was another door opening, if I'm not mistaken," Janis said.

Livella gulped loudly at the assassin's comment.

"You don't mean to actually follow this hallway, do you?" Livella asked weakly.

Janis raised an eyebrow before responding with cool logic, "Would you rather stand here forever while Magness—and potentially the rest of Lindrad for all we know—stay frozen in time?"

Livella stared at her, clearly not understanding.

"Look, gutless, I don't think that anything will get back to normal until this all pans out. I'm not an expert on this odd magic, despite what you may believe. However, I can tell when we don't have much of a choice, and right now, we *don't* have a choice."

Snatching the woman's hand, Janis moved forward heavily, expecting to feel resistance from the grip. Interestingly enough, Livella didn't pull back, she just surrendered along. Livella's face betrayed the fear that she was hardly trying to hide, yet she let herself be pulled along. Janis determined that she had painted the picture of the situation well enough that Livella didn't bother fighting against her.

Sound was more muffled somehow in the secret hallway. As they walked, their steps caused echoes that persisted longer than any sound should in a place like this. The symbols of blue continued pulsing brightly on either side, clearly lighting the pathway for them. As they could see from further back, the hallway turned slightly to the left. They followed this course leaving the open doorway and the frozen Magness disappearing around the gradual bend.

They walked for a few hundred paces before the Lights on the wall abruptly stopped, revealing a dark hole of a doorway and a matching set of large blue and silver symbols adorning the two halves of the wall that just slid open. Squinting, Janis tried to recall the symbols that she had seen on the first door. Her memory opened up and it was as if her body shifted in space. Her view rushed backward through the tunnel and her eyes saw the symbols on the first door.

A gasp interrupted her concentration and her view zoomed back to where they now stood.

"Your eyes—! What did you *do*?" Livella exclaimed, clearly shaken by something.

Janis looked at the woman skeptically.

"What are you talking about? I was just thinking about the first set of doors and the symbols there, and—"

"Your eyes *glowed*."

Livella was shaking now, and slowly pressing herself against the wall, away from Janis.

"That didn't look right. Your eyes went all blue and they glowed brightly."

Cocking her head, Janis took in the words that she heard. She recalled Marric, and even Rivelen, using their Seeing—the description matched.

"I don't know that I *did* anything per se, but I know what you mean. I suppose that I just used the Seeing ability. I just awakened into my powers last month and don't fully understand how they work yet."

A feeling tugged at her gut, a thrill for knowledge, for digging into the situation further to analyze what had happened.

Is that what I am, a Seer? she thought, *that couldn't be—wouldn't someone have discovered that by now?*

The exact parameters of her powers were unknown by all. Seers had spent hours trying to See into her past, her future, and what they managed to See was largely vague and unhelpful. The past was the clearest, and it irked her knowing that Seers had witnessed some of the less-than-glamorous events from her life.

Movement in the corner of her eye pulled her back to the situation at hand. Livella continued to quiver slightly, back pressed against the hard stone wall. Blue symbols pulsed just below the girl's head, one symbol shining behind her neck, emphasizing the outline of her body. Janis noted how skinny the woman was.

Muscle is fairly nonexistent on this one, she thought.

Again, movement caught her eye, though Janis realized that it wasn't the pulsing symbols in front of her that she noticed—it was movement in the dark of the archway that had opened when Livella had touched the other wall accidentally.

Ignoring the reaction of her companion, Janis stepped slowly forward to the threshold of the archway. She saw nothing but darkness inside. Expecting something odd to happen, Janis eased another dagger into her free hand. The moment she stepped through the door, blue Light sprung up everywhere, temporarily blinding her from the sudden flash.

Another gasp sounded behind her as Livella reacted to the flash of Light. Instinctively, Janis flung one of her daggers in that direction. Her aim was true and the dagger flew right through the face of a man that stood there staring at her. Janis's ears betrayed her understanding as the sound of metal to stone filled her ears. The blade hit the wall behind the man and fell to the ground with a clatter.

Janis whipped out another dagger before realizing that the man staring at her was not real. Instead, he was made of blue Light. The details of his face were intricate and fine, like that of a statue crafted by a very skilled artisan. Furrowing her brows, she looked to the side to see another man, much shorter than the first, but also made of Light.

"Livella," Janis said loudly, her voice echoing slightly off of the stone walls and floor, "do you see this too?"

Silence.

Gut wrenching, Janis spun to see if anything had happened to Livella. Urgently, but cautiously, she slipped back into the hallway to see that Livella hadn't moved, but she wasn't frozen like Magness.

"I'm not sure I want to even *try* looking in there. How can I trust someone like you—you, who have strange magic I can't understand?"

Rolling her eyes, Janis jumped forward and snagged the woman's hand in a tight grip. Livella yelped at the sudden movement and the grasp that Janis had on her hand.

"Get in here, you'll be fine."

Now there was resistance. Livella screamed and yelled as Janis yanked her toward the doorway and what she had seen there. For a moment, Janis debated just knocking the woman out and dragging her, but she had the feeling that Livella had to be conscious for this. Livella fought harder the closer that they got to the doorway. Blue Light grew brighter as they neared. Finally, Janis yanked Livella through, and the woman let out a strangled squeal.

Does she ever calm down? She's always so tightly wound, Janis thought, feeling annoyed at the fishmonger's daughter.

The two had paused just inside the door, as Janis figured she would take things slow with Livella so as to avoid having to drag her the whole time. Janis hoped the frightened woman would calm down eventually and come along of her own free will. Fortunately, this hope became a reality as Livella's grip relaxed on Janis's.

"Oh," Livella said, "this isn't what I thought it was."

Scowling, Janis shook her head. "How many times do I have to tell you that I can protect us if we run into any foggin' threats? I wish you'd just listen and stop making this harder for the both of us."

Livella's face turned pensive, and she met Janis's eyes while her breathing slowed.

"I'm going to let go of your hand now, and I'd rather you didn't bolt away. I'll just catch you if you try to run—but I want to focus on what's ahead, not chasing you. Understood?"

Livella nodded reluctantly.

As promised, Janis released her hand. Fortunately, the woman kept her word and didn't run. Turning, Janis pulled the second dagger into her hand again, preferring to have two weapons ready, should things get dangerous. Looking again at the strange Light figures, Janis observed the faces she saw. The taller of the men looked determined, with long, bushy hair flowing over his shoulders. His face was chiseled and strong. His arms flexed at his sides as if he was trying to display his strength in front of a crowd. The man next to him had a neutral expression. Balding slightly on top of his head, he looked to be older than the burly man. Oddly, no wrinkles were on his face, so Janis figured he couldn't be that old.

A Light flashed behind her and she turned to see that slightly further into the dark room, another pair of figures appeared, also made of the same blue Light as the first pair. Narrowing her eyes, Janis tried to determine what was happening. As she watched, more Light figures appeared periodically down each side of the room. Oddly enough, the room remained dark around the actual figures themselves, so Janis couldn't quite tell the actual size or shape of the space, but it seemed long and somewhat narrow, perhaps only three times the width of the hallway they'd just left.

New pairs kept appearing further into the room, with one person on each side of the corridor before it all stopped. Noting the lack of any apparent danger, Janis sheathed both daggers.

"Wait—you're putting them *away*? I thought you said that you would protect us if—"

"Relax, Livella. If there was a real threat, it would have surfaced by now. Besides, I can pull out my daggers so fast, it's like they are practically there already."

Livella huffed at the answer, but couldn't seem to think of an appropriate argument. Janis didn't feel the need to defend herself any further, so without waiting for a response, she stepped up to the next pair of figures.

As she moved closer, Janis noted how strange it was that despite being made of Light, the figures didn't shine brightly enough to illuminate the whole room like Light orbs did. Testing her theory, she held up her hand and summoned the small blue ball of Light she'd grown accustomed to. Gut wrenching slightly at the potential negative consequences of what she was about to try, she pulled her hand back and lobbed the ball of Light up and over the set of statutes. The ball flew right over the heads of the figures, stopping just a few paces behind them, revealing the actual wall and ceiling just above.

Well, that confirms my theory about the shape and size of the room, Janis thought.

It didn't mean that there wasn't something else odd lurking in the shadows behind the figures, but it was unlikely. Janis guessed that each set of figures were close to the walls and the low ceiling above. If the cavern had been bigger than her eyes could see, then it might have meant more trouble.

Focusing on the figures now, Janis saw the closest ones were a pair of women. One of the women looked upward at something, though it wasn't obvious what it could have been. Her face was young, but wrinkles betrayed her age. Her hair cascaded down her shoulders, long and straight. The other figure stood at about the same height, depicting a woman about the same age—perhaps slightly younger, though it was impossible to tell for sure. Her hair was tied up in a tight bun on top of her head and held in by a couple hairpins. She stood up tall, but her face pointed downward. For a moment, Janis thought maybe they were siblings, but their features were just different enough that she amended the idea.

Livella stayed quiet while Janis inspected the figures, opting to follow without comment. One by one, Janis observed the Light people, some men, some women. The first thing she noticed about each pair was how they were never mixed in gender. They were either pairs of men, or pairs of women. She could draw her own conclusions about that, but it was consistent.

After about the first ten sets of figures, Janis realized that she would gain nothing by looking at each pair, for though the detail was oddly very good, she didn't recognize any so far.

An urge came to her to reach out and touch one of the figures. The fact that they were made of Light was no longer an oddity since she'd come to understand Conjuring and how it worked. She reached out and paused, running through the list of risks in her head.

There was a chance that this was completely different than anything Janis thought she knew about Lightbearing, and that she and Livella would get hurt, but Janis didn't really care. She actually figured that if something adverse happened, it might actually be a welcome change to the odd and quiet room around them.

As Janis reached her hand out, Livella spoke suddenly.

"What in Lanser's name are you doing? You aren't going to touch that, are you? What if it hurts you—"

"Livella, sweetie. You may have not noticed, but nothing has happened to us yet. If you are that concerned about me, maybe you could test touching it, hmm?"

Livella blushed at the comment, but shook her head vigorously. "I most certainly will not."

"Fair enough," Janis spoke knowingly.

After the exchange, Janis inched her hand closer to the chest of the figure just in front of her. This woman was shorter than Janis and quite a bit plumper, face pudgy and round. She paused when her hand was merely a finger-width away from the personage. The pause was only brief, however, and she soon pressed her hand to the chest of the woman statue. To her surprise, her hand went through the apparition.

It was intuitive that such a thing would happen, considering light on its own wasn't normally a tangible medium. Janis had assumed that the constructs were Conjures of some sort, and therefore it would be possible to physically to touch them. What was surprising was the feeling that rushed into her hand. The moment her hand entered the chest of the woman, a tingling feeling burst through her hand like a fire rushing through a dry field, quick and consuming.

Gritting her teeth, she sucked air in sharply, causing a hissing sound. Janis pulled her hand back quickly at the same time. She instantly regretted it, as her action caused Livella to yelp loudly and jump backwards. As the woman did, she tripped herself and fell on her backside to the ground. Livella continued to yell, voice loud and screaming gibberish.

If there was any chance of them staying hidden from potential people lurking in this place or beyond it somewhere, their cover was now blown.

Realizing this, Janis tried to reason with her companion.

"Would you be *quiet*?" she hissed to the girl. "Do you want the whole world to know what's happening?"

Livella shook her head rapidly and then looked around. She eventually turned so that she was facing away from Janis, and then backed up just in front of the assassin.

"I am not hurt, but there was something odd, there. Hang on—let me try something."

A little quicker this time, Janis moved her hand to the conjured figure and put her hand through. Once again, the tingling sensation filled her hand. It didn't hurt, but it didn't feel comfortable by any means. Oddly, the tingling sensation didn't run up her arm like she expected it to, but instead it stopped at her wrist, where the edge of the figure ended.

Janis figured these couldn't be Conjures of any sort, for they would be solid-like if that were the case. She recalled Marric mentioning a similar feeling to her, a few days after she'd woken up. He had said that when he first arrived, he'd touched one of the Lighter's orbs and had felt a surprising tingling sensation. As she recounted his words, another idea came to her.

Holding out her other hand, she summoned the small ball of her own Light. Rather than emerging small yet intense like it usually did, it burst to life, at least five times in size and blazing even brighter.

Fascinating, she thought, *Marric had said something about Lighters enhancing the abilities of other Lightbearers around them.*

"What are we supposed to do here?" Livella said, interrupting Janis's thought.

Janis didn't respond immediately, which awarded her with a huff from her companion.

"Did you hear me? What do we need to *do* to make this all stop?"

Opting to not look at Livella, Janis instead cleared her throat to prolong the moment.

"You halfwit, I don't know any more than you what's happening right now. If I haven't made it clear that I don't, then I'll say it again—*I have no idea what's going on.* What I *have* been able to gather is that it all began when you got here and when we met. The door only opened after we both touched a wall, and I have a lingering feeling that we both have to be here, or else it will be bad for both of us. Questions?"

Livella gulped loudly behind Janis.

"I take that as a no," Janis said smugly. "Notice that these odd Light figures are all in pairs as well. That is obviously significant."

As she said this, her eyes gravitated toward the bottom of the personages. Each person stood on a sort of pedestal that was a handspan tall and about the size of a platter. The larger figures barely fit on the stand, toes poking over the edge sometimes. It wasn't unusual for statues of people to be on stands like these, but it was the symbols that she noticed on each one.

They weren't symbols that she understood by any means, yet they were familiar to her in some way. Turning around slowly, she saw that each pair of figures had the same two symbols. Each pair had one of each of the symbols, never were they repeated in one pair. Cocking her head, she walked more briskly to the end of the hall and the point where the pairs ended. A final pair stood there just before the room became too dark for them to see further.

Janis narrowed her eyes as she observed the final two figures in the hallway.

It was of Prost and Riln.

The scars were unmistakable on Prost's image. He was far larger in his depiction than she remembered him, but then again, she couldn't verify if the Light people around her were intended to be truly life-sized or if they were exaggerated in any way. Regardless, the two figures at the end were definitely Prost and Riln.

A flash of Light behind her made her quickly pivot around. Out of nowhere, a new set of pedestals sprung up just across the hallway from the Riln and Prost figures. Amazed, she and Livella watched as a flash of Light announced the arrival of two new figures in the hallway. Janis felt her stomach clench as she saw two familiar women standing as Light figures.

A figure with her own face looked forward, fierce and determined. Next to her own likeness was a depiction of Livella, young and innocent, staring to her left as if she was watching and waiting for something bad to happen. Immediately, Janis's eyes snapped downward at the symbols there. She turned quickly and compared them to the symbols of Prost and Riln. Sure enough, hers matched the one below Riln, Livella's matched Prost's.

They are labels of some sort, she guessed internally, *perhaps they mean something in the old language.*

"But—" Livella started, "—how is that possible?"

She was staring at her own image, arm outstretched slightly. It was as if she had seen a long-lost friend and was reaching toward them.

"I have no idea." Janis was flabbergasted.

She turned to Livella and summoned a ball of Light. The woman detected the new source of Light and faced Janis to see what was happening. Without hesitation, Janis tossed the ball at Livella's face. The girl gasped and tried to dodge, but was too slow. The ball dissolved against the woman's face and her skin paled. For a moment, Janis thought that her theory had been wrong.

Cursing, she moved quickly to Livella's side. Still, as Janis examined Livella's face, there was no sign of injury. Despite this, Livella started shaking and fell to her knees.

"Why did you attack me again? Didn't you get what you needed last time?" Livella sucked in air before glaring at Janis.

"It seems that you are in a bit of shock. I don't blame you—I didn't walk you through my thought process before attacking you."

Livella nodded, but her eyes grew distant. Her face was a bit green now, and Janis recognized the look as nausea.

"Sorry for the surprise. I couldn't well have asked you if I could just throw something at you, could I?"

Janis kneeled by Livella, wearing a look that she hoped would help the woman calm down.

"I had seen it before, but I had to be sure. You are immune to all Lightearing powers," Janis said matter-of-factly.

Livella just gasped, before spilling out, "But, I didn't know what you meant before—" she started hyperventilating then.

"Try not to speak, just breathe. Put your head down like this," Janis said, lightly pressing on the woman's back to help her bend forward. "It will help with the nausea."

Livella didn't recoil when Janis touched her, so either she was too shocked to react to the situation, or she trusted Janis. Either way, dots were connecting and Janis felt a hint of a thrill in her chest. If it was true that Livella was immune as Prost was, the symbol below their pictures was not coincidental. Riln was a powerful Lightbearer, apparently the strongest that Magness and Avryn have seen. That had to mean that the symbols below Riln's and her own statues meant they were the same.

I have all seven Lightbearing powers? That would explain the Destroying of my room, but why aren't my powers consistent for me?

To validate this, she summoned her Light dagger again and pulled out her own steel dagger. Rubbing them together, she heard the familiar metal-on-metal sound of two blades colliding. With all her strength, she slammed them into each other. As it had before, the Light dagger broke and disappeared into nothing.

Disappointment filled her.

"Tar'n Yiv'len videsk frinn K'alek Tar'n yrillnan grisk!"

The voice came again, this time practically yelling in their ears. Janis tensed and scanned their surroundings, fully expecting some mad man to come barreling out of the shadows with a sword.

Nothing came. Instead, the voice spoke again, repeating the same words.

"Tar'n Yiv'len videsk frinn K'alek Tar'n yrillnan grisk!"

They sounded very familiar to Janis, though she couldn't describe why. She recounted what she had heard, searching for their meaning. The strange voice spoke again, though this time, the words were Lindradian.

"The Prime Lightbearer and the Voidbearer must balance!"

Livella perked up at the words. "Did—" Livella started to say.

"—yes," Janis cut in, anticipating Livella's next words.

"How did we understand that? I swear at first I heard words that weren't in Lindradian and—"

Janis held up her hand and stopped her from continuing. Silence had followed the translated words, and Janis wanted to be sure that no danger would catch them unawares. After a short beat, a flash of Light announced the arrival of two women, also made of the same Light as the figures. One was a shorter woman with bobbed hair, a few handspans shorter than her companion. The taller robed woman had long hair that extended halfway down her arms as they hung at her sides.

Narrowing her eyes, Janis realized that she'd seen the women before. Looking to her left, she spotted the would-be-statues next to those of Prost and Riln. Sure enough, the depictions of the women in the figures were exact likenesses of the two women hovering above them in the air.

"Ummm, Janis, are you seeing this?" Livella had jumped up, and though a bit wobbly still, had managed to put herself behind Janis's person.

"I'm not blind, am I?" Janis retorted, stressed at not knowing what to expect.

Her mind analyzed what their options were. They could run, but having these strange Light beings at her back wasn't her first choice. The last thing she wanted was a Destroying ball smacking her between her shoulder blades and ripping her to bits. Attacking them wouldn't be wise for this same reason. Livella was crying behind her, obviously beside herself with fright.

Janis rolled her eyes. "Don't move, just wait."

The tall woman before them raised her hands up and spoke. Her voice echoed slightly, as if there was someone speaking the same words, slightly delayed. Once again, words came out that Janis knew she didn't recognize, yet she could understand them somehow.

"The new Prime Lightbearer and Voidbearer—how nice it is to meet you."

Janis furrowed her brow. This felt different than the first time she'd heard the voice in her mind, as it was now out loud, but the tone and timbre were the same.

No one said anything for a few moments.

"Oh, please don't say Lanser awakened a mute Prime, that would make this much less enjoyable for everyone."

Janis realized that the woman was talking to her and Livella, and that this woman wasn't a statue like the others.

"Who are you?" Janis said, voice hard.

A smile spread on the woman's face.

"Oh good, no mutes here. This will make it much easier. You can release your weapon, there is no need for that right now."

Confused at the use of the word 'release', Janis looked to her right hand, and realized that she had unconsciously summoned a dagger of blue Light.

"I'll keep my weapons out, if you don't mind. Now, I did ask a question, and I'd appreciate it if you answered."

The tall Light-woman squinted at a Janis, clearly not thrilled by her response.

"I suppose we have yet another snappy one, here. The first time in history there have been two Primes, and they are both snotty. What are the chances of that?

"She ain't as bad as the las' one, tha's fer sure," the shorter woman said, her voice thick with an accent.

"Yes, yes, I suppose that's true. This one hasn't tried to Destroy us . . . " she paused, eyeing Janis, " . . . at least, not yet."

The shorter woman snorted at the comment, but said nothing else.

"Can someone please tell me what the fog is happening right now?" Janis snapped, growing impatient.

Sighing heavily, the tall woman nodded.

"There is much to discuss. Please, if you don't mind, can you put your weapons away? We mean no harm."

Janis didn't move at the request.

"Answer, now," was all Janis said.

"Oh fine, we are the Prime Lightbearer and the Voidbearer of the past. Once, when we first awakened, we were just as you two. It is time for us to help you understand your place. If you please, we'd like no trouble. We are dead—there isn't much you can do to us."

"He din' listen an' tried ferever t' hur' us, but wasn' worth th'time," the shorter woman said, gesturing to Riln's figure.

They spoke with Riln before? Janis thought, intrigued.

"Fine, I'll put at least this one away," Janis said, letting her Conjured dagger disappear.

"As you wish," the regal woman said, shaking her head and smiling. "Let us begin, then."

10

Prost roughly pulled on his gloves. The Seers had said that the weather was a bit severe at the moment and that the travelers should prepare for the wet. Knowing that he'd be riding in the rain wasn't a problem for him, but Prost knew that he'd have to listen to his men whine about conditions the entire time. Anticipating their complaints, not the storm, is what put him in a foul mood for this mission.

Only moments after Riln shared his thoughts on the possibility of another Voidbearer existing, a courier had come in to tell them of another awakening. Despite all that was happening, Riln thought that their recruiting work must continue as before. More Lightbearers would be needed for their cause, and they couldn't let their efforts slow down. This awakening was expected in five days in T'Arren Vale, the capital city.

Prost balked at the thought of entering the city where he'd once lived. Whenever he was forced to do so, his mind rattled with memories, familiar sights, and smells that distracted him. Too much of his past was from there, and it pained him to have to relive his once fond memories, now overpowered by bitterness from all he'd lost.

Inevitably, memories of times before in the military would mean memories of his fellow soldiers at the time. First and foremost was Avryn.

Frustration filled him at the thought. He shook his head and instead focused on the knowledge that he'd be enjoying the thrumming of the rain and thunder around him as they traveled to T'Arren Vale. He would let the power of the storm invigorate him, drowning out the noise and helping block thoughts of his past.

One of their Seers indicated the mark would be a twelve-year-old boy, a common age for an awakening. He would be a Fixer, awakening in little more than five days. Riln was somewhat disappointed at the news, hoping for another combat Lightbearer, but anticipated leading the boy's choice of second-birth power to something more lethal.

T'Arren Vale was normally eight day's ride from Watchlight when they went at a slow pace, so they would need to hurry. Given the situation with Evenir and what happened the last few times they encountered them, Prost fully expected that they would have them as company when they reached the boy. It would have been preferable for the Seers to have given this information a week ago, but they didn't get to choose when they Saw awakenings, apparently.

Prost grumbled, irritated at this fact. He wasn't opposed to fighting—he wasn't even concerned for the most part, but it was inconvenient for them. Getting new Lightbearers in their ranks was easier when they didn't have any competition, but that was becoming less and less the case. Prost knew that Evenir had been tracking Lightbearers for years, but one usually made it first and escaped. There had been reports of Evenir troops scouring the forest all over the place. T'Arren Vale was the capital city of Lindrad; he would be shocked if Evenir didn't already have operatives there.

As he finished donning his travel gear, he heard footsteps echoing down the hallway. The footsteps weren't loud, but they were obvious. The sound got louder until just before the wooden door to his chambers, where he heard a hasty knock. Without missing a beat, Prost ripped the door open and glared at the smaller man.

"What?" Prost said, intentionally sounding gruff.

His words caused the messenger to jump.

"The party is ready to depart—sir . . . " the man paused when he saw the bulky man before him, "they are awaiting your instruction before departing."

"Fine, tell them to wait. I'll get there when I get there."

The smaller man gulped at the comment, but nodded.

"Is there something else?" Prost said, noticing that the man was not retreating as couriers normally did after completing their messages to him.

"Riln says you must take Jord with you."

Prost clenched his jaw at the comment.

"Did he say *why*?" Prost said after a moment.

"Ummm, no," the man said, shuffling on his feet side to side, clearly nervous to be facing Prost at this very moment.

Prost softened his features a bit; he found that if he intimidated his messengers too much, it took much longer to actually get his messages.

"Fine, I'm sure he has his reasons," Prost said, irritation clear in his voice. "Inform Jord that he must be dressed and ready to travel before I arrive at the stables. If he's not, he gets left behind."

The man shifted on his feet, but didn't leave.

"Ummm, he's already with the party, sir," the man said, face paling slightly as if he was afraid Prost might hurt him.

The little man is terrified of me, Prost thought, slightly amused. *He seems a nice enough sort of fellow; perhaps I can try to show him patience . . . leaders aren't always abrupt, are they?* he wondered.

"Ah, I see. Why did you bother telling me when I'd find out on my own anyway?" Prost tried to sound appreciative, but it wasn't coming across well, "send word to Riln that I will gladly be accompanied by Jord. Now, run along. If I don't see you again before we depart, I'll assume Riln had nothing else to say."

Nodding profusely, the man turned on his heels and sped off down the stone hallway. In a world full of complex powers of Light, Prost found it ironic that they still had to employ a system of runners to deliver messages to people in different parts of the lair. He realized then that perhaps those with powers likely received messages in a different way, which only made him feel more isolated.

Closing the door behind him, he swept his cloak aside and walked briskly in the same direction as the courier. His quarters were close enough to the stables that it would only take a few moments to get there. Prost felt that he should mentally prepare himself for the journey. The only positives he could think of were that he would finally get out of this stuffy cave *and* that Mert had managed to get himself captured by Evenir, so the insufferable man wouldn't accompany them. Of course, Riln wasn't happy about Mert's capture, but that didn't bother Prost. Mert was expendable, at least in Prost's mind.

As he entered the cavern that acted as their stables, his nose was filled with the pungent smell of wet manure. His stomach heaved at the smell. He had never liked the stables for this very reason. Sure, there were ventilation shafts blasted by the Destroyers, but it didn't help much, considering the hundreds of horses they held there. Only when they were leaving were the doors to the cavern open. Prost thanked Lanser that now happened to be one of those times. He looked over to see the thick wooden doors open with gray light pouring in, along with a fair bit of rain. The doors blended into the mountainside due to having taken on a gray color from weathering, which helped prevent outsiders from easily spotting the entrance to the compound.

It does look pretty nasty out there, Prost thought, a smile creeping onto his face.

Almost in response to his thought, a flash sprang through the doors, followed closely by a loud crack of thunder. Energy coursed through his veins and he felt excitement burst in every part of him. Adrenaline filled his muscles and he had the urge to run headlong out the door, letting the storm engulf him in its power. The thought was instantly quelled, however, when a black-robed figure moved directly in front of him.

"Riln thought we would have left by now. The fact that we haven't will not be lost on him. I'm sure he can See that we haven't yet."

Jord's narrowed brown eyes sat beneath wet hair that smoothed above a youthful face.

"Jord. I feel *so* lucky to have the pleasure of your company on this trek, but now that I *have* arrived, Riln will be Seeing nothing. Lest you forget who I am."

The sarcasm in Prost's voice hung thick in the air.

"Say what yeh want, dud. Riln will never approve of yous and yer lack o' power. I've only counted me blessings that I haven't 'ad to associate much wif yeh fer the past couple o' years."

Prost scoffed at the comment. "To say that the feeling is mutual wouldn't capture the truth," Prost said, jaw set hard. "You speak hard words for someone who can't even touch me with their power."

The corner of Jord's mouth tugged up at the side.

"Yeh may be immune to Lightbearing, but yeh ain't immune to steel." Jord continued, "I think tha' the scars on yer face are a righ' good reminder o' tha'."

Prost felt goosebumps crop up on his skin at the words. Anger filled him and he almost lost control. He wasn't able to stop himself from whipping out his sword and gripping the handle hard, knuckles white. At the same time, Jord held out his hand, an orb of red Light floating there. A wicked grin appeared on Prost's face at the boy's defense.

"If that's all you have, this would be an easy fight."

Jord growled at Prost, then spat on the ground.

"Yer threats are wasted on me, dud. I migh' not could 'urt yous, but I can rip apart everythin' yeh wear an' carry. Tha' would righ' make yer day worse, 'specially since we're late already."

Prost smiled darkly, "Your tongue might be sharp, but your threats are weak. You don't scare me."

Jord's jaw hardened, but he didn't have anything else to say.

"Now, now, boys, put yer tempers away, we still 'ave a long way t'go before we gets t' T'Arren Vale. Besides, t'isn't entertainin' t'watch a couple o' whiners waste time," Alts said, appearing out of nowhere.

The woman positioned herself between the two, casually fingering an arrow made of red Light. She didn't seem bothered by the fact that she was practically staring down the end of two lethal weapons held by equally lethal tempers.

She is an odd woman, Prost thought.

After a moment, the two put their weapons away, neither looking thrilled at the intervention.

"Good, now can we gets movin', please? I've already said goodbye to the blue in me 'air an' I don' wanna 'ave t'dwell on it much longer."

She flung her thick blonde braid over her shoulder as if to emphasize her point.

Something stirred inside Prost at the sight and he shoved it down quickly. He'd always felt a fondness for Alts, but now that Mert was held hostage by Evenir, technically no one was in his way of trying to woo the woman. However, he knew that would be a waste of his time. There wasn't any spare moment for that kind of stuff.

"We ride, now. Neera, you okay to Light the way?" Prost said loudly, unsure where their primary Lighter was, but knowing that she was likely near.

"Yes, of course." The voice came from behind him and he turned to see the dark-skinned woman prepping her own horse. "Have I ever let you down on that front?"

Prost shook his head at her, opting to say nothing else. She was probably the closest thing to a friend that he had here at Watchlight, but she wasn't even that. Her obedience was earned by almost everyone that she met at the compound, and Prost was no exception.

I should leverage that to my advantage, he thought, staring back at the woman for a moment.

"Thank you, Neera, for recognizing my authority in Riln's absence. He himself is unable to make the treks necessary to gather more Lightbearers to our cause, so he allows someone more hardened to do so."

Neera stared at him, looking slightly confused at the comment, but she just nodded.

"Ah, don' be such a baby, Prost. We'll listen to yeh. Even if we don' righ' like it much," Alts said, causing a few chuckles around her.

Slightly pained inside, Prost felt that he didn't have much of a choice at his response. Spinning around, he grabbed Alts by her neck and slammed her to the ground, holding her there. Eyes wide, she instinctively summoned a dagger and stabbed Prost in the side. Of course this brought no results, and she stared at him, panicked.

"Disrespect won't get you far in this world, Alts. And let this be a reminder that your wit and humor might entertain a few, but at the end of it all, I am still immune to your Lightbearing and can best any of you in a fight. Riln chose me as his second for a reason—don't you forget that."

Prost released her neck and she sat up, gasping for air. No one dared challenge his claim of Riln naming him as the second in command, but it couldn't really be questioned. He was, after all, with Riln more than anyone else, save perhaps Jord.

"For all of you coming with us on this little journey to T'Arren Vale, remember that I am in charge. You report to me. We don't have much time to get to the city, and when we do, know that Evenir will be there. Be prepared for a fight. With any luck, their Seers are behind our own and we'll beat them there."

He paced in front of the company as he spoke, looking each person in the eye and giving a nod. Inside, he hated this part of leadership. Riln was in charge and that had always been the case, but these days he was alerted to the fact that his authority was undermined constantly, and that he needed to gain it back before it got too out of hand. Reaching his horse, he stepped into the stirrup and kicked off the ground easily, swinging himself into the saddle.

"We ride now!"

At his words, the people meant to accompany him sprang into action, moving to their own mounts and jumping on hurriedly. Prost didn't wait for the last people before kicking his own horse into motion.

The world around him shifted as the forward momentum threatened to sweep him off his horse. He gritted his teeth as he approached the sheet of heavy rain just outside the large, arched doorway. Inhaling sharply, he directed the horse to plunge itself out the doorway, feeling the shocking power of the storm and the cold and wet of the pouring rain.

Adrenaline coursed through his body again, and his mouth pulled into a grin, the rain passing its strength to him.

11

The spectral women appearing before Janis didn't scare her too much. What really unsettled her was how unphased they were by her weapons. Shortly after appearing from nowhere, the two Light-created women directed Livella and herself to sit down, which Janis promptly ignored. This awarded her with another raised eyebrow from the long-haired woman.

Livella had quickly obeyed and had sat on the stone floor, each woman taking their own seats in front of her. The Light statues of Riln and Prost stood to the left of them, brooding.

"I am Tryvv, the *Prime Lightbearer* from the last age. This is Prileen, the previous *Voidbearer*," the long-haired woman said.

Janis felt an odd feeling inside as if the woman hadn't spoken in Janis's own language, but that she somehow understood what the woman said anyway.

I never learned the old language, how can I interpret it like this? she thought.

"Normally, the most recent Prime and Voidbearer address their replacements when the new balance is created and they meet for the first time, but these circumstances are—different."

Janis noted the pause in the woman's phrase, and gave her a questioning look.

"Have you met these ones?" Tryvv said, gesturing with an open hand to the figures of Prost and Riln.

Janis only chortled.

"Oh, I've met them all right," Janis said darkly.

Tryvv stared blankly at Janis for a minute before her eyes flashed down to the dagger that was still clutched in the assassin's hands.

"The times have shifted. Never in history have there been two living *Tar'n Yiv'len* and *K'alek Tar'n* existing at the same moment."

The tall woman looked over longingly at the figures of Riln and Prost. Janis looked at her face, then followed her gaze to the two men, glorified in their statuesque forms. She then looked across from them to her own likeness and Livella's standing next to her. It was clear that the figure was of her, but something about the way that she stood, looking up into the sky as if expecting Lanser himself to appear, made her look more authoritative. That, and the fact that it was made of Light.

"This also is the first time in history when a Prime Lightbearer and their Voidbearer chose a different path, one that disturbs the *Yrillnan*."

Even as she said it, Janis recognized that the word was not in her own language, yet she understood its meaning.

Balance, she thought, perplexed at the odd nature of her new ability.

"But we mustn't let time be frozen for much longer. I fear that there may be negative side effects from it all."

Janis loosened the grip on her dagger and held her hands in the air in front of her, the knife point directed at them.

"Now, wait just a minute. Time is frozen? How is that possible?"

Tryvv furrowed her eyebrows at Janis, clearly unimpressed with the interruption.

"Why yes, of course. This message is only for the two of you. As the Prime and the Voidbearer, you must understand the importance of your responsibilities in this world. Until we deliver our message, everyone in this mountain stalls while we give you the knowledge you need. How that is possible is unimportant at this moment."

Janis scowled at the comment. "I think I'd rather just be left alone, thank you very much."

As she said it, she slipped her dagger into its sheath and turned back toward the entrance of the cave. She gave a pointed look to Livella, indicating that she was leaving and it would be best if she followed. Livella returned with a look of fear and discomfort before following her.

"If you don't stay, it will mean the demise of many thousands of people."

Janis paused at that. Without turning, she spoke out loudly.

"What does *that* mean, exactly?"

Something in her stirred. Janis couldn't tell what it was, but she knew the strange Light-created woman was about to let her in on something significant. A piece of information so rare that apparently only Riln and Prost knew themselves.

A hunger opened up in her along with a resistance, something pulling her more strongly to the exit. Darkness coalesced around the hallway, engulfing the statues on each side with tendrils of shadow. She felt drawn to leave, to run away from all that was being said.

"He tempts you even now, I see."

Janis snapped to attention and began backing away from the tendrils of shadow that had appeared around her. As she did, they receded slowly, disappearing into the air and not returning. Everything felt wrong now.

I knew that I should have been watching my surroundings closer, she thought, frustrated at feeling trapped and caught unawares.

"If you leave now, the world will perish. If you stay, you'll understand what must be done. What you must become in order to keep the Yrillnan in check."

Once again, she knew that the strange word meant balance and it carried power, though the implications behind it were still lost on Janis.

Sighing, the long-haired woman stood up from her seated position. As she did, Janis noted that she looked regal and powerful, something that Janis recognized in kings and queens of the past. Her eyes carried something that Janis could understand: pain. Flashes of images from Janis's past came to her mind as feelings of her unfortunate circumstances came to her.

"For hundreds of years, Lanser, the all-powered, and Ugglyn, the anti-god, have fought for dominion over the world, but it began here, in Lindrad. Each empowered men and women with their own powers—Light and Void —to control the world."

Janis found herself enthralled at the idea. It felt ridiculous to her, as if she was a child listening to some false explanation for why the sky was blue. Unfortunately, she didn't have much of a choice. If she tried to leave, she suspected the odd darkness would come again. She had learned from past experiences that gathering as much information as possible was always in her best interest.

"All those who awakened as Lightbearers had to stand as one to combat Ugglyn's army of Voidbearers. Battles were fought and many died on both sides of the conflict, though Ugglyn's forces remained strong and active. In a last effort to push against Ugglyn, Lanser awakened a Lightbearer to lead them all, one with all seven Lightbearing powers. They called him Tar'n Yiv'len, or the Prime Lightbearer."

Tryvv paused then and gestured behind them to something there. Livella turned to see what the tall Light-woman was pointing to. Janis narrowed her eyes, expecting it to be a trick of some sort. Tryvv of course noticed Janis's reaction, and rolled her eyes in response.

"This isn't some ploy to get the better of you. How much of a threat can we be—we're dead," Tryvv said, sounding annoyed.

"She ain't very trustin', is she?" Prileen commented, "Prolly the reason she ain't dead, I s'pose."

It was clear that the shorter woman had dark hair, because the Light was a bit more tinted there than with Tryvv's hair.

"So that's him, then?" Livella spoke out, pointing at something behind them.

At last, Janis's curiosity got the better of her. Since it was clear the women were made of Light and wouldn't hurt them, Janis relaxed just a bit. She turned and saw the first figure near the entrance they'd come through to get here. Strangely, Janis realized, this figure was alone. Scanning the room, she verified that all of the other figures were in pairs.

"Iridian—he was the first Tar'n Yiv'len. He led the soldiers of Lanser to battle and ultimately to victory, but not without first knowing much tribulation. Iridian knew that he would die, for that was part of the plan. Little did Ugglyn know that this was to be, and he pushed his own forces forward with might. At the end of the conflict, Iridian and Ugglyn's last Voidbearer killed each other with a final blow. With these deaths, Lanser formed a Seal, made with the blood of both Lightbearers and Voidbearers alike. Lanser used a small part of Ugglyn's Void combined with his own Light to provide the Seal against Ugglyn's full powers."

"Yrillnan."

This time, Prileen spoke out, her voice sounding hard. Tryvv nodded as if she was expecting this, looking over at her companion.

"In modern Lindradian, it be like 'balance', so tha' is wha' we call it. Lanser's Seal locked Ugglyn's power away from freely enterin' the world. Yrillnan needed both th'Light and th'Void. From th'Seal came the first Prime Lightbearer and Voidbearer balance. The Voidbearer is no longer subject t'Ugglyln's rule, but does hold counterbalance to th'Light."

Once again, Tryvv gestured behind them to a set of figures immediately next to the lone figure at the front of the cavern. Janis saw that these two men were of the same height and build. They looked like they could be the same person. She cocked her head, considering what it meant.

"Yes, they are twins, as you can see." Tryvv spoke as if in response to Janis's thoughts. "Lanser awakened one as the Prime, and the other as the Voidbearer. This has been the only time in history when brothers were made Yrillnan. But it was their wealth and pride that doomed their Yrillnan rather than their siblinghood. Though their combined powers locked away Ugglyn's hold on the world, their actions weakened the balance. Their reign lasted only three years before they tore Yrillnan apart, each dying from their own stupidity and pride."

Janis's eyes scanned the long lines of figures on either side, back and forth until she came to Tryvv and Prileen's. These two clearly didn't live at the same time as the first men, so how did they know all of this?

Lanser's beard, there might actually be something after we die, Janis thought. She didn't have time for religion, and right now was no exception.

"After the self destruction of these two men, Lanser selected a new Prime and Voidbearer. Because the powers of the Prime became something beyond anything they could imagine, humility was required for the new Prime. Conversely, as it seems well known that opposites work well together, the Voidbearer would awaken from a rich life. Tar'n Yiv'len are born from adversity, while K'alek Tar'n are born from providence. This is by design," Tryvv said, looking serious.

Her eyes landed on Janis, and there was clearly something there. The strange tall woman seemed almost proud, though of what, the assassin couldn't know. Tryvv's gaze lingered on her for a while before Janis scowled at her and made her look away. All the while, Prileen observed her nails as if she didn't care what happened.

"What do you want from us, then? You don't know anything about me or Livella, here." Janis was gritting her teeth as she said it, impatient and uncomfortable with the situation.

Tryvv smiled at her then, and moved closer.

"Janis, I know you better than you can imagine. Your life has not been easy, it's true. But you've learned skills—behaviors that will aid you in the battle against Ugglyn and his followers. You are to be Tar'n Yiv'len. Though you have the powers, you must transform yourself to become the Prime."

As Tryvv spoke, unwanted memories cropped up in Janis's head. Once again, she was home in Port Lindle: her home broken, parents dead on the floor from the plague. Both her parents and brother had died, so the disease had stripped her of all companionship. Frozen, small, sick, and alone, it was a wonder she hadn't died then. To say that her life was full of adversity was an understatement. Regardless of what Tryvv said, Janis didn't want any of it.

"I'll pass, thank you," Janis replied.

Startled at the reaction, Tryvv furrowed her brow at her.

"I'm sure I don't know what you mean, I—"

"I said I'm not interested. Pick someone else. I am an assassin, I work alone. I don't want to be part of any of this. My job is simple: I get paid, I kill someone, I'm out. Next job. This makes the simple life I always wanted, and it's what I need. The history lesson has been interesting, but I'm not joining whatever cause you are championing."

Tryvv pursed her lips at the comment. Her eyes carried a sadness there, as if she understood something deeper about Janis's reaction.

"Unfortunately, that isn't an option any longer. You either transform yourself and become what the world needs, or you die, and. . . . "

Tryvv's face twisted as she said it, indicating to Janis that she was leaving something out, or hiding a detail that was important. Janis tucked this away for a moment, letting the words sink in. Though she didn't want to accept it, Janis somehow knew that they were true. She felt the hairs on her neck prickle and stand up as something stirred there. Janis didn't turn, but she somehow knew what it was.

The shadows, she thought. They had appeared out of nowhere and seeped out of the walls and dark recesses of the cavern. What were they?

Murmured speech alerted Janis to the fact that Livella and Prileen had retreated a number of paces away from them and were discussing something at length. Livella was white, probably still from the shock of everything that had happened and was happening right now. She nodded profusely to the Light-figure version of Prileen and was clearly hanging on every word that came from the woman's mouth.

"She is learning of her potential and her role as the K'alek Tar'n," Tryvv spoke quietly, nodding toward Livella. "The question now is, will you learn your own potential? Or will you run?"

Even before she said it, Janis could feel the strengthening pull of the shadows behind her, drawing her in to something that felt very wrong.

"What are the shadows?" Janis blurted out.

Tryvv didn't appear bothered by the abrupt and random comment; she just stared, a thoughtful look on her face.

"Even now, Ugglyn seeks your favor. Lanser has blessed you with the potential to become Prime, but you have the choice to submit to or fight against Ugglyn. You, my dear, are the wall between him and what he wants."

Janis winced at the sound of the words 'my dear' and forced her eyes up to look at Tryvv.

"And what does he want?"

"The world. If he breaks free, untold challenges will face the world. Many will die—he will push against Lanser. If he wins, suffice it to say the world will not be a better place for anyone. He knows you are in the way, so he will tempt you, try you, and attempt to kill you."

"What happens if I just join him?"

Tryvv clenched her jaw at the question. Rather than answer, she gestured to the figures of Riln and Prost.

"You'll become corrupted, an enemy to Lanser and his hold on the world. You desecrate Yrillnan, and you'll submit the Lightbearers to Ugglyn, and ultimately the world. Never before has a Tar'n Yiv'len submitted to Ugglyn's Void until now. There are laws and rules to this world. Only one

Yrillnan could exist at one time. Only one pair. Lanser has taken a chance on this world, his last chance. By breaking the original rules of the Yrillnan and sanctioning two, he is taking a risk."

Janis didn't really care. She had chosen her profession mainly because she was good at it, but also because it allowed her to stay out of the way of bigger problems. How she had ended up in this situation, she couldn't really understand.

"I don't understand what risk he's taken, other than picking the wrong woman for the responsibility," Janis said, narrowing her eyes.

Tryvv looked troubled, her eyes shifting downward.

"Janis," she said, looking up and staring directly in the assassin's eyes. "Lanser used the last of his power to break the laws of life and awaken another Prime. If you fail or die, there is no new Prime. The world will fall."

Janis's skin crawled at the words, but she didn't know what to say.

That is not a risk worth taking, Janis thought with disdain. Then she decided to shift the topic, not wanting to dwell on the mistake she believed was made in choosing her.

"Is that why their Light is red, then?" Janis gestured to the Riln-figure.

Tryvv nodded, but said nothing else. She looked worried, as if concerned her whole speech was lost on Janis and her efforts would all be for naught.

Technically that is still possible, Janis thought.

After Janis didn't ask any additional questions, Tryvv continued.

"For some reason, Lanser chose you as his Prime to hold back the powers of Ugglyn. Part of doing that is eliminating the other Yrillnan completely. They must be killed before they corrupt too many more Light-bearers. The powers were a gift to the world, and now they have become a curse to it."

Janis didn't mind *that* part of the story. If she could kill Prost right now, she absolutely would. Her mind raced back to images of facing Prost just before she'd awakened. He was a skilled fighter, and very arrogant in his own way. The kill. That is something that she could get behind. Unfortunately, she had a feeling that it wouldn't get her off the hook completely.

"Then what?" Janis asked.

Grimacing, Tryvv continued. "Then you continue to hold back the darkness, the Void. I believe that you have seen it now, no?"

The tall woman stretched out her transparent Light-hands and gestured around them.

"Even now, he watches. Even now, the Void threatens to tempt and consume you. I am no longer able to see or sense it, but Ugglyn knows that you are the key to his prison. You and Livella."

A look of concern came on her face as she glanced over at Prileen and Livella. The two looked quite a pair as they discussed who-knows-what. Prileen was taller than Livella, but seemed younger somehow. This was despite the fact that Livella looked fairly young herself.

"You must develop your abilities as quickly as you can in order to lead the Lightbearers of Lindrad against Ugglyn."

Tryvv's voice pulled Janis back to the situation.

"Your Prime Lightbearing is still in its infancy. It will take practice and a little time to learn what you must in order to be Lanser's warrior."

Janis squirmed inside. She didn't want to be *anyone's* warrior. Everything that had happened since she'd met Marric—actually, since she'd met Prost —had spiraled her down a path that she didn't want to follow. Janis knew that it had gone too far, and something about the shadows she'd seen around her alerted her to the fact that she was now in too deep. There wasn't any going back.

No, there is always a way to undo something, Janis thought.

The hope was small, but it was present.

"Throughout your life you will be tempted and approached by Ugglyn's power. He has nothing to offer you, nothing for you to truly gain. Don't fall to the Void. Use your Lightbearing for good. Bring in our brothers and sisters of power, and protect those who can't protect themselves."

The cave around her seemed to be pulling in, the walls and ceiling coming closer with every word that Tryvv said. Janis knew it was only in her mind, but the pressure and knowledge of knowing her life was changed and that she likely couldn't go back was getting to her. Her mind was reeling, her stomach clenching. She hadn't felt this helpless and stressed since her time before Macks. He had given her confidence.

Finally, Janis determined that she couldn't leave. Despite her reluctance, she somehow knew that she'd have to ride this all out. The moment she had the thought, the pull from the darkness behind her disappeared instantly.

Just then, the cave around her melted away. She felt her eyes expand as if they were being stretched open. All around her were blurs of color and movement. It felt as if her body were traveling at a quick pace until finally, the spinning stopped, the colors shaping into buildings and people.

Taking a moment to scan around her, she found herself in a bustling city. Four and five-story buildings stood around her, casting long shadows on the wide cobbled roads. People moved quickly on the streets, talking loudly and carrying all sorts of things. She recognized a pillared stone building to her left as the administration building for their monarchy. The king of Lindrad and his advisors met there to handle official matters. She knew this because she'd been hired to slay some of the king's advisors, and this is where they assembled.

It had been over a year since she'd been to T'Arren Vale, but somehow she was here in an instant. She had traveled over a week's distance in moments, somehow. It was daytime, but the sun was setting quickly, causing the shadows to extend far across the roads, almost connecting with the buildings opposite.

A young boy knelt in the middle of the road, eyes upward. A wide beam of blue Light surrounded him and extended far into the sky and the waning sun there. He looked pained, but at the same time, full of wonder. As Janis watched, she heard whispers of people around her as they gasped and stared. Women covered their mouths and stared with fright. Men held their wives and children, some blocking the path between the boy and their families.

Suddenly, the ground around the boy changed. It was as if the stones around him were moving backwards in time. The wear of the cobblestones disappeared, cracks sealed, mortar became new. Janis recognized the effect as Fixing. A wave of the blue power pulsed outward from the column of Light and ran through the closest people. Likewise, their clothing mended itself, looking new. The stones under their feet were Fixed and the road looked as if it was just newly built.

Janis stared in awe as she connected what she was seeing to what she knew.

This must be an awakening.

Sure enough, the beam of Light and strange Fixing of everything around the boy faded and he collapsed to the ground, stunned. The crowd around them backed away, most staring in awe and wonder. A few people, probably those that knew the boy, stepped forward and started shaking him lightly to see if he was okay.

A prickle on the back of her neck announced the feeling that she was being watched somewhere. She scanned the crowd, looking for something that was out of the ordinary. Her eyes landed on a black-robed figure, eyes bright and glowing with red Light, staring at her. It was a woman with short and curly brown hair. The woman nudged another black-robed figure beside her, this one a man. He had been staring at the boy as well, his eyes also full of red Light.

Janis turned to them and once again, crouched in preparation for a fight. The two figures didn't make any movements toward her, but instead closed their eyes and disappeared.

What the—? Janis thought, feeling even more uneasy.

She spun around, looking for others with red-lit eyes and black robes, but found none. As her eyes skimmed the faces around her, her stomach clenched when she recognized one of the faces that she had skipped over.

It can't be, she thought, looking back to where she had just looked.

Janis swore she had seen her old mentor, but Macks wasn't there. She didn't find him or his face anywhere among the crowd again. It made sense that she hadn't actually seen him. He had died long ago, after all.

The world began to swim with colors again as it spun into nothing. After a moment, the colors started combining again into images and people she recognized. She saw Livella and Prileen still chatting to the side about who-knows-what. The Light figures around her were there again, and Tryvv stood hovering before her, looking concerned.

"What did you See, Tar'n Yiv'len?" the tall woman asked.

"I was in T'Arren Vale," Janis answered, thoughtful. "I believe I just witnessed a boy awakening. I'm not sure why I Saw that just now, but there were others."

Tryvv looked at her, a bit of concern on her face.

"The visions will be clearer over time, but they will come more now that you know your nature. You must gather new Tar'n to your cause. This new Lightbearer needs to be found before Riln and his followers find them."

Janis connected the information quickly in her head, and suddenly it made sense why she saw two black-robed figures with red eyes. They must have been Seeing the same thing, although not necessarily at the same time. The Seeing world definitely played by its own rules. Internally, though, she somehow knew that what she was witnessing was around a week away. She wasn't exactly sure where Terris Green was, but she knew that they'd have to leave fast if they were to get to T'Arren Vale before the event took place.

"Why did I see that just now?" Janis demanded, looking hard at Tryvv.

Tryvv looked troubled.

"You are Prime. Lanser will lead you and your followers to new Light-bearers. You must have them join you in support of Lanser and the world," Tryvv said.

"I don't *have* any followers. I work alone."

Tryvv shook her head at the comment.

"That is no longer a reality, Prime."

"My name is Janis."

The tall Light woman pressed her lips in a thin line, clearly disapproving of Janis's tone and response.

"Janis, then. You must realize the importance of your new role as Prime. Gather the Tar'n, fight the Void. You and the new Voidbringer," Tryvv said as she glanced over at Livella, "the two of you are the only thing standing between Ugglyn and the world now. The Void knows that you are here. Take care, and be wise."

Tryvv said the words as if they were filled with finality. Janis's impression of an ending must have been correct, for the moment she said the words, there was a whooshing sound and wind sprung out of the cave in front of them. Prileen and Tryvv snuffed into nothing and the darkness of the cave pressed inward, threatening to swallow them. The shadows were inky black with a silvery hue. Livella screamed and ran to Janis. Instinctively, Janis raised her hands upward and a translucent blue Shield of Light sprang out of nowhere. The tendrils of blackness swirled around the statues in the room, plunging their Light into the darkness until it was just black around them. Janis didn't understand what was happening or how she'd summoned a Shield, but she was beginning to tire. Fear gripped her insides at the unknown.

All at once, the loud whooshing sound picked up. Janis felt her feet leave the floor, as did Livella's, and they both were thrown rapidly down the hallway back the way they'd come. As they flew, Livella screamed. Janis just grit her teeth and kept her hands raised. Symbols flashed along the walls as they flew past and through the doorway. The two women fell in a heap, and Janis lost her hold on the Shield around them. It snuffed into nothingness.

The two halves of the wall before them rapidly ground their way closed, blue Light pulsing more intensely as they moved.

Through the crack in the wall, Janis saw the black shadows advancing quickly, trying to make it out. They failed, however, as the two halves of the wall slammed closed with a loud boom. The two symbols of Light faded, and all was still.

Livella had passed out from the intensity of the situation and lay on the ground. Janis felt a twinge in her back from where she'd hit the hard stone floor.

"Now what in heaven's name are you two doing?" a voice said behind them.

Janis turned to see Magness advancing toward them with a confused look on her face.

"I thought I'd just seen you near the wall there, but you both just fell to the ground as if something knocked you down. What happened? Is Livella alright?"

"I think she just passed out, she'll be fine."

Crouching down, Janis pulled a small vial from a pouch attached to her belt. She pulled the cork out and held it under Livella's nose. The pungent smell of the bitter root stung her own nose even though she held it away from her face. Livella gasped and sat up quickly.

"Bitter gourd root's a good thing to have when you need to keep yourself awake," Janis replied, answering Magness's raised eyebrows.

"What in Lanser's name happened to you two?"

Janis winced at Magness's use of the god's name.

"That is a long story."

The assassin glanced at the wall behind them—no sign of any cracks or doorways any longer. She stood and walked to the wall where it had been moments before, and felt around.

"There were Light-statues. And—and strange women. Darkness and shadows were everywhere and—" Livella started to cry after she got the words out.

Magness stared at her with confusion.

Janis ignored the two women as Magness started speaking comforting words to Livella.

Feeling around, Janis couldn't find any indication of a doorway or the strange symbols they'd seen. This further validated her impression that this experience was only for Livella's and her own eyes. Something inside told her that she ought to keep some of these things to herself for a time. As much as she didn't like what she'd heard, she knew they had to get to T'Arren Vale fast.

"Someone will awaken in T'Arren Vale in seven days' time. We must hurry," Janis said.

"I beg your pardon, what?"

Janis turned, looking serious.

"Yes, I Saw it. I know where it is, and I need to go."

12

Marric stepped into the war room and found Janis and Magness having a spirited conversation. When the two women saw him enter, they immediately hushed their voices and looked up at him.

He felt as if he'd just walked in on something confidential. On instinct, he slowly backed away, muttering an apology.

"No—please stay, Marric."

Marric stopped his retreat as Magness spoke.

"We did call you and the others here, after all."

Marric inclined his head at the comment, and looked around the room. It was empty, save for Janis and Magness of course, and another woman with mousy brown hair and large eyes sitting in one of the chairs. Her hair was mostly pulled back in a ponytail behind her head, but some had escaped and was falling down to her shoulders. The free hairs looked a bit messy and disheveled, as if she'd had a scuffle of some sort recently.

He racked his brain to determine if he'd met her before and just forgotten her face, but his mind came up with nothing. After he had been sent away from Janis and Magness back in Janis's quarters, he'd watched them walk through the tunnels until everything went black. He'd assumed they'd entered a Shield, and he'd lost Sight of them. As he stared at the new woman, he had an idea.

Focusing on her face, he thought to See a bit about her. Maybe get a name or a bit of a history on her. Since he'd spied on Trease and Alsry earlier that day, he'd tried to See random people in the hallways, and sometimes he tried to See Avryn. At one point, he'd looked for Harmel and was able to see the man, looking a bit worn, trudging with a bunch of other soldiers through the woods somewhere. Harmel hadn't appeared to be in any trouble so Marric wasn't worried, but at the same time, Harmel had looked so tired and ragged.

As Marric focused on the new woman's face, he tried to let the feeling of Seeing come over him. Sure enough, he felt his eyes stretch open. The room spun around him with many colors, which were soon replaced by blackness. He Saw nothing.

Something irked Marric, and he felt like he should pull back. He did so, and found himself in the war room again.

It took him a moment to realize that Janis and Magness were staring at him.

"What did you just See, Marric? Is there something wrong?"

Marric blushed slightly, realizing that it probably seemed odd that he just lost himself in a vision. Right now, he had nothing to show for it.

"Erm, nothing, actually."

He felt like he'd done something wrong for it to not have worked. Choosing not to elaborate, he moved further into the war room. Marric couldn't help feeling curious, though. As he walked, his eyes shifted to the dazed-looking woman sitting in the corner.

Janis noticed the shift of his gaze and a look of understanding passed on her face. She looked at Marric and pointed to the woman in the corner while making the introduction. "That's Livella. She's like Prost. You won't See anything about her, because Lightbearing won't work on her."

Marric felt his skin chill and he faced the woman, stepping back in alarm.

Janis, seeing his reaction, chuckled audibly. "She's not like Prost in *that* way, Marric. The woman is as harmless as a kitten. I was merely saying that you probably couldn't See anything about her because she, like Prost, is immune to Lightbearing."

She had said it so confidently that the strangeness of the words almost didn't feel strange at all. Marric stared at her, disbelief on his face at how nonchalant she was about the situation.

"How? Isn't she dangerous?" As he said it, he felt a bit foolish, given the fact that the woman was untied and clearly in a daze. He wondered if she was drunk or sick or something of the sort.

"She isn't dangerous, she is . . . a friend," Magness replied, giving Janis a pointed look, to which Janis shrugged.

"We can talk about that later. Let's wait for the others."

Only moments later, Avryn and Turrin walked into the door, laughing and carrying a mug of some frothy drink in their hands.

Turrin spoke loudly in a pleased tone. "Roit. Now, what are we all meetin' for? Me an' Avryn were havin' a grand ol' time as it's our noit off. We got t'talkin' abou' the good days in T'Arren Vale. Did you know tha' he actually *knew* Prostafore—"

Avryn slugged Turrin on the arm, making the man wince.

"Now, what in Lanser's name was *tha'* fer?"

Marric noticed a strange look on Janis's face at Turrin's comment.

What was that about? he thought.

"Why do yeh care if'n Oi tell people abou' it?"

Magness spoke up, "Yes, I am well aware of Avryn's connection to Prost before he came here. That isn't why we are here. All we need is—ah, here they are."

Alsry and Trease shuffled into the room looking annoyed, as if they'd each just dealt with a defiant child. They entered one by one, far enough from each other that it looked like they might not have come together, but they came in too close together to have come separately. Marric interpreted the looks on their faces and their body language to mean they'd been fighting about something just before.

Magness appeared to notice the same thing, but ignored the situation and started speaking instead.

"Where is Rivelen? I asked for all the generals to attend that are present."

"Oi believe she is roit sick t'noit. She said t'get started," Trease answered before adding, "I don' roit think she's real sick, but if she wants t'miss th'fun, then fine."

Magness acknowledged this news before continuing.

"There is to be an awakening in T'Arren Vale, in a week's time. We must hurry there before Watchlight. Trease, given that you and your company just returned, we can send Alsry and her company. You can stay and watch. Turrin, I thought to send you, Avryn, and a few of your company to retrieve Marric's father. We have rough coordinates from what Rivelen could See about the man's location. Another part of Turrin's company will go with Alsry's." Almost as an afterthought, Magness added to Turrin, "We'll send Marric with them as well."

Marric jumped at the words. Not once had anyone mentioned that he would be able to leave Terris Green anytime soon.

"Unless of course you would rather stay here and just keep practicing," Magness replied, noting his reaction to her orders.

"No! No, not at all. I will go," Marric cut in, "But why won't I go with Turrin to get my father?"

Magness fixed her eyes on him and looked thoughtful.

"It may seem odd, but knowing that Watchlight may get there just before or at the same time as us makes me nervous. They are very persuasive, as you can recall, and I think that having you there to reason with the boy might be in our best interest. You are a more recent addition to Evenir, after all."

Just as she said it, however, she eyed Janis quickly before looking back at him. Marric processed the reasoning, and nodded his agreement. It was logical, though the idea of being in the same place as Watchlight agitated him intensely.

"The other thing we must note is that you are too valuable of an asset to keep hidden. I think that all of your fellow Lightbearers can agree you are never really ready to use your powers out in the world, so there is no point in waiting. I've seen the progress you have made in the past few weeks, and I believe that you have a lot to offer to the group."

For some reason, this made him feel proud; now he could prove he was worth all the trouble he'd caused his Evenir family in acquiring and training him.

"I think it would be best if you depart with your respective assignments as soon as possible."

Just then, a knock sounded at the wooden door behind them all. At the sound, the woman in the corner squealed in fright and hugged her midsection. Her reaction made the whole group look over at her. Marric felt bad for her, though he didn't know why. He didn't even know her that well, only that she was unaffected by Lightbearing.

The other generals looked at her curiously, a few opened their mouths to ask who she was, but then stopped, thinking the better of it. All except Turrin.

"Oo's tha'?" Turrin said, raising an eyebrow at the woman by the wall.

Magness looked at him, but shook her head. "We'll talk about her in a few moments. Come in!" Magness said loudly toward the door, eyes lingering on Livella as she did so.

A messenger came into the door, panting slightly from running. Pausing a moment, the slight man caught his breath before speaking.

"Varith is back with 'is men."

Magness smiled at the news.

"Is he well, then? Did they find anything?"

"No, ma'am. He din' find nuttin'. Should I bring 'im a message from yeh?"

The Evenir leader stood there for a moment, a look of thoughtfulness on her face.

"Yes, I imagine he is quite tired, but please have him as well as his lieutenants, Harmel and Shrell, report here to the war room immediately."

"Yes, ma'am."

The small messenger bowed his balding head and backed out the doorway to deliver the message. Marric saw Janis stiffen at the news of Harmel and Shrell being back at Terris Green, and he frowned at the reaction. Despite Janis's odd behavior, Marric was thrilled to get to see his friends again.

"I wish that all of the company leaders were here, but unfortunately many are out searching for new Lightbearers or Watchlight's compound. *Rivelen* apparently can't be bothered to join us here, though I can't understand why."

Magness looked annoyed. It didn't help that the small strange woman continued to gasp and quietly whine in the corner. Avryn spoke out then, gesturing to the woman.

"Perhaps I can see if there is something I can do about the poor woman over there. She looks beside herself with something."

Avryn moved off to a basin of water near the side of the room, and retrieved a cup of water before approaching the sitting woman. She still had her eyes upward, and was mumbling something that no one could understand.

"Actually, Marric," Magness said. "I think that I could use your help. I've just sent the messenger to get Varith and a couple of his men, but I failed to ask him to find Rivelen and request her presence, despite her supposed sick state. Given that he's just run off and I don't want to try to chase down another, can you please locate Rivelen and ask her to come?"

"Umm, sure," he replied with a shrug. "Though . . . I'm not sure where she is. Can someone tell me where her room is?"

Magness smirked at his comment. A couple of the others around him chuckled at his question. Turrin, who seemed to be the most amused, moved behind him and put his hands on Marric's shoulders. The man pressed down quite hard and Marric had to lock his knees so that they didn't buckle below him. It was an uncomfortable feeling; Marric hadn't associated Turrin's bulky, yet chubby size with strength. He'd seen the man Conjure a variety of weapons and prove his skill in combat with each of them, but he underestimated the man's strength due to his appearance of being a bit out of shape.

"Marric, son. She means to use yer Seeing. Yeh can find her roit well with yer Seeing powers."

"Oh—" upon realizing his mistake, he shyly nodded to her. "I'm sorry, I didn't know that's what you meant."

"That's alright, Marric. Just See if you can communicate with her. She's a Seer as well, so technically you can deliver a message to her."

Marric squirmed inside. It wasn't that he'd never found someone without knowing their location, but it was more the expectation that he had to deliver a message for the first time, in front of an audience.

"I can try, though I'm not sure how to do that, exactly."

Magness looked amused at the comment. "You have not had too much trouble doing that in the past. Trease here mentioned that Rivelen had caught you spying on Trease, Alsry and Avryn earlier today."

Marric blushed deeply.

"I—I didn't mean to intrude, it was an accident!" Marric sputtered, feeling like a child caught doing something naughty.

Magness raised her hand to stop him.

"You are not in trouble, boy. I am merely saying that you have the ability to find people that you need to, if you know them. Rivelen just happened to be searching for you, and came across your projected self while you watched them. Now, can you please contact her and let her know she is needed?"

Marric nodded at the request. Breathing deeply, he remembered the things he'd learned from Tynvel, the old woman with the missing teeth and the horrible slur in her speech. After a beat, the world spun and his eyes began to glow. Though he couldn't see it, he could feel it happening. Focusing on Rivelen's face, he felt a version of himself moving quickly through space before the spinning began to slow. Colors coalesced into real images, and Marric found himself in Rivelen's chambers. He suddenly felt very self-conscious. When he noted that she was merely reading a book at her desk, he sighed internally.

Rivelen's room was about twice the size of his own, and was filled with luxurious furniture and cushions. The walls had tapestries and other cloth strung up all over. If he didn't know that they were in a network of caverns, he might not have realized that's where this was. There was an overwhelming majority of the color pink everywhere, with some other colors here and there.

I suppose it's safe to say that she likes the color pink, he thought.

Given that he was Seeing her right now, she didn't turn to look at him. He would be hidden from her view unless she also stepped into her Sight. Marric's stomach clenched when he realized that he had no idea how to get a message to her if she didn't know he was there, watching her. He strategically shifted his projected self so that he was in front of her and waved his hand in front of her face. Of course, this resulted in nothing. He tried again, but she still didn't see.

Pressing his lips together in a thin line, he tried to think of what he could do. For a moment, he thought to pull back and ask the others how he could communicate to her if she wasn't Seeing him, but he thought better of it. For some reason, he felt like he had to prove himself and his training. If he asked, he feared that they wouldn't think he was ready to leave Terris Green and travel to T'Arren Vale. He'd heard of the Lindradian capital city, but had never had the chance to go there.

As he wracked his brain for what he could do, he opted to try touching her, even though he knew that she couldn't feel him and he couldn't feel her. The moment his hand touched her shoulder, it passed through. He had expected this, so it didn't surprise him. What did surprise him was Rivelen gasping suddenly as her eyes burst with blue beams of Light.

He sucked in his breath in shock and jumped backwards in the vision. The moment her eyes started glowing, a ripping sound announced a second version of herself coming out of the one sitting at the desk.

"Wha' in th'good Lanser's name are yeh doin' 'ere, boy?" she yelled. "Are yeh tryin' t'spy on me fer a good show?"

Her face was red as she said it, which made Marric feel even more embarrassed about it.

"I—I'm sorry! Magness sent me to tell you—I didn't know you would be here and—"

His own face blushed deep also, though it was a weird sensation. He couldn't technically feel the same things with his vision body, but he felt his physical face somewhere far away getting warmer. Regardless of the odd nature of the feeling, his vision self must have shown the same thing, for Rivelen narrowed her eyes as she noticed.

"So it be true, Magness sent yous, eh? Wha' is it she wants?"

Clearing his throat for fear of choking on his embarrassment, he spoke slowly so that he didn't stutter.

"She has something that she wants to discuss with all the leaders of Evenir. The present ones, at least. I know that you are sick, but she requested you attend the meeting in the war room as soon as you can make it there."

Rivelen pursed her lips, but nodded.

"Fine, bu' yeh better keep this t'yerself, eh? Ain't no one ought t'hear 'bout this, got it?"

Marric nodded vigorously. He stood there, staring at her for a moment before she shooed him away with her hands.

"If there ain't nuttin' else, yeh can leave!"

At that, he turned away and let his vision body flow back into his physical one. Once again, the room around him spun quickly, turning everything to a mesh of colors. This was particularly different, given the decorated nature of the woman's living quarters. Marric appreciated the beauty of it for a moment before the swirling stopped and he felt the hard stone floor beneath his feet.

"—have a lot to discuss and little time. I do hope Marric hurries this up," Magness said.

"Erm, I'm back now."

Magness startled slightly at his return before asking, "Good, is Rivelen on her way, then?"

"Yes, ma'am. I believe she is leaving now."

"Thank you. That was much faster than finding and sending a messenger. Now, Marric, I want to introduce you to Varith."

As she said it, she gestured to the side of the room where Marric saw a smartly dressed man with deeply dark skin and black curly hair cut close to his head. The clothing he wore was something that Marric often saw very wealthy men wearing when they took a trip to Wurren market. His vest and tunic were both deep purple and adorned with gold threading in beautiful designs. He wore white stockings stuck into smart-looking black boots. At his side hung a short sword. Marric marveled at the apparel of the man and how he had supposedly just returned from traveling.

"Ah yes, Marric. I have heard quite a lot about you from your friends, here," the man said, moving toward him. He extended his hand, which Marric took promptly. His grip was alarmingly strong, despite his lean figure. Marric could see toned arms bulging through the sleeves of his also-purple shirt.

"I am Varith, head Fixer and leader of companies twenty-two through twenty-six. I am also a second-born Conjurer. That comes in handy quite often. I believe that you are like Avryn, correct?"

Marric responded, "Yes sir, Seer, Mover and Conjurer."

"Ooh, that seems like quite a nasty combination, I must say. We're lucky to have you."

"Erm, thanks, I suppose."

Despite his endeavors, Marric couldn't help but look Varith up and down, observing his odd choice of clothing. While the rest of Evenir—save Rivelen—wore simple tunics and cloaks of neutral colors, Varith clearly cared for nicer clothing. Marric's eyes drifted to the side where a couple of Varith's companions stood, their clothes simple and dirtied, as if they'd had a rough go during their journey. It was obvious that they'd just arrived from their travels, but Varith's clothes looked clean and impeccable.

Before Marric could marvel any further, his eyes drifted up to the faces of the dark man's companions. Eyes widening, Marric realized it was Harmel and Shrell.

Rushing forward, he threw his arms around Harmel, feeling relief spread through his whole body.

"Harmel, Shrell! I'm so glad that you are back! I was concerned that I'd never see you again if you ran into some Watchlight men," Marric said, speaking so quickly that he stumbled on his own words.

"'Ey, Mar! Oi was wonderin' when yeh'd notice tha' was us. Yeh looked a bit confuzzled with Varith fer a bit. Are yeh sure *yous* are okay?" Harmel said, a twinkle in his eye.

The familiar sound of the man's voice and his jovial comments were so comforting to Marric. It was strange how he'd been able to get close to them so quickly. Marric thought about how he'd only known them for a couple months, but they seemed a constant, a security to him that he didn't want to forget.

Shrell said nothing, but instead bowed his head slightly. He smiled, but in his eyes, there was exhaustion.

"Yes, now that we're all happy to see each other, I fear that we must begin the discussion soon," Magness said, clearly impatient, "I do hope that Rivelen gets here soon—we can't really afford to wait much longer."

"Oi say we jus' start withou' her. She ain't goin' t'be much 'elp anyways, eh? Oi fink she'll jus' whoine 'bout 'er sick stomach, is all," Trease said.

Alsry jumped in then. "Oh please, Trease, we all know that she's faking it. I wager that she's been experimenting with her makeup again. Magness, why do you humor her fanciful and expensive tastes? They aren't going to do her much good if a Destroying ball flies into her face."

This comment was awarded with a hearty chuckle from Trease and booming laughter from Turrin.

"Tha's roit! Th'only thing tha' she 'as against tha' is t'See it comin'. But then it'd be roit too late," Turrin added.

Trease and Turrin continued to laugh, pleased with themselves, while Alsry rolled her eyes, annoyed at the interruption. Making a show of it, she flicked her hands in the air, causing two chairs wreathed in blued Light to quickly slide forward until they pushed behind the legs of the two laughing generals, obliging them both to take a seat.

"Sit down and take a breath before you kill yourselves with your annoying laughter," Alsry said.

Turrin kept laughing, but Trease had stopped and was glaring at her companion.

"Yeh know Oi don' loik bein' touched loik tha'."

As she said the words, a blue sphere sprang outwards from Trease, encasing her completely inside. Her Shield glowed bright and blue like the Lightbearing powers of all at Evenir, but it looked imposing for some reason.

Upon seeing this, Alsry just rolled her eyes.

Just then, the door sprang open and Rivelen strolled in. She'd messed her hair slightly and wore a night cloak over her blue gown, as if to emphasize that she'd just gotten out of bed. Marric gawked at her, knowing that when he'd Seen her just moments before, she'd looked fine; hair and clothing practically perfect.

Rivelen caught his eye and gave him a daring look that seemed to say, *tell them I'm not sick, and I'll kill you in your sleep.*

Marric held his peace.

"Well, now that we are all finally here, I believe that there is much to discuss. Please, Shrell, can you close the door?"

As the tall man moved to the door, it glowed blue and shut heavily on its own, causing a slight boom in the small war room cavern. Marric winced at the sound.

Everyone's eyes turned to Alsry, and she shrugged.

"I don't know why Magness always forgets that there are easier ways of doing things."

Sighing, Magness nodded. "I try not to take your powers for granted, but I also try not to promote laziness. Regardless, thank you for your help, Alsry."

The dark woman nodded, face still serious.

Marric remembered how intimidating she really was. For the most part, he'd had his Moving lessons from another Mover, Alsry's assistant, Tival, but she would step in and help him as often as she could. What she did with the rest of her time, he didn't know, but he was afraid to learn of it. Whenever she taught him, she never smiled, rarely joked, and treated him somewhat like a soldier of hers. Alsry was never rude or harsh to him, but she was still intimidating to be around.

"Janis has shared some important particulars that I feel we should all be aware of. After she initially told me, I thought to keep it to ourselves for a time. However, given the recent engagements we've had with Watchlight and the strangeness of Livella's arrival, I believe it's in our best interest to discuss this now."

Magness turned to Janis and nodded, giving her the go-ahead to speak. Before she could, Turrin jumped in, pointing heavily to the woman sitting next to Avryn, who was softly speaking to her and lightly squeezing her arm.

"Oi take it tha' is Livella, no?" Turrin asked.

Magness looked at him and nodded. "We'll let Janis talk about who she is."

Janis did not appear to appreciate having the floor to speak. She clenched her fists to the side as if this was the worst thing for her to have to do. When all eyes had turned on her, she stepped forward from her place in the shadows, eyes flicking to Livella. By now, Avryn had revived her to some degree, her eyes focusing now on what was happening with the group.

"I don't care for lengthy speeches or lots of words, so let's just get to the point," Janis said roughly. "Apparently, I am something called a Tar'n Yiv'len, or a Prime Lightbearer, and Livella is a Voidbearer. I'm not certain what this means, exactly."

She stopped then, eyes scanning the group around her. When she said nothing else, Turrin started laughing.

"Now, wha' in the blazes does *tha'* mean? Yeh sound loik a crazy person if tha' is all yer gonna give us."

Magness rolled her eyes and gestured to Janis to proceed.

Glaring, Janis continued.

"Earlier today, after Magness and I retrieved Livella—" Janis gestured to Livella in the corner, "—who mysteriously appeared here at Terris Green for no reason at all—there was a strange voice whispering to the both of us. We followed the voice to a dead end, here in the tunnel networks."

Janis launched into a confusing story that seemed completely ridiculous. In Marric's opinion, the only thing that made it even remotely possible is that it was Janis speaking. If Harmel or even Avryn had been telling the story, Marric would have assumed it was a joke, or just a story for entertainment. Not only did Janis tell it with complete seriousness, but she never joked, anyway. The idea of her making something up was just impossible.

When she spoke of the Light depictions of the various Primes, Marric was enthralled.

"Riln and Prost were there, among many that I didn't know."

Magness looked distant as she heard this, but then she spoke. "Watchlight and Evenir weren't always at war. It wasn't until Riln and Prost took charge that we became enemies. Before, we were two groups of Lightbearers separated only by different ideals. Now the divide between us is far more than that."

Marric started at the words. "You weren't always fighting? What changed?"

Magness looked at him, then continued. "It must be related to the bond between Prost and Riln that Janis just described. Talatha, your mother," the woman said this to him directly, "wrote of this in one of her last entries. There weren't any specifics, but I recall that she had written some strange symbols in her entry and I recognize the words now as Janis says them. Tar'n Yiv'len was something that she was trying to research in not only our archives, but in the archives of T'Arren Vale and the other towns in Lindrad. It appeared that she was trying to learn what it meant. I never had the opportunity to discuss this with her before she died."

As she said the words, a few of the others in the room looked at Marric warily, as if they might hurt his feelings.

He stared back at them, not feeling too much at the mention of his mother's passing. Part of him longed to know who she was and what she was like, but he couldn't necessarily mourn the loss of someone he'd already lost. Curiosity was the reigning feeling for him.

Magness gestured again for Janis to continue. Reluctantly, she did.

"Tar'n Yiv'len is supposed to be some champion for Lanser himself. The Voidbearer is for Ugglyn. Together, we are supposed to form some Seal for Ugglyn's powers, though what that means, I don't know."

Marric watched as Janis's eyes looked to Livella in the corner, eyebrows knitting together slightly. She paused for a beat, then looked to Magness, willing the woman to continue.

Sighing, Magness realized that she was lucky to have gotten so many words out of the assassin.

"Janis explained that Livella, like Prost, cannot be affected by Light-bearing powers. She is immune, like him. That means Janis, like Riln, is meant to manifest every Lightbearing class as if each one was her first awakened power."

Magness's words took on an accusing tone, and Janis didn't look amused at the comment. Up until now, aside from short bursts of power, Janis had shown little proficiency in all seven of the classes of Lightbearing. Marric felt bad knowing that this frustrated his friend.

"Riln and Prost were the only Seal locking away Ugglyn, until they fell to the temptations of power from Ugglyn. Their Light now shines red along with all their followers. Janis and Livella are the only Seal now holding Ugglyn effectively."

The silence that followed was practically palpable. Marric fidgeted where he stood, so decided it would be best if he sat down. He had heard and understood everything Magness had said, at least the *words* she had said, but none of it actually made sense. For some reason, he felt wildly out of place in this discussion.

"Wha' in the blazes is tha' s'posed t'mean? I sure ain't seen no Ugglyn marchin' 'round Lindrad, 'ave yous?" Turrin said, still sounding lighthearted, despite the news.

Magness looked thoughtful at the comment.

"I am not sure what the full implications are, but it seems like we should be partially glad that is the case. I am no prophet, nor are there any existing beings that can speak with Lanser himself."

Her gaze turned on Janis, who bristled at the attention.

"But now we have someone who has been blessed with his power to aid us against Riln. We always wondered why Riln could manifest all seven of the powers. Though I have a hard time accepting it, the potential power that Janis has received does make sense, logically. Riln must be this Tar'n Yiv'len, or at least one of them, now. Talatha would be thrilled to learn this. If only I'd been there to help her before she died."

Janis clenched her fists harder then spoke.

"The *problem* is that I have no idea what the fog I'm supposed to do. I didn't ask to be involved in this power war between two sides, but I guess I've been duped—snagged even—into dealing with all of this. My life was a lot simpler before I got caught up in all of this nonsense."

Magness looked annoyed at the comment. "Well, whether you like it or not, you are here, you *are* involved, and you can't escape it now. I have a feeling that you can run as fast and as far as you want, but you aren't going to escape Lanser. He sees all, knows all."

Clearing her throat, Trease interrupted the escalating argument.

"S'cuse me, ladies, bu' Oi 'ave t'ask. What are *we* t'do? This is roit strange t' learn an' all tha', but wha' are we s'posed t'do?"

Breathing deeply, Magness composed herself before turning to her companions. "I have a bad feeling that things are going to start getting more difficult for all of us now. Janis mentioned that she was told to keep gathering the Lightbearers together to build an army against Ugglyn's influence before he gets too strong."

Varith crunched loudly on something behind them. Marric and the others in the room turned their heads to see him eating an apple.

"What? I just got back from traveling. Can't a man eat?"

Alsry let out a frustrated sigh, almost a hiss. Turrin chuckled, still taking all the news with ease, while Rivelen stared at Varith, disgusted. The dark-skinned man merely grinned from ear to ear and crunched down on another bite. The apple suddenly glowed with a blue Light and was ripped from his hand, shooting up to the ceiling. It hovered there, far out of reach.

Looking offended, Varith gaped at Alsry.

"Now, that isn't right," he said, pouting. He held out his hand and Conjured a sword. Squinting his eyes, he stared at the blade as it grew longer and expanded up to the ceiling. As he swung his arm and the sword, he tried to skewer the apple. Alsry shifted her hand sideways, making the glowing apple shift just so that the sword missed it.

"Come on, Als, that's not fair," he whined.

"Please, can we try to focus?" Magness said, exasperated.

Alsry nodded in a satisfied way over her small victory.

Varith glared at her, but dismissed his Conjured sword dejectedly.

"Janis only just Saw, somehow earlier than our own Seers, an awakening in T'Arren Vale in a week's time. As I said before, Alsry and her company with half of Turrin's men should go to retrieve him before Watchlight does."

"I am going as well," Janis said, staring at Livella.

Magness shook her head, looking determined.

"I need you to stay here to talk more about what you saw and what we can learn from it. Plus, with the volatile nature of your powers, I fear that sending you will be more detrimental to the group than if you stayed here."

Janis smirked at the comment.

"Will all due respect, Magness, I don't report to you. I haven't sworn loyalty to your little band of whatever you are, and I will come and go as I please."

"Though you may not report to me, the rest of them do. If you want to leave here, fine, but I will not risk danger to my men and women because of your inexperienced use of Lightbearing—or lack of a humble attitude. The stakes are higher now, and I'd wager that Watchlight will send not a small number of fighters."

Her voice was rising now. Marric and the rest of the generals stared at the two, awkwardness filling the spaces everywhere.

Janis looked amused at the comment. "If that is what you wish, then I have no problem with it. I can just leave now and never come back. It probably would be for the best, anyway."

As she said the words, a screech sounded in the room behind Magness. Trease jumped back and summoned her Shield, the spherical shape expanding to block the war table and half of the war room. Avryn and Livella were the only two that sat outside of the wall. Turrin Conjured a broadsword and clutched it heavily in both of his hands. Janis whipped out her own daggers and jumped forward to get a better look at what had happened.

Avryn, hearing the scream, had Conjured his own short sword and snatched Livella out of the chair with his other arm. Marric couldn't see what the commotion was, but he felt his blood chill at the sound and the reaction of the room. Though he didn't really know if he wanted to see, he shuffled his feet to the side so he could look around the table with the maps and small figures on it.

When he saw what had made the woman scream, he froze, the chill in his body ramping up to a deep cold.

A black, mercurial form was wriggling its way out of the ground, four paces from where Livella and Avryn had sat moments before. There was something foul and foreboding about the silvery black form; the way it moved was strange and viscous.

"Wha' is tha' thing?" Turrin said, moving slowly so he was just outside the Shield.

"Avryn, get insoid the Shield, now!" Trease shouted.

Rather than looking over at the Alsry, Avryn kept his gaze on the black ooze that was quickly growing into something much larger. Inching closer to the Shield, he waited until Trease opened up a break in the Shield. Shoving his arm to the side sharply, he pushed Livella through the hole.

"Close it!" Avryn said loudly.

"Avryn, git in there, yeh piece of—"

"Now!" Avryn commanded Trease, who did so, grumbling to herself.

Avryn crept closer to the seeping form, but only after he ensured that the Shield had been closed. Drawing his real sword in his other hand, he moved slowly to the thing. The air around it looked to be slightly drawn in by the form, as if it was breathing inward. Marric couldn't tell if he was just seeing things or if maybe the Shield was convoluting the view, but the form looked to be smooth and completely without any variations in its texture. The silvery blackness of it was so stark against everything else, that it was easy to spot and follow. Finally, it stopped growing at about the height of Avryn's knees, and became as wide as two men.

Marric eyed Janis to see what her reaction would be. She stared, though she didn't look afraid. There was something in her eyes that looked like she recognized the thing, like it was familiar to her. Tearing his eyes from her and her odd reaction, he noted that the form crept slowly toward Avryn.

"Please, Avryn, don't do anything to it. Let's think this through."

"Magness, I think you and I both know that if we just leave it be, it won't go well. If something happens to me, at least it will just be me and not everyone."

With a quick sweep of his sword, he jabbed the shape-shifting form. The moment it connected with the strange ooze, it stuck there and Avryn grunted, trying to pull it back.

"Fog it!" he yelled, pulling harder. When it was clear that it wouldn't budge, he let go, the sword sinking quickly and completely into the ooze.

Weaponless save for his Light sword, Avryn held it aloft and jumped backwards.

"I have a nasty feeling that we shouldn't let it touch anything," Avryn said loudly.

The group stared as the otherworldly form expanded in size until it was to Avryn's waist.

"Move!" Janis shouted out of nowhere.

The assassin shoved her way to the front of the group and stood just before the spherical wall of the Shield. The silvery black form was almost to Avryn now, forcing him to paste himself against the wall. Janis quickly stepped through the Shield and faced the creature.

Letting out a loud yell, Janis held her hand out and created a ball of Light before lobbing it at the form. It connected with a loud crack, and a screech sounded in the air, raising the hairs on Marric's arms and neck. A flash of blue Light accompanied the sound, which made it more imposing on their senses.

Avryn shouted too. Once the spots had cleared from Marric's vision, he saw that the mysterious form was gone.

"*That*, I think, is what the Void looks like," Janis said, looking grim.

13

The air of the room was cold and serious, as the whole group stood their ground with weapons raised. Trease had pulled up her Shield again, this time encompassing everyone. Janis had moved closer to the others after she had dispelled the strange ooze that had attacked Avryn.

"Stay vigilant, friends. If more come, we need to work together," Magness said, sword drawn.

Janis, feeling her own adrenaline rush in her veins and roar in her ears, chuckled at the sight of it all. Facing Trease, she spoke.

"Did you not see what that thing did to Avryn's steel? I get the feeling that Lightbearing is our only defense against it."

Magness still looked determined as she gripped the hilt of her sword.

"Anything is better than nothing, even if all it does is provide a minor distraction," Magness replied.

"'Ow did yeh kill it, assassin?" Turrin spoke out, his own back to Janis. He held two swords of Light now, each impossibly long for actual combat. Janis knew that the blue glowing swords of Light could be sharp as ever and feather light.

"Instinct. I deduced when the steel was swallowed up inside that I would rather not lose my own daggers to it. Seems my instinct was right."

"Instinct, was it? Or are yeh knowin' more than yeh say? Did yous call tha' thing in 'ere?" Rivelen said, looking pale.

Janis opened her mouth to retort, but was interrupted by Avryn.

"Stop it! This is not the time to fight with each other. The best we can do is ensure that we are all safe. Now, keep your eyes open and look for signs of other dark patches."

His timing and reasoning were both right, Janis could agree with that. Whatever the strange Void form was, it was lethal. She suspected that if it touched any living thing, it would not be good. Doing what she did best, she analyzed the situation, scanning everywhere with her eyes. An idea came to her then. It wasn't something that she'd done before, but she thought to try it. Holding out both hands before her, she created a large orb of Light the size of her head. Unsure what exactly to do, she tossed it toward the floor. There were already about six orbs of Light in the room, but they all stood near the edges of the walls, while only one stood in the middle. Curiously, the Light bounced on the floor as if it was some type of children's ball.

When the Light connected with the ground, a shrill shriek screamed in their ears and a smaller form, silver-black and oily like the last one she'd Destroyed, squirmed up from the ground. In one startling motion, it engulfed her Light, making it snuff into nothing.

Janis snagged her long-knife from her side and almost rushed the black apparition instinctively. Memory reminded her that using steel was foolish, so she stepped backwards. Trying once again to create a Destroying ball, she held her hand out. Nothing happened.

Cursing to herself, she noted that the ignoble form had manifested inside the Shield.

"Look out!" she shouted, realizing that everyone had their backs turned, looking outward and not expecting anything inside the Shield.

Turrin turned and cursed, swinging his Conjured swords wildly. A few of his blows connected with the thing and it wailed in pain, writhing in agony while silvery black puffs of smoke hissed out where the blades connected. A blue arrow of Light spouted from the heart of the specter, causing more smoke to hiss out and more shrieking.

Janis looked up to see Marric with a Conjured bow and another arrow knocked. He looked terrified, but determined. With a smooth motion, he pulled the arrow back and shot the form again. This one went right through it, the arrow clattering on the ground on the other side, skidding just past Rivelen's feet, who also shrieked.

Her scream is almost worse than this thing's, Janis thought.

Frustrated that it wouldn't just die, she tried to summon something, anything. A flash of Light in her hand announced something appearing, but it quickly dissipated, causing Janis to grumble, gritting her teeth in frustration.

Alsry had Moved a few chairs into the path of the form as it moved slowly toward Shrell, Harmel, and Varith. The finely dressed man had Conjured his own sword, and a square shield like a knight's.

"Get, you black brute!" he yelled, jabbing the persistent form as it neared. This had little effect on the ooze, however, and it continued moving forward.

"Cover your ears, now!" Avryn shouted.

Janis turned to see him holding a small and intense blue orb of Light. He rushed the silver-black form and threw his hand forward. It connected with the thing and a flash of Light was followed by more shrieking pain and a blast that knocked many of them off their feet. Janis felt the wave slam into her gut, but she held her ground, gritting against the force and the pain.

Black and silver smoke expelled everywhere, inking the air around them and making it hard to see. Quickly, it cleared as if turning into the air itself.

Tension continued to hold the room as they moved closer to each other, looking everywhere. Trease, realizing the unearthly forms could manifest *inside* her Shield, pulled it inward until it disappeared.

"Non-Lightbearers, together, quick-loik!" Trease ordered them. Harmel and Shrell still had their swords drawn, but they moved quickly to stand next to Magness. Livella seemed to have snapped out of her daze completely with the commotion, and moved to the others. Trease held her hand up and summoned the Shield over the four of them. However, the moment it pulled up around Livella, it dispelled as if it couldn't hold.

Frustrated, Trease tried again, but with the same result.

"It's Livella, your Shield is too close to her. Make it bigger," Janis said, pointing at the mousy haired girl.

"Wha' does tha' mean? Oi 'ave seen Prost insoid a Shield 'afore—"

"But he always stands in the middle, away from the edges. This small Shield's edge is too close to her!"

Trease, looking determined, summoned another Shield that wasn't a perfect sphere. Instead, it harbored an oblong section that bowed out away from Livella, while the other side held close to the other three.

Marric had another arrow nocked and was spinning around slowly. Janis admired the progress he had made in the last few weeks. He had apparently gained some confidence with his powers. She recalled how he'd Moved the group of Watchlight men without hesitation when they were trying to escape their compound. She figured he had it in him, but this was proof that her thoughts were true.

"'Ere comes another!" Harmel said, pointing through Livella.

Varith cursed, noting that the dark inky patch was inside the Shield where it bowed outward, away from Livella.

Marric shot the arrow, but must not have thought about the Shield that stood between him and the form. The Light arrow ricocheted off it with a pinging sound.

"Drop the Shield, Trease!" Avryn commanded.

Trease concentrated and started to pull the Shield inward toward the congealing form above the ground. This one looked less like a shapeless blob and more like the trunk of a creature with two thick arms, which it used to slither forward. As the squat woman pulled the Shield in, the creature screamed when the wall got too close to it, and shuffled quickly toward Livella.

Livella was pale and stood there, frozen, as it moved to her.

"Drop the fogging Shield, Trease!"

Realizing that she was not helping the situation, Trease dropped the Shield. It was too late, however, as the form reached one of its arms out and grabbed hold of Livella. The moment it touched her skin, the form froze. Livella was screaming now, fear gripping every part of her. She didn't seem in pain, just scared.

They all watched as it grew in size. The air around Livella grew darker and her skin changed to oily black where it touched her leg.

Before long, Varith had jumped forward and sliced through the thing's arm with his Light sword. Shrieking pierced the air again and his sword shattered like glass. The creature's arm puffed into smoke, and Livella's skin turned to normal. Avryn lobbed another Destroying ball and the now one-armed thing exploded with another screech into black and silver smoke.

Panting, Varith spun around, scanning the areas around them. Trease had raised the Shield again, though this time it only covered Harmel, Shrell and Magness.

"Are you hurt?" Avryn asked Livella. The woman shook her head, still shaking with fear.

"Stay vigilant, people, I have a feeling that this is not over yet," Avryn said definitively. Crouching down, he pulled up the bottom of Livella's tattered skirt to inspect her leg. Janis could see that there was nothing there. No abrasions of any kind adorned the part of her leg that the strange creature had held just moments before.

"I—I didn't feel anything," Livella sputtered.

Expecting another form-creature to appear around them, Janis turned slowly, searching for movement or the contrast of the shiny black texture of one of the creatures against the stone floor and walls.

"Well—" a dismembered voice boomed from somewhere, "*That* was particularly interesting, wasn't it?"

The voice was low and deep, rumbling the very walls of the room they were in. Janis felt chills run through her body as she turned around and around, trying to find the source. As she did, she noted that the others around her had ceased moving. They didn't appear worried about the voice that had just spoken from nowhere.

Looking more closely, she saw that Avryn's frame was still crouched low, still looking at Livella's leg. He wasn't breathing. Normally, she could hear or even see the breath of another person, especially with the proximity that they were in now. One by one, she inspected her new allies to see that they were not breathing, either. Even Marric stood frozen, eyes wide with fear and tension. His body had frozen with an arrow nocked and pointed to the wall behind Avryn.

There wasn't anything there, from what Janis could tell. Likely he had also been scanning the area and had frozen with that position.

"It was an effective experiment, in the least."

Livella panted loudly a few paces away, and Janis stared at her. It wasn't overly surprising that she was the only person other than Janis herself who was immune to being frozen.

"Expending my energy for this was well worth it, in my opinion."

The voice intoned, vibrating the room and permeating every part of Janis's being. It felt as if the voice was sounding in her head, rather than through her ears.

"Are you hearing this?" Janis said, looking to Livella.

The woman nodded, jaw locked tightly in fear.

"Where the fog are you?" Janis shouted, feeling a little silly. She took comfort in knowing, or rather guessing, that the rest of the group couldn't hear her talking to nothing.

The voice chuckled, then hummed, the vibrations increasing in magnitude.

"I am the one that you are currently keeping at bay. Though my power is growing."

Well that's a rubbish answer, Janis thought.

"Is that supposed to mean something to me?" Janis replied, standing up a little straighter to show her confidence.

There was no reply. Livella stepped closer to Janis and grabbed one of her arms, clinging there tightly. Janis shook her arm sharply until Livella was forced to let go.

"No need for any of that, just stay close," Janis hissed.

After a few moments, a black spot of ooze appeared on the wall across the room.

Bracing for another encounter with the strange creatures, Janis positioned herself between the spot on the wall and Livella. She could hear Livella shivering from fear behind her. Steeling herself for the inevitable injury she'd get from the unknown beings they'd fought earlier, Janis crouched low.

The spot on the wall expanded until it had stretched all the way to the floor with which it connected. Congealing into a solid mass, the silvery black expanded from the wall, forming into a human-like shape.

Blast it all, why can't these things just stay consistent? Janis thought, annoyed.

The shape of the metallic black ooze was that of a tall and strong man.

Arms bulky and strong, torso wide and hard, it was still made of black matter that matched the oozes they'd just killed before. All of a sudden, the skin of the being changed color, turning into a light tan color as if it was a man that spent hours and hours in the sun everyday. Seeing the black liquid turn into a man might normally have been eerie to Janis, but in this case, it was a welcome sight. At least she could anticipate the thoughts and movements of something that was shaped and looked like a human being. The harrowing forms were largely unpredictable, given that they didn't have the same body construct or thought processes of a being.

Of course, Janis couldn't even be sure this wasn't just an odd extension of the strange viscous forms they'd just blown up.

The face of the being started clearing, the black ooze disappearing from one feature at a time, revealing different parts of a normal human man. A chiseled gray beard was cut seamlessly at his neck, kept short and tidy. Though it was short, the beard was full and looked very handsome. His jaw was strong and hard, the lines sharp from chin to ear. Black recessed to reveal a pointed nose, firm and resolute. Eyes came next, and they seemed to be almost closed, irises being cut off from view by the upper and lower lids of his eyes.

Overall, Janis thought the odd construct from the black ooze looked fairly appealing, for a man. Despite her lack of time for entertaining men she at least could appreciate good-looking ones, even in her job as an assassin.

Men or no, I'll be lucky to ever work again, she thought, eyeing the situation before them.

Where the man's clothes would be, the black continued to swirl for a time before expanding outward, filling in the space before and behind him. Janis watched in disbelief as black robes, thick and puffy in all sorts of places, appeared in place of the black ooze.

What horribly impractical clothes, she thought. *They make him look like a big-headed monarch.*

A memory of Riln twinged in her mind and she narrowed her eyes at how similarly dressed this man was to her apparent foil.

Once the clothes had formed, the man sneered at her.

"Yes, I'd wager that you don't approve of my choice of clothing, but I couldn't care less, Tar'n Yiv'len," he said, his voice a low thrum. "A king must be dressed in appropriate attire to express the magnitude of his power."

His use of the old language term wasn't lost on her, but Janis snorted at the comment.

"A king with that much ego should watch his back. With those clothes, he wouldn't get away from an assassin."

The moment she said it, she flung the steel dagger in her hand directly at the man. Without looking her way, his form shimmered in the air and appeared a few paces away. The knife flew harmlessly through the air in the space he'd been just before, smashing into the stone wall and clattering to the floor.

Janis glared, unsure of what just happened.

"If you believe that a physical blade could cause any harm to me, then you really must be the most dense Tar'n Yiv'len to ever roam the world," the man said, inspecting his fingernails casually. "I had wondered what Lanser was thinking, electing *you* to be the bearer of the next Seal, and now my curiosity has increased on the matter. An assassin is a ridiculous pick in my opinion, but that's just me."

Still crouched, Janis shifted her hand to pull out another knife to replace the first. Cursing, she realized that she hadn't packed all her holsters since the morning. Trying to look confident, Janis held out her hand and Conjured a knife, long and sharp. The blue of the Light pierced the room, and the man stepped back when he saw it.

"Ah, yes. You seem to be realizing your powers well enough now, hmm?"

He watched the Light with confidence on his face, but there was something hidden behind his eyes. Was that fear?

Taking the hint, Janis stepped forward and moved the Light dagger closer to him.

"Now, now, let's not get too hasty. You don't want to end your audience with me early, do you?"

Janis heard the words, but they made no sense.

"Audience?" Janis replied, "An audience with a black bucket of ooze? That's not something that I think would be any pleasure to me or my friend here."

Using 'friend' didn't seem quite right, but Janis didn't want to let on what her relationship was with Livella.

The man's eyes shifted slowly to Livella, who shrunk into Janis at his gaze.

"Yes," his voice purred, "I am aware of the new Voidbearer. How are you, my dear? I must say, you make carrying the Void within you look *good,* don't you?"

He licked his lips as he said it, awarding him with a shudder from Livella.

"The Seal does call for one carrying a small piece of my power. I'd give you more, my dear, if only you released me, ending this silly Seal that slows me down, but irritates me more than anything."

Janis listened to his words, trying to understand what he was implying. His use of personal pronouns did not go unnoticed by her, yet she couldn't fathom why he would speak them in regards to the Seal.

Unless, Janis thought.

Her mind shifted back to Tryvv and her comments on the Seal. It was created to hold back Ugglyn and what she referred to as the Void. Images in her memory of the sinister forms of silvery black ooze came to her. Though it happened so quickly, she noted how the air around the strange liquid moved, seeming to suck into the very matter of the forms.

"Ugglyn...." Janis said.

The man stood up taller as she said it, grinning at her.

"Yes, my dear, it appears that you are not as stupid as I originally thought. Then again, if you were truly stupid, I don't believe you would have lived to this day."

Livella trembled behind Janis, Ugglyn's name causing her to shake even more.

"How are you here?" Janis demanded, her tone impatient. "*Why* are you here?"

A pause.

"You find out that *the* anti-god is standing before you, real and in the flesh, and *those* are the first questions that come to your mind? I find that disappointing."

After finishing the words, he crossed casually to one of the stone chairs.

He walked with his shoulders high and an annoying confidence. Janis had to resist the urge to rush forward and stab the smugness out of him. But she knew this was an engagement far beyond her understanding. The man, Ugglyn, walked with purpose, feet slapping the stone ground and making an echoing clap as he walked. When he arrived, he turned and slumped into the chair, giving a glance to the war map at the center of the table.

"As I said before, I am growing in power. Lucky for your friends here—" he made a grand gesture with his hand, pointing to all the others in the room, "—I cannot fully manifest myself. Your Seal normally stops me or my Void from inhabiting the world at all. However, things have changed. Though your Seal remains intact, the loyalty of the former one has switched to me, allowing me more strength with each passing day."

"Ah, are you referring to the pompous piss ant that wears an equally ridiculous set of clothes?" Janis mused. "I'm more confused as to why Lanser would choose such a ninny in the first place. I take it that his choice of clothing is something he owes to you, hmmm?"

Inside, she felt uneasy, but something about the man's words about her holding him back gave her a surprising confidence. She didn't have much else as far as leverage went, so she decided to take hold of whatever she could.

Sneering, he waved his hands and his thick robe puffed into smoke, leaving him with nothing but a bare muscled chest and a pair of tight shorts.

"So you'd prefer this, then?"

"Sure, it means I can jab you through with my sword more easily. Less clothing to stop me from killing you."

Sighing, he waved his hands again, dark silver smoke coalescing around him, then dissipating to reveal a simple set of trousers, and a thin tunic and cloak that a professional hunter might wear. Under different circumstances, Janis thought the image before them might have been attractive, but unfortunately all she could see were the deep silver balls of ooze from whence the image came.

"Though I enjoy our playful banter, I don't have much time. It has taken months and months to save up enough power to manifest myself here in the physical realm. That can all end now, of course, if you simply give up your Seal."

He looked at Livella again and smiled, his cruel and wicked teeth showing as he continued beguiling Livella. "You can simply kill this ridiculous woman, my dear Voidbearer, and I can give you riches and power beyond your comprehension. You need only cut her down."

Livella continued to shake, her voice still gone.

Sighing, the man looked at her with pity.

"It seems a weakling has been chosen to represent my power. That is disappointing. I think Prost was an excellent choice, though even *he* fears letting me out of my cage completely."

Janis eyed him, waiting to see what he would do. For a moment, she thought it might be worth it to try stabbing him with her Light dagger, or even throwing a ball of Light at him, but she felt to listen instead. Something he said might give her an advantage. If not over him, then over Prost.

"Riln and Prost have weakened their Seal by letting me in over the years. I have yet to convince either of them to kill the other so that I may fully join the mortal realm. I believe that they are too distrusting of me. I promised both Riln and Prost power, yet they don't think it wise to free me completely. However, they did agree to build an army for me. I'll take what I can get," he shrugged as he spoke.

As he said the words, he summoned a ball of the silver-black ooze and threw it in the air.

"The effect of their choice was somewhat unexpected. It seems with each Lightbearer that steps over to their cause, I build a little more power. It is both pleasing and unbearably frustrating at the same time."

Ugglyn leaned back and put his feet up on the table. After a beat, he lobbed his summoned ball at the chair just next to Marric. The ball collided with the chair and fused with it. Slowly, like a spreading disease, it eased its way down the chair legs and up the back until the whole stone chair was infected with the black matter. With a whoosh, it disappeared into black smoke.

Janis's skin crawled at the sight. Livella whimpered and pulled herself closer to Janis, wrapping her arms around the assassin's midsection.

As much as she wanted to yell at Livella, she knew it wouldn't help. The woman's grasp around her was both uncomfortable and annoying, yet Janis had to keep her focus on the man before her.

"This is a mere taste of what my true powers will be when I am free. There was a time that I was free. Those were the days when men and women fought at my side, armies dying to either Light or Void. I must say, things have gotten boring since then."

The man's outline flickered slightly and he cursed.

"My limited power is waning. Before I leave, I will offer this one more time: Livella, my dear, I can give you more than you can imagine. Your life will never be the same. All weakness will be lost, all power gained."

Once again, Livella only cowered.

"Pity," Ugglyn whined. "I won't waste the strength I've saved for this moment any longer. I think I'll save the rest of my stored power to torment you, Janis," he practically spat her name out.

Standing sharply, the man summoned a sword of the swirling Void, silver and almost black. He strode over to Janis and she tensed, waiting for him to lunge.

"Inasmuch as I can, I will send my minions to pester and threaten you. Where you go, I will follow."

Suddenly, he swung his sword sideways, aiming for Janis and Livella. Janis had anticipated this, and flipped her Light sword to block it. The two swords clashed with a loud clang and her own sword puffed into nothingness. Cackling, Ugglyn spun around and swung his sword again. This time, Janis ducked and jabbed upward with her steel dagger. When the weapons clashed, his blade sliced her own completely in half. The dagger top clattered loudly to the ground, black ooze moving up and down the blade until it was fully consumed. With a puff, it disappeared into black smoke.

Janis cursed at her damaged weapon. Ugglyn laughed, amused at her meager attempts to defend herself.

"I did warn you that your steel would be wasted on me."

Chuckling darkly, he jumped forward with his black sword, jabbing at her abdomen. Instinctively, Janis let power course through her hand. Light poured out of her palm that clutched the broken dagger. Coursing up the blade, Light covered the entire dagger, hilt to the end of the broken half. Once it reached the broken blade, it extended outward, Light making up the broken end. Quickly, Janis parried his blow and swung at the man's side.

Before her blade could connect, he puffed away in a cloud of silver smoke, a maniacal laugh echoing throughout the room.

The moment he disappeared, the others in the room unfroze.

"See any more of 'em?" Turrin shouted, spinning slowly around the room.

Janis paused for a moment, observing her companions until she saw they all were moving normally.

"They are gone now," Janis said with confidence.

Everyone's heads turned to her, each with its own quizzical look.

"'Ow did yeh get over there?" Rivelen asked, looking annoyed more than anything.

Magness dismissed the question with a wave of her hand before asking one of her own.

"Gone? How can you be sure?" Magness questioned.

Janis stood up from her crouch and looked around.

"It's admittedly just a gut feeling, but I imagine that we would have seen more by now if there were to be more."

Beside her, Janis felt a nudge from Livella. Turning to look at the woman, she noted a look of distress on her face. In her eyes, Janis got the message she was trying to send.

Shouldn't we tell them about what we just saw? the face said.

Shaking her head slightly, Janis indicated no. She would have to talk to Magness about it later, but now didn't seem the time. With this room full of people, she didn't know how to explain what they'd just seen, let alone in a way that wouldn't cause capital chaos in the whole place.

Avryn noticed the exchange and furrowed his brows at Janis. In an effort to deflect his curiosity, she merely winked at him.

"Do you see any more of the Void creatures?" Janis queried.

Magness pursed her lips at the question, but acknowledged there hadn't been more.

"I believe she is right. We can't hole ourselves up in here forever. With any luck, we won't see any more of these strange dark creatures, but if we do —Lanser, just don't be alone. From now on, I am ordering each of you to have a companion, and those without Lightbearing, ensure that your chosen companion has a power."

Harmel grinned.

"Well, darn, Oi don' fink tha' Oi can't be wif yous, big brudda."

The jovial man smacked his hand heavily on Shrell's back, awarding him a wince from his taller brother.

"I don' think tha' I'll be too depressed 'bout tha' one," Shrell grumbled.

Eyes wandering to Janis, Harmel beamed at her. "Yeh 'ave some power to yeh, so Oi guess Oi choose yous fer my partner."

Her stomach fluttered as he said it.

What in the blazes is that? she thought.

"I don't believe I need a partner. Besides, I think it's best if Livella sticks close by, especially given the whole balance we just described and whatnot."

Her best attempts to shed the man's companionship were not successful, however, as Harmel sauntered over to her and linked his left arm in her right.

"We can be a roit good threesome, then."

Avryn chuckled at the scene.

Magness looked less than amused. "Yes, well, now that we all got to enjoy the show from such an unlikely pair, we must be off. Alsry, gather your company and leave with haste. Janis—and I suppose you as well—" she paused, looking at Harmel, "—will join Alsry. I thought that Harmel might want to rest, given your recent return with Varith, but if you do want to stay with Janis, then off to T'Arren Vale you go."

Harmel shrugged. "If Oi 'ave to, Oi'll jus' sleep in the saddle. Ain't no big problem fer me."

He turned to Janis and smiled again.

Pulling sharply, Janis removed her own arm from his. As much as she did not want the man sticking closely to her side, another part of her felt a bit of relief. With all of the people around her, she hardly knew any of them. Even though she couldn't claim to know Harmel much more than the rest, she had fought beside him many times on their journey from Wurren, and at least she knew what to expect from him.

"Let's go, then."

Someone cleared their throat loudly, turning a few heads. By then, Alsry had rushed off with Rivelen, Varith not far behind. The remaining few turned to Marric.

"I am to join Alsry as well, correct?"

Magness thought for a moment before shaking her head.

"Given the circumstances, and the fact that the journey to T'Arren Vale will have to be vigorous, I think it would be best if you and Avryn joined Turrin and his small band in retrieving your father instead. How does that sound?"

Marric's face lit up and he nodded enthusiastically.

"Oh, yes! Yes, thank you!"

Without hesitation, he rushed to Magness and threw his arms around her. The woman grunted at his momentum, looking a bit embarrassed.

"Yes—well you must get a move on. I don't expect you to run into any trouble."

The majestic woman turned to Turrin and addressed him quickly.

"Turrin, since you will have Avryn and Marric along, there isn't a need to bring many more men. I believe that a smaller group will move faster. Narim is not a Lightbearer, so I imagine that you shouldn't run into a large group of the enemy, if any at all."

Turrin nodded.

"Aye, ma'am. We'll git to it roit away."

Nodding to Marric and Avryn, the three men moved quickly to the wooden door and flung it open, rushing through to gather their men and leave. Marric paused just beside Janis and gave her arm a squeeze, looking a bit sad.

"Please be safe out there, Janis."

The boy opened his mouth to say something else, but shook his head and moved to the door.

Janis watched with curiosity, wondering what he had thought to say before he changed his mind.

"Go with Alsry, and please don't do anything stupid," Magness said to Janis.

Harmel laughed at the comment. Janis glared at him, not understanding why he would think such a thing funny.

"I can't imagine what you mean," Janis replied to Magness.

Magness narrowed her eyes. "I think it's obvious that I don't trust you. I wouldn't normally have you leave my sight for something like this, but given your potential power as a Lightbearer, I probably couldn't hold you back. Just don't get any of my people killed."

Janis looked at her, with a measured gaze. "I may be an assassin, but I only kill those that I'm paid to kill. Fortunately, your meager forces are not on my hit list."

Magness rolled her eyes.

"You know what I mean, Janis. Don't do anything that would get my men and women killed."

When she said the words, Magness stuck her hand out for Janis to take. Looking down at it, Janis almost didn't take it. Shaking hands wasn't something she was in the habit of doing. Either the person she was working with didn't want to get close enough to shake her hand, or they were trying to get her close enough to do her harm.

Against her better judgement, she took the hand and shook it roughly.

Magness winced at the tightness of her grip and let her own hand loose.

"Ugglyn's tail, Janis, it's just a handshake. You don't have to rip my fingers off."

At the mention of the anti-god's name, Janis felt her insides clench up. Fortunately, she was still practiced enough to not show any outward signs of her inward distress, and Magness didn't notice. Livella, however, gasped quietly at Ugglyn's name, putting her hand to her mouth.

Magness noticed the girl's reaction and leaned slightly toward her to see what was wrong. "Are you quite alright, Livella? You look very pale."

Janis cut in. "I believe she's just tired from the happenings of today. Perhaps it *would* be best if she stayed here while we rode to 'T'Arren Vale."

"Would that be wise? Given what we just learned about the balance and the Seal? I would have thought that meant you two should always stay together."

Janis shook her head. "If that were true, then we would have seen Riln every time we saw Prost. For some reason, the pasty man won't leave his dark cave. Perhaps he's allergic to the sunlight."

Magness looked unimpressed with her joke, but nodded anyway.

"Yes, yes, that is a good point. Livella, are you okay to stay here?"

"Erm," Livella said shyly, "I think so, yes."

She looked relieved at the prospect of staying. But as she realized she'd be left without Janis, her eyes darted left and right, as if she expected something to jump out of the corners and attack her.

"Of course, we can find someone to stay with you until Janis returns. I believe that Alsry will want to leave immediately. I would hurry before she leaves you two behind."

Nodding, Janis turned to the door and moved toward it swiftly, Harmel close behind. As she walked, she turned her head slightly, looking at Livella. She put her finger to her lips until their eyes met.

Livella looked concerned at the command, but subtly inclined her head in acknowledgement.

I can't wait to get out of this fogging stale air, Janis thought.

"Well ain't this gonna be roit fun," Harmel said.

They walked briskly to the stable room together, falling into silence.

14

The rain poured down on Prost and his companions at a steady rate. It wasn't the crazy torrent it had been four days ago when they had first left the lair, but it was still heavy enough to keep them plenty wet as they traveled. Each time their horses stepped, there was a sticky squelching sound of the mud as it was sucked upward by their hooves. Fortunately, the rain wasn't cold, but that didn't make it pleasant.

Prost had led the group on a mad dash until the horses couldn't go any longer. They hadn't been able to move as quickly as he would have liked, but he figured that they should still get there with plenty of time to locate the boy before the awakening. He didn't anticipate that they would run into any other trouble, but things could change quickly.

"Fog this stupid rain," Alts said from her horse just next to his, "Why does Lanser curse us righ' terrible every time we need t'be in a hurry?"

At the mention of Lanser's name, Prost gritted his teeth. Ever since he knew of the possibility of another Tar'n Yiv'len existing in Lindrad, he knew that a new Seal against Ugglyn must have been formed. Hearing Lanser's name struck a bit of fear inside him, knowing that he and Riln technically betrayed their own Seal by following Ugglyn. He thought back to when they'd first been together and their Seal began, and the events that led up to them meeting Ugglyn and ultimately taking over Watchlight, twisting the organization's ideals to fit Riln's own. The memory came to him as if it had happened yesterday.

"AND SO," *the majestic woman's voice spoke, "with you two begins a new Seal of powers. The new Seal against the power of Ugglyn. You are now the protectors of the world and everyone in it."*

Prost scoffed at the words. The deep gauges on his upper cheeks throbbed with pain as the memory of a few days before came to him. Riln had sliced his face so badly that the cuts had bled for hours. He felt lucky that he hadn't died that day. It was lucky that Watchlight had some medical staff who weren't just Fixers, as his wounds couldn't be healed by Lightbearing.

Having heard from Tryvv and Prileen that his Voidbearer status made him immune, he now knew why.

Prileen, the shorter of the two women, frowned at his reaction. Being that she and Tryvv were both made of nothing but blue Light, he had a hard time taking anything they said seriously. Unfortunately, he didn't have much of a choice. Any explanation was better than none.

Riln stared at them, his face calm and relaxed.

"So you say I have all the powers of Lightbearing?"

Tryvv nodded, looking pleased.

"You are the new Prime. You hold back the bringer of the Void, Ugglyn himself."

Opening and closing his hands, he smiled wickedly.

"So that makes me more powerful than my beloved leader."

Narrowing her eyes, Tryvv considered the statement.

"I suppose that is true, though I can't understand why that would matter in the least. Your power is meant to uphold the Seal and to defend the world from the Void."

Riln looked upward, an innocent look on his face.

"Oh yes—of course. We shall gather Lightbearers old and young to the cause of Lanser and train them to fight against Ugglyn. I understand my duty."

Tryvv relaxed at the comment.

"Go forth, and fulfill the Seal, Tar'n Yiv'len and K'alek Tar'n."

Prost grunted at the words.

"I didn't ask for any of this foggin' stuff. How did I get dragged into this? I don't give a fog about Lanser or about Ugglyn's plan. You people ruined my life."

Riln stiffened at Prost's words and spun on him, whipping out a dagger.

Fear gripped Prost at the sight of the steel blade that the pale man held in his hand, but then he remembered he'd trained for years to be a soldier. The only reason Riln had succeeded in disfiguring Prost's face was because of the distraction of Lightbearing.

Without any trouble, Prost dodged Riln and used the flat of his hand to smack into his pale wrist. The knife immediately fell out of it, clattering to the ground.

Prost felt powerful as he snagged the knife from the stone floor and held it to Riln's neck.

"The only reason I haven't killed you is because I've been half-conscious in the infirmary until today. Now that I have the energy, I think that it's time for you to pay for what you did to me. Unfortunately for you, the only thing that I want is your life."

He pushed the knife forward, pressing it into Riln's neck. The pale man's eyebrows raised in fear and he summoned a ball of blue Light, thrusting it into Prost's stomach. A loud crack and a flash of Light announced its connection. Bits of Prost's shirt exploded everywhere, fluttering to the ground. Of course Prost felt nothing. Riln's eyes widened and he began to whimper.

Prost looked at all of them—Riln, Prileen, and Tryvv. "You've taken everything from me, so now it's time for me to return the favor."

"Stop! You can't kill him! If he dies, the Seal breaks and Ugglyn will be freed!" Tryvv sputtered, "I know that he's done you wrong, but it's for the best of the world if you keep him alive."

Prost's eyes shifted to the women again.

"And what if I don't give a fog about this Seal? Then what?"

Tryvv looked sad at the question.

"Then you must not care about humankind being slaves to the power of Ugglyn. You must not care about your family, about your friends."

Prost chuckled darkly.

"My family has long forgotten me by now. They have all the money in the

world. When I left, they no longer had to worry about me failing to become a snobbish aristocrat like them.”

“No friends, then?” Prileen, the smaller woman said.

Prost froze at that. His mind flashed to a young man, just a few months younger than himself. Hair light brown and eyes of brilliant blue, holding a sword aloft and challenging him.

Avryn, he thought.

Immediately, his anger diffused and he stepped back, pulling the dagger with him.

Riln sighed, holding his hand up to his neck. A blue flash of Light emanated from under his palm. When he moved his hand away, the cut had been healed completely.

“And if Ugglyn were to be free? Then what? What exactly would happen?” Prost demanded.

Tryvv shook her head at the question.

“The Void would have dominance over the world. Everyone would be lost to darkness and would be subjugated to torment, forever. The Seal is essential to holding him at bay. If that Seal breaks, the world will likely end to his Void. For hundreds of years, men and women have been chosen to uphold the Seal. Only within the last hundred years has Lanser been able to bless others with the gifts of Lightbearing. This army is meant as a final stand against Ugglyn and his Void. For now, your Seal is the only thing in the way of him getting free.”

Prost ached inside, knowing that he couldn’t just kill Riln for revenge. He turned to see Riln looking at his hands, a look of wonder on his face.

LITTLE OVER A FORTNIGHT *after their encounter with the Light women, Prost and Riln found themselves in the throne room of their lair.*

The door to the throne room opened and in strode Goralt, Riln’s brother and leader of Watchlight. A thick mustache framed his upper lip. His eyes were striking blue, like his brother’s, and their faces looked very much the same. The only difference was that Riln was devoid of color. As a child, a sickness had drained all pigments from his skin and hair, only those in his irises remaining. Goralt paused at seeing Riln sitting on his throne, but seemed too curious for an update to immediately comment on it.

"How has your training been thus far? Are you coming well into your Lightbearing now?"

Riln stared at him from the throne in an attitude of a child playacting a mighty king.

"Yes," he answered Goralt, "I am coming along just fine."

Goralt smiled at Riln's words.

"That is very fine to hear. Though, it seems you've forgotten again whose throne you sit on." Goralt lifted his hand as he said it, gesturing for Riln to move. "Any progress on the rest of your powers? You are supposed to manifest all seven, correct?"

Smiling mischievously, Riln nodded and stood up.

"Yes, I have made significant progress while you were away fetching another Lightbearer. Did you get him, by the way?"

Goralt's face wore a disappointed look.

"Unfortunately, no. It seems Talatha's group convinced her that she should be living alongside normal people rather than convincing them to let us rule. It would have been advantageous to have her. Another Shielder would have done us some good."

Riln stared at him, unaffected by his answer.

"So, brother," Riln said measuredly, "at what point do we storm in and take what's ours? We've been training for years here and have nothing to show for it."

His brother chuckled at the question.

"You know that we seek a peaceful takeover of Lindrad. We can't be killing people left and right—how is that supposed to get us anywhere?"

Riln's jaw hardened. "Then why in Lanser's name do we develop our Lightbearing? What's the point of becoming stronger?"

Goralt narrowed his eyes at his brother's outburst.

"You know the answer to that. Leaders need to prove that they are able to take care of and protect their people. They may refuse to recognize our power right now, but we must show them why we deserve to be in charge. We are more than just soldiers, more than just killers. We can't maul, scar, and kill those that we want to follow us."

Prost flinched at that comment, eyes flicking towards Riln. He returned his hardened gaze to Goralt, hoping the man hadn't seen that. Unfortunately, Goralt was too observant to not notice the reaction.

"Remind me, Prost, how did those slices on your face come to be? I recall you saying you were attacked by a spine hog shortly before you arrived. Is that true?"

Prost froze. He was calculating what his answer should be. When his mind couldn't come up with anything good, he just nodded.

Their burly leader narrowed his eyes at Prost, but turned his gaze to Riln.

"It was you, wasn't it?" he said, glaring at his brother.

"The cuts were shallow; they'd have been easy to Fix if he wasn't fogging immune to us and our abilities."

"Riln! If I hadn't been out recruiting when Prost arrived, I never would have let this happen. You can't treat people like this. Just because we can Fix something doesn't mean you can go about hurting other people. You are a disgrace to Lightbearing and all that it stands for. It's a gift from Lanser, don't you see? By attacking and hurting others, you spit in his face."

Riln bared his teeth, hissing like a feral animal when backed into a corner. The purple orb of Light above them flickered slightly. Glancing upward, Prost noted that the orb was still intense and strong. He looked at Riln after, wondering what had happened. The lair itself was lit by the Lightbearing of the Lighter on duty, but Riln insisted on Lighting this room with his own orb. He claimed it was for practice.

"What is the point of us claiming power, claiming dominance if we can't display it? My Lightbearing was thwarted by that man's immunity, and I had to assert my power over him."

The scars on Prost's face stung at the words, as if they were cut open again.

Riln continued, "At what point are you going to realize that a leader should rule with power by displaying it? You speak of power, but you don't show it."

The Light flickered again, and Prost looked up just in time to see the orb shift back to purple from what looked to be a more reddish color.

Curious, he kept his eyes up at the ceiling, waiting for the flicker to happen again.

Goralt was practically yelling now. "I don't give a fog that you are meant to hold this 'Seal'—" he gestured in the air with his fingers as he said it, "If you continue to speak out of line, I won't hesitate to banish you. Watchlight doesn't need any infections like you."

This riled Riln up even more. However, only Prost was aware of the words' effect on Riln. The pale white man breathed in deeply, his demeanor appearing calm and collected. Prost, however, could see the fire burning in his eyes. It was the same look he'd seen the first day he'd met Riln, when Goralt was off recruiting Lightbearers. Prost had seen the look a few more times since he'd been here, given that he followed Riln everywhere he went and listened to every conversation. Goralt didn't catch on. The strong leader stalked up to Riln, closing the distance quickly, chest puffed out to assert his dominance. The air in the cavern became still; the only sound was their breathing while the two brothers stared each other down.

"You will listen. You may be blessed with all the powers, but that doesn't mean you're in charge. You're no leader, Riln. You must obey. Or so help me, I will Move your hide out of here faster than you can cry for mercy."

The fire in Riln's eyes intensified, and Prost instinctively grabbed the hilt of his short sword at his side. Since being here, it wasn't just once that Riln had lost his temper and blasted him with all the powers he had. Of course, none of them affected Prost, but it still made him extremely uncomfortable. It wasn't rational, not based on what he knew now, but he worried that his immunity would end just before a Destroying ball slammed into him, ripping him to shreds.

The storm was coming, and Goralt didn't seem to be aware of it at all.

"Get out of my throne room. Go cool off in the baths. I don't give a fog what you do, just get out."

Keeping his gaze measured, Riln took a deep breath and moved slowly around his brother's strong stance. When he'd reached a few paces behind the Watchlight leader, he turned and spoke again.

"See, I think you have it wrong, dear brother."

Conjuring a dagger out of purple Light, he lunged at the man's exposed back. Goralt was a fighter though, and he anticipated the attack somehow. Spinning around, he thrust his hand out, the purple dagger being wreathed in more Light before it was yanked from Riln's hand and thrown into a pillar.

"You dare attack me? You'll pay for that!"

Pushing both hands forward, Goralt threw Riln twenty paces back with his Moving. Prost stared at the two, unsure what to do. He could get involved, but he didn't know who to help. Riln's ideals weren't wrong. Prost agreed that power should be leveraged to gain control, but that didn't make Prost like Riln as a person. Prost wanted to believe they could achieve a peaceful overthrow of the Lindradian monarchy, especially since siding with Riln would already add to his inflated sense of ego.

"You dare use your Lightbearing on me?" Riln shouted, standing tall.

With a roar, he held his left hand out and created an intense ball of Light, purple and unwavering. Lobbing it forward, he aimed it at Goralt's head. Goralt easily Moved the ball to the right, where it slammed into a pillar, exploding its center to pieces. Rock dust and debris flew around the room, some shards pelting Prost in the face. He flinched at the stinging pain. Dust filled the chamber, beams of Light now visible from the orb above them. Once again, the Light flickered red.

Goralt now Moved his brother hard into a pillar to his left. He heard Riln's head smack the pillar with a crack, and the man fell to the ground, dazed.

"I have been a Mover for years, brother. You may be a supposed Prime, but your discipline is missing. You are weak. You cannot possibly lead Watchlight to victory. I am the leader, and you will follow."

Prost stared at Riln's body shifting slightly on the ground. His crimson cloak covered most of his body. Pushing off the ground with both hands, Riln coughed, bloody spittle splattering the ground.

Then, Prost heard something. Words sprouted in his mind from a disembodied voice.

Kill him, kill him and take what's rightfully yours.

Squinting, Prost looked around the room. He'd heard similar things before, but he couldn't ever determine where they came from. Shifting his gaze to Goralt, he noted that the man must not have heard anything, for he was focused on Riln and approaching him slowly.

He is weak, you are strong. Kill him and take control of Watchlight.

Prost spun around, looking for the voice again. He could hear it, but somehow he knew that it wasn't addressing him. Only once had Prost mentioned the voice to Riln, but his begrudging companion had only shaken his head and said to speak to no one of the voice.

Eyeing Riln, Prost knew that he could hear whispers too.

Riln began laughing maniacally. It echoed on the stone walls, bouncing from pillar to pillar as if there were other men laughing in the same way.

Goralt stared at him. Slowly but surely, he put his hands out, palms up, and lifted Riln with his Moving powers. Riln's body was wreathed in purple Light once again and he was pulled to his feet.

"My dear brother, how very sorry I am for this. I didn't mean to cause you any trouble. You are by far superior to me in Lightbearing, and I should have accepted that," Riln said humbly.

Grunting, Goralt let Riln fall softly to his feet, releasing his Moving hold on his brother. The pasty white man kept his gaze down at the ground, but Prost could still see the smile on his face.

"Hmmm, yes. I am sorry that it took some use of force for you to understand, but we are in agreement now," Goralt replied.

As Riln slowly raised his head, Prost could see blood dripping down his chin from missing teeth. A cut on his forehead also bled, blood spilling on his cheek. The view looked even more grisly because of the paleness of his skin. Hand behind his body, Riln summoned another ball of Destroying Light, the purple orb steady and piercing.

Prost realized what was happening, and thought to call out to Goralt a warning. Before he could, Riln jumped forward and lobbed the ball directly at his brother's chest.

Gasping, the Mover thrust out his hand, grabbing the orb and shifting it to the right. He wasn't quite fast enough, as the ball redirected from his chest, but still smacked into his left bicep. A crack sounded, echoing in the cavern, followed by a howl from Goralt as his arm, severed a handspan from his shoulder, fell to the ground. Blood spilled from his amputated arm, and he bared his teeth. Using his good arm, he threw Riln back into the pillar again. This time, the back of Riln's head smacked hard and he went down, unconscious. The Light around them flickered to red, and Prost looked up to see the large orb of Light shining a pure, unwavering red before snuffing out. Goralt yelled for a Fixer, grunting at the pain of his arm.

Seeing Riln unconscious and Goralt bleeding, Prost thought to help their leader find a Fixer and get healed. He knew that Goralt would blame him for not helping when he should have during the fight. He knew he'd be condemned with Riln and either thrown out with him or killed for treason. There was only one man who knew the truth of what happened.

Making a decision quickly, Prost pulled his sword and dashed to Goralt. He thrust his sword into where the man's stomach had been just before it went dark, and felt the blade enter flesh. A groan announced the surety of his aim.

Goralt fell to the ground with one last grunt.

What in Ugglyn's name have I done? *Prost thought.*

Riln stirred in the dark and Prost rushed to him, pulling smelling salts from his belt, ones to invigorate the body, their sharp scents very potent. Holding it out, he felt for Riln's nose and put the open vial just below his nostrils. Gasping, Riln sat up quickly. A Light appeared suddenly, making Prost squint as it hurt his eyes.

The first thing he noticed was the Light no longer shone purple. Instead, it was a shade of horrible red.

Riln noticed this too, a look of wonder on his face.

"Yes," the bodiless voice rang loudly in his head, "you are beginning to see what power will bring you now."

A dark silver, almost black circle of matter appeared on the floor just next to Goralt's bleeding corpse. Coalescing into something larger, the two men watched as a man formed from the dark matter, handsome and tall.

"True leadership comes from displays of power, from fear. I am glad you've finally given in to the whispers. Now, let's discuss this Seal that's getting in my way."

~

PROST SEETHED AT THE MEMORY. He'd been too weak back then. He had thought himself a hardened warrior, someone who could stand up to anyone and anything, defending the monarchy of Lindrad and defeating any that threatened it. Now that he knew of Lightbearing and Ugglyn, Prost knew that the soldier-in-training he'd been in T'Arren Vale knew nothing of real power and strength.

The pang of longing for his former life struck inside him again like an intense hunger. Knowing he was part of a Seal holding back the anti-god didn't make him feel any better about the fact that he'd never possess the raw power of Destroying. Even the power of Fixing was the focus of his envy some days.

He had never asked for his simple and directed life to be thrown into chaos, yet it happened, and at least the sense of duty in him kept him from killing Riln. That, and an inexplicable fear of the man. Even though Prost knew Riln couldn't hurt him with Lightbearing, his scars still reminded him of just how unpredictable Riln really was. Riln's power was founded in fear and the literal strength of his abilities.

That day, when Goralt had been slain, Riln took control of Watchlight. He fabricated a story of sickness in the leader, which the man had supposedly hidden for years. He had Fixed his brother's body so that it looked like his arm hadn't been blown off, and that his gut hadn't been ripped open by a sword. Riln couldn't bring him back from the dead, but he could at least Fix his physical body. They'd believed him. Everyone thought that the logical replacement for Goralt was Riln.

Since then, Watchlight had become more forceful and violent. Death had become a constant for Watchlight, and Riln didn't seem to care at all.

Unfortunately, Prost knew that the more forceful method Riln had introduced couldn't be denied. He'd come to terms with the new use of their powers—their 'attack first, talk later' methodology. Of course it wasn't always that brash, but it was different than Goralt's methods when Prost had first arrived.

"Hey, Prost. About how far out are we?" Neera's voice interrupted his thoughts.

He turned to see their resident Lighter a few paces behind him on her trotting mare. The woman's pitch black hair and dark skin looked even darker in the night air.

"We've been traveling hard for four days now. I think we'll be there in one day's time, maybe two if we have to keep going as slow as we are now," he answered, trying to remove the gruffness from his voice.

The feeling he'd been left with from remembering Riln's takeover of Watchlight and their subsequent betrayal of the Seal made him grumpy. As much as he knew the effectiveness of Riln's method, he still mourned his old self somewhere deep inside. He didn't bother trying to dig it up any longer. That would be a waste of his time *and* the time and aims of those around him. If Prost acted how he used to, Riln would most likely lock him up—only not killing him because of the Seal.

"I can' wait t'git somewhere I can put me feet up. My backside ain't doin' so good wif all the rushin," Alts complained on his other side.

"If yeh spent as much time riding as yeh did wif yer Conjurin', it wouldn't be a problem," Jord said in his monotone voice.

Alts stuck her tongue out at the comment, but went silent.

"Hey, at least the rain finally stopped. I think I've just started to dry off," Neera commented, trying to be positive.

Prost scoffed at her, looking up at the sky. The rain had finally come to stop during his reminiscing.

"Don't get too comfortable, I sense a storm coming again in the morning. With any luck, it won't be as bad as the last one," he predicted.

Those around him groaned at the news. They didn't like him or even respect him, but the one thing they trusted was his prediction of storms. He wasn't sure how, but he always could tell when they were coming. Prost guessed that it came from his upbringing. He'd had to learn to plan and handle the operations of their numerous workers and fields. Knowing when a storm would come helped them know best planting and harvesting times, not to mention when they should tell their workers to get out of the fields because of an approaching storm.

"I guess I'll just have to apply some more oil to my bag and gear to prepare," Neera said, sighing a bit at the revelation.

The group fell silent again, focused only on their travels and finding the soon-to-awaken Lightbearer.

Something nagged at the back of his mind, the voice that constantly seemed to whisper to him in the quiet times.

If any of these men so much as looks at you wrong, you should cut their hearts out.

Prost shook his head. Why his subconscious had taken on such a violent persona, he couldn't know. His only guesses were perhaps it was his frustration with Riln, or with his own lack of Lightbearing, or even more frustrating, why Janis's awakening had been able to hurt him despite his immunity.

The breeze rustling the trees intensified then, as if the weather reacted to his mood. He felt a mixture of anger, irritation, and anxiety at all these thoughts. Assuming control over these men and other Watchlight members was the only thing that helped him feel in control and like he had a place in all this, despite his problems.

You could lead them, you know, he thought, *You just have to kill Riln like you killed his brother.*

Shaking his head, Prost removed the idea from his mind. He chuckled bitterly to himself. It was a hilarious paradox. He was trapped in this horrible life—in this terrible position—but he couldn't really leave. He had tried before. Whenever he thought about leaving, the oppressive whispers came back to him, yanking him back to Watchlight and Riln's side. He couldn't kill Riln, for that would cause all sorts of chaos in the world.

The one time they'd faced Ugglyn, the anti-god had openly tried to get Prost to kill Riln so that the Seal would be broken. Riln had easily dismissed this suggestion, and Prost refused it as well. Riln cared too much about control and didn't want to relinquish it to Ugglyn. Prost's skin crawled at the idea of Ugglyn being free, ruling the world with his Void.

No, Riln had to live.

For years, Prost had thought of some way to get back at Riln, to show him that he couldn't control him. Unfortunately, there wasn't a clear way to assert his independence, and Prost knew he wasn't really free anyway. Riln *did* control him, and Prost didn't have a choice. Even with a new Seal in existence, Prost couldn't take the chance of setting Ugglyn free.

Prost looked to the sky. To the west just above the treeline, he saw the bright red light of Stellan setting. Looking to the east, he saw the light of Mallan making the treetops glow as if they were wreathed in the blue Light of a Mover preparing to throw them. Shifting his view straight up to the sky, he saw the darkness of the middle. It was poetic to see the red and the blue at the same time. Since Riln's reign began, everyone at Watchlight's Light had turned red. Although newly awakened Lightbearers' powers were blue, they eventually turned red as they adopted the violence and force of Riln's way, but those of Evenir stayed blue.

Why red, Prost didn't know, but when Ugglyn had been denied his freedom, he gave Riln some type of blessing, something that connected with his Lightbearing. He had spoken some words in the ancient language.

Prost thought back to the words, remembering them as if they'd been said yesterday:

Tar vil k'alek tarn videsk yulvan ivalis fron ick yar Ugglyn.

When the words were spoken, the air had been filled with power. Time slowed down; Prost was aware of every sound—his heartbeat, breath, even Riln's own heartbeat, thumped loudly and slowly, echoing. The air grew thick so that Prost could feel the weight of it while breathing, as if it was water rather than air. It didn't make him choke, but his brain panicked and he felt as if he might suffocate. The lone red orb above had grown brighter, the shadows deepening. Even the feeling of his clothes on his chest and limbs grew to be overwhelming, threatening to drive him to insanity. Stranger even was that he understood the words as they were spoken.

"Light with Void together pledge service to Ugglyn."

Ever since that day, Riln and those who followed him saw their Light changing from purple to red. It did make keeping track of the two sides easier. When out in the throng of battle, looking for the color of Light made it simple to know who to attack and who to help.

The air around him was cooling down gradually as the front of the storm approached them. Prost felt a thrill knowing the rain would soon be pelting them again. Inexplicably, the rain invigorated Prost, giving him more energy to push forward. At seeing the storm, his companions began grumbling, confirming Prost's expectation of their complaints about the wet.

Glaring over his shoulder, he noted the position of Jord.

He's so much like Riln, Prost thought. *The whelp better not try anything on me; I don't have the patience for a temper like Riln's right now. I know the boy well, but just watching the way he glared forward with a steeled look on his face is enough for me to know that the kid is trouble. The boy likely has a temper as volatile as Riln's.*

Prost shifted his gaze back at the rest of the group. Together, they were about fifty in number. Only around a third of the group actually had Light-bearing powers; the rest were just throw-aways. It was brutish to think of them that way, but he knew it was true. In a battle of power like this, a normal person found themselves dead before they could land a blow on the other side. At least the unpowered had been trained to recognize Light-bearers and their respective class and sub-class. Until they knew that, an unpowered couldn't hope to survive.

Grunting slightly, Prost felt grateful for two things. The first was that he never had to learn such training. It didn't matter what the person's class was for him, they couldn't touch him with their abilities, anyway. Second, he was grateful he hadn't had to train any new cadets. In all likelihood, Prost was the most skilled fighter for Watchlight, but his lack of training regarding Lightbearing made him useless for training the new recruits.

Cracking his neck, he thought positively about the battle they'd likely run into when they got to T'Arren Vale. Since the incident at Arrant Falls with Marric and the subsequent battle at the Evenir supply cave, Prost had been stuck in their blasted lair hidden from the fresh air *and* any chance of picking off any blue Lightbearers.

Fog, I'd even take a fight with a normal man if it meant getting to use my skills. And if Janis was there—

The burning thrill from knowing the storm was nearing flared up when he thought about his opponent in the last battle. He knew inside that he'd had the upper hand when he fought the assassin, but her awakening had ruined it all. Anger, anticipation, and adrenaline all mixed together inside him when thought about facing her again. He remembered facing her before and being thrown through the air when she awakened. Part of him hoped it had been a fluke—that her intense awakening was the only reason her powers had affected him, but he still doubted. When he'd been told that he was the Void-bearer, that no Light could touch him, it all made sense, to some degree. Unfortunately, he apparently had gotten overconfident and had paid for it.

Gritting his teeth, he imagined the upcoming fight in T'Arren Vale and hoped she would be there. Janis wouldn't get the better of him this time. Narrowing his eyes at the path in front of him, he shouted back to his group.

"We are just over a day's journey from T'Arren Vale. Be prepared for *anything*. Evenir likely had the same visions, and if we are lucky, theirs came later than our own. We are still unsure from what direction they'll be coming, but as we get closer, our paths are more likely to converge. If you see any blue Light, kill the foggers and call out a warning to the rest of us."

Heads nodded around him at the words.

Turning to his right and a few horses back, he found Vint focusing on the road in front of him.

"Alts," Prost called, not turning to see the woman, "you know the way. Keep us moving in the right direction."

The blonde woman nodded curtly, glaring at Prost. Apparently, she wasn't over his treatment of her back at the lair.

"Aye. Got somethin' to be dun, eh?"

"Just using my resources," Prost answered.

She shook her head and shifted her horse to be in the front of the group. Those just behind him—Jord, Lathe, and another whose name he couldn't recall—all heard his words, staring at him.

Prost guided his horse to fall back a few positions until he was just next to Vint. They had brought one other Seer, as was customary in a group like this, but Prost preferred to work with Vint. Despite their scuffle in the lair a few days back, he knew that he could trust the stocky man.

"Oy, Vint. I need you to See where we are going. If there are Evenir men in our path, I'd like to know about it as soon as possible."

Vint turned his large head to look at Prost. He didn't look thrilled to be listening to Prost, but Vint heeded the command.

Focusing his sea-green eyes forward, they started to glow in the pupil, the red Light spreading until his whole eyeball was filled. While they glowed, Prost could only guess what the man Saw during the vision. A few people had tried to describe the feeling to Prost, but he couldn't ever understand what they meant.

"I See a clear path to T'Arren Vale. The approaching storm will shift sharply west and we'll only get rain on our path for an hour or so. That will allow us to move forward more quickly than you anticipated."

Prost grunted. While it was a good thing that they wouldn't be hit by the storm, it also meant they wouldn't continue to have the rain as their companion, a companion which Prost preferred to sunny weather. Prost knew that despite the complaining, his men were more motivated to move quickly during inclement weather.

"Is something wrong, Prost?" a higher, almost lilting voice asked on his other side.

Prost turned to see Jord eavesdropping on their conversation.

The boy's expression was patronizing. He seemed to understand what Prost was thinking and was mocking him.

Just kill him, Riln will forgive you, something in Prost whispered.

Rather than comment on Jord's words, Prost raised his voice and shouted to the others.

"Vint has confirmed our clear and direct path to T'Arren Vale. We'll hit rain for about an hour, but it will end after that. We'll drive forward slowly during the rain, and then quicken the pace once we are through. I think that we'll make it before Evenir."

With that, Prost directed his horse away from Vint, nodding to him in approval. He shot a pointed glare at Jord, who looked unaffected by the gaze.

Wishing Riln hadn't forced him to bring the boy, Prost moved to the front of the pack and gestured Alts back again as he assumed the lead.

15

When they'd left Terris Green, Marric hadn't expected the weather to be too severe. Being inside for so long, he'd forgotten that they were in the middle of spring and that rain was common during this season. Normally the rain didn't bother him, but it was a deluge that soaked through every layer of clothing he had. Silently, he prayed to Lanser that his things hadn't been wetted too badly. Every time he traveled, he prepared his sack with the necessary oils to protect from the wet, but with rain like that, no number of applications could protect his belongings. The chainmail under his shirt was cold against his skin. Avryn had insisted that he wear some for the journey, as all the fighters for Evenir did.

There were only the three of them as Lightbearers, plus another Seer woman whose name Marric couldn't recall. The four others bore no powers at all. The idea was that they'd move rapidly to Narim's location for less chance of Watchlight getting there first. They had learned of his whereabouts from the Seer that rode with them now, who knew enough landmarks within the forest to lead them to where she'd Seen Narim resting.

Marric wondered how his father had made it out of Wurren alive. He recalled the images of his house burning to the ground, and had assumed that his father hadn't survived. Despite his father's appearance of spryness,

Marric knew his father was getting older and slower. Marric also wondered how his father had been able to make it so far in the wilderness alone. Given that Narim never liked when Marric went out alone to practice and learn survival skills, he wondered where Narim had picked them up.

The group's horses clopped along loudly in the night. The rain had slowed to a drizzle and appeared to be slowing even further. He thanked Lanser that he'd finally be able to check out the insides of his bags. Glancing around, he noticed the others' hoods were starting to come down with the slowing rain. Taking their lead, Marric pulled his own hood back. Turning around, he saw the female Seer with them. As he watched, her eyes began to glow the steady blue while she rode her horse. The Light in her eyes only lasted a few moments before fading.

"We are still moving in the right direction. Looks like he's just got a fire started," she said.

Marric felt a bit guilty that he couldn't remember her name. He was also too embarrassed to ask again. When Magness had told him she'd changed her mind about him going with Turrin to get his father, he'd been too excited to pay attention to much else. Although he was an awakened Seer, they still had to bring another, as she could more easily locate Narim.

"Thank you, Gila. I appreciate you regularly ensuring that his location has not changed. Let's hope the fact that he hasn't moved since last night isn't a bad sign," Avryn said.

Ah, Gila, that's her name, Marric thought, a little relieved now.

"Meh," Turrin exclaimed, "We'd blast 'em t'pieces if'n we saw 'em, anyways." He chuckled at his own comment, as if it were a hilarious joke.

Marric stared at him, smiling awkwardly.

"I would rather you not Destroy them directly. You know I don't like that," Avryn said.

In the fading light, Marric could see a disappointed look on the man's face.

"Ah, yeh always ruin the fun. Oi din' pick Destroying as me second-born class fer nuttin'."

Avryn grimaced at his words.

"I also don't believe that you took it to blow people up, though maybe I don't know you as well as I thought I did." Avryn cocked his head to the side as he said it.

Laughing again, Turrin responded, "Aye, Oi'm just messing' with yeh. Was mostly curious, is all. Moit 'ave picked the wrong one fer how un-useful it is. Me Conjurin' is roit enough fer me most o' th'toim."

"You know that many people including myself believe you don't choose your second-born class, it chooses you. Why Destroying was your path, I can't say, but we'll use it to our advantage." Turning his gaze to the Seer, Avryn smiled. "And I find it perfectly convenient that Shielding is yours, Gila. It made it so we could cut two out of this party. With my Fixing and your Shielding, we are well equipped for whatever might pop out of the woods at us."

Marric felt a twist in his stomach, his eyes now frantically scanning the trees around them. Avryn had said it so smoothly and comfortably, but Marric didn't like the idea of something attacking them.

Noticing the change in Marric's behavior, Avryn continued, "There isn't need to worry. We all have a lot of practice with our Lightbearing. Gila can Shield us in an instant, and you know my reflexes are not slow. Fog, Turrin might be faster than me with his Conjuring."

Turrin shook his head, grunting loudly. "Ain't it at all. Yer just flatterin' me so tha' Oi won't let yeh get stuck wif nuttin' during an attack." The older man turned to Marric and winked.

"You're just being modest, you old man," Avryn joked. "I am glad that Magness decided to keep this operation small. I think we can move a lot more quickly, given the circumstances."

Marric agreed, though not necessarily because of the same reasoning. Sure, he was happy to move more quickly, but large groups actually unsettled him. Marric wasn't a socialite by any means, and having that many companions would make him feel exposed and awkward. Even now, he could feel the eyes of the men and women behind him on his back. It wasn't that they were actually staring, but he often imagined being scrutinized.

I need to show them that I am capable of a lot more than they think, he thought.

At that, he let the conversation around him fade into the background while he focused on his father's face. Breathing evenly, he let his Seeing take over and felt his eyes open wide, inevitably filled with the now-familiar blue Light. The forest around him blurred as his vision zoomed forward quickly through the trees. After some time, the images cleared up and he saw his father sitting down next to a flickering fire. It was barely alive and based on the wood, had only just started burning. A canopy of trees above Narim blocked much of the drizzling rain, but some drops still fell down. Marric assumed that his father had only just been able to start a fire since the rain had slowed. Narim looked half-dead. His hair was disheveled, his clothes muddy and ripped in numerous places. Deep purple bags hung under his eyes as if he hadn't slept in days. He was skinny, likely because he hadn't had time to bring food along or to forage as he fled.

Marric felt a pang of sadness at the sight. He moved his vision-self forward so that he stood just in front of his father. Knowing that the man couldn't see him, yet still wanting to comfort his father, Marric knelt down just before his face.

"We are coming, father. I am sorry that we didn't make it before now. Avryn and I are on our way, please—just hold on."

A rustle in the trees to the right made Marric jump, and his father reacted similarly, though with much less movement.

Forgetting momentarily that he was invisible and untouchable, Marric stepped backwards and unconsciously prepared his hand so that he could Move whatever might come through the branches.

The rustling stopped, and Marric's breath caught when something leaped out of the bush a moment later. Narim's breath sucked in sharply indicating his own surprise. A fat hare sniffed its way up to the fire and sat on its hind legs, looking up at Narim.

"Well, Oi'll be pickered—yeh scared me roit good," Narim said, a weak smile adorning his face. "What are yeh up to in this 'ere rain? Should be hidin', if yeh ask me."

Marric's whole being filled with relief knowing that it wasn't something that would attack his father. Watchlight had burned their home and driven his father out of Wurren. Marric knew that they could have eyes on his father; he just hoped they were so focused on getting the new Fixer in T'Arren Vale that they wouldn't bother coming for Narim.

A slight flash of blue Light to his left made Marric turn to see Gila there, staring at his father.

"Just watching over him while we travel, hmm?" she asked, a caring look on her face.

"Erm, yes, something like that," Marric replied.

"He does look in rough shape. Based on the path that I saw, we should be able to reach him by late morning, after we pause briefly for rest. I only hope that he can last one more night before we get there."

Marric nodded, feeling a bit of dread at her comment. Seeing his father this way, he had a hard time believing Narim could last in the forest alone for another night. The man looked as if he'd pass out from exhaustion at any moment.

There was silence between the two of them as they watched. Narim was muttering something to the hare as he held it in his lap, petting its ears backwards continuously.

"I—" Marric started to say.

Gila turned with a curious look on her face and watched him.

Deciding exactly what to say, Marric continued.

"I was trying to prove to myself that I can be a useful Lightbearer by coming here, Seeing where he is."

Gila looked confused at his words. For a moment, there was silence again. Finally, Gila seemed to understand.

"Oh Marric," she said softly, "you *are* useful. I only came along because I know the forest better than you. Magness knows that you can See well enough now, but when it comes to guiding a caravan like this, it's helpful if you know the forest as well as its landmarks. Don't feel bad that I am here. Your time will come."

She smiled warmly as she said it, moving to stand next to him. Putting her arm on his shoulder, she tried to assuage his insecurities. The sensation was odd to him. He could see that she was there, her hand on his shoulder, but he couldn't feel a thing. Marric knew that she couldn't feel him either. In fact, her hand was depressed slightly *into* his shoulder rather than resting on the top.

"I hope that you are right."

"I am, trust me," she replied. "Now, I haven't done this for a few hours so it's probably a good idea to check again. I'm going to shift my vision into the future to make sure nothing ill befalls him."

As her image began to fade, Marric called out to her. "Wait! I would like to come," he said resolutely.

Gila smiled again, her curly blonde ringlets falling to either side of her face underneath her hood.

"Of course."

She held out her hand for Marric to take. Once again, he moved his hand to hers and tried to clasp it, but felt nothing. Marric wondered if he'd ever get used to the sensation. His concern at their lack of ability to touch each other causing problems was squelched when the image of Narim sped up quickly. He apparently would sit with the hare until sundown, when he would retire. Marric watched his father rapidly put out the fire and lay down in the darkness. Stellan flew overhead, the red light streaking quickly through the small break in the trees before Mallan streaked by. Fog thickened in the air around them, hiding the forest from their view. Marric furrowed his brow as he lost sight of his father in the fog. Darkness ruled the sky above until Isllan's orange light streaked through the trees, a dull orb through the fog.

"No need to worry, the fog will be gone in just a moment," Gila said, reading his reaction.

It was an odd thing seeing time move so quickly. In all his practice using his Seeing, he'd never advanced time during a vision like this. Soon after Isllan's light spun through the quickened night, the fog disappeared and the breaking of the sun lit the sky into a brighter blue through the canopy of leaves above. Marric shifted his gaze to Narim, who still lay sleeping. Normally by this part of the morning his father would be awake, but his father was likely exhausted from the rapid travels, and needed the extra sleep.

"Fog!" Gila exclaimed, "They're closer than we are." Her curse and frustration caused Marric to snap back to attention.

At first, he didn't know how she knew the other party was closer, but then he noticed that time had slowed back to its normal flow. Given that his father had slept relatively unmoving, and in the darkness you could hardly see anything, the only indication of time speeding by were the moons.

When the sun rose further, the forest and its life came into view. Marric had only just noticed birds, rabbits, and even deer moving past at an impossible pace just before a bird slowed down to a normal pace. Then Marric saw them. Three figures wearing dark cloaks with their hoods up slunk toward a sleeping Narim. They moved so slowly that Marric wasn't alerted to them right away, until he followed Gila's gaze into the forest.

Marric watched as the three figures moved into the clearing, the front one holding out a dagger coated in some silver-black substance. He felt his hairs stand on end when he realized it was likely laced with something lethal. Instinctively, he shouted to his father, trying to wake him.

"Stop that! It won't do you any good here," Gila hissed as if the sound he made would give away their position. "Blast, what time is it? It can't be much more than an hour past dawn tomorrow when they'll reach him. We can't afford to wait until tomorrow afternoon to get there."

Narim slept, unaware of the danger that lurked just over his figure.

Creeping closer, the man leading the other two made a gesture outward with both hands, indicating that their companions should fan out and check for other dangers. Quickly, the two slipped back into the forest on either side of their leader. Stopping just short of his father, the man paused for just a beat. In a flash, he dove toward his father, Marric letting out a scream at the sight. All at once, the world spun and Marric felt his vision-self being tugged back to his body.

The slow-moving forest around him where he sat on his horse snapped into view as he landed back in his physical body. Marric felt a bit dizzy, though he couldn't tell if it was from the rapid change in scenery or the fact that he just saw his father killed in some future possibility.

"Avryn! Watchlight is too close to Narim! We need to get to him before they do," Gila said loudly.

Avryn cursed to himself. He then asked, "When will they get there?"

"A couple hours past dawn tomorrow morning. I'm not sure we can make it before then. We still have so much ground to cover."

"We'll have to push the horses to a run and hope that they have the energy to get us there in time."

Gila looked unsure, then pointed to a fallen log in their path just twenty paces ahead.

"But S'ren, there are too many obstacles and trees. Perhaps if we had a straight course and nothing in the way, we'd get there in time. But having to weave and dodge prevents us from pushing the horses to a run."

Nodding, Avryn summoned a small orb of blue Light, about half the size of his palm. In a practiced throw, he lobbed the ball into the fallen tree. A loud crack pierced the otherwise quiet forest around them and splinters from the trees exploded in all directions. Marric winced at the loud sound and a few splinters that pelted his face, but when he looked back, a clear path had been blown through the fallen tree.

"We'll have to take the path down by brute force, unfortunately."

Gila stared at him. "You can't be serious. Everyone from here to Terris Green will know where we are!"

"We don't have any choice," Avryn said grimly before turning to speak to Turrin, " I'll need your help."

Marric noticed a wide grin on Turrin's face and he felt a little uneasy at the sight.

"Fog, yes! Oi roit loik this plan," the older man said, summoning a blue orb of his own.

"It takes a moment to summon the Destroying orbs, so we'll each take turns moving every other obstacle, and then maybe we can move at the pace we need."

Gila groaned.

Despite her complaints and worry, Avryn whipped his horse into motion and the others followed suit. Marric felt his stomach drop with the new speed, the stinging of the small slivers on his face more potent than before.

Then the explosions began ringing out, scattering animals away in all directions.

16

The sun was dipping in the sky again and the caravan kept pressing forward. Janis didn't mind pushing fast and hard. For her, she wouldn't have stopped at all except to sleep for a few hours during midday. Traveling at night was always more effective in her opinion, but then again, she normally traveled alone. Right now, their group contained around twelve men and women. They had left Terris Green with a larger group, but just yesterday they split off into three groups to approach T'Arren Vale from different directions to account for Watchlight's likely approach. Evenir knew the general direction of their opposition's lair, so they anticipated they'd be traveling from the north, but what they couldn't account for was all the operatives that were already out of their base.

Gone are the days when I could be alone during travel, she thought.

Trying not to mourn the loss of the past, she focused on the path before them, shifting energy into her senses to listen and see things that others might not. The sun was getting lower, darkening the forest around them slowly. Regardless, it was still teeming with life from the animals and bugs that normally roamed during the day. A steady sound from her left indicated a small river that flowed from one of the mountains nearby, probably ending at the sea, far beyond them to the east. Janis knew that it would turn away from their path soon, and she was glad. Perhaps then her hearing could be more effective. The constant bubbling of the water was starting to bother her.

Janis had traveled this route many times. Staying near the brook was advantageous for many reasons, but the primary reason for her was ironically the noise. She was a fairly silent traveler herself, but having the extra mask on her tread allowed her to move just a bit quicker. The unfortunate side effect was that it also masked potential ambushers. Despite this, Janis was pleased that Alsry led them this way. It showed their leader's sense for stealth was much better than Janis expected. Thinking of Rivelen and Turrin, she shook her head. Based on how they were always loudly lumbering around Evenir's base, apparently neither had any stealth abilities whatsoever. She marveled how they had received the positions which they held.

Earlier, Alsry had ordered the whole group to be silent. No speaking of any kind. The hooves of their horses clopped fairly loudly, sure, but minimizing the noise would ensure that they were less likely to be heard and more likely to hear something around them.

"Paltrel, what do you See?"

Janis turned her vision to an unassuming man. He was of average build, had common light brown hair, and dark brown eyes. His nose was a bit crooked, as if he'd run into a wall as a child and it stuck that way. Thick brows covered his large eyes, which glowed with a steady blue.

"I See no danger ahead in the forest. But—"

He paused, pressing his lips into a fine line.

"Looks like Watchlight is going to get to T'Arren Vale around the same time. I see mostly blurs, which means that they have a Seer watching us in the city as well. The future keeps shifting from each of us making different decisions based on what we See."

Janis listened, a bit aghast. What use was seeing the future if it was this much guesswork?

Part of her knew that she could technically use the same ability, but she hadn't dared to seek it out. She had slipped into the in-between a few times on this journey to review their surroundings during their travels in the forest, but this hadn't been overly helpful, as there was nothing to report.

Janis furrowed her brow.

Except that Macks kept showing up, she thought, a disconcerting feeling entering her chest.

Macks had died years ago. She had received reports from one of her employers that he had a bounty on his head for so long, that enemy assassins took him out. This was not long after he'd abandoned her eight years ago. She had only been eighteen, and had just learned to survive in the cruel world. Five years she'd spent with him, learning his ways, and he had abandoned her on a job to save his own skin. His lessons had paid off and she was doing alright now, but she still loathed the man. Hearing that he'd died was both satisfying and saddening at the same time.

Shaking her head, she focused on the road ahead. They would arrive at the borders of T'Arren Vale within an hour. Looking up into the sky, she saw that the sun had already tipped past its highest point and would be setting within a couple hours after they got to the city. Remembering the vision of the awakening she'd had back at Terris Green, she thought about how the sun was below the taller buildings and closer to setting. They would make it, but only just.

Janis scoffed at the revelation, earning her a look from Alsry who rode beside her. Knowing that the vision had waited until likely the last possible moment for them to make it there was ironic. An ability to see the future could have given them a bit more time, couldn't it?

"Is something funny?" Alsry whispered next to her.

"According to Harmel, there is *always* something funny," Janis deflected.

To her right, Harmel grinned from ear to ear and winked at her. She answered him with an exaggerated eye roll. The fact that he'd opted to come without even resting irked her somewhat. At the same time, it felt nice to have someone she knew around who could handle a blade.

Behind them, the group of ten additional people rode on their steeds. Janis couldn't understand why such a large group was required to retrieve the boy, but Magness had insisted. There were some arguments, mainly from Janis, and eventually she had negotiated the number down significantly. Apparently, Magness anticipated some type of large fight to happen at the scene, though she couldn't understand why. Hearing Watchlight would be there made her ears buzz. She'd been itching for a fight for over a week. Sure, they had sparring rooms and there were a few men who had tried their hands at fighting her, but that was just practice. The real thrill came when either your life or theirs was at risk.

Alsry immediately held up her left hand, halting the group. Hoof patters stopped in a slow wave until there was silence, other than the bubbling water to their right. Alsry made another gesture and the group responded immediately, dismounting their horses and moving toward the water.

Janis, having not been trained on the group's hand signals, stared at the dark-skinned woman.

"We go by foot now. The horses will give us away."

Feeling a bit of relief at shedding the noise, Janis urged her own horse to the river and dismounted. A few men tied their horses off to trees, ensuring that they could reach the water, but a majority of them just left the horses untied.

"Most of the horses are trained to come at a signal sound. These," Alsry said, gesturing to the few that were tied, "are still young and haven't yet learned to not run off."

"And the hand signals were meant to keep your men and women from wandering off as well, I presume?"

Harmel, having just started drinking water from his waterskin, spat his mouthful out loudly, choking as he laughed at her joke.

Alsry looked less than impressed. "I am not sure if I find it more annoying or disconcerting that Harmel's sense of humor appears to have rubbed off on you. I don't think it becomes you."

"Tha' ain't my humor there, tha' is 'er own bit. Oi must say Oi roit loik it," Harmel said, still trying to contain his laughter.

Fire smoldered behind their leader's eyes, and Janis stared at her, almost feeling the woman's mood exuding from her being. Janis knew that she was a Mover, but there was another Lightbearing power hidden inside that she didn't know. At one point she had asked Alsry, but the woman simply didn't answer.

I've got to try not to get her on my bad side, Janis thought.

She was confident that in hand-to-hand combat she could probably survive against the woman, but Janis definitely didn't want to be thrown about by her Moving, or even take a Destroying orb to the back if that turned out to be her second-born power.

Alsry made another gesture that Janis didn't recognize, and the men and women around them shouldered their weapons and waterskins, leaving the rest of their provisions with the horses.

Looking about, Janis's only thought was that this was a goldmine for a band of thieves. Unattended horses and provisions were enough to make any simple thief drool at the easiness of it all.

"We move in groups from different parts of the forest, like we practiced. The awakening is to be in the square at the center of the city. Make your way from the different entry points and set up as soon as you can. Keep an eye out for Watchlight. If we're lucky, we'll get to our positions before they get to theirs."

Silently, the group separated into roughly even groups, some moving off to the left, and some to the right. The river wouldn't turn off to the right for some distance still, so that group would have to follow the bank until it did before they could move farther toward their entrance.

"And we," Alsry continued, still whispering, "take the forward path."

Of course, Janis hated the idea of coming on the main road. It was sure to be a trap, an ambush already set by someone. The only reason why she didn't argue further (other than some light pushing back) was because she knew that *someone* likely had to be the bait, and she didn't mind the idea that she could use her daggers for some real fighting again.

The men and women around them took a few moments to shift their weapons, hiding them under cloaks and in belts. They had changed their cloaks and picked up baskets and crates of random fruits, vegetables, and foods. The plan was to go into the city via the main road, acting as a caravan of merchants. A few of the men got to bring their horses while the rest walked. They wouldn't be able to act the part if they weren't traveling with at least some of the beasts. Harmel and Alsry had covered their own battle-worn cloaks with some more simple, merchant colored ones. Simple, brown, no embroidery of any sort.

Janis just wore her normal black apparel. Seeing her with the others, she knew that she stood out. Alsry held out a dress, simple and pink with a white apron, and Janis shook her head.

"I'm not in the mood for playing dress up, thank you very much. I thought you were the type of person who didn't require me to repeat myself."

Alsry looked less than pleased with her response.

"I am the commanding officer of this company. Whether you like it or not, you need to follow my orders," Alsry said flatly.

Janis smiled at her condescendingly.

"Of course, I understand you can't take chances on some rogue ruining the operation. But you needn't worry; I'll stay out of sight."

At that, she winked at Alsry and ran toward the city boundaries and the guards that stood along the pathway just before the main gate.

"Fog you, assassin, get your behind back here now!"

Not stopping her momentum, Janis turned her head slightly and yelled back to Alsry, "I won't blow your cover or anything! See you in the city center!"

Feeling her heart race at her quick run was incredible. It had been so long since she'd been able to run at a breakneck pace like this. A short bend to the left brought the yawning gate far ahead into view. The entrance was still far enough off that the guards likely hadn't seen her yet. Before they could, she slipped back into the trees and began running at a diagonal from the gate toward the wall to the left. If she remembered correctly, the trees were allowed to grow a bit closer to the wall a few hundred yards from the gate. It wasn't the first time she'd used the tallest trees near the wall to leap to the edge. As it was, the wall wasn't necessarily intended to keep assassins like her out. If it was, they'd have built it far taller. Janis believed the wall was more to act as an automatic funnel for traffic to the few open gates into the town.

Smiling to herself in anticipation of the jump, and from the memory of her past jobs that required her to enter here, she paused and put her back against a tree at the edge of the forest line. The wall stood about ten feet away, twenty-five feet tall, gray and quiet. The guards didn't bother to patrol the grounds continuously along the base of the wall surrounding the city. There were going to be guards atop the wall, however, and Janis had to be prepared.

Shifting slightly, Janis pulled a pouch from her bag. Sucking in a deep breath, she closed her mouth and opened the top of the pouch to peer in. Inside was a powdered substance, bright green.

I should have plenty to get where I'm going. It's been a long time since I've had the pleasure of playing with you, my friend, Janis thought fondly.

Ground of klout root was a very fast-acting and intense tranquilizer. There was a misconception throughout Lindrad that klout root was poisonous, but that's all it was, a falsity. Macks had taught her that the root could be sun dried and ground up into a fine powder. Inhaling even a small amount could knock someone out for hours. The best part was that the symptoms from the powder very much resembled someone inebriated with alcohol. Also, given the fine nature of the powder, it often left little trace of itself once used.

Pulling the drawstring tight, she breathed out and tied the pouch to her belt at the ready. In many cases, she wouldn't bother with the powder, opting to just kill the guards, or even slice them with poison-coated daggers to kill or knock them out. In this case, she didn't get the feeling that causing a commotion would be in anyone's favor. With Evenir's large group and Watchlight's supposedly large group, killing some guards would not make finding the new Fixer any easier.

Turning back to the tree, Janis pulled out her long dagger and put it in her teeth. She likely wouldn't run into any trouble in the tree, be it animal or person, but it wouldn't hurt to be prepared just in case.

Jumping slightly, she caught hold of the bottom branch six feet above the ground and hoisted herself up. Then she fell into the familiar rhythm of climbing a tree. Her leg and arm muscles tightened at the extensive use and her heart thumped in her chest. Fortunately for her, she was very light on her feet and had little trouble scaling the tree in good time.

She hadn't made it to the top of the tree, but she knew that she didn't need to. The branch on which she stood was three feet above the height of the wall. Judging the distance, she opted to climb up one more branch to give herself two more feet of height. Creaking slightly, Janis knew the branch would have a hard time, even with her slight form. She didn't dare move higher, for the chances of the smaller branches not being able to hold her weight were too high.

Breathing deeply, she took a moment to enjoy the fresh air and gather the energy to launch herself from the branch. The top of the stone wall was typical for a battlement, with patterned crenels or indentations like a king's crown. Two feet up, then two feet down they went, across the top of the wall. Technically, she was only three feet above the top of the crenels, but she was aiming for the indentation, not the top of the crenels. Even with her skill, this jump was risky. She would have to use a lot of leg strength to jump the distance and give herself a bit more height to make sure she landed it. Gritting her teeth, she thought back to the other times she'd made the jump. The first time, she'd landed on her chest and had to drag herself up, fingernails breaking at the scramble. It wasn't glamorous, but it was thrilling. The second time, she'd got just the tips of her toes on the top of the wall. Those, of course, couldn't hold her full weight, so she'd slipped and had to resort to dragging herself up again.

This time, she was determined to make it. Taking another breath, she readied herself for the leap. Just before she could make it, however, the wall disappeared completely, as did the tree underneath her and the branches around her. Scrambling, she grabbed around until her hand felt a branch about the size of her wrist. The world around her spun, colors blending together in an odd assortment. Her eyes felt like they were extended to their fullest and she felt a soft warmth there.

What in Lanser's name is happening?

Before long, her vision began clearing and she saw Marric and Avryn crashing through the forest, explosions of blue Light and splintering trees coming every few seconds. She flew behind them, observing the artful organization of Turrin and Avryn throwing Destroying orbs at perfectly timed intervals. It looked like they were clearing a path to somewhere and moving their horses at a fast pace. The ruckus that they were making caused Janis to flinch, suddenly nervous that the noise she was currently hearing would be her undoing and give away her location in the tree just outside of T'Arren Vale.

Shaking her head (which felt very far away), she realized how unrealistic that thought was. Her vision blurred again and suddenly they were in a small clearing, a fire smoking in the center. An old man, who Janis could now see was Narim, lay next to the fire. Three figures in black cloaks emerged from the other end of the clearing, most hidden in hoods. The first to emerge was holding a blade coated in something dark, almost black with a hint of silver.

Distant explosions behind her grew louder until the sound of splintering wood was close enough to cause the man to look up, his face slightly visible in the emerging sun. The forest was still fairly dark, given the height and density of the foliage, but the clear sky above was lighting up, which gave her enough of a view. Seeing his nose and mouth, Janis recognized the features slightly, an image buzzing somewhere in her mind. Perhaps he was one of Luden's lackeys?.

Just then, a loud crack announced the tree immediately behind her exploding into thousands of shards and pieces. A few of the larger chunks flew straight through her midsection, careening toward the hooded man. He jumped back just in time for the large chunk to miss him. Janis spun on the sound, feeling a bit queasy at just seeing something go through her body as if she didn't exist.

If this is what to expect from Seeing, I'd rather stick to the in-between, Janis thought, her disconnected body gritting its teeth somewhere far away.

Avryn and Turrin flew through the newly opened space in the trees behind her, both tugging roughly on the reigns to halt their horses.

Each man summoned a sword of Light. Janis watched with annoyance as they jumped from their horses. Marric came through the trees then, followed by the woman she'd met just before they'd all departed.

Gila, she remembered.

"Lay no hand on this man," Avryn spoke loudly, moving slowly to Narim's form. The fact that Narim hadn't risen suggested he wasn't just sleeping. Janis thought for a moment that Narim was dead, but looking more closely, she could see the steady rise and fall of his chest. He must have been deep in something, for the explosion hadn't woken him up.

Laughing, the figure in front crouched lower.

"May the best man win, then."

Without hesitation, the man lobbed a dagger right at Avryn while still clutching his coated knife. Luckily, Avryn's reflexes allowed him to dance out of the dagger's pathway. The blade flew past him, barely missing his horse before it bounced off of a translucent Shield that had sprung up quickly. Shifting her gaze to Gila, Janis assumed it was her creating the mystical

Shield. Janis then looked at Marric, noting the steady fear in his eyes. It wasn't as obvious as it used to be, but it was there. He'd Conjured a bow and arrow out of the blue Light.

"May he, then," the figure spoke.

Avryn and Turrin charged forward, yelling loudly.

The world spun again and before long, she found herself back in her body atop the tree. Steadying herself, she couldn't help but note that the sensation was similar to waking up from a dizzying blow to the face, without the pain, of course. The fogginess of the spinning world cleared quickly, however, and she mentally logged what she'd seen. She couldn't quite pinpoint the timing of the strange vision she'd seen, but given the time of the day, she assumed that either that had just happened this morning, or would happen tomorrow.

Fog the visions, I need to learn how to control when they come so it's not such a risk during fights, Janis thought.

She didn't allow more time for herself to consider the dangers of that timing.

To her right, she could hear a few horses and footsteps approaching the city gates. A guard yelled to the approachers, urging them to report their business. Alsry and their caravan had made it to the gates.

Looking across the way, Janis could see that a guard would soon make it to the turret at the far end of the wall and would be doubling back soon. His mail and plate looked heavy, and she anticipated that he couldn't move as quickly as she could. Just before she could jump, she gasped as her eyes were forced open by another vision. She cursed, but couldn't do much about it.

The odd thing was that she knew she was Seeing something, but she was still in the tree. Her vision showed her leap the distance to the wall, and she could See the bottom of the notch she aimed for coming up quickly. Her trajectory was slightly off, and half of her body collided with the higher crenel, while her foot barely caught the down notch. She tried to right herself, but before she could, her balance was lost and she fell, hands grasping desperately for the edge. Without success, she saw the ground rush up to her and everything went black.

Suddenly, she was back in the tree. Looking to her left, she saw the guard in the same position he'd been before the odd vision. Clutching her dagger, she shook her head and focused on her path. Knowing that it was now or never (for waiting for the guard to pass would put her too far behind) she leapt out. As she flew, it all felt familiar. It was a déjà vu, but she knew why.

Fog it! she thought desperately.

Just as she'd Seen, her position wasn't quite right. Bracing for the wall, she grit her teeth as her right side slammed into the upward notch and her toes desperately sought friction on the edge. Instinctively, she threw the long dagger she'd switched to her left hand mid-air, the blade slamming into a wall notch diagonally across the top of the wall, sticking in a few inches. As she slipped, she felt her downward momentum stop suddenly, her toes still barely attached to the lower notch, her other half dangling in the air.

Confused, she looked up to see a blue Light rope wrapped around her wrist, holding her in place. She traced the line and saw it tied to the dagger she'd instinctively thrown just before.

How in Lanser's name—? she thought.

Knowing the guard would be turning around any moment if he hadn't already, she yanked herself onto the wall and crouched low into the three-foot notch so the guard couldn't see her.

The Light rope was still wrapped around her wrist, and she cursed when she realized it was visible in the open space. Panicked, she scrambled to remove it from her wrist. When she couldn't immediately get it untied, she tried to hack at it with another small dagger. As she sliced through the material, which strangely felt exactly like a normal rope, it melted along the whole length into the air.

Janis heard the approaching thunks of the guard's plated feet, and she formulated a plan in her mind. His movement was slow, so he hadn't noticed the Light rope or her dagger stuck in the notch across the path. The wait was agonizing as he moved closer to her. By now, Alsry and her group were likely through the gate and moving to their destination. Janis hoped that she'd be able to get there first to check out the area to make sure it was safe. Finally, the guard got close enough.

"Wha' in blazes is tha'?" he said as he noticed her long dagger protruding from the stone.

The guard sucked in a breath to shout to his companions, but Janis sprang out from the gap in the wall and dashed to him, her hand simultaneously pulling a small bit of powder from the pouch at her belt. Throwing it into his face, she caught the latter end of his breath and his eyes rolled in his head as he fell heavily to the ground with a loud clunk.

Janis moved quickly to her dagger and yanked it free from the stone. Sheathing it, she turned and sprinted along the wall until she made it to the tower to the left of the gates her group had just entered. A lone guard stood in the room. The man hadn't heard the commotion on the wall, likely because of the constant noises that were coming from the market below just inside the city. Janis thought to knock this one out as well, but decided to leave him be.

Peering over the wall, she located a cart full of hay close to the bottom of the wall where she stood. She'd practiced jumping from walls this height, and could likely do it without breaking anything, but she knew it would still hurt and that it might cause more of a commotion.

She took a breath and took aim. Launching herself lightly from the wall, her stomach lurched and air whipped about her hair as she landed in the cart full of hay. Janis tucked her knees to block some of the momentum, and rolled out onto the ground. No one noticed, given the bustle of the market, other than a poor runt child that sat eating the discarded core of an apple.

The little boy stared at her, wide-eyed. Janis just winked and moved off into the crowd. Her apparel was a bit odd for a woman, but she wasn't the only one dressed oddly. This was the capital of Lindrad. People visited from far and wide for diplomacy and trade, even from other continents. Only the guards at the gate would have questioned her validity, especially since she didn't feel like coming up with a lie convincing enough for them to let her in. Now that she was in, however, she wouldn't look any more out of place than the other outsiders.

Just as she'd had the thought, another woman stalked by wearing an extremely exposing dress, the bottom line cut above her knees. Her top was a full fur coat, thick and brown, with a bronze breastplate covering it all.

Considering the horrible impracticality of the dress, she shook her head and quickly headed off in the direction of the main square.

Another reason she didn't want to move with the caravan was because she wanted to get a good vantage point over the square. If Watchlight was here, they may have set up small groups like Evenir had to keep an eye on the square from afar. Janis didn't want these pockets of Watchlight to get the better of them and attack. Alsry and her group were disguised, sure, but a group of that size moving *away* from the market wouldn't be able to fool their enemy.

Getting to the square was easy, as Janis had been to T'Arren Vale on numerous occasions. Tall four and five-story buildings ran on either side of the cobbled roads, making her feel both exposed and hidden at the same time. The streets were wide, so it wasn't too much trouble to move in them, but it was very crowded. People moved in all directions, chattering to each other, calling out for buyers of whatever wares they carried. Shops and pubs had their doors open, odd smells wafting out from some. Janis passed a store that sold herbs for healing and spells and she wrinkled her nose at the stench. Looking through the window, she saw dried onions and garlic hanging from twine decorating the inside. Underneath the smelly vegetables, she saw bowls full of powdered herbs and other concoctions. One bowl held a small parchment with fancy writing on it that said, *for the one you love*. Coincidentally, the bowl next to it had a parchment that said *for your enemy*.

Shaking her head at the thought of the false witchcraft, she moved down the shadowed cobbles as quickly as she could, scanning for signs of black cloaks. It was unlikely that Watchlight would be roaming in large groups wearing their uncommon pitch black cloaks, but she looked nonetheless.

After dodging a few people as they bustled by, almost knocking her over, she realized that being down on the road was only slowing her down. Angling for a narrow alleyway across from one of the many bakeries in the city, she slipped deeper into the shadows. The sun was moving down in the sky, so the road she walked on wasn't too bright, but the narrowness of this alley made everything more shadowed and dark.

Moving further into the shadows, Janis found a place where she could climb. The trim on this building looked sturdy enough, and it protruded from the walls with half an inch of space for her fingers. To make the climb easier, she pulled out one of her smaller daggers, sharp and smooth on one end and serrated on the other. This building was four stories tall and would be a bit of work. Putting her left fingers on the small trim, she jumped and used her hand to pull heavily until her foot caught on the lowest of the trim.

Janis immediately dug her dagger into the wall with a thunk and held on to it so that she could release her other hand and grab the higher trim.

She continued this way, a rhythm taking over, steadily, yet still fairly quickly. Janis knew that if there was anyone inside these walls, they'd hear her knife thudding into the outside wall. Judging the wall's thickness, she wasn't pushing the knife too far in. There would be gashes from her knife, but they shouldn't draw too much attention.

Just as she had the thought, her foot slipped on the trim below and she instinctively shoved the dagger in more heavily. It thudded loudly, the sound echoing down the small alley. Looking up, she noted that she had accidentally pushed the knife all the way through.

Cursing, she pulled her knife out and realized that she hadn't checked what the building was before she'd started climbing. Janis only hoped that it wasn't something very occupied and that no one had heard her noise. Carefully, she scaled the rest of the way to the roof and put her dagger away.

She stood only a couple streets from the square now. As she looked to the next building, she observed the position of the sun. Based on what she could recall from the vision (that now seemed ages ago) the boy should be awakening in the next hour, if not sooner.

Janis sprinted to the next building and vaulted herself easily over the small alley between the two. She kept her momentum, air whooshing in her ears and pulling at her hair. The weather was warm and humid. T'Arren Vale wasn't necessarily close to the ocean, but it stood directly in the path of the wind from it. The sea breeze amazingly found its way over here, cooling the city on most days. Of course down in the streets, the wind could only be felt occasionally given the height of the buildings, but up on the rooftops, Janis could feel it and smell it all.

Janis leapt one last time to a shorter building just outside the square. She crouched down low when she noted a group of four figures wearing dark cloaks just one building over. Scanning to the sides, she ensured that there were no other people on the roof before she crept closer to the small group.

"I finks this is righ' dumb. 'Tis only one Fixer t'be awakened. We gots tons o' them. Why send so many of us? In the rain an' all tha', toos," one of them said.

"Oh shut it, Yorv, yeh ain't gonna die. Lanser knows yeh needed the wash since yeh been stinkin' a bunch these days, anyway," a woman next to him answered.

"'Ow's 'bout yeh both shut it?" another man hissed at the two.

Janis saw that the group did look somewhat ragged, as if they'd moved at a quick pace through some heavy forest. Of course, the Evenir group she'd come with looked relatively the same, the difference is that these men and women wore black cloaks. Janis moved her hand to her pouch, ready to knock them down before a large man stood up and turned in her direction. Dashing to the side, she slipped behind a chimney.

"Hey, did you see that?" the large man asked.

"Wha'? Are yeh seeing' things again, Tripe?" the first voice chuckled. "Yeh need to relax. T'ain't no one else up heres."

"But I know I just saw something."

A heavy sigh sounded. "Fine, I'll go check fer yeh," the female voice said.

Janis heard a blade get pulled from a sheath.

"Nah, nah. Just in case, let's try something else."

The group went silent then. For a moment, nothing happened. Suddenly, a flash of red Light lit the shingles of the roof, shining from the direction of the group. Realizing what it was, Janis dove out the other side of the chimney before the shingles on the other side exploded with a loud bang. Jumping to her feet, she spun on the group of men and women. There, a man held his hand out with an orb of red Light hovering there. His teeth were bared and he looked pleased with himself.

"Well, Oi'll be fogged, Tripe actually 'eard somethin' real this time."

His oily hair was black and looked messy, as if he never took care of it. A tattoo sat on his forehead above thin brows. Janis recognized it immediately. It was an eye wreathed in beams of light. It looked horrid placed on his forehead like that, but seeing it was a relief to Janis.

I hadn't planned on killing any of them for fear of causing a commotion, but as they are Watchlight men. . . .

With practiced ease, Janis pulled her long dagger out in her right hand and a smaller one in her left. Jumping forward, she closed the distance quickly between herself and the four black-cloaked figures. Two of them pulled swords from their sides, while one of them still held a red orb in his hand. Grinning as if he knew a joke that Janis didn't, he lobbed the orb not at her, but to her side. An explosion on the rooftop blasted splinters and shingles outward. The force of the blast pushed her to the side and she flew toward the edge of the roof. Cursing, she twisted in the air and jammed the smaller dagger into the roof, holding on tight. It was enough to keep her from falling. Just then, the woman in front Conjured a large pole of Light in her hand, at least seven feet in length. She jabbed at a Janis, trying to push her from the roof.

Janis dodged the jabs and yanked her dagger free. Rolling to the side, she quickly ran away from the edge. She turned and noted that the other man and woman hadn't used any Lightbearing. That meant that they either had unhelpful abilities, or none at all. Acting quickly, she shifted left and threw her small dagger end-over-end toward the group. A small dome of red Light appeared out of the air and deflected the knife to the side where it flew off the edge of the roof.

Lanser's might, I hope that doesn't strike someone below, she thought.

The ugly black haired man summoned another orb of Light and prepared to throw it. Janis watched where he aimed and jumped in the other direction right as he let it fly.

As she landed, she heard a commotion from the square across the way. Looking over, she saw a Shield of blue Light spring up, blocking a small group of men and women that looked to be from Evenir.

Looks like I'm not the only one that ran into some Watchlight operatives.

Focusing on the group again, she realized that the three wielding weapons—two steel swords and the woman now with a Conjured red Light sword—hadn't left their positions near the edge of the wall. The Destroyer was a few paces in front of them, away from the edge. Her thoughts shifted to when she Saw Avryn and Turrin facing the men in the forest. They'd come in displaying their Lightbearing freely, giving away their advantage. No matter how fast she was, she couldn't get the better of two Lightbearers without evening the fight. The Shield suddenly disappeared, and Janis cocked her head, wondering why they took it down.

Lanser, if you blessed me with whatever the Fog you say you did, make sure this works.

A flash of red Light snapped her back to attention as she saw another

Destroying orb headed right for her. Twisting her body just right allowed her to narrowly miss the orb's touch. It passed behind her and slammed into the slanted roof, the explosion rocking her forward and toward the group. The roof of this building was very large, but there were holes blown everywhere. Janis knew that there wouldn't be much left if she didn't end it quickly.

Sucking in a breath, she used the forward momentum from the explosion to her advantage. Imagining her physical hands pushing the four figures, she shoved her free hand forward. All four of the figures were wreathed with blue Light. Eyes wide, they all flew backwards as if she'd pushed them simultaneously with her hands. The three closest to the edge flew off the roof and tumbled to the ground below, screaming loudly.

Shocked that her Moving trick had worked, she paused before realizing that the Destroyer hadn't been close enough to the edge. Scrambling up, he'd summoned another orb and lobbed it at her. Cursing, she ducked as it flew over her head, this one breaking a large hole in the roof.

Looks like he's getting desperate and giving them more oomph, Janis thought.

Focusing on her task, she imaging shoving him off the roof again and threw her hand forward. To her disappointment, nothing happened.

"Fog it!" she said, as the man noticed her unsuccessful attempt to Move him off the roof.

By now, people on the ground were getting loud, noticing the event across the street with the Shield and the three people fallen on the ground below. The building they were on was tall enough that Janis couldn't see the group on the ground, but she could hear the yelling. People from the center of the square were congregating in a group around her building, and some backed up to look at her and the man fighting.

"So, yeh gots a bit of some Lightbearing yerself, huh? Well, no matter. Yeh can' live through *this*!"

The oily man gave a battle shout as he summoned an orb in each hand and threw them both at her. Unfortunately for her, his aim was true. Instinctively, she dodged one direction, but that put her right in the path of another. Fear dug into her stomach as she braced for the Destroying orb to collide with her midsection. At the same time, she threw her hand out desperately to block it, knowing it was fruitless.

A flash of blue Light shocked her as a translucent wall of blue Light appeared just before her. The orb crashed into it with a loud crack and disappeared into nothing. The one she had dodged just before landed and blasted her with splinters and debris again, her face and hand stinging from the shrapnel.

The man looked shocked. He stared at her, trying to understand what had just happened. Taking advantage of this, Janis threw her long dagger at him. He gasped as the dagger pierced him right through the chest. Falling to the roof, he died moments later.

Janis was out of breath. Her face stung and the backs of her hands were ripped to pieces from the debris and explosions. She stared at the dead man for only a moment before redirecting her vision to the ground, where some people were shouting at her. Most looked scared, some stared at her in wonder.

Deciding that she didn't want to have to explain this, she moved to the man and pulled her dagger free before spinning around. Janis ran to the back of the roof and easily jumped to the next one. She ran full out over two more roofs before landing on another, two stories shorter. Janis tucked her knees and rolled forward to account for the drop. There she lay flat, so that no one from the ground could see her.

The commotion from the square was still happening, from what she could hear. Another disturbance had sprung up a few streets over, and Janis guessed it was another Evenir-Watchlight scuffle.

Gritting her teeth, she ripped a part of her sleeve off and began wrapping her right hand. After getting it settled, she tore her other sleeve to wrap her other bleeding hand. As she touched the fabric to her hand, a blue Light appeared, small, yet intense. Before she could wrap her left hand, the skin knit back together and the blood stopped. Her stomach writhed at the unusual Light, and she pulled her hand away.

While she appreciated the convenience of what just happened—Lanser be thanked—it irked her at the same time. She felt like a child with a weapon that she couldn't control. Janis knew that she ought to try Fixing her other hand, but she couldn't bring herself to do it.

Why did my life have to become so complicated? I didn't ask for these unnatural powers, fog it! Janis thought, annoyed.

A warm drop of blood dripped down her cheek and she remembered that there was damage there. Whatever wounds she had would cause looks, but she didn't have time to wait. Sitting up quickly, she moved to the edge and peered down. The street wasn't empty, but people were too focused on moving either to or away from the square where swords clashed and yelling could be heard.

Janis jumped from the two-story building and cushioned the fall by once again bending her knees. She opted to not roll with this one, given the population of passersby on the road. Even so, she drew a confused look from a few people who were passing just as she landed. Without much pause, Janis turned and rushed to the square where the sounds were getting louder. The moment she entered, she could see the fighting was pretty intense. Carts had been knocked over, some blown up completely, some bystanders lay on the ground, unconscious or dead from the battle. Flashes of red and blue Light lit up the buildings on the side of the square where the shouting was coming from. To her right, another group of blue Light-wielding people rushed to the aid of their companions.

Janis almost threw herself into the fray before she realized that the time for the boy to cross the square was drawing close. Looking up at the sky, she had a sense of familiarity that she hadn't had when she first Saw the situation. When she'd been here before, there hadn't been fighting, just the crowds moving with the normal city throng. Now that there *was* fighting, it could likely have changed how things would play out.

Spinning to the center of the square, she saw the statue of their last monarch, standing regal and made of white stone. She recalled Seeing the boy near the statue when he awakened, but as she scanned the crowd, she saw nothing, no sign of the boy at all.

Instead, her eyes locked on a tall man wearing all black, scars running from nose to ear on either side.

Prost.

17

Prost gritted his teeth at the chaos of the square. When they'd made it to T'Arren Vale without hindrance, he should have assumed they'd run into small groups of Evenir men and women within the city. After all, they'd assigned their own small groups to hide in various places as well.

He ducked as a man wearing simple brown clothes swung a steel sword at him. With ease, Prost dodged it by twisting his upper body before jabbing his short sword through the man's midsection. Sticking his foot out, he kicked him off his sword and looked to the center of the square. People were panicking and running in all directions. Likely, most of them had only heard rumors of Light powers such as these. Lightbearers had been in hiding for so long that he was sure this would cause all sorts of political ruckus.

Riln is going to be angry, Prost thought, chills running through his body at the thought.

The fact remained that his master couldn't hurt him through Lightbearing, but the man's anger still made Prost uncomfortable. When he thought about Riln's anger, Prost's scars itched as if they felt the blade entering his flesh again.

A flash of blue warned of a Light weapon coming at his face. As he'd practiced many times, he let the sword hit him. The blade passed through him without effect. The owner of the sword looked shocked, her eyes wide before he easily cut her down.

"Prost!" a voice yelled to him.

Turning, he saw a shorter woman with dark skin and pitch black hair. She glared at him, her hands at the ready. Prost thought he'd seen her before in one of his past encounters with Evenir. Having never engaged in combat, they didn't know each other, but she obviously knew *of* him. He smiled at her menacingly. The idea that his reputation preceded him was pleasing to him. It wasn't altogether surprising, but still pleasing.

"I don't believe we've met, have we?" Prost said, casually teasing her.

The woman looked annoyed at his question. Rather than reply, she growled and brought her right hand to the side. One of his men battling there glowed with a blue Light before he was thrown directly at Prost. Grunting, Prost shifted sideways to avoid being slammed by the flying man. The man barely missed Prost and slammed into the ground, crumpling from the blow.

"Angry now, are we? Upset that your powers are useless on me?" Prost spat at her.

With a measured look, the woman picked up some cart debris with her powers and Moved them directly at him. He dodged them easily and was about to say something else to her when he noted her left hand pulling back toward her. His eyes shot up when he recognized the motion and he tried to jump sideways. It was too late; she was pulling the now-unconscious man directly into his back. Prost grunted as she slammed the full weight of the heavy man into him from behind. Using the momentum, he fell to his knees and let the body fly over him. The woman easily stopped her Moving, and the body fell back to the ground.

"That's a bit brute, don't you think?" Prost said, annoyed.

"Well, I have to get creative now, don't I? Voidbearer."

Prost's skin chilled at the term. Not once had he or Riln shared that term with anyone in Watchlight. Of the numerous times he'd fought Evenir men and women, never once had he been called 'Voidbearer'. It meant she knew something about the Seal—about the balance. He clenched his jaw and stood up. Knowing he and Riln had betrayed the blessing of Lanser left a somewhat raw spot for him. He hated that he was the one cursed to know of Lightbearing's purpose, only to be loathed by the wielders of it.

"Why did you call me that?" Prost yelled, anger boiling in him.

She smiled, looking pleased with herself.

"I see I've hit a sensitive spot, hmm?"

A Watchlight man suddenly came screaming at her, his sword raised. As he barreled toward her, she kept her eyes on Prost and held her hand out. The man froze, body glowing with blue Light. With a flick of her hand, he went flying back into the wall of the building just next to them, his back slamming hard into the brick there. With a quick motion, the woman Moved the man's own sword downward, still in his hands, so it pierced his midsection. His body stopped glowing and he fell to the ground, a shocked expression on his face.

"You can call me Alsry, love."

A smile spread on Prost's face as he recognized a worthy opponent.

"I will call you whatever I fog well want, wench," Prost spat.

With a small roar, he lunged at her with his sword. She made to Move the sword out of his hand, but her powers didn't work as she expected. Prost didn't understand it himself, but for some reason, anything he held in his hands became immune to the Light, just like his person. It had nothing to do with what he touched in general, for if that were true, Riln couldn't incinerate his clothes when he threw Destroying orbs at him, or even Destroyed his clothes directly.

The woman's face gave away some slight surprise before she composed herself and dodged his swing. Whipping out two short swords of her own, she slashed them forward, forcing Prost to step back to avoid one while parrying the other. Prost felt the thrill of an evenly matched fight. Lightbearers often got cocky with their powers and never learned combat. This woman was another exception.

At this thought, he considered whether Avryn would be among their ranks. Part of him still wanted to best his old friend with the sword while the other part dreaded the idea. They had too many memories together for Prost to feel good about killing him. He suspected Avryn felt the same, for when they'd fought before, each one had not taken advantage of moments when they'd been able to kill the other.

His thoughts flashed back as quickly when the woman flung another piece of debris at him. The large wheel of one of the exploded carts flew right at his head, forcing him to duck again. More pieces of the cart flew at him, one after the other. The woman's hands worked furiously to throw things at him, and his reflexes were being pushed to their limits in order to avoid each object. A grunt behind him announced some debris colliding with a body. He spun through the next volley to see who it was. A man wearing a brown cloak was apparently trying to sneak up on him before a cart plank had smacked him in the face.

Prost almost laughed at the irony of it.

"You'd better be careful what you are throwing, my dear," he said patronizingly, "It seems you are far more effective at hitting your own men than me."

She looked annoyed at his comment, but her eyes still smoldered with determination.

"Perhaps we should up the stakes, then."

The swords which she had sheathed before her last onslaught glowed blue before flying from their scabbards. She directed them at Prost with speed. Prost flipped his own sword up and parried the swords as they flew at him. One twisted at his left side while the other targeted his head on the right. He ducked and lifted his blade to parry the other. Inside, Prost marveled at the woman's control. She appeared a bit older than him, and given that Lightbearers awakened in their early teen years, she'd likely had a lot of practice.

Unfortunately for her, Prost was well practiced at fighting two swordsmen at the same time. The only difference was that he couldn't kill one to relieve the pressure. Instead, the pressure was constant. As he ducked, twisted, and parried the blades, he knew his energy would run out if he couldn't neutralize the woman controlling the operation.

He dodged a few more blows before he turned at an unnatural angle to swipe one of the blades away behind him. The motion caused his side to ache from the exertion, but it had the intended effect. The blade spun away from the strength of his blow. This allowed him a small break, so he fluidly pulled out his loaded crossbow. She'd used her powers to seize the blade he'd knocked behind him, and was pulling it back toward Prost. Sword still in hand, he managed to take aim and let the bolt fly at the woman. Her eyes widened, realizing the danger. Despite that, she managed to shift sideways just enough that the bolt didn't enter her shoulder completely. Instead, the bolt barely pierced her arm, pushing right through her flesh.

Gasping in pain, her hold on the sword closest to Prost faltered. He whacked the blade away, seeing the Light fade slightly as her attention was distracted. Rather than pull it back, she let it fly away and put her hand to her arm. Prost watched as blue Light pulsed under her hand, intensifying, then quickly disappearing. When she removed her hand, the wound was healed completely.

Fog it. Of course she's a Fixer, too, Prost thought, gritting his teeth.

The sword to his left flipped back at him and he continued to fight with it, angling his body so that he could still see the other sword lying dormant. She didn't grab it, but instead began to throw debris at him from all directions.

Disappointed that his ploy had failed, he considered his other options. He had been forced to drop his crossbow to keep up with the blows of the sword. That didn't matter, because he wouldn't be able to nock another bolt with her barraging him like this. A thought flashed in his mind, and he knew it was likely the best option.

Prost continued to dodge the debris and the sword while slowly advancing his position toward her. With her brow knit in determination, she took a step back here and there, trying to keep away from him. He was moving faster, however, his work required less focus than her own. She was running out of debris and was forced to reuse what she could. She ended up having to pull objects from further away, which took more time and effort on her part.

He knew that there was one thing the woman wasn't expecting, and he needed to catch her off guard with it. Fortunately, he soon reached a few paces from her. Prost could feel his body slowly growing tired and didn't want to let it get worse.

The sword battled him from the left, the debris flying in from the right. Rather than blocking the next sword swing, he turned and snatched the sword from the air with his hand. As he expected, the moment he grabbed the blade, the Light controlling it faded immediately, and she lost power over the sword. Prost's palm burst with pain from grabbing the sharp blade.

A shocked expression flashed on her face, but it was too late. He dove for her, hand now bleeding profusely, and slashed with his own sword. Her reaction was fast, but not fast enough. Prost's blade was headed right for her midsection.

Just before his sword could enter her flesh, his eyes spotted movement to his left. Reacting, he grunted and tried to dodge a small projectile coming at him from afar. His last-minute evasion allowed him to narrowly miss what he could now see was a small dagger. Unfortunately, it meant his sword flew off course, missing his opponent completely.

Growling, Prost looked in the direction of the flying dagger.

Fog it, he thought at the missed opportunity. Inside, a combination of dread and thrill flourished when he saw who had thrown the knife. Without any surprise, his eyes fell on Janis, standing across the square on the other side of the statue.

It was only a matter of time before the assassin would show up.

Janis stood confidently across the way, staring at him with amusement in her eyes. She looked gruesome, as blood dripped down the side of her face where she'd been wounded. Blood also dripped slowly down her right hand, the stones wetting below her.

Prost made out a small crowd just to her right that had gathered next to a few bodies lying on the ground. The bodies wore Watchlight black.

So, she got the better of one of our groups, hmm? Prost thought, *It won't be without consequence.*

He watched as members of the group started pointing at Janis with angry expressions.

"Alsry!" Janis yelled across the way, "The boy!"

Prost turned to see the woman he'd been fighting. She had Fixed her injuries, but looked very depleted from their fight. Prost could tell that he had more in him, and confidence filled him at the revelation.

"Leave Prost to me! Get the boy!" Janis shouted, running toward Prost.

For a moment, Prost didn't understand what she yelled, but her words reminded him of the awakening that they had come for.

"Alts! Jord! Get the boy, *now!*"

Alts, fighting another female Conjurer with blue Light daggers, distracted her opponent with a well-placed but miniscule Destroying orb at the woman's feet. The cobblestones exploded with debris and dust, making the woman jump back. Alts turned and rushed to the other side of the square where the Seers had told them the boy would come.

Jord was preoccupied, and must not have heard his command. Either that, or he completely ignored Prost altogether. The hood of his cloak had fallen backward, exposing his buzzed head and the dead look in his eyes. One by one, he flung perfectly placed Destroying orbs, sometimes into the walls of buildings or into the ground. Right as Prost watched, he saw an orb collide with a man's arm, exploding it to pieces.

Prost's gut twisted at the sight. He was no stranger to blood and death, but the scenes caused by Destroying were still enough to unnerve him.

After Moving her remaining sword away from Prost and into her hand, Alsry had turned and rushed in the same direction as Alts. Prost hadn't realized it, but his left hand still clutched her other sword by the blade, cutting into his palm as he held it tightly. Cursing at his distraction, he flipped it over in his hand, catching the handle. The wetness of his bloody palm threatened his grip, but he held tight. Looking around, he found the eyes of the black-clad assassin.

Her hand moved to her face, a blue glow just disappearing from under her palm. Prost glared at her when he realized that she was Fixing the wound there. Blood no longer trailed down her cheek. Curiously, however, he noted that her hand still bled, dripping on the stones.

Shouts and clashing steel sounded behind him as he and Janis both readied themselves for a fight.

So it's true then, he thought, *could she really be Tar'n Yiv'len like Riln?*

Despite her amused look, Prost saw something else there. A reservation, something he hadn't seen before. The fact that she hadn't Fixed her hand and didn't hold a Conjured weapon of any sort made him wonder what state her powers were in. He recalled hearing about when Riln had first gained his powers. It had taken weeks, almost months for him to gain full use of them.

It mattered very little in this case, for he was unaffected by the Light, and Janis knew it.

"Shall we begin, then?" Prost said, knowing that even with the ruckus around them, she'd be able to hear him.

Janis nodded, then rushed toward him.

SEEING Prost with his hand bleeding was somewhat satisfying to Janis. It was satisfying to see such an arrogant man injured in battle, and her only regret was that it was Alsry and not herself who'd done it. As she ran toward Prost, she glanced to her side, where Alsry engaged the long-haired blonde woman.

Janis thought back to her fight with the same woman at the falls ages ago and hoped Alsry was good enough to stay alive.

Focusing back on Prost, she made inventory of his movements, his injuries, and his attention. He looked completely energized and unaffected by anything, save for the cut on his palm, which dripped down the sword he held in his hand. Janis hadn't yet seen him fight with two swords, so she ran through the differences to account for in this engagement. She'd have to split her focus differently to ensure she could block each of his blows with the two swords.

Just before she got to him, however, he lifted the tip of the sword and flung it away from him, the sword clattering to the stones nearer the statue in the center of the square.

Or not, I suppose—Janis thought, *at least that takes out the other variable.*

Raising her long dagger above her head, she jumped and pulled the blade downward, aiming for his head. He effortlessly blocked the swing with his own sword. Anticipating this, Janis kicked outward with her foot toward his chest. He managed to swat her foot to the side with his free hand. With the momentum, she spun around and aimed her dagger at his midsection, which he avoided by jumping backward.

"This time you won't have an awakening to keep you alive," Prost hissed at her.

She glowered at him, taking his own words and using them to her advantage. She summoned a ball of Light and put everything that she mentally could into it. As of yet, she hadn't been able to Conjure or create any Light that did what she wanted it to, but that didn't matter. All she needed was the brightness. As the Light flashed into life, he squinted his eyes at the intensity and yelled, swiping his blade around. Janis dodged his sword and let the orb fall to the ground. It snuffed into nothing there.

And that *is why I don't try Lightbearing more,* she thought, noting the unreliable nature of the orbs she'd tried summoning before. If it *had* been a Destroying orb, it might have helped by distracting him.

Prost blinked quickly, his vision likely swimming with some spots while Janis repositioned, trying to get behind him.

"Your tricks will only delay your death, assassin," he growled, his sight apparently returned as he spun on her and stared her down.

Diving at her, Prost tried to skewer her stomach, but she easily danced away. Flashes of blue and red Light continued everywhere, the fighting getting more desperate as the sun started to set. Janis and Prost continued to whirl around each other, trying to get the advantage. Her hand still stung from the roof debris earlier, and some of her blood was flicking around as she blocked her opponent's blows.

Faster than Prost, Janis ran some distance while stealing a glance to the other side of the square where Alsry was lobbing various glowing objects toward Alts. Alsry's attacks were proving only a distraction to Alts, for she easily evaded them, one by one. Alts quickly flung a red dagger at Alsry, which the latter deftly dodged. Neither woman was getting the upper hand at the moment.

I might think that was a beautiful scene if I didn't know otherwise.

Her moment spent, Janis felt Prost approaching heavily behind her and she turned just in time to block his sword with her own long dagger. Three quick blows followed, his sword flashing in all directions, adrenaline likely ruling his movements. Unfortunately for him, Janis was used to this type of combat as well, so she easily blocked and parried each of the blows.

Prost didn't look *mad* per se, but he was determined. Something in him was more determined than he had been when they'd last met. Something in him was off.

Janis jumped backward, giving herself some distance from him. She summoned another bright ball of blue Light, hoping to blind him again, but he knew this trick and wouldn't fall for it again. Rather than looking at the Light in her hand, he averted his eyes and flicked his sword toward the Light orb in her outstretched palm. She was forced to let it go. It fell to the ground and exploded, debris and dust blowing everywhere. The force of the blow rocked Janis off balance and she redirected her body to soften the blow of her fall. Rolling through the momentum, she came back to her feet.

There was a new look in Prost's eyes now. It was subtle and quick, but was that—

Fear? Janis thought, *That's unexpected.*

PROST SHOOK off the stinging from the rocks that had just blown from the ground. He glared at Janis, annoyed at the fear that blossomed in his chest. Up until this point, Lightbearing had proven non-threatening. Seeing this woman brought back the unfortunate memory of how her own awakening had affected him.

He shook the memory off. That feeling of being thrown through the air without being able to do anything about it was just wrong. No one liked feeling weak or out of control, but her awakening had been the first thing in a long time—besides Riln himself—that made him lose his confidence.

He knew that he couldn't let the assassin see it. That's how they worked, exploiting whatever weakness they could and using it to their advantage.

Prost wasn't exempt from that method, but he knew assassins were annoyingly skilled at it, and he didn't want her to get any advantage.

Just as he thought it, he noticed her eyes narrow as if she noticed something.

Fog it, she knows, Prost thought.

With a curious look, Janis Conjured a small dagger. It wasn't perfectly formed; the pommel and the blade appeared fuzzy as if she couldn't quite get the concept together, but it would likely be as lethal as a normal blade. At least, to someone who wasn't immune.

He had a sinking feeling knowing that her Light had hurt him before. Shaking his head, he rushed forward, his blade coming quickly toward her.

She blocked with her steel blade and swung her Light dagger at his head. His instincts fought each other in that moment. For years, he'd trained against his soldier instincts to treat everything as a threat, as Lightbearing hadn't ever been one. Precious moments were lost in fights until he got used to ignoring the reflexes to dodge Lightbearing.

But then, there had been their last encounter.

A new instinct shoved its way into his brain, held up by his experience of being hit by her awakening Light.

Despite the warring instincts, Prost stood his ground, opting to let her roughly Conjured dagger slam into his face. The sharp edge connected with his face and went through without harm, her fist smacking his head instead.

Relief blossomed in his chest and stomach. He shoved his free hand out, taking advantage of Janis's close proximity. His palm slammed into her gut and she grunted, body pushed back. Rather than fall to the ground, however, she just winced and stumbled slightly back before regaining her balance.

Her brow knit in confusion. She was clearly putting some pieces together, though which ones, he couldn't tell.

While Janis recovered from his direct blow, Prost's gaze flashed left to where Alts fought Alsry. He could see blood on the dark-skinned opponent he'd fought just before, and felt a bit of pride at Alts's abilities. Turning his gaze to his ally, he saw Alts had bruises on her face and arms from glancing blows caused by the debris Alsry had been Moving at her.

Movement from the corner near the fighting women caught his eye. A young boy, perhaps eleven or twelve, stepped into the square holding a basket of bread. Seeing the commotion in the square, he stopped and stared, eyes wide.

There he is, Fog it! Prost thought.

"Alsry! There he is!" Janis shouted to her friend.

Cursing, Prost took a gamble and lobbed his sword at Janis. She hadn't expected this. Gasping, she jumped backward to avoid the large sword flying end over end toward her. Just as the sword left his hand, Prost barreled toward the two women. While he ran, he scooped up his crossbow, quickly loaded a bolt, and shot it directly at Alsry's neck.

Almost in slow motion, the bolt flew toward the woman's neck. Just before the bolt could connect, it glowed blue and was pushed aside just enough to only graze her, a shallow cut opening there.

Quickly, the dark woman shoved her hand out, causing Alts's body to glow blue and fly down the street. But the dark Mover woman had carried Alts too far, losing control. The blue glow left Alts's body, and she managed to soften the blow by landing awkwardly on her hands and knees. Grunting, she jumped back up to her feet.

Prost was in the process of nocking another bolt when Alts shouted something at him.

It took a moment for him to understand the words, but he turned to see his own sword glowing blue and flying directly at him, not end over end as if it was thrown by a hand, but like a spear instead, moving straight and true. Prost immediately abandoned his plan, dropping the bolt he'd just pulled out. Instead, he watched the blade, gaze measured, before grabbing the blade from mid-air as he'd done before.

The moment his hand connected with the blade, the blue Light faded, but a force hit his body, unseen and unexpected, knocking him backward. He fell to the ground, his other hand bleeding now that he'd used it to intercept another sword.

What in Ugglyn's name?

The uneasiness in his gut returned.

～

Janis felt a thrill fill her.

Was that Light I just saw around Prost?

It had happened so fast, it was almost imperceptible. Not having control over her supposed Prime powers was frustrating for her. She'd thrown the sword at Prost just to distract him from shooting Alsry through with his crossbow, but just as she had let go of the handle, it had glowed blue with Light. Though completely unintentional, it had worked to her advantage.

Janis knew that she'd Moved it toward him, but she didn't know how. When he touched it, the Light faded in the sword, but it had transferred to him somehow.

The look on Prost's face was a combination of disbelief, anger, and a little fear. His body hadn't been Moved far, more like a light shove from a person standing next to him, but the implications were far more grave. He was supposed to be the Voidbearer, immune to all Lightbearing, but the Light had worked on him.

Two sets of movement behind Prost made her shift her gaze there. First, she noted the boy who would soon awaken. He turned on his heels and ran back around the corner. The other movement was not far from where the boy just stood. Her hair stood on end when she saw it was another of the Void forms that had plagued them in Terris Green, though this one looked more smoke-like, as if it struggled to exist.

Prost noticed her eyes flicker behind him, and he turned his own head momentarily to see what she was looking at. His brow furrowed as he turned back to her. He looked confused, as if he couldn't see anything.

Immediately, the form flowed ominously toward Alsry. It left a trail of silvery black liquid on the cobblestones behind it.

Janis felt panic rising in her chest. Only she and Avryn had been able to reliably get rid of them in Terris Green, and Avryn wasn't here.

"Alsry!" Janis managed to shout.

It was all that she could manage, however, since Prost had flipped the sword he'd caught and was now rushing at her. Janis side-stepped out of his swing and went to dig her own dagger into his side. He spun out of the path of her blade and attacked again. He was so fast that Janis didn't have time to dodge this one, instead having to use her own dagger to deflect his swing. Pain lanced up her arm as the blades connected and she almost lost the grip of her own weapon. His sword edge skimmed the ground where she'd redirected the momentum with her block.

The maneuver had put Janis's back toward Alsry, Prost now facing her. Rather than wait for Prost to regain his composure after her artful block, she spun on her heels and sprinted in Alsry's direction, who was now dodging more Conjures being thrown at her from Alts. The form seeped slowly but surely, and was only a man's height away from her.

"Alsry, behind you!" Janis shouted again, out of breath but desperate to alert her comrade.

The company leader dodged another dagger made of red Light before turning her head to see what Janis was shouting about. Just as she did, Alts took advantage of it and lobbed another Light dagger right at her. Brow furrowed in confusion, Alsry passed her gaze across to a galloping Janis, her face questioning before looking back at her opponent and a dagger coming at her. Gasping, she shifted to the right just enough that the dagger flew right into her forearm. She dropped to the ground then, panting. Her dark forehead was beaded with large drops of sweat and she looked haggard, as if she might pass out from exhaustion at any moment.

The form inched closer behind Alsry and Janis saw another flash of red in her left peripheral vision as she ran across the cobblestones, nearing the two women in combat. Alts had summoned a bow and arrow and was aiming right for Alsry. She let the arrow loose and Janis did all that she could think of—she pushed her hands out in front of her. Alsry's body glowed blue and she was flung ten paces away. The Light arrow, aimed true, collided perfectly with the evil form. The red arrow sliced right through its center and an unholy high-pitched screech rang through Janis's ears. She winced at the sound, but rushed to close the gap between her and Alsry. Footsteps pounded behind her and she knew that Prost was not too far behind. She could do better once she reached Alsry and they could fight back to back.

In a flash, she assessed her threats. Alts to her left, the Void form to her right, and Prost behind her.

Fog, this isn't going well.

Alsry moved to pull the Light dagger from her body when it snuffed into the air. A blue glow announced her Fixing of her wound. It was a deep cut, and Janis figured it would take time, considering how tired Alsry was. Knowing that the Void beast, though more terrifying, was a lot slower than Prost and Alts, she opted to neutralize them first. Gripping her last dagger firmly, she spun around and flung it at the approaching Prost. He growled and dove to the side to avoid being skewered. Taking the brief moment this bought her, Janis unstrung the pouch of powder and with a grunt threw the whole thing at Alts. The blonde woman had just summoned another arrow and was about to shoot Alsry when the pouch slammed into her chest and exploded, powder flying everywhere. The Conjured weapon disappeared as she fell immediately to the ground, unconscious.

Janis was out of daggers now, and she felt naked.

She could hear that Prost was up and hot on her heels now. Assessing the situation with the Void form, she noted that it still crept toward Alsry, who wasn't paying it any attention.

Why isn't she getting away? Janis thought, exasperated.

Another thought struck her. *It's as if she can't see the Void beast at all.* Prost had looked equally confused when she'd spied it behind him earlier.

If she truly was the only one who could see it, then she had to do something. She scrambled to put her hands together.

Let me create a Destroying orb, a Lightbearing orb—fog, even a Conjure. Blue Light flashed in her hand, but quickly disappeared.

Prost was almost on top of her, and she spun to see his sword coming at her head. She ducked and felt the air whoosh around her hair. Without any weapons, she clenched her fist and shoved it right into Prost's stomach, pushing with all her might. He took it with a grunt, the air rushing from his lungs in a heavy gasp.

It was just enough for Janis to jump out of his reach again. He shook his head and spit on the ground.

"What's wrong, *Janis?* Out of knives?" Prost taunted.

Opening her hand, she focused hard on Conjuring something and managed to create the rough form of a blue dagger. His eyes glared at her.

"That won't work on me," he said. Though he tried to sound confident, there was doubt in his tone.

It's not much, but it's all I have.

"Then why don't we test that theory?"

Janis Conjured another dagger of Light in her other hand and lobbed them right at him. Prost's face hardened as he clearly debated whether to let them hit him or dodge. While he was distracted with this inner conflict, Janis focused as hard as she could on something else. With a bright flash of Light, a giant orb of Light appeared in her hand. Just as the daggers flew harmlessly through Prost's shoulder and side respectively, he looked up and growled as the flash of Light blinded him.

Janis, eyes squinting from her Light, could barely see Prost covering his face from the brightness. Taking advantage once again of his hesitation, she turned and threw the large orb at the Void form.

Somehow, she knew that it wasn't a Destroying orb, yet it appeared equally as effective. The large orb connected with the dark form and it let out another loud and long screech before melting into the ground. The dark ooze pools left in its path also disappeared. Alsry didn't even seem to notice.

"The Capital troops are here! Run!"

Sure enough, down the streets leading from the square marched even rows of soldiers, spears in hand, full armor covering their bodies.

Fog it! We need to leave!

Janis thanked Lanser that the troops hadn't come until now.

"Evenir, retreat! Get out of the city, *now!*" Alsry shouted.

Men and women in brown scattered at the words, some flying up ropes dangling from building walls, some down empty alleyways. Black-clad Watchlight operatives followed their lead and fled the large army headed toward the square. Helping Alsry up, the two women shared a look and understanding flashed on their faces. Both of them raced down the street after the boy who would be awakening any moment now. As they turned the corner, they ran straight until there was a crossroads.

"Lanser's beard, where is a Seer when you need one?" Alsry said, breathless.

"Wait," Janis thought, hoping her theory would be right. She glanced up, looking for Light, noting that the sun was at exactly the right place from her vision. To their right, a flash of brilliant blue Light flicked around the corner.

"There!" Janis said, running toward it.

Her body was tired now, and her hand still stung from where it bled. Alsry was panting next to her and she could see in the woman's eyes that she didn't have much left in her either. Despite the Fixing she'd been able to manage, it was draining energy from her with each use.

The two women turned the corner to see the boy kneeling on the ground. The stones around him all glowed blue and were being changed, Fixing themselves to their perfect state. The wooden walls of the buildings around him were sprouting branches and leaves, as if they were turning back into the trees from whence they came.

"We'll need to grab him. This awakening isn't dangerous like that of a Mover or a Destroyer." Alsry said.

Janis nodded, and moved closer to the boy. He was oblivious to the world around him. After a few paces, Janis stopped when a flash of black came from above, a new figure landing just behind the boy.

The Light was fading now from the awakening, and the boy's eyes began to roll back in his head. After a moment, he fell to the ground. Pounding feet and a huff behind them announced Prost trailing in their wake.

Janis and Alsry watched as the strange black-cloaked man smiled at them, his face menacing. Though shadowed from his pulled-up hood, Janis could see the wicked smile under a sharp nose and two dark eyes. Pulling a knife from his belt, he held it up so that they could clearly see it. Janis jumped forward, grasping at her now empty belt, cursing when she found nothing there. When she looked up, her skin crawled.

The blade the man was holding was *moving*.

No, when she looked closer, she noted that the blade itself wasn't moving, it was covered in silvery-black liquid which appeared to be writhing up and down the steel. The substance looked identical to the odd Void form she'd just blown up only moments ago.

With his teeth still bared, the man shoved the blade of the knife into the unconscious boy's side, his eyes flying open, a gasp sucking in through his mouth. The man dropped the boy and then jumped backward, seeing that Janis was close.

"Alsry! Fix him!" Janis yelled backward, not bothering to turn her head. She dashed after the cloaked man as he spun and barreled toward the next turn. Pausing for just a moment, she readied herself for an ambush. The hooded man could easily have stopped just around the bend. When she moved around, however, she saw that he had not, but was running down the narrow alleyway. Janis pursued the man as fast as she could.

It wasn't long before she could see that the alley ended with a wall. The man was trapped.

Right as she had this thought, the man jumped against one wall, his foot on the narrow trim jutting out. He pushed himself off the trim there to higher trim on the neighboring building, then back to the first. In moments, he'd jumped himself up high enough to grab the lip of the roof and hoist himself over.

Janis wasn't overly surprised to see him do this; she'd been forced to perform similar maneuvers before. For a moment, she thought to follow his lead and jump up, but then she remembered Prost and Alsry back with the stabbed Fixer boy.

"'Ey!" a voice called from above.

"Luden says 'ello, luv," the man said from the roof above. Then he was gone.

Her mind reeled at the words.

That wasn't someone from Watchlight.

She didn't have time to fully process what it meant. Instead, she spun on her heels and ran back to the street where the boy had been stabbed. Just as she turned, she thought she'd see Prost and Alsry fighting, but Prost was gone.

"The coward split the moment he saw the boy take a knife. I guess he figured he'd be useless on this one."

Alsry had a concentrated look on her face as she held her hands over the stab wound on the boy. Sweat still beaded her brow and she looked exhausted.

"Why aren't you done? Isn't Fixing normally fast?" Janis said, an annoyed tone in her voice.

Alsry shot her a look.

"Normally, yes, but I've taken quite a beating, in case you haven't noticed."

Just as she said it, she spat to the side, a bit of blood in her spittle.

The street around them was quiet, commotions finally dying down in the square behind them. With any luck, the other Evenir men and women would have fled from the soldiers and headed back outside the walls to where their horses were waiting. They'd hoped to stay the night, but given the fight they'd just had, there was no chance they could find a place private enough to hide from the soldiers.

Janis looked at Alsry and furrowed her brow.

"Something—" Alsry said, straining, "—something is pushing back."

Looking more closely at the wound, Janis could see black veins running up the skin from the wound. She moved in and ripped away the boy's shirt. He was still unconscious and couldn't protest. He was still a boy, his chest small, but growing from adolescence. Veins of dark silver-black were spreading slowly up his skin.

"I'm not sure what's happening, but my Fixing isn't taking," Alsry groaned.

She looked like she would pass out at any moment.

Janis looked at the boy, his face suddenly reminding her of Marric. They didn't really look anything alike, but his youthful features were enough to make her think of him.

Fog it all, what is happening?

She looked at Alsry and saw the woman was losing consciousness. She'd spent herself too much with the last battle.

"We need a fresher Fixer, where can I find one?" Janis asked, annoyed that they were alone.

"Can't—no—time," Alsry gasped.

With those words, she passed out, her body collapsing to the ground. She didn't have external gashes or cuts, but she'd fought long and hard with Prost and Alts, then had to Fix herself numerous times. Her energy was lost.

Janis panicked slightly. She didn't know why. It wasn't like she had an attachment to this boy. His life being lost hadn't necessarily even been her fault. But there was something else.

If I'm supposed to be this fogging Prime or whatever, Lanser, this better work.

Concentrating, Janis put her hand over the wound, the warmth of the blood on her palm. Since Alsry had passed out, the veins of dark silver were moving up and down his body even more quickly. The boy was panting now, still unconscious and clearly dying.

Come on, come on! Janis thought.

Anger boiled inside as she watched the veins move into his neck. For a brief moment, a blue Light burst in through her hand, entering the knife wound. The skin began to knit together there, even some of the silver-black veins disappeared a handspan above where the cut had been only moments before.

Then the boy's chest fell and didn't rise again.

The Light in Janis's hands faded and she sat there, shocked.

"FOG IT!" Janis yelled, anger bursting inside.

He was gone, and she hadn't been able to do anything about it. If she was supposed to gather these new Lightbearers, if she was to build an army for Lanser, how could she if her powers did nothing?

Turning, she noted that Alsry's chest was rising and falling still, an indication of her retained life. Knowing that their time was short before the soldiers caught up with them, she reached down and hefted the unconscious woman over her shoulder with a grunt.

Time to get my best dagger and get out of here, Janis thought, moving as fast as she could back to the square.

18

The forest around them was beginning to lighten with the rising sun, but Marric couldn't afford to focus on that right now. Avryn and Turrin had just charged the cloaked men standing on the other side of his father, Narim's unconscious form still on the ground. The group had blasted their whole way through the forest, their horses running as fast as they could through it all, but they'd made it just in time.

Panting, Marric shivered slightly at the destruction that lay behind them.

Marric still panted from nerves after the journey they'd just taken through the forest. He felt that he might be jumpy for a few hours if not longer after having to hear explosions and be pelted with debris from the exploding trees and shrubs. Marric scarcely had time to even consider recovering from the adrenaline of the journey when Avryn and Turrin had charged into battle with the three black-cloaked figures, only moments before Gila had blocked a dagger from slicing through her horse's leg with her Shield. The two of them, plus the non-Lightbearers, still were encompassed within the Shield.

Marric sat atop his horse, a Conjured bow-and-arrow in his hands. He watched Avryn spin his Light blade in the air, colliding with the steel of the enemy fighters. They'd only just begun, and Marric thought to drop one with a well-placed arrow. Gila had warned him not to, and he could see why.

He wasn't as skilled with the bow as he would need to be in order to not hit Turrin or Avryn. Each was moving so quickly with their swords that Marric likely would be more a hindrance than a help with his weapon.

"Get your father, Mar. I'll cover you. Go!"

Marric was aware of what she said, but for some reason it felt like she was talking to someone else, not him.

"GO!" she said more forcefully.

Snapping to attention, Marric dismounted, his bow and arrow flashing away into the air. Just as she said, her Shield expanded out as Marric moved cautiously forward toward his father's body. He moved slower than he normally might for fear of touching Gila's translucent Shield. He'd never thought about what it would feel like to touch it, but he didn't want to take the chance.

"More in the woods!" Avryn suddenly shouted. Marric's head snapped up at the fighting men just in time to see arrows flying in from the surrounding forest. Avryn threw up a small Shield, an arrow piercing through it easily, but getting deflected so it missed his head by a hair. Turrin, not as quick to see them coming, took an arrow to his shoulder while one grazed his leg.

Yelling loudly, Turrin spun on one of the men and came at him with brute force. The smaller man blocked Turrin's Light sword, but the burly Conjurer was much stronger. When the swords collided, the small man's arms buckled under him and Turrin took the moment of imbalance to swipe his leg from under him. In a flash, he dug the Light sword into the man's gut and pulled it free, blood dripping from the blue weapon.

The former of the three figures had lost his hood, his oily black hair reflecting the blue Lights of their Conjures.

"FIRE!" he shouted, just before another volley of arrows came flying at the men. The Shield around Marric and the others snuffed away and appeared around Avryn and Turrin. The arrows thudded against the Shield harmlessly, some bouncing in his direction.

It was then that Marric realized he'd stopped to watch, mesmerized.

Wind whistled just passed his ear and his hair stood on end knowing that the arrow just missed him.

"Marric, fall back!" Gila shouted, her Shield appearing around him again just as a rain of arrows fell around. The archers in the woods saw her Shielding pattern now, and they appeared to be firing in halves, some at Turrin and Avryn, some at the others. Marric wanted to listen, but his father was only fifteen paces away. Gila's Shield snuffed away and appeared back and forth around the two leaders of their group and the others, the woman trying desperately to Shield them all while Avryn and Turrin fought the two sworded men.

Seeing the pattern himself, Marric waited until the Shield snuffed away. Then he dashed toward his father.

"Marric!" Gila gasped behind him before she was forced again to focus on her Shielding tactics. Avryn had taken an arrow in his side, but Marric also noticed that the one of the black-cloaked men had too, right through the thigh. This made him feel better about deciding not to fire his bow. Gila's Shield sprang to life behind him, and he knew that he was outside of its reach now.

I've got to hurry! he thought as he rushed the last few paces. He crouched by his father's body and shook the man vigorously.

"Pa! Wake up!"

Nothing.

Marric's stomach sank as he thought they were too late. Before the sorrow could fully hit him, his father groaned loudly.

"Pa! You're—"

Loud footfalls pounded in front of Marric and he looked up to see a cloaked woman, short brown hair and a large nose, baring her teeth at him. She ran with her bow pulled back and Marric's eyes went wide when he realized what she was doing. Instinctively, Marric threw his hands outward at the woman. Her eyes widened when she glowed blue and was thrown backward twenty paces. This made her release her arrow, however, and it flew right through Marric's shoulder. Gasping from the pain, Marric felt tears well in his eyes. Adrenaline coursed through his veins, however, and he remained focused on the woman who lay on the ground. She was not moving, and Marric thought he'd knocked her unconscious.

Standing up now, Marric flinched as two more arrows from the forest zipped past his body. Cursing, he focused on his father and continued moving forward.

Marric ducked down as more arrows flew around them, Gila still performing her Shield acrobatics to try to block them all. Turning to her, he saw that their non-Lightbearer soldiers had drawn their own weapons. Two moved into the lightening forest while two others shot volleys blindly from their crossbows.

Without the sun fully extended, they wouldn't be able to hit any of their enemies without sheer luck.

Turrin and Avryn had managed to down another of the enemies, this one a woman. The leader of the group who had thrown the first dagger at Avryn still fought. With a shout, two more figures came from the dark forest around them.

How many of them are there? Marric thought, fear gripping him again.

His father was still unresponsive, other than some groans. He knew that he would not be able to pick up the old man, at least not without being hit with the arrows flying around them, so he opted to try something else. Conjuring his own bow and arrow, he nocked the arrow, aimed into the forest, and let it fly.

The arrow's Light flashed through the trees, shadows flickering around as it passed the trees and shrubs. Realizing now how he could help, he Conjured arrow after arrow, nocking them and shooting them into the forest at different angles. His Conjured arrows didn't make it far, but it was enough to give their allies a little Light. A curse came from one of his shots as a figure had to dodge it. Other shouts were likely from surprise at the blinding arrows now being thrown at them.

A thud sounded from the forest as a bolt from one of Evenir's men found its mark now that they could see through the intermittent flashes. Pride flared in Marric's chest as he felt useful for the first time since he'd been with Avryn and his companions.

"Yeh crafty little git," a voice came from behind him.

Body locking from fright, Marric spun to see a man barreling toward him, a sword outstretched.

Yelping, Marric pushed his hand out and the man grunted as he was lifted off his feet a handspan. Marric hadn't had time to put much into the Move, so the man only stumbled backward. Recovering quickly, he swiped his sword through the air at Marric, almost cleaving off his arm.

Marric's bow and arrow snuffed away and a sword appeared. Dread filled him as he remembered that he had little sword training. Turrin had only just begun to teach him the simple moves last week.

The black-clad figure, face handsome and young, narrowed his eyes at Marric. He was blond and couldn't be more than three years Marric's elder.

"Let's see 'ow yeh do wif tha' fancy sword, eh?" he rasped out.

Marric's stomach clenched as the man came at him with his sword. Instinctively, Marric parried the first blow and dodged the second before the man's blade skimmed Marric's cheek.

A stinging sprouted there, making Marric suck in a breath. Resisting the temptation to reach up and feel it, he swung his sword wide at the man. This made him chuckle.

"Ah, so yeh ain't as good wif the sword as the bow, eh?"

The dread spread in his body as Marric knew he would likely die in this type of combat. This was soon verified when the man came at him with a few successive jabs. Marric managed to dodge a few of them but he gasped as he saw one of the latter jabs come right at his stomach. A flash of blue blinded Marric and he heard steel clanging on something hard. Squinting, he saw that Gila had thrown up her Shield just before he'd been skewered by the man's sword.

Oh, thank Lanser for her.

Narim had rolled over, the commotion likely pushing its way through his unconsciousness, but he still didn't look too aware of the situation. Just as Marric's eyes flicked over to his father, the man noticed this and spun on the old man laying there.

With a grin, he ran toward Narim, sword raised. Marric gritted his teeth at his mistake. If he hadn't looked over at his father, the man probably wouldn't have focused there. Panic rising inside, he shoved his hands out again, this time with enough concentration that the man was thrown forward ten paces where he landed with a loud thud, rolling away.

An explosion to the side brought Marric's attention to Avryn and Turrin, who had been joined by a few more black-clad figures. No more arrows were raining down from the forest, so Marric assumed that Evenir had either killed the bowmen or with the lightening of the forest, the black-clad men and women had given up and rushed in with hand weapons.

The path was now clear to his father, so Marric nodded to Gila, who dropped her Shield around him so he could run to his father's side.

"Pa! Wake up!" he said, desperately shaking his father.

"Erm . . . mgalrt eh?" his father mumbled. His eyes rolled open for a moment, staring at Marric before they closed again.

Even with his thinner frame, Narim was still considerably larger than Marric. Marric knew he wouldn't be able to drag him fast enough, but a thought came to him from long ago. Avryn had said that Movers could often Move things much larger than themselves. Putting this to the test, Marric focused on his father's form. Body glowing blue, Narim was slowly lifted into the air and began floating toward Gila where she still sat atop her horse. Marric thought if he could just get his father close, she could Shield him better from there.

Loud footsteps behind him made Marric lose his concentration and he let his father fall six feet shy of Gila. His body landed with a thud. Marric would have winced from seeing his father fall as dead weight, but he was too distracted from the sword flying at him. The man he had thrown was up again and swinging his weapon at him. Marric dodged, unable to focus enough to Conjure anything. A few times he'd manage to Move the man's sword away from him, but the man was too fast for him to make any progress.

"Marric, fall down in three seconds!" Gila shouted behind him.

Marric heard the words but didn't register them at first. He went limp as soon as he realized her meaning, just in time for a bolt to slam into the chest of the man he was fighting, the force of which pushed him onto his backside. Blood spilled from where he'd been hit, and Marric turned to see Gila holding an empty crossbow.

His stomach churned from seeing the man die right in front of him, but the adrenaline kept him from losing too much sanity in the situation.

He stumbled over to where his father lay, and Gila opened the Shield up for him to enter. Marric collapsed next to his father, who was now looking up at the trees above.

"Wha' is 'appenin?" he whispered, talking to some unseen being.

"Pa, we've got you. Just rest for now."

Avryn shouted and Marric's attention was drawn to the fighting there.

Apparently, there were more men and women hiding in the forest than they thought. Avryn and Turrin were now surrounded by at least ten of them. A few lay dead at their feet. Avryn had an arrow through his arm and Turrin was sliced in a few places on his back, with another cut on his neck.

"'Ow's 'bout we even the odds, eh?" the apparent leader of the group said before pulling out a vial of dark silver-black liquid. He popped the cork and poured some on his blade.

Marric watched, chills running in his body. Something about the liquid just looked wrong, though he couldn't say why. It looked familiar somehow, but he couldn't put his finger on it.

The men and women around his friends backed away slightly, as if they were afraid of the concoction. Suddenly, Marric felt his eyes widening, and the scene before him changed. Figures of Avryn and Turrin fought black-cloaked people from all directions so quickly that Marric could hardly follow. Then everything stopped and went in slow motion. Marric saw Avryn and Turrin fighting three figures slowly with their Light swords. The man with the dagger coated in the silver-black grime slid in swiftly between his men and stabbed Turrin right in the chest. Black veins sprouted immediately under his skin and he fell to the ground, eyes wide. Marric's mind screamed, but it was a distant thing, something he wasn't actually hearing with his ears.

Then it was all gone, and the fighting continued. Confused, Marric looked to see Turrin still fighting alongside Avryn. It all was happening so fast, it took him a moment to realize he'd seen this before. A woman spun this way, her sword being blocked by Avryn's sword. Another man swung his dagger overhead, looking to stab Turrin in the face. The older man blocked it easily and kicked the man away.

Marric's sense of déjà vu was deepened, and his blood chilled at the sight. Looking to the right, he saw the leader of the group poised and ready to pounce.

"Turrin, watch out!" Marric managed to shout, but it only distracted the man, who turned to see why he had shouted. This awarded him a cut to the arm where he would have blocked a blow. The déjà vu ended there, Marric's shouting causing a change in what he'd Seen. However, the man with the dagger still came in for the killing blow. Marric Conjured his bow and an arrow, nocked it with a fluid motion, and shot it right at the man with the dagger. His aim was off, but it was enough for the man to see it and have to shift away from his course. Growling at his unsuccessful attempt to stab Turrin's chest, he instead threw the dagger. It flew true and thudded into Turrin's thigh, sinking in up to the crossguard.

"Retreat! Git outta 'ere, now!" the leader shouted.

Most of the men and women managed to slip away quickly into the trees. Avryn stabbed the lead man through the chest before he could retreat, letting the rest run.

"Let them go!" Avryn shouted to their couple non-lightbearer men who had survived the attack. Marric scanned around them, noting that two of their companions were missing.

He gulped, trying not to see their bodies, for that's likely all he'd find if he were to look for them.

Turrin let out a loud groan and fell to the ground. The dagger stuck out of his leg like an unhealthy growth of some sort.

"Somethin' ain't roit, Avryn."

Turrin's brow was sweating, which wouldn't be altogether unusual, given the fight they'd just had, but his face was also pale and turning green as if he was ill. Avryn had pulled the arrow out of his own arm and was Fixing his wound there when he noticed Turrin's state. He stopped his own healing and rushed to his friend. By then, Turrin's head had fallen back and he was barely conscious.

"Don't worry, I'll Fix you up good," Avryn said, firmly grasping the handle of the dagger and ripping it free. When he saw the thick veins of silvery black running up Turrin's leg, he cursed.

"It looks like some type of poison. We must hurry."

Without hesitation, Avryn Conjured a dagger and cut away the top of Turrin's pant leg, revealing the stab wound there. Black veins ran up and down his leg as the poison spread. They were moving alarmingly fast.

"What in Lanser's name. . . . " Avryn gaped.

Quickly, he positioned his hand over the wound and his Light began to glow, intense and bright. It pulsed gently, and Marric could see the open wound on his leg start to knit together, the blood flow stopping. In only moments, the wound was closed completely, but the dark veins kept spreading, and Turrin kept getting paler.

His eyes rolled back in their sockets and he groaned before mumbling something incoherent. His breathing increased, getting more and more shallow. The vein trails had traveled up the man's leg and Marric imagined them going up into Turrin's chest, moving toward his heart.

"I Saw this happen. Well, not *this* exactly, but it goes everywhere and kills him. Avryn, you have to Fix him," Marric said desperately.

A determined look on his face, Avryn put his hand over where the wound had been before, the origin of the silver-black veins attacking their friend's body from the inside. The Light glowed again, pulsing faster now, but the veins receded only slightly. Gritting his teeth, Avryn increased the intensity of his Fixing, the veins pushing back a little further from his efforts.

"Something is pushing back. I can't—" Avryn gasped through his teeth, "—I can't push it away."

He locked his jaw, the muscles in his cheeks tightening up visibly. The Light got even brighter, the flashing increasing in pace.

It wasn't working. The veins were not receding fast enough, and Marric figured the poison would be reaching Turrin's heart soon. He didn't know what would happen after that, but such a vital organ couldn't withstand a poison like this. Turrin's mouth foamed a grey spittle and he was unconscious now, the poison taking its course.

An idea snapped in Marric's mind that was unlikely to help, but he had to try something.

"Gila, quick! Come here!" Marric shouted to the woman still holding the Shield around them.

Her face was white from watching the scene. The black veins did look grisly in the increasing light of the morning and against the bright blue of Avryn's Lightbearing. Avryn was sweating again, droplets running down his face. The Light was so bright under his hand that Marric had to squint even when he looked in the general direction. Avryn's efforts were working a little more now, the veins beginning to disappear up and down Turrin's leg. Despite that, the poison was about to progress under Turrin's pant leg and out of visibility. Even with the increased intensity, Avryn's Fixing wasn't fast enough, and they all knew it.

"Drop the Shield," Marric ordered.

Gila gave him a look of annoyance and frustration at the order, and she opened her mouth to protest before Marric cut her off, his face flushing from his rudeness.

"I'm sorry, but we don't have time—we need you putting energy into your Lighting."

Her face changed to curiosity then, the anger and frustration leaving her. Regardless of her thoughts, the Shield around them sucked in and disappeared.

"Marric, I'm not a Lighter—I'm a Seer and a Shielder! I don't have much Light to give."

"Please! We can't wait any longer. We need to try!"

Marric had not practiced his Lighting at all really, but he'd been able to summon a Lighting orb, small but intense, to guide him through some of the darker hallways of Terris Green. Since they'd left Wurren, he'd been less comfortable with darkness than he had before being chased by black-robed people from Watchlight.

Putting his hand up, he summoned what he could: a small Lighting orb only the size of his thumbnail, but so intense that it rivaled the brightness of Avryn's Fixing powers just before them. Gila followed, her orb hovering above her right hand, looking about double the size of his own.

"Put it closer to Avryn's hands."

By now, Avryn was lost in concentration and was not paying much attention to what they were doing at all. He'd moved his other hand over his first as if to put more power into his Fixing. It must have done something, for that's when the veins had started receding faster.

Gila and Marric moved their Lighting orbs closer to Avryn's hands and sure enough, a pulse of Light rippled from their small orbs and into Avryn's Fixing. His powers flashed and the pulsing quickened again, flashing more brightly. The three of them stood there, Gila and Marric averting their eyes, Avryn staring through the brightness with grim determination, before one final flash rocked the scene around them. Even with his eyes turned away, Marric was blinded by the brilliance.

Avryn collapsed on the ground, conscious, but breathing hard. Gila and Marric's small orbs were gone, somehow extinguished by the Fixing power's odd pulse at the end.

Still lying down, Turrin gasped and shot his eyes upward, scanning their surroundings with a panicked look.

"Wha' done 'appened? Did Oi die?"

He turned his head to see Avryn lying down and cursed, his face worried.

"Wha' did they do t'yeh? Oi'll cut 'em through if'n they 'urt yeh bad-loik."

Turrin jumped to his feet, spinning around. His brow knit in curiosity, then he looked down.

"Someone lookin' fer some fun, eh? Din' need to cut me pants off to Fix the stab, did yeh?" he asked, addressing his exposed thigh and leg where the pants were cut.

Marric blushed at the comment, and Gila chuckled out loud.

"Leave it to Turrin to make jokes after almost dying," she snorted.

Turrin looked confused. "Almost dyin'? Wha' in Lanser's good name are yeh talkin' 'bout? Was jus' a flesh wound."

Avryn sighed, sitting up and holding his head.

"If my head would stop pounding, I might be able to tell you. I've had to do an unusual amount of Fixing on you, and never before has Fixing been that tiring."

Turrin cocked an eyebrow.

"Was I really tha' bad? Huh, sorry fer tha'," the burly man said, shrugging.

"It wasn't the wound itself that's troubling, but what they used to enhance the injury. I've never seen or experienced anything like it before. It was some type of poison, but—"

Avryn paused, worry adorning his face. Marric didn't often see negative emotions from the man, though he didn't think that Avryn lacked the feelings. Normally, Avryn was confident, happy, and focused on the objective; for him to be so worried and even show it so clearly made a pit grow in Marric's stomach.

"Whatever they used was pushing against my Fixing—it was as if it had a power and a mind of its own." Shaking his head, he stumbled to his feet.

"We'll have to take time to analyze the event as we travel back to Terris Green. Your father doesn't look like he's doing very well right now."

Marric snapped to attention and turned again to his father lying on the ground, eyes scanning the trees above.

"What's wrong with him?" Marric asked, panic creeping into his voice. He cleared his throat and shook his head to try to get a control over himself. "Is he poisoned or something?"

Standing unsteadily now, Avryn shuffled over to Marric's father and collapsed there, the exhaustion obvious not only from his gait, but how he let himself fall to the ground.

"From what I can tell, he's just exhausted and hungry. I wouldn't be overly worried about him in all honesty, at least not now that we're here. We should be off. Though these Watchlight men have fled the area, I somehow doubt they will leave us alone much longer."

Gila's eyes suddenly glowed bright blue and she hummed to herself.

"Actually, from what I See, they retreated completely. It doesn't appear that they'll be coming back here anytime soon. It seems we've killed most of them."

Nodding, Avryn continued. "Thank you for checking, Gila. Despite what you Saw, I still don't like the idea of unreasonably delaying ourselves."

It took longer than Avryn hoped to get everyone back on their horses and ready to go. Given that they'd lost two of their non-Lightbearers, they did take a moment to give a small tribute and dig shallow graves. Avryn was still too weak to really help with the digging, so he was forced to sit and watch while the others dug for their friends. Marric and Turrin Conjured shovels for everyone to use so that Gila and one of the other men could help. Words were spoken in tribute of the two, then they headed out.

The sky was darkening with clouds again as they moved through the forest. Fortunately, the path was cleared from their earlier destruction, and they could move fairly quickly without pushing the horses to running speed. Avryn dozed in the saddle almost instantly, Turrin leading his horse and staying unusually silent. Their journey there had been full of talking and laughter, at least during the day. Now, they all thought about what had just happened. It took hours for Marric's body to stop shaking fully. The adrenaline and excitement from the fighting was new to him. Before, he would have frozen up completely. Though there were still times when he probably wasn't in control of his emotions, he did far better in that exchange than he'd ever done before.

Marric wondered if he'd ever get used to the feeling. When he'd finally stopped shaking, his muscles ached all over, not only from the fighting and running, but from the constant shaking and spasming for hours. The wound in his shoulder still throbbed as well. Avryn had barely enough energy to make it stop bleeding, but that was all. Marric groaned quietly through the pain.

The forest was humid, the musty smell becoming even more distracting. There hadn't been any rain since it had stopped the day before, but the dark clouds above threatened to pour showers on them at any moment. Marric wondered if he'd welcome the feeling of the rain on his sore muscles or if he'd just be sick of being wet again. It didn't matter in the end, for the storm never started.

Animals went about their business, the forest alive around them. Turrin had commented how that was a good sign for them. A lack of animal activity normally meant that there was trouble afoot. In time, they came to the spot where the forest was still intact, and Turrin joked that they should just Destroy the whole way back to Terris Green. The idea of resuming the breakneck pace they'd forced on the way here made Marric nervous. Avryn had woken only thirty minutes before, looking a little more fresh.

"While the speed might be nice, I don't think it's in our best interest to carve a specific pathway directly to our sanctuary with its location intentionally hidden," Avryn teased.

"Meh, yer prolly right, as usual. Was only commiseratin' tha' we can' be as quick no more."

As they entered the unbroken trees and shrubs, the darkness dimmed the cloud-lit sky. This unsettled Marric more, and he suspected his companions felt the same way. Gila shifted her hand over her side sword and Avryn tensed visibly on his horse. It wasn't too dark that they couldn't see the way, but it was dim enough that some movement might be obscured.

"So wha' d'yeh think abou' tha' nasty poison, Avryn?" Turrin blurted out finally. They'd all wanted to broach the subject, but Avryrn slept for so long that they didn't want to have the discussion without him. Marric had been tempted to bring it up the moment Avryn awoke, but he thought better of it.

Avryn was quiet for a few beats before he spoke. "I can't say for sure what it was they used, but I can assure you, it was quite potent. I've been exhausted before from Fixing too many things and people in such a short time, but never from a stab wound like that."

Another pause.

"The best way to describe it was that it *fought back* against my power. My Fixing was almost not strong enough to get through it."

Avryn's head jerked, his face looking thoughtful.

"How did I get through in the end? I was so focused that I didn't realize what happened until my concentration broke and I fell back."

"Marric's a clever boy, that's how," Gila spoke out. "He got me to drop my Shield, and we gave you a bit of a boost."

"What do you—?" Avryn began to ask before he stopped. "Ahhh, your Lighting. How clever. What made you think of that so quickly? Neither of you is a Lighter by awakening, so it's a bit surprising to have you come up with it on the spot."

Marric shrugged, unsure if the motion was seen by his companions or not. He was blushing, but they definitely would not have been able to see that.

"When I was watching you, for some reason the memory of Narinda boosting my Conjures when we first got to Terris Green came to mind. I was panicking because we didn't have a Lighter with us, but then I figured we ought to try what we had, even if it was in our weaker form. I honestly can't believe it worked."

Turrin snorted.

"Remind me to always 'ave a Loiter along. Could roit well be the difference between life an' death now, couldn' it?"

"Well your quick thinking definitely changed the course of what happened," Avryn praised.

Marric shrugged again before continuing, "I'm just glad that it worked."

"Likewise," Avryn said, looking happy as he usually did. "What perplexes me most is how Watchlight could get their hands on something so horrible and potent as that poison. They have always been brutish, but that was beyond what I thought their capabilities were."

"Meh, dun' surprise me much. They was desperate when they realized tha' we were much better than them at fightin'," Turrin said, still not turning back to them as he talked.

As he said it, another thought came to Marric.

"Why were they there at that specific time?"

"Hmm?" Avryn questioned.

Marric's eyes furrowed as he thought through what had happened.

"My father has been traveling for days—why didn't they find him earlier and kill or take him?"

The question brought more silence to the group. Marric turned to look at his father, who was sleeping again, riding one of the horses left over from their lost companions. Regardless of why the timing was the way it was, Marric was grateful that his father was alright. If it hadn't been for the chaos of their travels through the forest, Marric might have been more emotional at seeing his father again. Now that things were calming down, tears welled in his eyes.

Clearing his throat, Marric turned away and feigned a yawn, hoping that if anyone noticed his teary eyes, he could say it was just from yawning.

"No matter how I think it through, I can't come up with an answer. Perhaps their Seers didn't find him until the same moment that ours did? It wouldn't be the first time that's happened. There isn't really a good explanation for when a vision becomes available for a Seer. Unless they are specifically seeking a person or a moment, they do come at random, it seems."

Turrin grunted at the words. "Yeh all can' be *tha'* dense, can yeh? It's obvious, really."

The rest of them stared in silence at Turrin, who made a show of being shocked. When no one laughed, he furrowed his brow.

"Oh—yeh really don' see it." He chuckled to himself as if it were a private joke.

"They 'ad to 'ave timed it jus' right. They *wanted* to be there when we got there. Don' yeh see? It wasn't no coincidence. Nah, they meant fer us to clash like tha'."

Avryn shook his head slightly. "I did have that thought, sure, but Watchlight doesn't have anything to gain by waiting until we arrived."

"If'n they could thin our numbers, 't might be worth it fer them."

"If that really were their design, we'd have far more encounters with them. Also, their battle prowess isn't that much better than ours—what really matters is which Lightbearers happen to be more skilled. Riln may be barbaric, but I don't believe he would sacrifice his Lightbearers so readily like that."

Marric thought on that before sharing his next thought.

"There weren't any Lightbearers, though. Isn't that strange to anyone else?"

Avryn cocked his head.

"I suppose I didn't even think of that. They were skilled enough fighters that I was focused on not getting killed. I did keep my guard up, as usual, just in case they sprang a hidden ability on us, but it never came."

Turrin grunted again. "Makes it seem less loik it was Riln's doin'. Don' think tha' group goes anywheres wifou' a whole lot of 'em."

The conversation ended at that, no one wanting to conjecture more on the situation. The sky above still held dark clouds, and the humidity in the air rose enough that Marric thought the storm would fall upon them at any moment. Still, no rain fell.

After staying the night in the forest, Marric was surprised to see his father still sleeping. It was only on the second day of their journey to Terris Green that his father finally awoke. His joy in seeing his son again was full and almost took the tiredness away from his face. It didn't last long, however, as his father soon fell back asleep on the horse. Before drifting off, Marric's father told them that the house was set afire while he wasn't home. He'd happened to be at the market getting supplies when it happened. Narim didn't bother to stay to put it out. Something felt wrong the moment he'd seen the fire, so he fled after grabbing some personal effects.

There wasn't more of a story to tell on his front, so when he awoke again, Marric shared with his father their journey to Terris Green and how Marric had awakened in an unusual fashion.

"So, let me say it back to yeh. Yer a special Lightbearer guy, cause yeh gots three of 'em, eh?" Narim asked on the fourth day of their travel back to the sanctuary.

Marric blushed, but confirmed his father's query with a nod. "Yes. I was able to survive the awakening. I believe it had something to do with the rabbit foot the old Seer woman gave me in Erisdell."

"It doesn't really make a whole lot of sense to us, but I am grateful that whatever it was protected Marric. The time of his awakening was unexpectedly chaotic, and I couldn't be there like I hoped to just in case Fixing would have saved him." Avryn smiled after he said it.

"By jove, t'all seems odd t'me. Can' believe my son 'as odd powers of Light such-like."

They had discussed Lightbearing at length already on their journey back to Terris Green, but his father still was in awe at his son's new gifts. He'd asked Marric to Conjure all sorts of things. Each time he did, his father just gazed at him with an astonished face.

"Roit unlucky tha' Oi din' get no powers such like. Imagine 'ow easy life'd be if we din' need to buy tools fer the work!" Narim exclaimed.

"Tha' roit there is a good an' practical man," Turrin said, chuckling to himself.

They arrived at Terris Green later that evening, and immediately let Narim rest from the journey. Avryn disappeared as they entered, likely to report back to Magness about what had happened. Marric tried to not be offended that he wasn't going to be included in the debrief, but he let it go. The only other thing on his mind was food. Gila was thinking the same thing, so the two of them moved off to the mess hall.

"How long do you think before Janis and Alsry are back from T'Arren Vale?" Marric asked as they walked.

"Oh, they will still be a ways out. We only traveled four days to retrieve your father. Even if they moved quickly it would have taken seven days to get there. I think they'll be fine, they are likely on their way back now."

Marric paused as they walked down the hall. "Mind if we take a look at them right now?"

Gila smiled warmly at him. "I think that would be fine. Would you prefer to sit? Or are you alright standing here?"

"We can stand. Unless you think there is a reason for us to sit—"

"No, no. It should be alright."

They each took a synchronized deep breath and Marric imagined Janis's face in his mind. Eyes widening with blue Light, the world around him melted away, gray stone walls blurring in a spin around him. Colors and images zoomed around as if he was flying through the air over the forest. The vision slowed and stopped in the middle of the forest on a band of traveling men and women.

Marric froze when he saw them. Janis's clothes were torn up, the sleeves of her shirt missing completely. She was bleeding from a spot on her hand, which was bandaged by a linen cloth. Alsry looked exhausted. Purple bruises adorned her face and arms all over as if she'd fallen down a steep hill. Her eyes looked distant, and she appeared lost in thought.

There wasn't any sign of a wound anywhere on Janis's head, but her hair was slightly matted with blood. "Lanser's beard—" Gila said, suddenly appearing next to Marric.

"What happened to them? They look like they've been attacked."

Gila didn't answer his question. Instead, she looked behind the two women leading the party and nodded her head slightly. Marric glanced over to see what she was doing. It took him a minute to realize she was counting them.

"Fog it, they're missing at least half of the numbers they left with."

Marric's stomach turned. It was daytime outside of the sanctuary, though the night would soon come. Judging from the light filtering through the trees, they were looking at the group in the current time.

Without warning, Janis perked up and drew a dagger from her waist. Her eyes scanned the forest and Marric felt dread inside. He knew Janis had incredible senses and she had heard something. Her eyes moved around, Alsry perking up, herself.

"What is it? Do you hear something?" she asked Janis.

"No, but someone is watching us."

Marric and Gila both looked at each other, curious.

"You don't think—" Marric started to say. Before he could say anything, Janis gasped on her horse and he spun, terror filling Marric despite the fact that he wasn't physically there and couldn't really be harmed. The sound of

Janis gasping like that never meant anything good. When his eyes fell on her, her eyes widened.

Janis sat up straight, a grimace on her face while her eyes shone with bright blue Light. An image of her separated from her current body, standing on the ground to the left of her moving horse.

He hadn't realized it, but he and Gila had been hovering above ground, somehow moving at the same pace as the horses.

"What in the fog is happening now?" she growled in frustration. Looking up at the figures on the horses, her face scrunched in annoyance. "How in Lanser's name am I supposed to be prepared for this happening—"

Before long, she noticed Marric and Gila and she moved to pull daggers out of her holsters.

"Wait! It's just us, Janis!" Marric shouted, trying to get her to stop.

She relaxed when she realized who it was.

"Sorry, I've had run-ins with dangerous enemies in visions like these before and don't really relish the idea of it happening again. What are you doing here?" she questioned, her own vision self moving along the ground with the horses, just as Gila and Marric did.

"Umm, we were just checking on you and Alsry to see how you were. What happened?" he asked, eyes flicking to the company leader, who looked ragged and exhausted.

"Run-in with Watchlight—pretty much what we expected would happen, but worse."

Gila stared at her for a moment before speaking. "Where is the new Fixer? I don't see anyone new traveling with you."

Janis stiffened at the question. "We lost him—it's a long story. To be honest, I don't really feel in the mood to talk about it right now, if you take my meaning."

Gila pursed her lips at the comment, but nodded politely.

"How in the fog are we floating like this? I wish it would stop, it's creepy," Janis said, looking disgusted.

"I—I don't really know," Marric replied, looking to Gila for explanation.

"It's a frame of reference thing. You are moving, so that means we are as well."

Janis scowled. "Well, that's clear as mud. How do you fogging get a handle on this Seeing thing? I—"

Just as she said the words, her image went fuzzy and then sprung back into her body. Janis's eyes went dim and the vision ended for Janis.

"Fogging Seeing. How is that supposed to be helpful if you can't keep control of it all?" Janis growled loudly.

Alsry perked up at her words.

"What are you talking about? What does that have to do with anything?" Alsry asked, perplexed.

Janis pointed up at Marric and Gila, or roughly in the direction they were floating in.

"Marric and the other Seer woman that went with Avryn are watching us right now."

Alsry jumped at the words and examined the air above them. "How in Lindrad do you know that? I don't see a thing there."

"My Seeing reared its ugly head for just a moment. They're there."

Staring flatly at the space between them, Janis shook her head and said to the now-unseen Marric and Gilla, "It's a long story. We'll tell you when we get back. Just pray that we don't run into more Watchlight goons right now. I could probably kill them, sure, but I don't feel like being messed with by my shoddy Lightbearing anymore."

Alsry was looking at Janis from the side. "The fact that you can See now makes being with you insufferable. Tell them we'll be fine and we'll see them soon."

Rolling her eyes, Janis retorted. "Tell them yourself, they can probably hear you."

Janis noted how terrible Alsry really looked, then spoke again. "I hope you don't make a habit of almost getting yourself killed. I can't always be there to watch your back."

"Hey now—" Alsry had begun to say before Marric's view began to spin and they returned to the hallway on the way to the mess hall.

"What happened?" Marric said, confused.

"I can't be sure, but I think someone put up a Shield and we lost them. They heard Janis and realized they weren't doing their job."

Marric had been pushed back by a Shield before and it did feel similar to that experience.

"Anyway, we can't be sure what happened until they are back, so let's just go eat something."

The two continued on to the mess hall, but Marric's stomach wasn't hungry anymore. Something felt so ominous about what Janis had said. That, and the lack of the new Fixer with them made him dread hearing their report. Privately, he was just relieved they'd been successful in getting his own father.

Despite his loss of appetite, Marric followed Gila to the mess hall to fill the void in his stomach.

19

Prost's body ached.

He was well acquainted with intense battles and his energy wasn't really lacking, but cuts and bruises adorned his face and limbs, not to mention the deep gashes where he'd caught the swords Moved at him. It wasn't the wisest of choices to catch them, but it had done the trick. He'd done crazier things since being with Watchlight, so his companions weren't overly surprised to hear how he had been hurt. The only thing he felt at the moment besides this pain was regret.

It wasn't enough.

Riln would think it wasn't enough. They were coming back empty handed. The only solace he figured Riln would find was that Evenir didn't have the new Fixer, either.

He recalled the situation while messing with the scraps of linen they had for bandages. Medical supplies weren't high on their list of importance, given the Fixers they had along, but a few bandages were present as an extra back-up. Most of the other men and women didn't care to check the supply regularly. That fact made Prost more annoyed. Since he was the only one who couldn't be Fixed, he was normally the only one who used the medical supplies.

The wounds stung even more at the knowledge that he was the only injured person in the group right now.

A sound to his right made him turn to see a smirk on Jord's face.

"Is something funny to you?" Prost snapped.

Jord shrugged. "Yeh might wanna think twice 'bout gettin' yerself hurt like tha'. 'Ow long 'ave yeh been immune to Lightbearing?" Jord asked, a fake look of inquisition on his face. "Oh yah, forever."

Prost's emotions boiled inside and he clenched his fist, imagining smashing the boy's face in.

"Say what you want, boy, but you and I both know the only thing keeping me from killing you is Riln himself. I'd wager you fight like a child. Take your Destroying away, and what do you have? A pale, sick-looking boy only good for target practice."

Jord's eyes narrowed at the comment, but he didn't say anything else. Prost knew then that his words cut the boy deep. He hadn't even seen Jord use anything in battles other than his Destroying, so he assumed that in a hand-to-hand fight, the boy would crumple easily.

"Perhaps we can save all idiotic comments like this until we get back to the base and I don't have to listen to you lot," Prost said more loudly this time, so that the men could hear him from behind.

They'd lost a lot of men and women to Evenir today. Prost didn't enjoy seeing his comrades fall in any situation, despite not being close with any of them. When he'd first arrived in Watchlight's compound ten years ago and determined he'd be there to stay, he'd tried to make friends. Unfortunately, the moment any of the Lightbearers realized he was immune to their powers and was well-practiced with weapons, his congeniality had dropped sharply.

Since the first years, he'd just given up, and most just left him alone. Even though he'd given up making friends, it didn't mean he didn't resent his lack of social standing. Prost resented most people around him; doing so distracted him from the fact that many of them disliked him first.

His mind wandered back to before the curse of the Void. He had grown up wealthy. His father was a plantation owner, and had been for years before his birth. Growing up, his life had been easy and comfortable. Part of him regretted this. Sure, his parents were fine and kind and all that, but the lack of challenge had frustrated him. That, and the jealousy and judgement he constantly got from his peers—the other boys and girls in school. He'd begun to hate his heritage and how everyone thought him to be soft. To prove them wrong, he'd joined the military when he was only sixteen. It was somewhat uncommon for a boy so young to join the Lindradian militia, but they had let him. The years of training had hardened him to a point where he was practically a shoo-in for general, or at least assistant general for a few years.

Then the fogging whispers had come and ruined everything.

In the militia, he was respected, not feared. He didn't have many friends per se, but his reputation preceded him as one of the most advanced and skilled fighters of their companies.

With the lack of war between Lindrad and the neighboring continents, deaths, and thus general vacancies, were low. If there had been many casualties, he figured he'd have climbed the ranks much more quickly.

His mind reeled at the memories he had with Avryn. He'd met the man three years after he had joined, Avryn coming into his company after completing his own training. They'd become friends almost instantly, when they happened to band together against some idiotic soldiers harassing some locals in T'Arren Vale. They'd each stepped in with unspoken agreement and from then on, they'd been friends.

His mind drifted, the cloudy sky above and distant rumbling thunder filling him with a sense of power.

Avryn chuckled beside him as they drank ale at the famous pub in T'Arren Vale, the Trilistan. They'd each already had too much to drink, but the bartender was still urging them on, trying to get them to drink more, looking only to fill his own pockets with their commissioned silver fronds.

"I think that we should probably call it a night, don't you?" Avryn said, hiccuping.

Prost laughed at his companion's inability to hold his spirits. He was a lot bigger than Avryn, but that only aided him in competition with his friend when it came to drinking. Each had just fought their way up in a training exercise with the other soldiers. In the absence of any wars, the militia commissioned their soldiers to

fight in tournaments to keep their skills sharp. Prost and Avryn were still unde-
feated in both the single and the companion events.

"If you are too lightweight to handle more, then sure, we can call it a night. If
only it was a drinking competition we were in, I'd slay you good," Prost teased.

Avryn rolled his eyes, his body titling slightly as he almost lost balance on his
stool.

"Lessjusssssay that's too bad for the others we're paired up for the tourney.
We're the top! No one even comes close to us with the—" he paused to belch, "—
sword," Avryn said drunkenly.

Prost chuckled. "Right, only because you've got me watching your back!"

Avryn raised an eyebrow, confidence on his face, but a distant look still in his
eyes from inebriation.

"Oh? Then explain th'cut on your face from our sparring jusyessterday?" Avryn
teased.

"Luck, that's all. Besides, you can't disregard the bruise you've got on your chest
from where my staff slammed you good."

Avryn winced as he apparently remembered the still-tender blow.

"Fair enough, we're evenly matched. So far, we've both won and lost th'same
amount in all our sparring seshions over the years, no?"

The bartender tried once again to fill their glasses, but Prost stopped him with a
glare.

"You put any more ale in that without us telling you to, and I'll dump it right
on your head, hear me?" Prost threatened.

Chuckling, Avryn smacked Prost on the shoulder.

"A simple 'no thank you' would have sufficed, my frien'."

Prost shook his head and glared at the bartender again.

After paying their tab, Prost paying this time, they wandered down the street,
the crowd having lessened with the night. The alley and cobblestones were bathed
in a pleasant gleam from Mallan as it neared setting. The second moon was dipping,
which meant the night was still young, but theirs was close to ending. Normally,
soldiers were expected in their barracks long before Mallan was about to set, but
Prost and Avryn were pushing their limits. Unnecessary infighting always occurred
when soldiers were out during Isllan and the fog, so rules had been put in place.

"We'd best get some sleep before our bout tomorrow. We've got our comp fight

against Yilan and Ovrot tomorrow. Should be easy, even with a drunk head like this, but still, we'll want to make a show of it."

Avryn grinned at Prost's words. They were, as of yet, not even closely rivaled with any of the other soldiers, so they'd intentionally made a show of it, ramping up the entertainment as best they could.

"True. We'll be a better show if we aren't ssho drunk," Avryn chuckled. "Not shure we can beat you cutting the trousers off the last pair. Crowd went wild for that." He burst out laughing at the memory.

Prost joined in with his own laughter. "I couldn't resist. They were so slow—I just had to mess with them a little bit."

They stopped for a moment, composing themselves before their eyes met. Immediately, they burst out laughing again.

"Oh dear," Avryn said finally, "I think we've lost ourselves in ale. We've still each got a tricky opponent tomorrow for our individual fights."

Prost grunted. "Maybe you do, but Riglan is slow as a longbird flitting leisurely through the air."

Avryn gaped. "How poetic of you! Have you begun to read?"

Prost made a show of scowling and punched his friend hard on the shoulder.

"Ow, fog you," Avryn pouted, jokingly.

In retaliation, Avryn sloppily kicked Prost right in the side, causing the bigger man to grunt in pain.

"Ow, Lanser's might."

The two laughed again at their jabs. A few passersby stared at them, looking worried. It wasn't uncommon for men to be walking the streets drunk, but they suspected there were likely few who were laughing after bruising each other. It made them look a certain kind of crazy.

Avryn bowed deeply to an older man carrying a few books under his arm.

"Don't mind him, he has no side vision, y'see. Poor man was born crippled like tha'."

The book-carrying man stared at him blankly, unsure what to say. Prost glared at Avryn and turned to the stranger, who jumped the moment Prost's eyes landed on him.

"Scram," was all he needed to say to make the lone traveler run away, mumbling to himself.

"If you weren't big, I think you'd look quite kind and squishy, don't you think?" Avryn jested.

Prost was a head and a half taller than Avryn, and quite a bit thicker. It didn't mean much in a sword battle for them, however, for though he was stronger than his friend, Avryn's speed made up for it all.

They turned the corner down a deserted but wider street leading away from the square. Though they hadn't passed through it, they could hear a larger crowd talking and bustling about the tables set up there. It was market day, so the selling and bartering would push the limits of Isllan and the impending fog, but really only in that section of the city. The rest of the city would stay as it was just outside the pub, slow and dead.

"You know at some point we'll be fighting each other, right?" Avryn said in a surprisingly sober tone.

Prost paused. "Yes, I believe that it's likely to happen."

"I don't plan on going easy on you, that's for sure."

Prost nodded, considering the likely future. "I wouldn't expect anything less of you. As long as you don't force me to kill you."

The air took on a tense nature, not physically, but something that was mutually felt. Despite their friendship, their egos were too big to not fight for the tournament title, even against a best friend. Killing wasn't allowed in the tournament, but it had happened where soldiers died from resulting injuries or when they didn't know when to quit. Disqualification for killing wasn't always the outcome, especially in the final rounds of the tournament.

"Fair enough, but I say the same to you, my friend. I imagine we'll put on quite the show."

The two men lapsed into silence as they walked to the barracks. A breeze funneled down the street, whipping the hair about their heads. The cold of it bit at Prost's cheeks and he inhaled to revel in the feeling. Winter was over, but the remnants of the cold had not quite left the city. It sat at a higher elevation than the other townships near the sea, so the cold took a bit longer to vacate the vast streets of T'Arren Vale.

"Well, it's soon to come, so let's just get to that point and see what happens. How's that sound?" Prost offered.

"It's the best we can do at least. Then the decision for general should be close to follow."

Not only were the men competing for the title of tournament winner, but also for the title of general or assistant general. It wasn't necessarily true that the winner would gain the position right off, but it could likely happen.

"It's been ages since we've had a proper battle," Avryn said, his face thoughtful.

Prost changed the subject. "What do you have going on in that mind of yours? You've been distant for days now."

Avryn pressed his mouth into a thin line, face straining slightly as if he was deciding whether or not to say something to Prost.

"Erm, well," the man started.

Prost raised an eyebrow in surprise. "Since when do you feel like you can't tell me something? I thought that was the point of us being friends. It's easier if you just spit it out, in my opinion."

Avryn sighed. "Yes, that's true. I guess I'm not sure how to say it. Do you remember when that group of people came to talk to me in the pub last week?"

Prost scrunched his eyebrows, barely remembering it.

"Oh, yeah, I'd forgotten about that. It was just before I smashed Triliv right good in a single fight. I was so focused on not getting crushed by his massive sword and fists that I'd lost track of where you went. What about it?"

Avryn looked nervous about something.

"Sorry, my head isn't right. I think I've had too much drink to talk about this right now. Maybe we should try tomorrow—"

Prost stopped walking and turned to his friend, putting both hands on his shoulders. He stood quite a bit taller than Avryn, and his chest was so much broader that he felt he was talking to a much younger boy, though Avryn was only three years his junior.

"Let's just talk about it now. It's obviously bothering you, and I think it'll be easier if you just spit it out."

Avryn smiled at his friend's words.

"Yes, I think you are right about it being easier to just say it, but part of me wanting to wait is that you need to be more mentally prepared for it."

Prost frowned.

What the fog does that mean? *he thought.*

"Ummm, okay . . . what did they want to talk to you about? Give me a hint."

Sighing again, Avryn took the bait. "They wanted to talk about some 'change'," *Avryn gestured in the air with his fingers, wiggling them to make it seem ridiculous* what they said, "something that might happen to me. They were loony and I didn't want to talk about it. That was until another man, a black-cloaked man, came to tell me the same thing."

Prost stared, completely lost. Avryn didn't continue though, instead he trudged on. They were almost to the barracks then, running out of time before there would be other ears to hear what he had to say.

Deciding to help out, Prost piped up.

"So, you had a bunch of crazies tell you the world was going to change or end or something? I don't see how that's a big deal, there are always doomsayers claiming the world will end every day."

Avryn still looked worried, as if he was about to offend Prost. "No, no it wasn't that," Avryn said. Then his eyebrows shot up, a new thought coming to him, "Do you remember a few days back, when someone blasted the armory walls and doors to pieces?"

Prost scoffed. "Yeah, the blooming idiots almost killed all the horses in the stable next door as the weapons were flung all over the place. How'd anyone get a hold of that much explosive material, anyway?"

Avryn was white now.

"Fog it, man, don't say that was you! You'll be flogged for that, killed even."

"No, no it wasn't me . . . well, it wasn't me on purpose. Ugh!" Avryn slammed his palm to his forehead. "I didn't do anything, something just happened to me while I was there and—"

"Oi! Yeh lilly-white loons, what are yeh doin' over there? Grishnon's 'bout to down a half keg o' ale; don' wanna miss it, I reckon," a voice shouted from the doors.

Prost looked up to see one of their fellow soldiers gesturing them in. Anger boiling inside, Prost opened his mouth to tell the man off, when Avryn shook his head.

"No, I would rather like to see this. Grishnon can't hold his ale even as well as I can, so I bet this will be a good show."

Avryn's face was getting color again, but he still looked worried. He forged forward, but Prost stopped him.

"What happened there, Avryn? You were gone for almost two days after it happened. If it weren't for the general vouching for you, I'd have thought you were to blame for the armory. Now you are telling me that you were involved?"

His friend pulled away from his powerful arms, wincing.

"I will tell you more, in time. Perhaps tomorrow, even. But right now I just need to see Grishnon make a fool of himself before I pass out on my hammock."

Prost rolled his eyes, but didn't press the issue further. He trusted his friend, and he knew that Avryn would tell him when he felt it was right. If that was tomorrow, then tomorrow it would be.

"Last one there is a gaggle of geese," Prost challenged, then vaulted to the door.

Cursing, Avryn ran after him. Without the head start, Prost knew that Avryn would have beaten him easily in a foot race.

As he ran, Prost reflected on what Avryn had said. Not once had he seen his friend that rattled before, even when they'd been slammed hard by their officer's training or even on the losing end of a group battle in their novice days. He marveled at what could have happened at the armory, at who the odd people were who had spoken to him at the pub, and apparently another occasion.

Shaking his head, he focused on walking to the pub, looking forward to the next day when he'd learn more about what happened.

Little did he know that his life would change—for that night, the whispers started.

~

PROST WAS DRAWN from the memory by Vint's loud grunt.

"We're almost back to the compound, Prost. If I were you, I'd be thinking about what to say to Riln about how we lost the boy. So Riln doesn't take it out on all of us—we aren't all immune to his Lightbearing."

Scowling, Prost made a rude gesture at Vint.

"I'll be fine, and you know that I'll take the blame in whatever I say to him. That's what it means to be second in command: everything is *my* fault. Now, calm down."

Vint glared at him, but pulled his horse back to where his sister, Lathe, was riding on her horse.

Receding back into his own thoughts again, Prost recalled the memory of Avryn the night before the whispers came.

At the time, Prost didn't know that the reason Avryn was missing for a couple days was due to his own awakening. When he'd finally told Prost, it made him somewhat resentful. While his friend had gained some extraordinary and unexplainable power, Prost was being distracted by voices leading him away from everything he'd ever wanted, or they'd drive him insane.

His stomach turned knowing that he'd have to approach Riln with the news of the lost Fixer. Only whispers sounded around him as his group, now cut almost in half, stressed and worried about Riln's reaction when he saw that not only had many of their ranks been killed in the battles with Evenir, but also that it was for naught. The boy was gone. Prost didn't know if it was worse that the boy was dead or better knowing that he hadn't joined Evenir. Despite their betrayal of their Seal when receiving their gifts, it was a disservice to the world for the boy to have died like that.

Who the fog was that man anyway? he thought.

When they'd started back to the compound days away, Prost had asked one of the Seers to scour the city and surrounding areas for any sign of the man who had poisoned the boy. They came up with nothing. Unfortunately, without any information about the man other than the color of his garb, they could only See random images. Such images might not have been the actual person in question, especially since Watchlight's main wardrobe was a black robe as well.

Prost knew that once Riln was through the anger, he might have some other ideas on what to do to learn more about this man. Whether he was working alone or not, Prost didn't know. He assumed that the man couldn't be working alone, but it was only a guess. Perhaps a paid assassin?

Cocking his head to the side, he thought on that. Only months ago he'd intercepted Janis from receiving a job to kill Marric. At the time, Prost didn't care to know much about her employer for that job, but now it was coming to light. Sure, there were a lot of men and women who would hire an assassin to kill someone, but a Lightbearer? That was more uncommon.

Lightbearing still wasn't well known in all of Lindrad, despite occasional public fights like they'd just had. The people often had odd explanations about witchcraft and evil to write off what they saw. It would be hard for someone to explain away the battle they'd just had, but Prost didn't care. If more people knew about it, that didn't really affect him much.

Squinting forward, he thought back to when he'd seen Janis in Arivan, the small coastal town to the east. Could her former employer be connected in all of this? Prost shook his head. It was something he would have to dig into further.

His mind shifted to Janis, who was a failed experiment. The Seers had come across Janis once or twice in their Sight and she'd stood out. As far as assassins go, she was one of the most skilled and crafty. Her reputation preceded her, though her name did not. She'd had so many false names, it took Prost a long time to learn her real name. It wasn't surprising for her to be pulled in on a job to kill a Lightbearer despite her apparent lack of knowledge about the powers. And now she'd somehow awakened too.

When they first employed her, they had no knowledge of her future. Apparently neither had Evenir, given the deaths of some of their men and women during her awakening. In spite of this, it made the failure of recruiting her that much more poignant. Not taking the opportunity to test her skills and ultimately offer her a place in Watchlight was not just a failure, but a devastation.

Riln hadn't taken well to that one.

Prost shivered slightly when he recalled the destruction of the room and those around him. Riln had shredded a few non-Lightbearer workers who were bringing him food for lunch while he was lashing out at an immune Prost. Losing Janis was not something he could tolerate.

It was as if his thoughts were magnified to the group following behind, as the whispers increased and the air around them seemed to thicken with nervousness. He looked up to see that the mountain entrance to their stables was within half an hour's time.

Knowing Riln would be angry, Prost knew he needed to take the blame. He commanded respect by anger, but he knew taking responsibility built loyalty. After all, no one else could withstand Riln's wrath like he could.

Pulling the reins of his horse, he turned the beast around so he faced the men and women with him.

"Soldiers!" he shouted, "We are almost upon our home, our sanctum, and our leader. We know he will not be pleased with the news of our lost companions or of the boy, but this is my responsibility and his wrath will fall on my shoulders, alone. When we arrive, retire to your beds, get some food —fog, some drink too."

The words were bitter in his mouth, for he also feared Riln's wrath. Some eyes hardened at his words, respect lacking in their eyes, while some looked grateful. Regardless of their thoughts, they would obey. Whether out of fright or loyalty, they would obey. Those who were not scared of him were at least scared enough of Riln.

He felt like an imposter, for he really didn't care that much about the men. Most of them had treated him with contempt since he'd been there, but he knew if he was to be considered second in command, he would need to get some respect by giving a little. He cared about being respected more than he would have liked to admit. Something inside told him that the news of Janis's awakening and the existence of another Voidbearer would spread soon.

Prost seethed at the thought of Janis. For the second time, she'd somehow been able to use her Lightbearing on him. The pit in his stomach deepened before he shoved it away.

During the fight and even just before, no Lightbearing touched me—I'm immune, of the Void. . . . Except for that one moment.

It was brief, but it was enough to rock his confidence yet again. When he'd grabbed her Moving sword, the Light had faded instantly just as he expected it to, but it *had* shoved him. There wasn't any strength behind the shove, but it was still an invisible force he'd only felt once before—and from the same woman.

Shaking his head, he focused on the task at hand.

Within the hour, the horses were stabled and Prost stood in front of Riln, hands behind his back, silence filling the cavern. The lone red orb pulsed slightly above him, indicating his master was agitated, which wasn't surprising to Prost.

"You had one simple job, Prost, and you failed. How many times has that happened in the last weeks? I've made a point to not count, but it's obviously enough times to not be in your favor."

Riln stalked around the room as he spoke, his voice steady, eyes piercing through Prost. The shadows of the pillars flickered with the pulsing Light above, making the red sheen on the rest of the cavern even more eerie and unnerving. Prost waited for the lash-out of power. Riln hadn't slammed him with anything yet, but it would come.

"We were prepared with adequate numbers and Lightbearers; we knew that Evenir would be there. They failed in their claim on the boy because of a variable neither side accounted for—a potential third group. I have reason to believe it is Luden and his band of thieves who are to blame for the death of this new Fixer. I overheard his name spoken to Janis by the one who killed the boy."

Riln cocked his head.

"Luden, the rich man without a spine, the one you insisted would be no trouble for us when we hired Janis months ago?"

The fire behind Riln's eyes intensified and Prost's skin tingled, preparing for the anger from his master.

"Yes, that's the one. Though I don't know that this is retaliation for what we did. The cloaked man only attacked the Lightbearer—then he was gone, as if he'd only been there to kill the new Fixer."

Riln pursed his lips, which were pale enough that they were hard to see in contrast to his bone-white face.

"Intriguing."

Silence followed.

Prost watched as Riln's eyes burst forth with bright red Light, beams extending from them about a handspan. In moments like this, Prost considered just leaving, getting away from the madness before it could manifest itself in his leader.

The vision Riln saw took a bit longer than the normal ones, which only lasted for a few minutes. In this case, Riln was entranced for just over ten minutes, his body stiff and his head angled upward as if he was communing with Lanser in the sky. Suddenly, his eyes dimmed and he eyed Prost.

They stared at each other for just a beat before Riln roared and lunged at Prost, a sword of red flashing into existence as the white man shoved the blade right through his chest. There was a ripping sound from his shirt and cloak being punctured by the sword, but Prost felt nothing. He thanked Lanser for unlimited access to tailors to replace all the clothes Riln ruined. A successive Destroying orb followed, shredding the sleeve near his shoulder, the rest fluttering down to the floor.

Prost stood there, trying to breath evenly. He didn't want Riln to know of his experience with Janis. He had left out the details of how her awakening affected him personally. For some reason, saying that he'd been affected by

Lightbearing would make it real—make it true. So he kept it to himself. Due to Riln's lack of ability to See him or any events in his proximity, he gathered that Riln hadn't and would never see that it had happened.

"Of course, due to your *ailment*," Riln spat, frustration evident in his tone, "the vision I saw was fuzzy. All I could see was the unclear image of a cloaked man."

Riln stepped back and his face looked a bit calmer, though not enough to ensure he wouldn't lash out again at any moment. Prost clenched his jaw, anticipating another blow and praying that he was still immune, even though the thought of him not being immune was ridiculous.

"I did, however, look for Luden. While his image is foggy, I could See that he operates in Stilten and he has quite the network. I can't be sure how he knew about the boy in the square, but it seems only logical that he'd have a Seer with him telling him when awakenings will happen. It's also unclear why he wanted the boy dead—or Marric for that matter—but you will find out for me."

Riln turned then, his back sending the message that he was done.

Prost bowed slightly and turned to leave.

"And Prost," Riln said, inevitably hearing Prost's footfalls as they moved away, "do not fail me again."

Anger continued to boil up inside of Prost, hearing Riln threaten him like this. He knew he could attack the man and kill him in an instant, but it was the unknown that kept him from doing it. Despite their communication with Ugglyn and his urging them to kill each other, Prost couldn't let the monster free. He couldn't know what it would mean if he did, but when something was locked away like that, he figured it was for a reason.

Prost did allow himself the luxury of imagining burying a knife in Riln's chest or even injuring the small man to prove that he could. Instead, he refrained, letting Riln escape his wrath.

As he stalked out of the room, Riln gasped.

"Wait!" he called, a sort of desperation in his voice.

Prost stopped, his ears roaring from anger that peaked inside of him.

"Yes, Riln?" he asked in a measured tone.

"Well, this is interesting, isn't it?" Riln said.

The man's voice had lost both the subtle and the obvious tones of anger and had adopted a more curious timbre. Prost knit his eyebrows, wondering what could have changed his master's mood so quickly.

He turned, ready to see what Riln was thinking, when he saw that he was having a vision. His glowing eyes gazed upward, Riln's arms extended outward.

"What is it?" Prost asked, unwilling to wait for Riln to just tell him.

The pale leader's eyes still glowed red and he was nodding.

"It appears that for the first time ever, we have eight awakenings happening all at once throughout Lindrad."

Prost froze.

Eight? Prost thought, *Fog it, we just got back!*

"Eight, sir? Are you sure they aren't just within a close period of time—?"

"No!" Riln shouted, cutting him off. "Given your lack of Lightbearing, you should trust someone that actually does have it. I'm getting their names and faces now. Prepare five groups of men, small bands—save for one—and prepare to leave immediately."

Prost nodded at the command. For a moment, he thought to ask why only five groups, but he opted not to, assuming that Riln wouldn't take the question well. Turning swiftly, he moved to the doorway.

"And prepare my horse as well, to join the largest of the five groups."

Pausing, he thought on the request, turning once more Riln. "You're coming."

It wasn't a question, but it wasn't quite a statement. The idea of his sickly-looking master joining them on one of their speedy expeditions was ludicrous. Ever since Prost had awakened as K'alek Tar'n, he had only come with them a handful of times to get any newly awakened individuals. Knowing this, Prost didn't want to question Riln's request outright to join them, but at the same time, he had to ensure he'd heard correctly.

"Yes, I don't think I'll want to miss this one. You see, there will be four awakenings in Stilten alone, and I intend on ensuring that we secure all four."

Prost nodded curtly, but dread filled his being. Knowing he would have to travel alongside this man for a long period of time annoyed him. He was tired from having just returned from T'Arren Vale, but even knowing that he could get away once more from this horrid pale man made it worth it, even if he was exhausted.

"I'll ensure we are ready to go within the hour."

"Good, see that you do. I'd rather we not get off on the wrong foot with this journey."

Prost turned and said nothing more, quickly leaving the throne room.

Silently, he marveled at Riln's ego. Images of beating him to death or rigging his saddle to tear apart when the horse got going too quickly flashed in his mind. He kept them there to assuage his anger, even while knowing they were an impossibility.

20

They'd arrived back at Terris Green, and within minutes, Janis retreated to her room to get a nap. Alsry, having rested from the journey, had insisted on heading to the war room to discuss what happened with Watchlight in the city, but Janis had other plans in mind. She had an appointment with the in-between to determine why their mission had failed.

She'd thought about entering the memory while they traveled, but given the size of Watchlight's operation, Janis knew she needed to be on her guard the entire journey, lest they get ambushed by black-cloaked men.

Her mind had reeled at what the man had said before running off along the rooftop.

"Luden says hello."

Fog that man, why does he think he has to have his hand in all this? she thought.

A memory of Luden came to her mind and she almost laughed. The man was a prim and pompous child. He was extremely wealthy, which was obvious not only by the way he dressed, but how he acted. He was entitled, weak, and egotistical. She couldn't think why he would want anything to do with the death of a Lightbearer, either. Then again, he'd hired her to kill

Marric, and with all the commotion, she hadn't been able to do more than wonder why someone like Luden cared or was even aware of Lightbearers.

She knew there was something there, and she needed to try to find it. The stone hallways of Terris Green were mostly empty as she walked back to her room. Despite her efforts to move quickly and quietly, she could still hear faint echoing of the friction from her boots on the ground. Without others in the hallway to drown her sounds out, her footsteps sounded loud and obvious.

Janis glanced up at the blue orbs the size of her head, steady and glowing every four or five paces. It was a marvel that one person could power all of them at once. She couldn't understand how they managed it. It was even more frustrating to realize that she apparently had the ability to produce the power herself, but she'd had little success.

Reaching up to her head, she felt around where the cut had been days ago. There was nothing there, not even pain. How she'd been able to Fix that, she didn't know. Looking down, she noted the spot on her left hand where some debris had sliced her. Of course, a Fixer had healed it soon after they left the city, but she wondered why she hadn't been able to do it first. Janis still felt disappointed that she couldn't get a handle on the powers. If she'd had a choice, she would just give them up altogether, but she didn't think that really was a viable option. Right now, the only thing she could do was try to control them, or to at least keep them in check. She counted herself lucky that she hadn't accidentally summoned a Destroying orb or fallen into a vision which would have rendered her defenseless during the fight.

Despite her survival and obvious lack of success in retrieving the boy, one of the most distracting events of the day was that Harmel had gone missing.

After the rendezvous of their group at T'Arren Vale, they'd waited almost an hour for all the Evenir people to escape the city. By then, the trickle of Evenir members had slowed to nothing and they realized they couldn't fully escape the soldiers without leaving the city entirely.

The hallways were even more lonely at the thought of Harmel being gone.

He was likely left behind as nothing but a corpse.

It was a macabre thought to have about a person, but it was the reality of life. Part of the reason Janis wasn't religious was due to her constant proximity to death. If she wasn't the one killing, which she often was, she was at least around it. Her only hope in life was to survive to live another day, which she'd succeeded at, so far.

Still, a pang of something wrought in her gut at the thought of Harmel being dead. Never at any moment would she admit to calling him a friend, but he had gained something from her that most people couldn't: her trust, at least to some degree. Janis never could fully trust anyone, but she could at least know that he had her back and would be there to call out an attacker from behind.

He's dead, no need to worry about it now, Janis thought brusquely.

Her trust had only ever really been extended to one other person, and he'd left her before dying to a knife during a reckless job he'd attempted.

Macks.

Janis's mentor and teacher of all things assassin had left her, despite all the things they'd been able to accomplish together.

A burning rushed into her chest and made it feel tight. She'd not experienced the plague of love since her parents and only brother had been taken by sickness all those years ago, except for Macks.

Janis let her mind drift off into the memory of their last mission together.

MACKS LEAPT *from the wall to the ground, landing so softly that Janis thought it impossible. Grinning, she made a show of jumping high into the air, her body becoming weightless for only an instant before gravity tugged her heavily downward. Deftly, she took the weight of her fall with bent knees, her landing even quieter than his own.*

"Showing off does no good to an assassin, unless you are trying to get yourself killed," Macks said flatly, amusement showing in his eyes, regardless of his tone.

"Humility isn't harmful to a master either, I think," she replied, staring at him directly.

He smiled at the comment. "Neither is an ego, which it would appear you have in excess."

"Let's just say you've taught me pretty well."

And he had. For years, she'd traveled with him and learned the ropes, become experienced in intrigue and acting, lying and fighting with daggers and whatever else. Now she was eighteen and could more than keep up with his antics.

"Regardless, let's just focus on this job and not get ourselves—or more importantly, each other—killed."

He grinned then, his chiseled jawline defined by the street lamp hanging a few paces away.

The night was dark, save for the growing light of Isllan on the rooftops and tops of buildings. Mallan had set only minutes ago and the third moon was making its way along the sky. Stilten was a large city, perhaps even the same size of T'Arren Vale. So many thieves, assassins, and other criminals housed their operations in the alleys and cellars of the city. In other places, people stayed in their homes to hide from the fog and its horrendous effects, but not in Stilten. Here, people hid from the dangers of the people roaming the streets, seeking their next victim of theft or death.

"This should be a clean and easy one," Macks whispered as they stood there. "We move in, eliminate Ulivarin, then leave. He should be here alone, save for his bodyguard. You drop the guard, I drop him, then we're out for the bounty. Clear?"

Janis nodded. "Less talk and more moving."

His eyes twinkled at the comment. "Fog, I taught you well."

"Pat yourself on the back again for that one. You're clearly not even a little proud of it."

He glared at her for show, then crept forward.

Janis's eyes fell on the back of his neck, his black hair lengthening there. He pulled up his collar as he shifted into the shadows of the street.

Her heart thumped loudly, a tingling filling her stomach and chest. She let the feeling run through her, endorphins energizing her. Then his voice rang in her head.

Rule number one: don't give your trust to anyone.

Despite the rule, and despite the many times he'd tried to remind her, they'd been together for five years, but only as ward and master. Not once had he indicated or shown any feeling for her, but that didn't matter. He was attractive, he was skilled, he had given her a new birth —a new life from when she was orphaned all those years ago, and now he was more to her than she could explain.

She followed him, pushing the thoughts away and shifting her senses from the infatuated feelings that were pulsing through her now. He was quick, but she was quicker. In no time, she'd caught up to him and he turned to look her in the eyes. With a quick nod, he pointed to the tall building on their left. The lamps had been extinguished already, but that was unsurprising. Gangs often didn't want anyone poking into their business, so they'd make sure there was little to no light exposing their actions.

Ulivarin was the ringleader of one of the Stilten gangs. They'd been paid to kill him in an attempt to cause a war between the few groups as they speculated who killed their leader. While Janis felt uneasy about the job, Macks assured her that their involvement would be discreet and lucrative. Still, something pulled at her gut and she didn't like the feeling. It was Macks, though, and she'd come to trust him more than he'd taught her to trust anyone.

They both startled at the movement of the fog coming around the corner, and Janis alone paused to deal with the effects. Macks had continued unhampered, and had almost made it to the door at the top, but she caught up quickly. Under normal circumstances, the door would have been guarded from the outside, but the guards would have moved inside during the fog so as to avoid the oddness from the mist and the other strange things that could happen in it. With a twinkle in his eye, he knocked softly on the door. When nothing happened, he rapped on it again.

After a few moments, the wood door slid open slowly.

"Prolly jus' a bird. Grit, jus' leave it alone."

A grunt was all that was heard before a man started to move out of the building. Before the guard made it even a few inches, Macks lashed out with his dagger, slicing a shallow mark on the man's exposed and beefy forearm.

"What in Lanser's—?" was all he managed to say before collapsing forward, the poison quickly taking hold. It wouldn't kill him, but it would make him ill for at least a week. Anticipating the thud of the large man, Macks dove in front of him to brace his fall. He grunted with effort when the larger man landed on him as dead weight, the poison having knocked him out.

"Grit, what's goin' on?" the other voice said. Macks gestured with his head to Janis, but she had anticipated the command. She pushed off of the unconscious man's back and spun in the air, eyes scanning quickly for the guard's companion.

Spotting him instantly, she sliced his cheek with the same poison and he fell straight down, Janis barely catching him before he could loudly thump to the ground. He had given a small yelp of surprise just before going unconscious. A quick scan of the area showed that no one had been alerted.

Macks slipped in behind her, face red from exertion.

"Fog it, that man's three times my size. Lucky you weren't first in line—he'd have crushed you to bits," he whispered, the sound barely audible. The only reason she could hear it was because of her extensive training on hearing focus. She'd learned to tune out all other sounds but ones that didn't match the regularity of the location.

She didn't respond, but rolled her eyes to ridicule her mentor. He threw a real punch at her, which she easily dodged. Macks didn't play; when he attacked, he did it in earnest. He'd said that it was better to train that way because it was more effective. Real pain caused real reactions.

She returned with a quick chop, which he easily dodged. They then moved along the wooden rafters of the building. The floor, rather than being covered with containers and supplies, was full of tables, chairs, and other furniture for lounging. There was a muffled conversation taking place below.

Macks gestured enthusiastically to get her attention and she looked over at him. He pointed to the guards on the other side of the rafters, then moved his finger over his throat to indicate she should take them out. Smirking at his gestures, she slipped around to where the other two guards were standing. As she moved toward them, she noticed something odd, something that seemed off. They each stood firmly upright and unmoving. Before getting too close, she stood in the shadows and observed them, unsure what to think. Even after a few minutes, the men still hadn't moved. Normal people—even assassins—couldn't hold still for that long. Her gut wrenched as she realized something bad was about to happen. She spun around to see across the rafters where Macks was preparing a dagger with lethal poison. He eyed the group sitting at one of the tables below, Ulivarin right in the center of the group, boasting about something Janis couldn't hear. Janis suddenly realized these were dummies, put there as a distraction.

Movement behind Macks caught her eye, and she saw a guard advancing on him. Her mentor was too distracted taking aim with his newly poisoned dagger to notice anything. Janis grit her teeth and gestured wildly, resisting the temptation to yell at him. Thinking quickly, she drew a small dagger. She knew she didn't have time to lace it with anything, so she aimed right at the man's eye. In the dark it would be tricky, but there wasn't time.

Janis flung the dagger over the open space below, watching it fly almost true. In her haste, she miscalculated the aim and rather than it slamming into his eye socket, the dagger took his left ear clean off. Regardless, it had the intended effect and the man stopped his advance, howling in pain. Macks jumped at the sound and turned, quickly slicing the man's neck to stop the scream and kicked him to the ground with a thump.

The room below exploded into action even before Ulivarin could shout about invaders. Loud thumping behind Janis caused her to turn and see a large man barreling toward her. Panicked, she jabbed forward with her long dagger, right into the man's chest. His momentum was too strong and he slammed into her, pushing both of them over the railing. Terror filled Janis and instincts took over as she wrapped her arms around the large man and twisted in the air so that he would break her fall. Bones cracked in his back as they crashed to the floor. The wind was knocked out of her lungs and she gasped in surprise. Without hesitation, she sprung to her feet and yanked the dagger from the man's chest. He lay there, unmoving.

Three men appeared from the shadows, one of them Ulivarin himself.

"Well, well. We wondered when you'd show up."

Janis's blood chilled at the words. Shuffling feet and grunting indicated that Macks was fighting up above. That was confirmed when a woman's unconscious body fell from the rafters onto one of the rickety tables, crushing it under her weight.

"What? No smart words from you this time? Yurifal said that you had quite the tongue on you when he hired you for this."

"Fog you, that's all I have to say," Janis said, just before flicking her long dagger at the head of one of the men. The man was large and brutish, but his speed contradicted his appearance as he dodged her throw. The large dagger thunked loudly into the wooden post there. Before she could grab another dagger, strong arms wrapped around her and gripped her tightly. She grunted in surprise, but couldn't do much else.

"Yes, hold her just like that. I want to carve her to pieces for her interference."

Janis glared at him before looking upward.

Her eyes met Macks and he looked at her, pain in his eyes. She stared at him, *shifting her eyes back at the man holding her to indicate that Macks should knock him out.*

Macks looked at her, unmoving.

"Get the other one, now!" Ulivarin ordered some of his men.

Janis watched in disbelief as Macks looked at her and shrugged before turning into the darkness and disappearing.

Her stomach sank.

Suddenly, words rang again in her mind: Rule number one, don't give your trust to anyone. Even me.

Rage filled her being, along with terror. She was stuck, and Macks had left her to die.

Yurifal had set them up. Janis couldn't say she was surprised, but she was angry. When she had told Macks that getting involved with the gangs wasn't going to end well for them, she meant something like this.

"You stole something of mine a few months ago, I'd like it back."

Janis froze, thinking back to the only other job they'd done in Stilten in that time frame. They'd been hired by Stilten's local government to recapture stolen goods and the head of the thief.

"I see your mind working there. Careful, might get you into trouble."

Forcing down the fear, she opened her mouth and spoke measuredly.

"If I remember correctly, that was a recovery job. You stole that first, tripe."

Ulivarin advanced quickly and punched her heavily in the face. Pain lanced up her jaw into her head, her vision going blurry. The world spun for a minute and she heard Ulivarin shouting now.

"You killed my sister, wench, and took her head! Thing is, gangs know something about family and taking care of their own. Yurifal agreed that having the likes of you and that other idiot running free wouldn't stand." He smiled, teeth stained from excessive ale consumption, his breath putrid.

"And now you will die."

Janis eyed a glint as he pulled a dagger from his belt and thrust it toward her. Thinking fast, she pushed heavily with her legs to the side. The man holding her from behind hadn't expected it and grunted. It wasn't perfect, but it was enough. Ulivarin's blade grazed her side, causing it to sting. A majority of the blade slid into her captor and he gasped. She took the moment to throw her head back, knocking him in the nose. His grip loosened and he fell to the ground. Janis dipped low, her head still aching from the Ulivarin's punch, and tripped him to the ground. In quick successionshe slammed her hand into another man's shin, breaking it easily. In the process, she took a sword in the shoulder from one of the other guards.

Gasping from the pain, she pulled out her last dagger and jumped toward the man, the sword still in her flesh. It slid further through her shoulder and the man, completely shocked at what she did, stood there as if petrified. The dagger entered right through his eye, and he fell to the ground. Janis yanked the sword out of her shoulder, gripped the handle, and swung it wide into Ulivarin's legs. He screamed in pain as it severed one of his legs with its sharp blade.

Janis heard footsteps from the stairs in the darkness. She saw people advancing from all over. Her injured arm was losing strength, but she knew she still had her other arm. Running forward toward one of the tables, she saw an ugly woman, face scarred from what looked like burns, appear out of the darkness in front of her. She raced to one of the many tables, leapt onto the bench and then the table itself before she pushed off the top as hard as she could. She flew into the air and caught the railing of the rafters with her good arm, grunting.

Curses from below gave away their surprise while she struggled up onto the balcony. Her injured arm was no good, so she had to put her leg up and shift her weight onto the edge. She could hear footsteps in the dark pounding up the stairs to her and she stood up as fast as she could before pushing hard and fast to the door. She slipped out quickly and blended into the shadows, barely escaping the gang leader and her death.

While she ran, her terror turned to sorrow and anger as she remembered the image of her mentor, her friend, and the man she'd grown to love—turning aside and abandoning her.

THE STONE FLOOR and walls of the wide hallway on the way to her quarters were even more depressing after the memory. She'd learned a few days later that Yurifal and Ulivarin had caught up with Macks and slit his throat. Janis had left Stilten and hadn't been back since. She'd received jobs from people who lived there, but she had made a point to not go back since the event. Gangs didn't forget a vendetta and she anticipated they wouldn't soon forget their grudge. Coincidentally, Luden's base of operations was Stilten. His band wasn't a gang, but he had enough money to keep any potential gang enemies quiet and away from him.

A distant sorrow tried to pierce her chest at the loss of Macks, but it was fairly easy to ignore and push away. She'd become too attached to him. She'd ignored his advice and not only trusted him, but had fallen for him in ways she was embarrassed to admit. Since then, she hadn't bothered with letting herself love or even trust anyone else. It was a lonely life, but it was required for her to do the job of an assassin.

She rounded the corner, moving more quickly now to ensure that she had some uninterrupted time to look back on the memory. As she turned the bend, she paused, seeing figures at the end of the hallway. Avryn and Marric were talking as they moved in her direction. She froze and almost jumped back around the wall to hide from them, but decided not to. Janis wasn't in the mood to talk to them, but she didn't really have an alternative if she was to get to her quarters fast enough. The back of her mind itched with the sensation that someone was probably on their way to ask her to talk to Magness. Of course she couldn't really know, but her past experiences indicated that it was probably true.

Hardening her resolve, she stalked toward them. They didn't see her right away because they were deep in a conversation about something, but eventually Marric turned her way, seeing movement there. His face lit up when he saw her.

"Janis! You made it back!"

Marric rushed to her and opened his arms to hug her. At the last moment, his face changed to more thoughtful and he paused, putting his arms down.

"Sorry, just excited to see you. I know that you aren't keen on hugs."

Janis raised her eyebrow at him, surprised.

He's changed somehow, more serious.

"Yes, I believe I've mentioned that a few times. Glad to see that it's finally sticking."

Marric blushed and Janis noted that some things hadn't changed, despite his sudden seriousness when he approached her rather than just hugging her.

"Regardless, yes—we made it back safely, but I regret to say that it wasn't without consequence. Alsry and I made it out, but many of those with us did not."

Marric's face transitioned from blushing to pale at the reminder of the loss. "What happened?" he asked.

Avryn was studying her, his demeanor unusually down. "I suspect that there is a longer story at play. Rather than have you repeat your words, I imagine we should go to Magness in the war room and discuss there."

Marric nodded, showing he understood but saying nothing else.

"I think Alsry can talk through whatever Magness needs to hear—I'm retiring to my quarters for a bit to rest up."

"Rest? I thought you never had to do that," Marric replied. It was clear he was trying to make a joke, but it came off awkward, as if he wasn't completely himself, either.

Apparently they have a story of their own, Janis thought.

"Yes, well, as much as I wish I wasn't human and could go with no sleep forever, that isn't the case. I'll need only an hour or so to sleep. I should be fine after that."

Marric looked at her incredulously.

"An hour seems hardly enough, but I know that you have some reason to disagree with that," Avryn said flatly, echoing the feeling that Marric showed through his face.

Janis shrugged and walked past them.

"Regardless of what you think, I believe it's enough."

Technically, only a few minutes was probably enough. Time was odd in the in-between. Janis had tried to understand how time worked inside the place, but it was never consistent. Many times she'd relive a memory that lasted only a few minutes and an entire day would pass outside the in-between. Sometimes she'd be in the in-between for hours and come out with only minutes having passed in the real world. Somehow, remembering her memories always lasted exactly the amount of time she had. She couldn't even begin to understand how it worked, but it definitely made the skill even more helpful.

"I say take more time, if you need. Unless you ran into something like we did while you were out, there isn't a need for rushing."

Janis smirked at the comment.

"That intentionally cryptic comment isn't going to draw me back to the war room right now. It was worth a try, but I'm set on something and I'm going to do it."

Avryn scowled at her. "While it wasn't intentionally so, the comment was cryptic, sure."

Making a show of it, she sighed and shrugged.

"Talk to Alsry—we had quite a scuffle and yes, I'd say we encountered something very odd, but she can handle it fine."

At the comment, Marric's eyes wandered down as he once again inspected her state. Clothes sliced and tattered in places, she had a bandage on her hand and worry in her eyes. Seeing his review of her, she held up her bandaged hand and wiggled her fingers.

"Just a flesh wound, don't worry a bit. Unfortunately, Harmel disappeared. I can't say if he died or not, but he didn't return with us."

This time, Avryn's face flashed with sorrow and a bit of anger. He opened his mouth to say something, but shook his head before softening what might have been a scolding tone. "Then you must have run into something terrible, indeed. Take your rest, then come to discuss the events."

Avryn nodded curtly with his words and put an arm around Marric, who looked confused. Janis assumed that he was trying to process what happened: the news that one of his friends was possibly dead, the knowledge that others had died, and even Janis had been hurt. It was apparently too much for him. Janis wondered if she ought to feel bad about dropping that all on him so suddenly, but it couldn't be avoided. At least Avryn knew she didn't intend on elaborating.

The moment the two turned away, she flipped around swiftly and moved to her doorway just around the next corner. Moving the curtain aside, she felt annoyed again that she didn't even have a proper door to keep anyone out. To account for that, she took a dagger and slammed it through the curtain edge into the stone behind it. Rock cracked and debris flew from where she'd stuck her dagger in. With a quick motion, she scribbled the words *Resting, leave me alone or die* on a piece of parchment and slammed another small dagger into the wall on the other side of where she'd secured the curtain.

There, if they don't get the message, then they deserve to die.

Moving to her cot, she sat down and focused on what she needed to. She didn't really need to relive all the events of the fighting in T'Arren Vale, she just needed to get back to the moment when the man had appeared and killed the boy. She lay down and thought about the instance while closing her eyes and breathing evenly. Being able to control her mind and memory while sleeping had taken years for her to master, but the time had been well worth it. Thoughts of Macks mingled with the fighting days ago, but they were only residual from the memory she'd recounted just moments before running into Avryn and Marric.

She slipped into sleep and the world around her went black. Janis knew it was because her eyes were closed and she was reverting her attention to the memory. Before delving in, she followed her normal practice of checking her connection to the outside world. She could still feel the cot under her in the back of her mind. The room around her was quiet, but she could feel the air faintly moving from vents built into every room for natural air flow.

Satisfied, she let her consciousness fall, not physically, but figuratively into the memory. Her feet landed on the cobblestones and pain erupted in a few places on her body. Her hand stung, the memory of the debris slicing the back of it tempting to pull her away to that moment. She held strong and didn't let the in-between pull her away.

Janis relived the events of her fight with Prost in the T'Arren Vale square, feeling satisfied with her small wins against him each time they happened. Soon, her past self ran toward the boy.

Janis took a moment to check her peripheral as she ran, just in case she spotted something useful. For just a flash, she saw Harmel fighting with another man. Harmel gained the advantage, but instead of killing him, he bounded down an alley with some retreating Evenir men.

Harmel, she thought, *he had been there the whole time. What happened to him?*

Something panged within her and she balked at the feeling. As much as she hated to admit it, she'd grown fond of the man, which in turn increased her concern over him. She hadn't had to worry about anyone but herself only months ago; now here she was worrying about others and forming relationships with them.

Before long, the peripheral of Harmel fighting disappeared as she and

Alsry rounded the corner. Soon enough they were there, watching the boy's awakening from twenty paces away.

"*We'll need to grab him. This awakening isn't dangerous like that of a Mover or a Destroyer.*"

Her past self moved toward the boy, but this time she saw the man fall and smile at her through his hood. The man brandished the knife, obviously teasing them before he stabbed the boy right through.

Suddenly a tugging sensation pulled at her gut and her memory froze. Another memory slammed into her, almost dragging her out of this one. The only time she'd felt this type of tugging was in that cave ages ago when Riln had appeared to her for the first time.

Her senses in the real world tingled, and she mentally reached out to that line. The only feeling that had changed was something in her eyes. Somehow she knew that a vision had started, her Seeing being activated by something. Despite her in-between self being frozen, Janis heard a ripping sound and as a new iteration of herself, she fell to the ground, stunned. Turning quickly, she saw her past self still frozen, a bit of shock and anger in her eyes as she watched the man stabbing the boy. The familiarity of her separating from her body meant that she'd slipped from the in-between, the limited view of her reliving her memory, into a full-on vision as a Seer.

Everything started again. Janis took immediate advantage of being separated from her past self and sprung to her feet, vaulting to the cloaked assailant. She jumped at him and threw a fist into his face. Unsurprisingly, it went through harmlessly.

Was worth a try, she thought.

The hooded man didn't look familiar at all, not even when she was this close to him. He turned, oblivious to her vision-self and ran toward the alley. Janis easily kept pace with him. It was as if she had unlimited energy. She couldn't really even feel herself running, which was disorienting to some degree.

Loud footsteps behind announced her past self in pursuit.

Lanser's beard, I was loud, wasn't I?

It didn't matter, for she wasn't trying to hide.

The man reached the back of the alley and jumped quickly from the wall of one building to the neighboring building with such speed that even

Janis marveled. It was as if the man was weightless for a moment before he grabbed the lip, pulling himself up and landing deftly on the roof.

Janis cursed to herself that she couldn't follow, but then gasped slightly when her body, free to move as a Seer, rose suddenly in the air, flying upward until she was level with the man.

Well, that was unexpected.

Turning, she was face-to-face with the man now. He glowered down at Janis's past self and then spoke, his voice heavily accented.

"Ey! Luden says 'ello, luv."

The idea that Luden sent this man to kill the boy frustrated her. She still couldn't understand why the rich man cared about this boy, let alone Marric. The fact that the two most recent assassination jobs she knew of from Luden were both Lightbearers wasn't a coincidence. Teenage boys weren't a threat to anyone, save for their abilities.

Just like she remembered, the man turned and her past self lost sight of him instantly as he moved to the other side of the roof and leapt to the next building over. Janis rushed after him, her feet moving, though she couldn't feel the hardness of the roof under her at all. She gritted her teeth at the oddness of having practically no normal physical feeling.

She jumped easily to the neighboring building and followed the man, keeping pace without trouble. It was then that she remembered she didn't even have to run. Her vision-self would follow him at his pace if she willed it. His movements were quick and unfettered, as if he'd been doing this for years. Janis wasn't surprised; she knew she wasn't the only one in Lindrad who could move that quickly and fluidly, but it frustrated her that she hadn't been on her guard more. The man stopped suddenly and froze where she was.

Movement to her left caused her to suck in air loudly and flip in that direction. Another black-cloaked man stood there, hood up, staring at her and the assassin who'd just murdered the boy.

Eyes narrowing, she assessed the situation. Why the assassin had stopped, she didn't know, but the other black-clad figure wasn't approaching, speaking, or doing anything, really. He just stood there. Janis could tell it was a he, or rather, she assumed it was, based on his build and how he stood.

Shifting her focus to the original subject of her chase, she noted how odd it was that he just stood there. Taking her chances, she kept her other eye warily on the figure on the other roof and moved to get a better look at the assassin. Her gut still clenched and her senses remained on edge. Anything could happen to her, and once again the knowledge of her incorporeal state was not giving her much comfort in the situation.

She was finally able to move around the assassin to see his face. He looked determined and mirthful. What she noticed immediately was that he hadn't stopped at all, he'd frozen. His body wasn't moving with any breath or even the slightest shake, which even the most skilled person couldn't achieve. Her senses heightened the moment she saw his frozen state, and she turned to the figure across the way. Somehow, she knew it was his doing.

"Who are you? Why did you freeze this?" she asked bluntly.

The figure shook his head and began laughing. It wasn't a scornful or dark laugh, it sounded genuinely mirthful. Janis noticed in the waning sunlight that blue and red Light shone in the distance back where she'd just run from. Apparently, some Lightbearers from both sides hadn't made it out fast enough before the militia got to the square. The distant Light lit up the left side of the cloaked figure, as if both Mallan and Stellan had somehow fallen to the ground in the middle of the city, lighting the surrounding buildings and streets.

No answer came from the man, so Janis moved closer. Finally, seeing that she moved closer to him, he lifted his hands slowly, making her stop to see what he was doing. He reached up and pulled back his cloak hood, showing a face with a few small scars on the cheeks and forehead. His eyes were strikingly green, his messy black hair and chiseled jaw lit up by the distant Light from the square.

Even with the scars and the rugged appearance of his hair, the man was quite good-looking.

It wasn't his looks that made Janis's heart skip a beat, however. It was a familiar pang that struck her like an unexpected fist to the gut, the force knocking the air out of her, both in shock and almost pain.

Macks....

Seeing him here again somehow mingled with the memory and felt like slamming hard into a wall. The fact that he'd slipped into her memory again was so unusual. When she'd entered the in-between every time before, never had she seen memories mixed like this. Whether it was her losing control of her in-between or the fact that now she had Seeing to mess up her normal flow in the memories, she couldn't tell. There he was, the man she'd fallen for just before he died, exactly from her memories.

Before she could analyze the situation much further, she felt her external senses perk up, sounds of footsteps approaching her. A hard hand grabbed her shoulder outside of the in-between and she clenched her fists, wanting to stay but needing to address the danger outside of the memory. The world spun in a whirl of colors and then she was staring up at a man's face. Immediately, she threw out her fist, catching him in the gut.

Grunting, he jumped back and shouted.

"Lanser's own, Janis! It's just me!" Avryn yelled, holding his stomach. "If I'd known you'd assault me, I would have Conjured a wall between us."

Janis smirked at his comment. "You've known me for how many weeks now? You really thought you'd be able to lay a hand on me, even in my sleep, and not expect me to slam you? It's clear you still know nothing of me."

Avryn pressed his lips into a thin line, the look on his face obviously agreeing with her words, but not wanting to admit it.

"Magness needs you, now. You've rested for an hour so it's time to share what you know. Alsry started to share what she knew, but it's clear that you have pieces she is lacking."

He still held his hand over his stomach, but he didn't appear to be in too much pain anymore. It appeared he was trying to process what just happened.

"Fair enough, my rest was sufficient."

Even as she said it, she knew it wasn't true. Still, she hadn't needed the rest for her own body as much as she just needed more time to look back. The quest to the in-between revealed nothing to her other than the assassin was really skilled at roof-hopping and that she couldn't keep her memories from flooding together. If anything, her time in the in-between had made her more frustrated with herself.

If I can't get a hold on this Lightbearing rubbish, then it's going to get me killed, she thought.

Regardless of her inner turmoil, she looked at Avryn condescendingly and grinned.

"Shall we, then? Perhaps you'll need a salve for that bruise," Janis mocked.

Avryn rolled his eyes, but beckoned her. "Just come, but don't swing any more fists. I'm not as patient as you're used to seeing me."

Janis raised an eyebrow at the threat, but took it seriously. She didn't fear Avryn, but she knew he could be someone she didn't want to mess with.

"After you, then."

21

Marric sat thoughtfully in the war room. He wasn't there alone, but the silence was palpable as others processed the information Alsry had just given them. After hearing how they'd lost half of the T'Arren Vale party, Magness immediately sought Janis and her side of the story. She'd indicated to Alsry that it wasn't out of lack of trust, but because she needed to hear every possible detail.

The chair beneath him felt extra hard for some reason, as if he'd been sitting there for an extended period of time. However, he'd only been there for less than an hour. Something about hearing of all the dead made him more sensitive to his surroundings. That must have been the case, for the blue orbs of Light in the war room were melancholy to him. He suddenly missed sunlight and fresh air.

Sadness still hovered inside his chest and stomach at the thought of all the death. They'd only lost two with their company to retrieve his father, but that had been enough to shake him. Alsry and Janis had left with a lot more men and women than that.

Marric's chest constricted with regret. He felt guilty for what had happened, though it made no sense. Even if he'd gone with them as originally intended, he was a brand-new Lightbearer and likely couldn't have done much more to protect them than Janis and Alsry had. The worst part was that Harmel had disappeared. Harmel's smile flashed in his mind and Marric felt tears welling up in his eyes. He quickly forced the thought of Harmel being dead out of his mind, clearing his throat loudly to forget it. The sound caused a few of the others in the room to turn and look at him. He flushed, not liking the attention and stared hard at the wooden door to the library outside the room.

He allowed himself to get lost in the pattern of the large tree carved into the door. The artisan had somehow been able to capture the faces of many men and women inside the branches and leaves of the tree.

His eyes immediately wandered to a face at the center of the branches. The woman there was beautiful and looked so young. He didn't know how it was intended for her to be portrayed, but she looked to be only a few years older than him. Magness had told him that it was his mother, Talatha. Apparently, she had led Evenir for years before she died only months before Marric had arrived. Regret filled him that he hadn't awakened earlier and been taken here before his mother had fallen.

Had she known that I'd awaken? he wondered, allowing himself to be distracted.

When he'd learned his mother was a skilled Shielder, he immediately asked if Lightbearing was hereditary. Magness had shaken her head and indicated that though it happened sometimes, it wasn't often enough to be considered hereditary. There still wasn't a pattern to the awakenings, as far as anyone could tell.

"She was quite a woman, I must say," a voice to his left said, making him jump.

He turned to see Varith studying the door alongside him. Marric didn't know how he'd managed to get there without Marric noticing.

"Mmmhmm," Marric said, at a loss for words.

"I was grateful to fight alongside her. I can't even tell you how many times she saved not only my life, but many of our lives with her quick reflexes and Shielding. She was quite something," Varith said in his deep voice.

Marric furrowed his brow, suddenly realizing he'd never taken the time to learn more details about his mother and her time as Evenir's leader. When he'd first arrived and found out that the woman on the door was his mother, he was so astounded that he'd been forced to push it from his mind to save himself from overwhelm. That, and Janis, Shrell, and Harmel had been in danger of being attacked by Watchlight any moment.

"You knew her, then?"

The question sounded stupid, given that Varith had just said he fought with her, but Marric didn't know what else to say.

"Yes, I did. We all did. She was an incredible leader, probably the best. No offense to Magness over there."

Magness apparently had heard the conversation and perked up.

"I could never take offense to hearing that my sister was the best leader. I myself would have followed her anywhere. Not only was she wise, clever, and bold, but she was gentle and cared deeply about all of us."

The dark-skinned man put his arm around Marric and the two continued staring at his mother's carved face.

"I probably am not the only one to say this, but I loved your mother, Marric," Varith said wistfully. "Not only was she a great leader, but adored by all who knew her. It was a terrible loss for Evenir."

The doors at which they stared suddenly flew open, the bang causing Marric to jump. In strode a tired-looking Janis and Avryn.

Lanser's beard, she looks weary.

Marric was struck by the sight of her, especially because ever since they'd been traveling together, not once had she looked so haggard.

The room suddenly came to life as everyone was pulled out of their thoughtful state. The group was small; only the major generals of the companies attended. This plus Avryn, Shrell, and Janis made up the whole group. Turrin sat next to Rivelen across the room, the backs of their chairs against a topographical map of Lindrad. Shrell had been whispering quietly with Varith before the company leader had come to talk to Marric.

"While I'm glad to hear that you are recovering from your injuries, I think we must talk about what happened."

Janis looked at the Evenir leader skeptically, then raised her eyebrows.

"All business and no fun. My kind of woman, there."

Magness rolled her eyes and gestured inwards to the others in the room. She had been inspecting something on the map while they waited.

A few moved closer to the table in the center of the room, while most stayed where they were and listened from a distance.

Unsurprisingly, Janis was one of these, as if she was apprehensive about getting too close. Most of the group didn't notice her intentional distancing from the others, but Avryn and Magness did, exchanging curious looks. Despite their interaction, Magness began talking anyway.

"Alsry has given me a brief summary of what happened in T'Arren Vale, but I felt that we should have Janis come explain any other details that might have been missed. Dear Alsry is still exhausted from the trip, and I fear that her fatigue has prevented her from sharing intelligence that could be key to the situation."

She turned to look at Janis, who was fiddling with one of her dagger harnesses as if she didn't care what was being talked about. There was something about her that Marric couldn't put a finger on for a moment. She was different, though he couldn't really describe why.

Janis, noticing the group watching her, finally spoke.

"Oh, is it my turn now? Well, don't you want to share what Alsry has already given you so that I don't repeat myself?"

Magness shook her head, her short mousy hair swinging around her head slightly as she did so.

"No, I think it is prudent for you to share whatever you have in whatever detail. I don't mind hearing duplicate words, and I think the others would agree."

Heads bobbed around the table as the others showed their affirmation.

"It better be a roit good story, tho'. Oi ain't gonna stick aroun' fer it if yeh ain't gonna make it good," Turrin joked.

Janis stared at him flatly.

"I suspect you should just leave now, then. Storytelling—other than to disguise and endear myself to someone I'm about to kill—is not something I care to develop."

"Okay now," Magness cut in, "let's not detract from what you have to say."

The leader shot daggers with her eyes directly at Turrin, who feigned fright, putting his hands up to protect himself. Then he chuckled and gestured grandly with his arms out for Janis to start.

They stared at her as she considered what to say, a thoughtful look on her face.

That's it, Marric suddenly realized, *she's distracted by something.*

Marric didn't really know Janis that well, but her demeanor had changed from when they saw her just before she rested to now. Something was clearly on her mind and it must have been complex, for she was a bit distant, as if whatever else she was thinking about was splitting her attention. It was eerie to Marric, for he'd never really seen her that way before. Janis had a way of always being vigilant and focused in even the most stressful situations. He wondered what could have shaken her like this.

"While I don't like the idea of telling you all that happened, I will tell you what I think you should know."

Magness opened her mouth to protest, but Janis glared at her.

"With respect, you don't all need to know my life history. Know that I don't withhold any information if I think it would be a detriment to you or anyone here."

Magness's face hardened and she narrowed her eyes at Janis. "You may not consider yourself part of Evenir, but this is *my* home and these are *my* people. If you are hiding anything that will harm them, I will expel you from here without any regret. If you can't respect me or my leadership, then you can leave, Prime or not."

Janis stared at Magness. The assassin didn't look angry, but rather impressed. Janis gave a slight nod, then continued.

"Understood. I will tell you all the important details. When we got to the city, I split off from the main group in order to scale the wall and find my own way in. Wearing disguises, though sometimes I am prone to do, is not my style. Thus, I scaled the wall from one of the taller trees on the outskirts of the city. Just before I jumped, however, I had some sort of vision."

"So you are developing your Lightbearing, then?" Magness cut in.

Janis looked annoyed at the interruption, but nodded, looking away.

"It's not worth talking about too much, but I Saw Avryn and Turrin displaying their Conjuring readily to some black-robed figures standing in a forest somewhere."

Avryn stared at her curiously. "You Saw us with Narim, then?"

Janis nodded, looking down at a scuff on her boot.

"It wasn't much, but it looked like you were about to have a good bout with them. Judging by the look on your face, it didn't go as well as you hoped it would."

Avryn's look immediately melted into a more annoyed one, but he didn't say anything else. "We'll get to our part, just keep going," he said, curtly.

Janis either didn't notice, which Marric assumed wasn't the case, or she just ignored his tone.

"After the vision, I jumped to the wall and snuck to the square where I had Seen that the boy would awaken. I happened to run into a small group atop a building in the square, which I took care of pretty quickly."

"'Ow very specific of yeh," Turrin chuckled, fingering a roll he'd procured out of nowhere.

"It wasn't much of a fair fight, but I did get cut in a few places on my hands and face. There was a Destroyer and a Conjurer up there that made things a bit more interesting."

Magness balked at the words. "And you managed to kill them, alone?"

Janis shrugged.

"Turns out that Lightbearing doesn't prevent people from dying from a fall. I just tossed them off the roof, and that did the job just fine."

Avryn looked like he wanted to ask more questions, but he didn't bother. His eyes had suspicion in them, and Marric knew why. Janis's story thus far had been vague in many ways. She was always short and to the point, but there were times when it was obvious she was leaving details out intentionally.

Marric guessed that he as well as Magness and the others were thinking the same thing. She'd revealed before all these incidents that she was some type of Prime Lightbearer and yet she hadn't talked at all about her powers, other than the odd vision she'd seen. When she talked about the group of Watchlight she'd run into, there was something else there, but she hadn't said anything.

Had she used her Lightbearing and she just doesn't want to admit it?

"After taking care of that, I ran to the square where the fighting had begun. The sun had set and I knew the boy would be appearing soon. Seeing Alsry locked in a fight with Prost, I evened the odds and made it possible for her to run to the other side of the square. Unfortunately, the blonde Watchlight woman got in the way and Alsry had to engage with her for a time. I saw the boy enter the square, see the fighting, and turn around quickly. I'd have caught up to him long before he awakened had Prost not been a crafty git, keeping me busy. That, and if the Void form hadn't suddenly appeared, I'd have made it to the boy first for sure."

Magness's eyes narrowed at her words, while Varith's widened. Turrin dropped a piece of his roll, mouth open as he gaped at what she said.

"Wait, *what*?" Alsry asked, her head perking up at Janis's words.

Janis looked from face to face.

"This must have been a part that Alsry left out." The Evenir leader looked to the shorter, dark-skinned woman, eyes searching for an answer from her.

"I didn't see anything of that sort while I was there." Alsry turned to Janis, still looking exhausted, but something coming alive in her after hearing what Janis said. "You saw a Void creature like we all experienced here in Terris Green?"

"Yes, you didn't see it?" Janis had her brow furrowed as she said it, "It was obvious enough that anyone could have seen it, even from far away."

"I saw nothing, though now it makes sense why you were shouting at me to watch from behind."

Janis pressed her lips to a thin line. If she truly had been the only one to see that creature, then there was something else going on entirely. Looking down, she paused for a moment, apparently considering something.

"Ugglyn spoke to me and Livella before we left. He said something like, *Where you go, I will go.* At the time it didn't make much sense, but maybe that's what he meant. If Alsry had truly not seen the creature at all, then—"

"Hold there. Ugglyn—as in the anti-god himself, spoke to you and Livella? What did he say? How can that even be possible? And this is another piece of information that you apparently kept from us," Avryn said, jaw clenched.

Janis rolled her eyes.

Marric considered the implications if Janis had allowed the creature close to their companions, and his stomach dropped a bit. Now that they knew she was the only one there who could have seen the creature, there had to be something missing, a piece of knowledge that they'd have to go digging for.

"Well, that makes sense why you weren't running away when I told you to look out behind you." A bit of amusement came into Janis's voice.

"What doesn't make sense is why you didn't mention anything about this the entire journey home," Alsry said, obviously annoyed at the situation.

Janis shrugged.

"I just threw some Lightbearing at it and it went away, that's all that matters. My mind was more focused on what happened next. Taking down the blonde woman and keeping Prost one step behind us wasn't too difficult with a good throw and some poison powder. After I took care of them, we ran and found evidence of the boy awakening. Light was shining about the rooftops. When we got there, a cloaked man dropped to the ground and stabbed the boy right through the chest."

Marric started at the words. Of course he'd just heard the same thing from Alsry, but the way Janis said it was so brash and forward that it was off-putting. His gut twisted at the thought of a boy, barely past ten, being killed so publicly.

This isn't a world I ever thought I'd be a part of, Marric thought.

"And then you ran off," Alsry said, "While I barely had enough energy to try to Fix the boy."

Nodding, Janis focused on a spot on the wall behind the group. Marric almost looked to see what she was staring at before realizing she was just thinking about what happened.

"Yes, I chased the man down an alley. He slipped away by jumping from wall to wall in the alley and shimmying up to the roof, where he disappeared."

She paused, something else coming to mind which she opted to keep to herself, apparently.

"I lost him there and don't know where he went."

The thoughtful look was back on her face, and Marric knew she was keeping something.

"Before he disappeared though, he told me, 'Luden says hello.'"

Silence.

The room froze at the words, everyone dropping into their thoughts.

"'Oo th' fog is Luden?" Turrin finally said.

Magness cocked her head, looking thoughtful.

"I myself don't know anyone by that name, but then again I don't know every member of the Watchlight group. Is this a new leader of some sort?"

Janis stared at them incredulously.

"I suppose it shouldn't be that much of a surprise that you don't know about Luden and his crew—until now I didn't even realize they had any connection to Lightbearing, but Luden is the man who originally hired me to kill Marric long before he awakened."

Marric's blood immediately ran cold.

She was there to kill me, he thought.

Avryn started at the words. "Wait, *what?*" Avryn said, looking more angry than Janis had ever seen him. "You were hired to *kill* Marric at one point? Why didn't you tell us this?"

Janis shrugged, folding her arms. "You didn't ask. Besides, I never even got the chance to think about killing Marric because Prost came in and gave me a better price to keep Marric alive. Now here I am, caught up in all of this."

Avryn pointed a finger at Janis, anger still apparent in his body language, though his face had softened a bit. "I know this isn't your normal world, Janis, but I believe you would have awakened whether or not you'd been caught up in all this. Just be grateful that you hadn't been on a job when it happened and gotten yourself or others killed because of your ignorance of Lightbearing."

The words were forward and Marric could tell that Avryn intended them to be stinging, but Janis looked unaffected.

"Well, you are right there. I would have certainly been surprised when my body started glowing and I could see the future and whatnot." Janis's tone was light and she appeared to not care about what they were discussing, but her face betrayed her actual interest in all this.

"So, this Luden man paid you to kill Marric before Prost came in and asked you to keep Marric alive?"

Nodding, Janis finally looked up from her hands. "That sums it up, yes."

Avryn's mouth hung open for a moment before he closed it, shaking his head and putting his hands to his forehead. "I don't understand why you didn't tell us this beforehand, but we know now. Why would Luden, whoever he is, care about killing an awakening Fixer? Fog, even a Light-bearer at all?"

Magness stared at Janis the whole time, her face unmoving. Apparently, she was processing something that she didn't feel like voicing to the rest of the group.

"What do you know, Janis?" Magness asked measuredly.

Magness didn't look annoyed, but there was something there Marric wondered about.

"Luden hired me for dozens of jobs before this one. It wasn't unusual for me to meet his men at night to get a job and the name and location of the mark handed off to me. Everything was normal and fine until Prost swooped in and slaughtered them, then quickly threatened me. As far as I know, none of the other marks I'd killed for him had anything to do with Lightbearing. I think if they had, I'd have learned about it already. I don't have any idea why Luden is targeting Lightbearers now...."

The answer was apparently acceptable to Magness, for she nodded and finally looked away.

"Alright, so we know that there is now another group seeking awakening Lightbearers, though it doesn't appear for recruitment. We need to understand why this Luden cares about killing Lightbearers. With Marric it could have been a coincidence, though I doubt it. By killing a second awakening Lightbearer, it had to have been intentional. Were there other non-Watchlight people attacking our men and women?"

She directed the question at Alsry, but the woman looked about to fall asleep. When no answer came, she turned to Janis, eyebrows raised.

"The man wore a black cloak, similar to Watchlight, so it is probable that in the chaos of the fighting there could have been Luden's men, but there isn't a way to be sure."

With a curt nod, Magness turned to Varith. "I know that it's been scarcely two weeks since you returned, but I'll need you and your men to deploy part of your company to learn of Luden. We need to understand what his motivations are and where he operates. Start in T'Arren Vale."

"That won't be necessary," Janis spoke out.

Everyone's heads turned to Janis.

"He operates out of Stilten, where he and his family are from. Luden is incredibly wealthy due to his family's past operations, and he flaunts it. The majority of his men and forces reside and stay there. He's come to the top of thieving crews, and though his ragtag group of mercenaries aren't considered a gang, even the established gangs fear him now."

"Well—" Magness said, "I guess that solves that. Varith, prepare to take your men to Stilten and ask around there."

"I really wouldn't do that if I were you," Janis interjected. "It's not a good idea to go snooping around in a town like Stilten—you could easily be spotted by a Luden informant."

Varith smirked at the words.

"I believe I could hold my own, my dear. Contrary to my appearance, I am quite an adept fighter and can take care of myself."

Janis didn't look impressed. "You look like a pompous rich man to me, but perhaps that qualifies you in your mind," she said offhandedly.

The comment was obviously intended as an insult, but Varith brushed it off.

"Now, now, let's not be like that. My clothes and appearance look immaculate at all times by nature of my awakening. Being a Fixer has more uses than just healing people. I don't see a point in looking dirty all the time or wearing clothes with tears and rips."

Janis burst out laughing. "It is really hard to take you seriously now."

"Stop, you two. We don't have time for squabbling like this," Magness interrupted. "If Luden's man sought to kill the boy, why didn't you just Fix him when the assassin ran away?"

She had turned to Alsry, whose eyes were a bit unfocused. Somehow, the question had gotten to her anyway, causing her to perk up slightly.

"He used some—poison or something. It was pushing back against me."

Marric's insides twisted at her words. The moment he had the feeling, he saw Avryn and Turrin reacting similarly.

"What kind of poison was it?" Avryn asked immediately.

Alsry just shook her head. It was apparent that she was having a hard time grasping reality. A disturbance started outside the wooden door suddenly, and most of them looked up, as if expecting someone to enter.

When no one did, they continued. At that point, the group had fallen silent, save for Turrin.

"Did it glow all odd-loik?"

Alsry blinked and nodded slowly. "I can't be sure, but I think so."

"Yes, it honestly looked like it was made from the same stuff as the Void form I'd seen moments before he appeared," Janis said.

"The form that only you could see," Varith mused.

"Yes, that's the one."

Marric's eyes darted between the two. Neither appeared to like each other, but somehow they had friendly interactions laced with something like malice.

"'Ow could they be th' same? It don' make no sense t'all," Rivelen said.

"I don't know that we can write it off that easily yet," Avryn cut in, awarding him a mean stare from Rivelen. "What happened here in the cavern was so fast, I'm trying to recall what the creatures looked like. They had been a deep silver, almost a black liquid of some sort. The man who stabbed Turrin—his knife glowed a similar color."

Avryn turned to Alsry. "And it fought back. It pushed against my Fixing unlike anything I've ever experienced. I would not have been able to Fix Turrin without Gila and Marric boosting my powers with their Lighting. It was a brilliant thought from Marric."

Marric blushed at the words.

I really need to get better at taking compliments.

Avryn opened his mouth to say more but the doors banged open, Livella striding in.

"Oh, thank Lanser—there you are," she said, looking at Janis.

Janis turned to her, then stepped back. "What do you want?" Janis said, letting her hand fall to her dagger.

"For this stupid voice to get out of my head!" she exclaimed, moving closer to Janis and slumping into an empty chair there. Janis followed Livella with her eyes until she was settled in the chair.

Marric turned, looking out the open wooden doors to see a disgruntled-looking man staring at Livella. He was the Lighter on duty at the moment. Marric had seen him on occasion when he came to the war room, but he'd never stopped to talk to the man because he always looked like he would rather be left alone. Now was no exception.

"So sorry, ma'am. She insisted on coming in, despite what you said. I've been fighting with her for five minutes, though I'm sure you could hear us. The whole of Terris Green likely could."

Magness eyed Livella, who sat in the chair casually and held her hand to her head. "No worries. There shouldn't be any harm in her being here—" she paused then, "considering her role in all of this."

The man cocked his head, apparently not having been filled in on Janis and Livella's connection and the Seal against Ugglyn. Magness soon realized this, and turned to the Lighter with a smile. "No need to worry. She can remain here."

He nodded curtly and shut the doors with a loud thump that echoed in the stone room.

The room stood silent as they watched Livella massage her temples and forehead. When no one said anything, her eyes popped open and she grimaced.

"Don't mind me. I don't really know or care all that much about what you are talking about, I just need the voices to stop. Now that Janis is back I think they might, but I'm going to stick as close to her as possible to make sure."

Janis looked less than pleased by the declaration. "You certainly can try, but I guarantee that I'm faster and more slippery than you are," Janis said, smirking.

Livella finally stopped massaging her head and looked to Janis, her eyes pleading. "Please. I know that you probably don't want me skulking around, but the voices haven't stopped plaguing me since the day after you left." She paused, smiling wistfully, then slumped back in her chair.

"They are finally gone. Don't let me interrupt. Now that I'm here, I think they'll stay away."

It took a few moments for the group to recall where they were going with the conversation, but it soon picked back up.

"Where were we, then?" Magness said, "The poison that was used on both the boy and Turrin must have the same origin. If we know that the boy in T'Arren Vale was killed by Luden's man, why did they care about getting to Narim? These are questions we need answered, Varith."

The smartly dressed man nodded, and moved to the table where a bit of parchment and quill sat.

"The question, then, is what is the poison that they used?"

Marric thought back on Janis's words on the odd creatures that had attacked them a couple weeks ago in this very room. A shudder ran through his spine at the memory. He himself hadn't been that close to the dark forms to really be in danger, but seeing them move toward Avryn had been cause enough for him to panic.

Closing his eyes, he thought back on the memory and felt his eyes change, as if they were expanding while they were closed. When he opened his eyes, he was still in the war room, though the people around him had changed and they were all frozen, as if time had stopped. Marric saw a translucent blue Shield hovering in the air like a wall between most of the group and the Void form that was turned to Avryn against the wall. Marric squinted to inspect it, then realized that he must be Seeing a memory. Just as before, he moved his body knowing that his physical self was in its place back outside of the vision.

As he moved closer, he noted that the color of the odd creature shifted as he moved toward it. Light reflected off of its surface to some degree, but it came off almost metallic-looking. At the same time, the form was dark, almost black. There was no face or limbs that he could see, just a globule of viscous material. Marric then noticed that it left a trail of silvery substance behind it as it seeped across the ground.

How could something like that be turned into a poison? he thought incredulously.

Still, the liquid behind the odd creature did resemble the color and glow of the knife that the man had brandished before he shoved it into Turrin.

"Marric, are yeh there?" a man's voice echoed around him, as if from a dream.

He started in the vision, then realized his friends must have noticed him Seeing. He intentionally released himself from the vision and let the world around him spin into blurs of grays and blues, though a distinct black spot remained there, staining the vision until he came back to the war room.

"Erm, sorry." His face flushed slightly when he saw that Shrell had moved closer and he was the one that had spoken.

"What did yeh see? Anythin' bad-like?" Shrell inquired.

Marric shook his head vigorously, probably a bit more exaggerated than he intended.

"I'm sorry, I was just remembering, well—Seeing the moment when the creatures attacked us here in the cavern."

Rivelen looked proudly on from behind Magness.

"Clever one, tha' boy is. What'd yeh see, then?"

Marric pressed his lips into a thin line, recalling what he'd just noticed. All eyes were on him now, and he realized that he didn't know how long they'd been staring at him. He'd just entered the vision mid-conversation and lost track of it all. He immediately forced his mind off the thought for fear that his already red face might deepen in color.

"Um, the Void form that was here looked very similar to the knife that the man used to stab Turrin. It even glowed with the same odd metallic color. I can't say for sure that they are directly related, but I don't know why they couldn't be."

Magness smiled and nodded, pleased with his words.

"You needn't be embarrassed at your powers, or to speak up, Marric. I asked you here because you are ingrained in this all as much as we are," she said.

Marric returned the smile. "I am just trying to help in whatever way I can."

Avryn nodded to Marric, then turned to Magness. "How possible is it that these creatures would be related to Luden?"

Magness raised an eyebrow, then gestured to Janis. "I believe you are asking the wrong woman here."

Janis shook her head. "I can't imagine there being a connection at all—" Janis paused then, considering something. "They are from Ugglyn—the creatures, I mean. I know Luden, and I cannot imagine him being anyone of interest in a situation like this. He's a rich kid. He whines and gets what he wants by paying someone for it."

Avryn gawked at her. "And you are one of these people that play into his childishness, then? How can you be proud of doing what you do knowing that people like him employ you?"

Janis shrugged, genuinely uncaring. "You work for pay. That's how life is. I'm an assassin; I take what pay I need to keep out of trouble and to keep myself taken care of." Her expression darkened suddenly. "Unfortunately, that hasn't been the case for far too long, now that I'm caught up in all of this."

She opened her hands and inspected them warily, as if they might suddenly explode something.

"You may as well get some rest, along with everyone else," Magness suggested, interrupting Janis's reverie, "I can't have my top people exhausted, should something urgent come up."

Marric couldn't say he disagreed; glancing at Janis and the others, he saw deep circles under everyone's eyes.

Looking forward to a good night's sleep, the meeting broke up as everyone trickled out to the hall, making their way to their respective quarters.

~

MARRIC HAD DRIFTED off after a time, but had woken and sat in bed, thinking about the previous day's events. He was just about to see what he could find to eat when something strange started happening.

Suddenly, the room began to spin and colors blended into a whirl of motion. His eyes had expanded and he knew he was being pulled into another vision. It had been a while since he'd been pulled into a vision against his will, but he tried to let it happen on its own. He'd found from experience that pulling against it was distracting and actually took more energy than it was worth.

The world finally stopped spinning, and he found himself inside of a building made entirely of wood. The furnishings were nice and people milled about, eating and drinking. A serving girl, perhaps only twelve or thirteen, wove through the tables, handing out drinks and food. Marric scanned the room and jumped when he saw cloaked figures standing periodically among the tables, eyes red with Light. His insides tingled knowing that something big was happening. There were also blue-eyed Seers in the room, and they were all facing the girl who was serving.

She lithely put a few drinks on the table before her face contorted in pain and she dropped her tray, reacting to the feeling. A sudden burst of Light flew from her, tossing tables, food, drinks, and men all over. Marric winced as a mug flew right through his face. Another blast of power flung from her, and everything and everyone slammed against the walls, a few windows shattering.

She must be a mover, Marric thought.

Finally, a third burst of power flew from her, shattering the rest of the windows and breaking a supporting beam of the roof. Then a portion of the roof fell down, coincidentally on a couple red-eyed Watchlight Seers.

Marric turned to see who else was there, and gasped to see Janis standing beside him, her eyes aglow with the same blue Light. Her face was scrunched together as if she hated the experience. Next to her was Rivelen, blonde hair perfectly quaffed, as usual.

The world spun again, and Marric prepared to fall back into his body in Terris Green, but the world around him formed into another place, this time of an eleven-year-old boy drawing water from a well. The hair stood up on Marric's arms as he knew somehow that the time was exactly the same as what they'd just seen in the bar. A woman called to the little boy from inside the house and he put down the bucket, turning to head in when suddenly he grabbed his stomach in pain. The air around him flickered with blue Light as a large Shield flickered into existence. He strained with the pain in his gut and looked around, confused. As he fell, he'd yelled out—a woman, likely his mother, emerged from the house, screaming at what she saw. Just before everything spun into colors again, Marric spotted men and women with both blue and red glowing eyes watching the scene.

Lanser's beard, is every Seer in Lindrad Seeing this right now?

The thought couldn't be possible, yet somehow it had to be. While he hadn't memorized the faces of all those he'd seen in the pub vision, he had the feeling that the Seers who were with him now were completely different people than those from before. It was a different combination of Evenir and Watchlight seers every time.

Once again, the world spun. Marric felt slightly nauseous in his body back in Terris Green from the changing of the scenes.

He felt disappointed again when he didn't drop back into his body. Now he stood before the bed of a child, sweat slick on her forehead. She couldn't be more than ten. Marric knew what would happen, but the mysterious blue glow still was startling, in part due to the fact that the room was holding a doctor and many other people, likely family members, as well as numerous Seers watching the scene. They all gasped and shouted, jumping away as the Light seeped from the unconscious girl. Plants grew from the wood planks, the air was rid of all dust and dirt, cracks in the windows disappeared as the wave of Fixing flew everywhere. The girl sighed in relief and opened her eyes, the sweat disappearing from her brow.

In a flash of more color, Marric stood next to Janis again, though there was no sign of Rivelen. The many Seers all stood facing two blond boys who looked like twins. They sat cross-legged in a square, telling stories animatedly to a group of smaller children. Each of the two doubled over in pain at the exact same moment, holding their stomachs. Light burst around one of the boys, rings of blue Light appearing around him, spinning slightly. The other gasped and his eyes flashed beams of Light, his eyes looking upward at something. Children screamed and ran across the cobblestones yelling for their parents.

Marric turned to look at Janis, who also noticed that he was there as well.

He couldn't see the pupils in her eyes, but the look on her face showed the same thoughts that he had.

What was happening? Five awakenings all at once?

Soon, the world was changing again. Two more awakenings appeared before him. The first was another girl, likely from a small town due to the nature of the roads. They were made of dirt and held heavy tracks from wagons passing through. She had been carrying a basket of bread somewhere when she fell to the pain in her stomach. Marric almost felt the pain himself, remembering what it had been like before he awakened months ago. Orbs of beautiful and brilliant blue Light flung all through the sky, floating and illuminating the building and homes around her. People watched, mesmerized at the scene.

Another boy appeared, and Marric cried out in shock. Dread filled his stomach as he stood there watching Crents in his home, taking care of his drunken father back in Warren.

It can't be.

Sure enough, just as Crents offered his father a new mug of ale, he gasped and dropped the mug in his father's lap. Cursing, his father stood up and yelled something at him. The older man reached out his hand to smack him in the face when a burst of Light flew from him, throwing his father back with a grunt. He slammed into the wall and slumped down, dazed. Another force of Light pushed him back into the wall and he fell unconscious.

Thank Lanser he isn't a Destroyer, Marric thought, seeing Crents crumple to the ground as the last pulse flew outward.

The scene melted away, along with the other Seers that stood around watching. This time, he was on an old cobbled street somewhere. He scanned quickly for Janis, and found her once again beside him. Rivelen to her left. They looked on at a teenage girl, likely twelve or thirteen, trying to sell lumpy woven socks and other wares. Everyone ignored her by passing her on the street. Just as a man and his wife walked by, she cried out in pain, dropping the socks she was holding and falling to the ground. She began to glow blue.

Marric felt sick. Instinctively, he shouted to the man and his wife to run, but of course they couldn't hear. A burst of Light sprung from her and before his eyes, the man and woman shredded into pieces. His stomach convulsed at the sight and he felt like his real body would throw up back in Terris Green. Another blast flung from the girl and more carts and buildings around her exploded, most of the people having already retreated upon seeing the first blast.

Somewhere a few streets over, Marric heard glass shattering and he somehow knew inside it was the same girl he'd seen serving in the bar at the beginning of the vision. He turned to see Janis gritting her teeth, Rivelen looking green next to her. Marric turned and inspected the other Seers around him. Some looked sickened, some oddly pleased with what they saw. His eyes stopped on a man wearing a bulky red robe, hair pure white and his skin even whiter. He froze, fear gripping him.

It was Riln—the man who'd tried to kill him all that time ago. The man who'd tried to recruit him into Watchlight stared at him from across the road, eyes lit with blinding red Light. He smiled cruelly, sending another jolt of fear through Marric's whole body before the vision melted away and he was back at Terris Green.

Eight awakenings at once? How can that be?

BACK IN THE WAR ROOM, the energy was chaotic. An emergency meeting had been called on account of the recent visions from Rivelen, Marric, and Janis.

"—let's hear about these visions—" Magness stopped to wait for them all to settle down.

Rivelen spoke in urgency, "Magness, somethin' big is about to 'appen."

The Evenir leader inspected them, turning to each of them and looking for a moment.

"You all saw the same vision?"

Rivelen spoke first. "Yes. There will be eigh' awakenin's all over Lindrad a' th'same toim."

Magness stiffened at the words.

"*Eight*? Are you certain? Did you See them all at once, then?"

Rivelen opened her mouth to continue, but Marric spoke up now. "It's true! I Saw them too, and Janis was there."

Janis didn't look thrilled to be involved in this at all, but she nodded as she reinforced the report. "Yes. There will be eight all at once. At least four were in Stilten, alone. Somehow I don't think that is coincidental, considering the conversation we had yesterday about Luden hiding in the city." Her jaw hardened as she spoke.

"Well, what are yeh waitin' fer? Let's go get 'em!"

Magness held up a hand, stopping Turrin as he leapt from his seat to stride out of the room.

"Are you absolutely sure that this is true? Never have we seen even two awakenings happening at the exact same time, yet here you say that there will be eight?"

Janis's eyes narrowed, something going on in her head that she wasn't sharing. Marric wasn't concerned that she was having thoughts and keeping them to herself, but given the most recent revelations, he wondered if she ought to be telling them more. He stared at her and then noticed Livella paling nearby.

"She said this would happen, didn't she?" the young woman said suddenly.

Magness stopped speaking and turned to her. "I beg your pardon, who said what?"

Livella didn't look up at Magness, but kept her eyes low, staring at the ground. "Tryvv, the last Tar'n Yiv'len—she said that Ugglyn was getting stronger and that more awakenings would happen." She looked up and jabbed a shaking finger at Janis. "That *she* would have to get them and take care of them."

Janis, now hiding her emotions better like she normally did, looked at the woman skeptically.

"Despite whatever powers—or lack of powers, apparently—Lanser gifted me, I cannot be in eight places at once."

Livella shook her head. "You can't leave me here again. I just barely got rid of the voices in my head. Wherever you go, I am coming too."

Magness opened her mouth to protest, but Livella shouted her down. "You can't leave me here! I won't take it!"

Their leader pressed her lips together and nodded curtly. "Then let it be so," Magness said. "Varith, fetch some more appropriate travel clothes for this woman and get her something to fight with." She turned to Livella and asked, "You know how to use a blade? A crossbow . . . anything?"

Livella shrugged. "Closest thing I ever used was a pen knife."

Magness looked less-than-pleased at the words, but told Varith to get a dagger, any kind.

"You'll go to Stilten with Janis, then."

Janis rolled her eyes. "When will you stop trying to order me around? I don't report to you," Janis said bluntly, "however, given that there will be four of the eight awakenings there, I agree it would be good to have another pair of hands."

Janis paused and regarded the woman slumped in the chair next to her with skepticism.

"I suppose I'll have to tend to you, then. Can't have you killing yourself over the whispers because I left you behind. It wouldn't bode well for the balance."

Livella nodded, but her eyes were distant as if she were in a different place altogether now that they'd agreed to let her go with Janis.

Marric listened while Magness told Varith and Turrin to mobilize their companies to two of the awakening locations. She ordered Rivelen to write down the locations and whatever else she knew about the future Lightbearers. Rivelen was already madly scribbling down the details on some parchment before she was given the command.

"And Rivelen, you will take half your company and give the other half to Shrell to retrieve one of the new Lightbearers."

Rivelen looked up sharply from her work. "Yeh mean to send *me* sommer? Yeh know I don' like—"

"We don't have time for your arguments, Rivelen. I made you a general for a reason, and you know how to fight well enough."

Marric stared at the tall blonde woman as her face grew hard. She wasn't angry per se, but she was annoyed at the orders. Rivelen didn't like getting her hands dirty.

"Yes, ma'am, as yous request."

She returned to writing down the locations and names. After a moment, she paused and looked up from her writing. Janis, seeing this, moved to her side and stared over her shoulder.

"Ah, you forgot the one in Wurren—you know, the scraggly looking boy?"

Marric's breath caught at the words. "Crents, he's a friend of mine! I can't believe he's going to awaken as well—I would have never thought—"

Magness held up a hand to silence him. "You know one of the new Lightbearers?"

"Yes, he used to work with me in my shop."

Magness frowned. "Then I think it best if you accompany the group headed there. Shrell, take your men and women there with Marric."

Shrell nodded curtly, clearly still upset about his brother. "Yes ma'am. Yeh alright to go wit me, then, Mar?"

Marric forced a smile at him. "Yes, of course."

The doors swung open and a messenger came running in. "Erm, the old man is awake now and he wants to see his son."

Marric felt a thrill inside. He had traveled back to Terris Green with his father, but the man had been so delirious, he was hardly good company.

"And, erm . . . " The messenger turned his head back into the library behind the door and muttered something to an unknown presence there before returning to relay a new message.

" . . . erm, the lord of all humor is proud to be alive and well."

They all stared at the messenger, no one saying anything. He reddened at the staring eyes and bowed, retreating from the room.

"What in the blazes was that supposed to mean?" Avryn said, nonplussed.

The doors flew open once again, and a man walked in with a broad smile.

Marric's chest flared at the sight, and he jumped from his seat. "Harmel!"

Avryn rushed to his friend and threw his arms around him. Harmel looked well groomed and fairly rested, despite the craziness of T'Arren Vale.

"By Lanser's name, you didn't die, then!"

Harmel's grin widened somehow, which didn't seem physically possible. Shrell didn't react as openly as Avryn, but relief showed in his eyes at seeing his brother.

"Yeh can' get rid o' me tha' easily, yeh old git! Got in las' night. Had roit proper toim t'clean up and whatnot."

Harmel turned to Janis and something changed in his eyes. He held up his hand and tipped an imaginary hat to her. "Good t'see yeh, lass."

Janis's jaw hardened at his words and she shook her head. "Call me lass again, and you'll get a knife in the back," she said casually.

Her face and resolve remained hard despite the threat, but there was something else there. Marric couldn't quite be sure, but it looked like Janis was relieved to see the man.

Marric looked at Harmel, seeing what he meant about cleaning up. His clothes were fresh and he didn't look dirty at all. Marric thought back to when he'd seen Janis and Alsry just after they left T'Arren Vale and how bad the looked. Harmel didn't look at all that way, but considering the fact that he'd likely arrived during the night and had time for a rest and a wash, this fact didn't make Marric think the man had been through less than his other companions.

"How did you manage to get out? Janis said you'd been cornered by the soldiers."

"Les jus' say tha' th'T'Arren Vale troops ain't that great at knowin' their own men. I just knocked one o' 'em out and took his clothes. Was an easy ride out from then on, fer the most part." He cocked his head, clearly remembering something but not saying it. Janis raised an eyebrow and scanned him up and down.

"Yes, you look like you made it out of there clean as a whistle."

He grinned at her. "Yeh knows Oi've 'ad a wash, but glad t'see yeh, too," Harmel said, winking at her.

Janis rolled her eyes before turning to Magness. "The visions of the eight awakenings were within a week's time. It's probably in our best interest if we save this celebratory moment for later."

Magness pursed her lips at Janis, apparently not pleased with her veiled order to the Evenir leader. "Yes, you are right on that point. Harmel, perhaps you should stay here for some additional rest, you've been on journeys nonstop for some time now."

Harmel smirked at her. "Wif all due respect, Mags, Oi fink Oi'll be going wherever she goes."

Janis stiffened when she saw he was pointing at her. "Oh fog it, man, do you have to follow me *everywhere* I go?"

Harmel feigned a hurtful look and held his hand to his chest. "Now, now, ain't no need t'be rude an' all that, no? Everyone needs summon t'be there fer 'em." He smiled again and turned to the side, gesturing grandly. "Shall we goes t'get new horses and whatnot?"

Janis shot a look at Magness, but the leader obviously thought it was hilarious and wasn't about to intervene.

"Look at me all you like, assassin, I've learned with these three men—" she gestured to Shrell, Harmel and Avryn, "—that they do not listen to orders for rest. You'll have to get used to that."

Janis regarded Harmel crucially, then sighed. "Just don't get in my way."

"Jus' don' run off loik yeh did at T'Arren Vale, eh? T'ain't easy t'follow yeh up on the walls and whatnot."

He kept saying something, but Marric had shifted his attention to Magness.

"I think this is a situation where I'll need to come with a group. Avryn, you'll lead the largest of the convoys with myself, Janis, Harmel, and. . . . " She eyed Alsry, who had received a cup of hot something from which she was sipping. Trease sat behind her, patting her heavily on the back. Alsry looked a little dazed, her black hair frizzed and unkept in many places, but her eyes were gaining more focus now.

"I see you looking at me from over there. Yes, I will be fine. I've eaten and slept, so I'll be able to come with you. We're short on company leaders and you'll need more support if you're going to Stilten for four awakenings."

Magness nodded curtly, looking a bit uneasy at the words.

Trease chuckled out loud as she nudged Alsry roughly in the shoulder.

"Yeh'll be foin, Oi'll watch yer back roit good. Won' be bad t'have a Shielder wif yeh fer the trip."

Marric shot out of his seat.

"Do I have time to visit my father quickly?" he asked hurriedly, realizing he hadn't had the chance to talk to his father much since Narim was always sleeping recently.

"Yes, but please hurry."

THE TRIP to his father's room was short, so it wasn't too long before he knocked on the board nailed into the stone wall outside his father's curtained quarters. When he'd first arrived, Marric wondered why someone had bothered to cut and fasten blocks of wood outside all the rooms, but he knew now. The blocks of wood were the best way to notify someone you were there while maintaining privacy.

"Eh? 'Oo's there? Mar, is tha' yous?" Narim said from inside.

"Yes, Pa, it's me. Can I come in?"

"Of course! Don' be silly."

Marric smiled, hearing more life in his father's voice now. As he entered, he jumped slightly when he saw another person sitting next to his father's bed. It was a woman, one of the Evenir medics. She wore a white armband and a white hat with a flat top like a plate over her red hair.

"Ah, I didn't realize you had someone with you already—"

"Hmm?" Narim said, taking a spoonful of broth from the woman as she offered it to him. "We ain't doin' nothin' but eatin', is all."

Marric saw immediately what they were doing when he entered, but he still blushed.

"Yer face is right red now, son, t'ain't nuttin t'be red fer."

"Yes, I've been trying to get your father to eat for the better part of the day, so you may speak with him, but please don't ask too many questions; I've finally got him to take some down."

Narim scowled at her, but it was only in jest. Marric rarely if ever saw his father angry.

"I wanted to see how you were doing . . . " he paused, considering what to say, " . . . and to tell you that we are about to leave again."

Narim looked at his son, turning his head just as the spoon neared his mouth. Half of the contents spilled down his chin and shirt as the woman clicked her tongue at the mess.

"I wasn't given this job for target practice. If you'd just hold still," she said curtly.

His father swatted her away and she rolled her eyes.

Marric cleared his throat. "I thought that they Fixed you all up? Did it not work?"

"Nah, they Fixed me alright. They can' Fix me age, though," he chuckled at his own words. "Turns out I ain't up t'such a long, 'ard journey like tha'. Still gots to get me energy back, an' all tha'."

He took another spoonful of liquid then made a face at the woman.

"'Ow much more o' tha' is there? Goes on ferever, seems like."

The woman crossed her arms. "You know, if you would just take it down yourself, you wouldn't need me here. You have enough strength to feed yourself, and have for a while."

"Yeh knows tha' if yeh left, there'd be a spill and it'd go t'waste."

Looking annoyed, the nurse gave him one last spoonful before sighing and standing up.

"That's probably enough at this point," she said, then huffed out the door.

Marric raised his eyebrows at his father.

"She didn't seem all too pleased with you."

"Meh, don' worry 'bout 'er. She likes me roit well. Nice lady, tha'."

Narim gave Marric a meaningful look, then wiggled his eyebrows at him in jest.

"Oh Pa, she's way too young for you! Don't even think about it."

"Love don' 'ave age limits, do it?" Then he chuckled. "I'm just poking fun, Mar. Don' know if I could marry again after Tins. Think I'd like to keep a good memory of her and yer mother."

Marric winced at his words. There was nothing good about any memory he had of his stepmother Tins, but his father was in denial of that fact. Narim sat up further, the wooden frame of his cot creaking loudly. The room was small and held no furnishings, other than a small side table and a single chair, which Marric took the liberty of sitting in now that the medic had left.

"Pa, I need to leave again. There are eight awakenings happening at once and they need me to go get one of them. Pa, it's Crents who will awaken!"

Narim gave him a curious look; he was reacting to the news, yet his eyes were still glazed over it as if it didn't matter. "I thought they 'ad enough Light people. Why'd they need yous? I can' lose you, Mar, not after yer mother."

The words stung a bit as his father said them. Not because they were rude or insensitive, but because Marric had recently shared their mother's true fate with Narim only the day before. His father hadn't taken it well. Sure, he sat on the cot and tried to be his normal, joking self, but he wasn't the same.

"Yer mother—" Narim's voice caught in his throat for a moment before he could continue, "—yer mother died doin' this. Chasin' people like this, gettin' 'em 'afore they awakened and whatnot. It's no' safe fer yous."

Marric held up his hand to stop his father. "I know, I know. But Pa, I've gotten so much better already. Look—"

He held up his hand and a burst of Light made Narim flinch. When he looked up, Marric held a bow, the one resembling the size and weight of the one he'd spent years practicing with.

"I don't need to think as much to Conjure anymore. And Moving—"

Rather than say the words, Marric stood and shifted his hand over the chair he was in. The wooden seat suddenly glowed blue and moved across the floor as Marric moved his hand.

"It's becoming part of me faster than I expected. Plus I'll have Shrell and a lot of others with me and—"

"Yer magic show ain't gonna make me feel much better, Mar. Those black covered men, they got this too. Yer so young, let summon else go instead."

Marric pressed his lips in a thin line. "Pa, I can't. I'm too valuable to leave behind. I promise that I'll be fine. I'll come back to you."

Narim's eyes welled with tears. "Tha's what yer ma said all those years ago. Said she'd be back righ' fast, but then she was gone. Though' she was dead. Instead, I 'ad to suffer 'er death again yesterday." Tears were falling down unrestrained now. "If'n yeh die, Mar, I'll kill yeh."

Marric looked up at his father. Though tears were still running down his cheeks, he wore a wry smile.

"I can' stop yeh, yous know tha'. But come back t'me. Now go."

Marric felt apprehension that had been building there for some time. Despite having returned safely from retrieving his father, Marric felt it was due to luck and other people's skills. How long would it be before he couldn't rely on that anymore?

"I love you, Pa. Rest up, I'll see you again soon."

Narim formed his hand into a claw and shifted it over his heart to ward off all evil. "Don' git yerself blowed up."

Marric could tell the words were intended as a joke, but they actually sent a jolt of fear through him. Having seen the power of Destroyers, he knew how easily things could end. An image of his short-haired friend, Jord, flashed in his mind. The boy had been hardened, brainwashed by Riln somehow. Part of Marric longed to see him again, but another part feared that he would.

"I'll try, Pa."

Marric waved goodbye to his father, his mind still revolving around Jord and their encounter weeks ago. Before he'd come to see Narim, he'd Seen into the future, looking on their journey to Wurren. Though much was blurry and dependent on Watchlight's decisions, one thing was clear: Jord would be there to get Crents too.

22

◇

L uden sat in his armchair before the empty hearth, a woman standing beside his chair, massaging his shoulders. The sun was still high in the sky and it was too hot outside for a fire to blaze in the hearth, but he faced it still. He felt it showed dominance. People could see he intentionally left his back facing the rest of them. He'd paid them all well enough that a betrayal was unlikely. He had been threatened plenty of times, but he kept his money well hidden in various places. If he was killed, their source of wealth would dry up. Despite that, he eyed Triliv, the large peon he'd hired, sitting against the wall to his left.

Triliv sat with his arms folded and stared at the room behind Luden. A few men and women milled about, chatting among themselves.

"A bit higher on the left side, dear. And you can go a bit harder—no soft hands on this back."

The woman massaging his shoulders nodded and pushed harder. Luden sighed in relief but winced at the pain from some of his knots.

"How you can spend so much of your time being idle, I can't understand," a voice spoke from behind.

Luden's muscles tightened at the voice and its sudden appearance behind him. He shot a glare at Triliv, who looked sheepish.

"Tis jus' the Seer. Ain't no reason t'worry."

Luden waved his hands to the side, shaking off the woman's hands.

"That's enough now, Trudy, you can take a break."

She dipped her head, turning and retreating behind the bar and into a door there. Luden stood and faced the man. The Seer's face was mostly hidden by his hood, as usual. Only his strong chin was visible beneath the shadow of the fabric.

"It sounds like you are jealous of my ability to relax. I have offered you such niceties, and yet you deny me still."

The Seer grunted. "I don't take well to people touching me. Most that try get a knife stuck in them, regardless of their intent." He grinned as if this was a joke.

"While fascinating, that is horribly macabre."

The man shrugged in response. "As for your niceties, money is enough for me. But take my funds away, and I'll not only stop finding Lightbearers for you, I'll take something else from you. Perhaps a hand."

Luden laughed for show, but inside he was shaking.

"Your jokes are always appreciated," Luden said, trying to shrug off the comment.

Ugglyn's tail, he's serious. I can't let him know how nervous he makes me.

"You hired me for my skills, and I have delivered, have I not?"

"Yes—yes, you very much have. I only wish I'd found you a long time ago. I've wanted to hunt down every Lightbearer in Lindrad for a long time and you've finally given me the ability to do that. It's been more than handy to know when they'll appear, and take them out before they do."

Luden twisted his neck to make it pop, trying to appear casual and uncaring in front of the unsettling man.

"Like I said, keep paying me, and I'll make it happen."

Nodding, Luden pulled a pouch from his side and handed it to the man.

"There's your pay for the last bit of work. Remember to let me know about the next awakening as soon as—"

"There are more. In a week's time."

Luden paused, eyeing the cloaked man. "Already? How convenient."

The Seer chuckled. "Even more convenient is that there will be eight at once—four here in Stilten. Names and locations of the awakenings are already listed on this parchment. I Saw this only an hour ago. Send men to take out the four here, but you'd best hurry."

Luden stared at him for a moment, then raised his hand to his chin. The Seer held out a piece of folded parchment, but Luden pointed at Triliv and the cloaked man reached over to hand the list to the giant man. The Seer grimaced at having to interact with the large and stupid Triliv, but he did so anyway.

"There is something to consider, though. We could find the children and kill them before they become the monsters I know they will . . . or, we could wait." An idea was forming in his mind, and Luden felt pleased at his cleverness.

"Krilat returned from taking care of the boy in T'Arren Vale, and let me know that this—poison of yours worked all too well on the new Lightbearer, despite his ability to heal. Likewise, the men I sent to retrieve Marric's father, though unsuccessful, did manage to wound one of the Lightbearers with the same poison. They raved at its effects."

Luden's gaze wandered as he picked his teeth with a jeweled toothpick while the man answered the report.

"I've been told it would be, so I'm not surprised." The Seer seemed wary of what was coming next.

"Yes, well, I'd like to meet the supplier. I need more. If I'm to kill more of Evenir and Watchlight, I need to equip all of my operatives with it."

The Seer stiffened. "That is easier said than done."

Luden snapped his head up, scrutinizing the man before him. Something was off. Was that apprehension?

I've worked with the man for six months now, and he's always been perfectly confident. What has him shaken now?

"Then make it easier to do than say, that's why I'm paying you, is it not?"

The Seer nodded curtly, but still looked stiff and worried.

"You see—" Luden drawled on, "—learning how effective the serum was with the others and the timing of when my men met the resistance made me think that we can use the next awakening to our advantage. Could we kill them all now? Easily, but why not take the opportunity to pick off as many Lightbearers as possible? We'll wait until Evenir and Watchlight come, and then we'll use this poison to kill as many as possible."

Snorting, the Seer folded his arms. "While clever, I believe you underestimate the power of these people."

Apprehension sparked in Luden's chest while anger boiled in his gut.

"I believe you underestimate my operatives. With your poison, they can kill more than you might think."

The Seer shrugged, then put his hand up in surrender. "Make it worth my time, and I'll get more poison."

Luden rolled his eyes. "Price isn't an issue. Get me the poison and I'll pay you whatever you wish."

The Seer nodded, then pulled another vial of the silvery liquid out of his trousers.

"Here, it's the last bit I have. I'll find more for you. Why you want to put your men at risk just to take out some random Lightbearers is beyond me, but for the pay, I'll do what you ask."

A servant boy scuttled to Luden with a tray holding a piece of paper. He was small, likely only a child. Luden nodded to him and procured a small coin, worth practically nothing, holding it out to him. The boy snatched it and shoved it in his mouth, pushing it to the inside of his cheek. Luden raised an eyebrow, but took the piece of paper from the tray.

The moment he took the paper, the boy ran quickly back where he'd come from.

Rather than open the paper to read it right away, he eyed the Seer, considering something. Luden still didn't know his real name, but that normally didn't matter. Pay was always his protector, so he didn't really have trust issues. This man, despite sucking gold fronds from Luden numerous times already, didn't seem loyal to the money. It was as if he had some other agenda.

Perhaps a spy for some of the other gangs? Luden thought.

As they spoke, a shadow was cast on the window as the sun started to dip behind the roof. Luden gestured to one of his servants to get a fire stoked and started. It was a little early, but the heat of the day would leave soon enough. Besides, the crackling of the fire was a good thing to listen to while thinking. Seeing the unspoken command, the servant went to work setting wood for the fire.

"Is there something else? You are still here," Luden said dryly.

A pause.

"What I don't understand is why you care so much. Waiting until the Lightbearers come will put you and your men at risk. If they didn't know about you already, they do now. Why do you care so much about killing Lightbearers? They normally stick to their own, not causing any harm to people like you."

Luden raged inside. "I don't pay you to question my motives, do I?" he said measuredly. He was angry at the question from the Seer, but he worried that displaying such anger too readily would get him a knife in the gut. This man seemed the type to not handle anger diplomatically.

Breathing deeply, he closed his eyes and turned away from the Seer, just in case his face showed the hidden emotions.

"It is—a family matter. You wouldn't understand."

"Then I will try not to, sir."

Luden stayed turned away from the man but he heard footsteps retreating. Triliv watched and nodded to Luden.

"Yerp, 'e's gone a'right."

Relaxing, Luden cracked his neck again, grateful that his small gamble of turning away from the man and snubbing his question didn't get him a blade in the back.

The fire in the hearth was starting to spark and crackle, invigorating Luden. The room would get very hot and muggy soon, but he didn't care. At this point, he just wanted to relax and think for a time.

A thought struck him and he snapped a finger at Triliv.

"Have him followed."

Triliv cocked his giant head and stared. "'Oo?" Triliv opened the list he'd been given and squinted at the names. "I don' read righ' well, so 'oo needs followin'?" the oaf of a man said.

Luden growled and turned sharply to the giant man. "The Seer, you idiot!" He smacked Triliv on the forehead, but the large man didn't even flinch.

"Ah, okays." He stood up as if to follow him.

"Not by *you*, you idiot! You're too loud and large to hide! Send one of our servants or children to tail the Seer. If we can identify the source of the poison, then we'll have won the day."

Triliv cocked his head, taking a moment to fully understand the command before lumbering off to find someone to execute it.

So who'd the rich entitled guy send to follow me today? the Seer thought, moving down a small alleyway in Stilten.

He considered just turning around to see the tail, but determined that surprising them would be much more fun. It would also instill fear in them that despite the money Luden paid them, nothing was worth crossing him.

The Seer, as he was so aptly called by Luden and the rest of his men, reveled in the fact that they all knew very little about him. Other than his skill as a Seer, they didn't seem to care much about his past. That was clearly an oversight on their part, for if they knew how truly lethal he was, they might not have employed him in the first place.

The sun was still high in the sky but not shining directly above, making the shadows of the small alleys still dark in contrast to the bright cobbles of the streets outside of the alley. He didn't really have any reason to hide, but he disliked moving about in the day if he could help it. There were likely men in the city who disliked him from past jobs he'd performed or people he'd killed.

He smirked as he walked. He wasn't overly worried that he'd be in too much danger if caught by an enemy, but it wasn't worth the trouble. As of now, the only thing he needed was more funds. All of his money had been left behind in a hurry when an assassination job went wrong in T'Arren Vale six months ago. It was the kind of blunder that made him seriously trust the truth of the visions he Saw with his Lightbearing. He'd come into his Lightbearing so many years before, but did his best to stifle and hide it.

Once he'd gained enough control for it to not spring itself on him in the middle of a fight, he'd just ignored it.

Now it was his main source of income. He didn't really like depending on it, but ever since he'd given in and used it on pretty much every job for the past few years, the money had been a lot better. Turns out when you can predict most everything that's going to happen, it validates your skills to your employers.

Except when your mark has Lightbearers of their own.

The Seer gritted his teeth, remembering the encounter with the man he was supposed to kill in the capital city. It had all been exactly how he'd Seen it, until he was ambushed by a large group of other men, one of them being a Lightbearer who could blow things up.

A Destroyer, apparently, he thought.

Luden had given him a lot of information on Lightbearing, which he'd had to extract delicately in order to not reveal how little he knew about the powers. Now that it was a part of his life, he had to learn more about it *somewhere.*

He paused at the end of the alley, a line of sunlight on the ground introducing where the shadows ended. People milled about thickly on the roads to and from the center of the city where many of the popular shops were set up. Knowing he was hidden by his cloak wasn't comforting enough, but it would have to be. Shrugging his hood lower over his face, he scanned the street and rooftops across the wider, cobbled road. Directly across from the alley opening he could see a bakery, one of the finest in town. Next to that was the local bank, and on the other side, a brothel.

He snorted at the irony of the bank being directly next to the brothel. It was convenient for rich men that the two were so close, he imagined.

Glancing over his shoulder, he saw a shadow shift quickly behind a part of the building that jutted out, forming a small wall.

Must be a child then, no one else could hide behind that small of a wall. I probably shouldn't be too harsh on him.

The Seer stood there for a moment longer, taking the time to pull out another mostly empty vial with a small bit of the dark silver glowing liquid. He wasn't thrilled about how he was going to have to procure the poison, but if he wanted to acquire enough to retire as an assassin, it was necessary. Now that Luden had seen it work, he was too tempted by its effectiveness to give it up.

The pause was enough that the tail could properly see him enter the sunlit road, heat almost instantly entering his black cloak, making the air inside his hood musty and hot. Turning sharply to the right, he stalked casually down the road, nodding to some women staring at him curiously. Given that it was nearing summer and starting to get fairly hot during this part of the day, his current dress would definitely draw more eyes. It wasn't against the law to dress like this, but it was a bit odd to do during the heat of the day.

And yet, he didn't care. No one would stop him. Sure, he looked suspicious, but mostly people would think him a lunatic for intentionally wearing clothes that would be unbearable in the heat. For a moment, he thought himself a bit crazy as the sweat poured down his back, his clothing not tight enough to soak up all the liquid. Drips fell down his face as the heat intensified, soaking him.

Though he didn't turn around, he knew that the child saw him and was following. Another group of rich people, this one made up of a few couples, eyed him warily.

Oh, fog it all, mind your own business.

He focused on another alley twenty paces away and sped up slightly, knowing that the tail might have trouble keeping up with their small legs.

At length, he made it to the alley and turned quickly back into the shadows. The temperature change was stark, not only due to the shadows, but because of the wind that flowed through the small alley. This one ended at a dead end a hundred paces back, but there was something there which others didn't know about.

After the turn, he stopped abruptly and pushed his back heavily to the wall.

Any moment now.

Just then, a small form turned and peered around the edge of the corner. He whipped his hand out and snatched the child by the lapel, holding tightly so that he couldn't get away. A yelp came from the small child. The boy couldn't have been more than eight. His red hair stood up in all directions as if he'd never bothered grooming it at all. Freckles riddled his entire face so that from far away, his skin there looked a shade darker than the rest of him. Wide, dark brown eyes stared at him in terror. The man carefully lifted the boy by his tunic so that their eyes were level.

"It's rude to follow people without their permission, you know."

The boy just stared at him, completely stunned.

The Seer grinned, trying to lighten the mood.

"Fortunately for you, I knew that you were following me from the moment I left Luden's hovel."

He slowly lowered the boy down, feeling him shaking like a leaf in the wind, then reached for a pouch at his side. Keeping one hand firmly on the boy, he opened the pouch and pulled out three gold fronds. The boy's eyes widened as he watched, likely expecting him to pull out a dagger and slit his throat. Instead, his jaw dropped when the Seer proffered the money to him.

"How about you take this, go buy yourself something really nice, and then tell Luden that I returned to my room at the inn. He doesn't need to know anything about this."

The boy nodded absently, but kept his eyes on the money.

"What do you think, then? Do we have a deal?"

Jumping slightly at the question, he looked up at him.

"Uhh, yeah—yeah, roit okay wit' me." His nods sped up and became a bit manic.

Chuckling, the Seer poured the money into the boy's hand, then loosened his grip. Before the boy could pull away, the man pulled back on the lapel of his shirt and spun him to look at his eyes.

"And don't you go betraying me, now. Luden may be rich, but he doesn't scare me. I don't normally like killing children, but it's not out of the question."

The boy's small face paled at the words and he nodded again. He tried to say something but choked on his words, his eyes watering.

"Good, good. Now run along, lad."

The Seer released the boy and gave a small kick to his backside as he ran away. He didn't bother watching where the boy ran, for he figured the threat was sufficient to keep him from telling Luden the truth. Instead, he turned down the alley and moved quickly to the dead end, the stone wall which surrounded the city. Even though he knew the boy had retreated and he didn't sense any other followers, he looked back to ensure he was alone, then pressed a small piece of the wooden wall of the building to his left. The small section depressed easily and he maneuvered it to the right, where it slid along a track. The Seer had learned about this little door many years ago as he ran from the authorities after one of his jobs. Since then, every time he came to Stilten, it was the place he went for privacy.

It was likely the door had been intended as an escape route for the building owners, should there be a fire or other emergency, but the ownership of the shop had changed multiple times since it was built, and the new owners had no knowledge of its existence.

He had to duck through the low doorway, about the height of a small child, but he slipped through easily. Turning, he eased the piece of loose wood back into place and slid a board over the back to secure it in place. No one had followed him, but having the door secure wouldn't hurt anything. Once inside, he turned and crept down the hidden staircase that stood behind the back wall of the shop. The stairs led to an overpacked basement full of extra expired stock for the shop above, and myriad other random things. He came here regularly and even had a bedroll stashed away in case he needed to stay for a while. Fortunately, this and a few of his other belongings were hidden behind stacked tables, chairs, and other random artifacts that the shop owners never used. Light filtered down another set of stairs from the windows above in the shop, so it was fairly dim, but he was used to seeing in the dark already.

Settling down on the bedroll, he steeled himself for the vision. He'd grown used to Seeing things, but this wasn't going to be a normal one.

He breathed deeply and let himself fall into the vision, his eyes snapping open, wide and glowing with red Light. The world began to spin around him, blurring into color and shapes before they formed back into reality. There, right in front of him, sat his body.

Seeing the present version of yourself was relatively un-useful in most cases, but all he needed to do was leave his body and consciousness to See what he needed. Still, he inspected his surroundings to ensure that everything was alright. Voices were speaking above, but were quiet due to their distance. He looked on his body, sitting with legs folded and face pointed upward. His eyes were aglow with the bright red beams, causing the items around to glow with the same hue.

"Vilick fritlat Ugglyn ug yasnin," he said, his voice echoing in the air as if he stood in a stone cavern rather than the crowded basement of a shop.

For a moment, nothing happened. Then the air in front of his vision body started rippling and getting darker, forming into a cloud of silver-black air that looked like discolored smoke. He felt the hair on his arms raise back in his physical body while nervousness sprang in his gut.

In his whole life, he could only remember a few instances when fear ruled him. As of now, he could still count them on only two hands. This encounter, plus the ones before it, were easily pushing that number higher.

The inky black substance hovering in the air coalesced into a man wearing dark clothes of the same color. His beard was fully gray and cropped smartly against his skin. His hair was equally gray, yet his face was young, albeit drawn in some ways. He looked as if his age would be impossible to guess, for he could be old or young depending on which of his features were noticed first.

The Seer gritted his teeth, preparing for the question.

"While I'm honored to have been summoned *already*, I sincerely hope you haven't done so for idle reasons. My power grows weaker each time I expend it on visits like this. So get to the point!"

The Seer flinched at the anti-god's words before replying, "The poison—we need more."

The black-robed man stiffened at the request. "Blasted man, you wasted it already?" A pool of the silvery-black ooze appeared on the floor next to Ugglyn and fear blossomed in the Seer's stomach.

Fog me, he's summoning another one.

Standing up straighter, he tried to look as if his resolve was stronger than he felt.

"It was not squandered, no. We used it to kill a new Fixer, which I believe was the condition of you providing it. Your intent is to kill Lightbearers, is it not?"

Ugglyn's face twisted into an evil smile. "So you got one, then? That's something, at least. As for the rest?"

The seer stiffened. "Not as successful—"

It was all he could say without the anti-god careening into anger. Regardless of the vagueness of his response, Ugglyn roared loudly, the pool of ooze next to him exploding upward into a creature made of the substance. It was round with spikes and two large tentacles flailing outward. They grasped at the ground, trying desperately to move toward the Seer. He gasped and stepped backward.

"Killing me will do you no good! What other Seers have you recruited?"

That was a gamble, but the Seer didn't have any other cards to play at the moment.

Ugglyn's eyes glittered wickedly as if he knew a secret, but he waved his hand over the creature, causing it to calm.

"Consider that your only boon, *Seer*. Your power is of Lanser, yet you've betrayed him for your own greed."

The Seer shrugged, still quivering slightly from fear but breathing as normally as possible to hide it.

"Money's all I need in this world."

Ugglyn grinned at this. "Then I'm glad your corruption has allowed me to find you. Despite our meeting in a vision, I cannot hold this form much longer. I've expended too much energy. Yrillnan is pushing back again."

The Seer cocked his head. He had read the word in the book he'd found, but Ugglyn had never really mentioned it until now. Apparently, something kept the anti-god from being restored—though he didn't know what. All he could be was grateful. His loyalty wasn't to Ugglyn, but instead to the money.

"I need more of this Void substance. As much as you can provide."

Ugglyn's form faded slightly. The anti-god closed his eyes and growled until his image formed again.

"Fine, I've not the energy to argue. Know this: you may speak the forbidden words again, but I won't be able to come. Yrillnan is strong again. Kill the woman. She's holding me back."

His form was flickering like the flame of a fire. Opening his mouth, the anti-god tried to say something again, but no sound came. His eyes rolled back in his head and his body aged so quickly that his skin became transparent, a skeleton showing behind the fake flesh. Just before he melted into the same silvery black liquid, he waved his hand over the stilled Void creature and it melted into a pool. The Seer watched as twelve vials of the Void poison appeared next to his physical body on the bedroll.

Only moments after the vials came to be, Ugglyn's form flickered and disappeared into nothing. The Seer shivered slightly at the encounter, knowing he had been lucky this time. He focused and allowed the world around him to spin, blurring into colors and nothingness before he was back in his body. Looking down at the floor next to his knee, there were the vials of odd poison.

He stared at them for a minute, willing himself to pick them up.

How I got myself in this mess, I'll never know.

With two fingers, he gingerly picked up the vials one by one and stored them in a bag to wear over his shoulder. Each had to be properly wrapped in cloth to protect them from bumping into each other as he moved. For a moment, he imagined what would happen if one of them broke. A chill ran through him at the thought.

He never clarified which woman to kill, the Seer thought. Even though the anti-god hadn't said her name, a feeling in his gut told him he didn't need to ask.

Shrugging, the man felt relieved that Ugglyn hadn't been too angry at his request and had allowed him to stay alive. There hadn't been too much evidence that the anti-god really could have killed him, but there was something there—a power that The Seer didn't like to feel when he summoned the creature.

He stood and made for the door before stopping. A pull in his gut behind him beckoned to him and he gave in. The feeling wasn't unusual, for the book had the effect on him ever since he'd found it in the city. He didn't know where it had come from, but it felt extremely old.

Turning, the Seer moved to the wall where a curtain hung next to his bedroll. To anyone who might venture down here, it would just look like an odd tapestry or a forgotten cloak. Moving the fabric aside, he saw it. It was thin and small, bound with dark leather and completely covered in inscriptions. Some words were written so small that he couldn't read them, some were larger. Only one word stood out on the front, or at least what he assumed was the front. The rest of the inscripted words were all in symbols that he couldn't read. He recognized them, for he'd seen ancient texts in libraries. The symbols on this book appeared to be written in the pure old language, before the current system for writing came into play. Oddly, the one word written on the front wasn't in the old symbolic language, but instead in the new conventions, allowing him to read it.

Yrillnan

The Seer gaped at it, the pulsing feeling inside pulling him closer to the book even though it was in his hand. The power was unmistakable, but hidden. That is what drew him to the book seven months ago. Though he'd checked many times before, he still opened it, ensuring that most of the pages were filled with images and words all made with the old symbolic system of the ancient language. All of them were illegible except for the one phrase he almost regretted uttering those six months ago, just before finding Luden.

The words that had summoned Ugglyn.

Another shiver ran its course through his body before he put the book in his belt. It felt awkward there, but the pulsing in his brain stopped whenever it was in his possession. Given the impending battle, he couldn't afford any distractions. He'd avoided too much killing up until this point in Luden's service, and though that had been his profession for most of his life, he had left it behind. His Seeing provided a more lucrative offering and it had been much easier than being an assassin.

Moving quietly to the stairs, he quickly scaled them, careful to hold the bag over his shoulder so as to not disturb the vials. He unlatched the hidden door and slid into the alley. Though his vision with Ugglyn had only lasted moments, the sun had set completely. Dropping into visions had a strange effect; normally they were long inside and quick outside, but when he met with Ugglyn, the effect was always the opposite.

Just another reason to not have any more meetings with that creature, he thought.

Not that he needed to really keep a list. Meeting with the anti-god wouldn't under any circumstances have been a good thing.

Except for the money.

Pushing the thought of his recent and past meetings with Ugglyn out of his head, he returned swiftly to meet with Luden. This time when he entered the pub, it was full of men and women drinking and talking loudly. It wasn't surprising to see all the people there—it was often how they all spent their nights, using the money that kept them all from knifing their leader in the back.

The Seer pushed through some men laughing raucously, one of them turning to punch him for the trouble. He side-stepped it easily and slammed the side of his hand into a pressure point just under the man's neck. The offender fell with a loud thud. The now-unconscious man's companion glared at him before turning away, clearly unwilling to engage in a fight.

They all hated him. Apparently, Luden had done a decent job of brainwashing them to hate all Lightbearers. The Seer had been forced to kill a few of Luden's men who got too passionate about him and his abilities. He'd eliminated them without much feeling, and without much consequence. Fortunately, that type of thing worked, given how violence is was what called the shots around here, next to money, of course. Despite their hatred, they did fear him.

The Seer strode up confidently to the large armchair where Luden spent most of his time. He didn't bother letting Triliv mention his arrival, but made a rude gesture at the large oaf, making him look perplexed while he processed the information.

"Still lounging away your life?" Macks said suddenly.

The blond man shot up from his chair, spun and tripped on his feet, falling to the ground.

"By Lanser's robe, you scared the fog out of me!" Luden shouted, standing up and trying to save face by pretending it hadn't just happened.

"I don't care for subtlety these days. You'd think you'd have learned that by now."

Luden just glared at him. "Remind me why I don't just kill you."

The Seer stared at him casually, then gestured backward to the huge unconscious man on the floor.

"You couldn't even if you tried. Plus, I'd just See you trying before you did."

Luden stiffened at the reference to Lightbearing. The Seer still didn't fully understand, but the leader hated all Lightbearers. He wouldn't give any information other than it was a family matter.

The Seer grabbed the bag and lifted it from his shoulder, setting it on the seat of the armchair.

"I'd best be careful with that. Hate to see your good arms taken by one of the vials breaking."

Luden's eyes flashed with surprise. "You were able to get more *already*? How? Who is your supplier?"

The Seer chuckled. "If you think I'd give up my supplier so you and your men could cut me out, then you really are stupid," the Seer said shrewdly.

The effect was instant and exactly what he was going for.

Luden's face reddened, and he looked as if he would explode. Despite his anger, he said nothing else. Instead, he opened up the bag and peered inside.

"That can't be more than a dozen vials. I asked for more than this."

The Seer snorted. "It's what you get, and you'll get no more from me. "

Luden spun on him, a dagger flying from his belt toward the man's gut. The Seer easily side-stepped the thrust, snatching Luden's wrist and twisting it to the side, the dagger spinning to the ground and into the wooden floor with a thunk.

"Just a little tidbit about me, *Luden*," the Seer said his name with false familiarity, "I am a trained assassin. You can try to take what you want from me, but you won't get anything other than yourself as a corpse. This is what I brought, and I don't think Ugglyn cares that you want more."

Luden's eyes narrowed at the words, but the Seer knew they wouldn't mean anything other than a threat. The rich man couldn't even possibly imagine that's where the poison indeed came from.

"Fine. But you will be here to fight the Lightbearers."

The Seer pressed his lips into a thin line, considering the command. He could opt out and slip away with what he'd earned to pick something else up in another city, but then he'd spurn Luden. Given the magnate's unlimited resources, such an action would likely haunt him for the rest of his life.

"Fine, but on my own terms."

Luden countered, "Fine. But I keep all the poison." As he said it, he moved his body to block the way to the bag sitting on the chair.

The Seer laughed, then slowly shook his head.

"Eleven should be enough for you and your men, then. I'll just keep this one for a rainy day."

He held a vial in front of Luden's face, the leader's eyes going crooked as he tried to focus on it. Luden's face reddened in anger, but the Seer kept his calm and cool demeanor. He swiftly tucked it in a pocket at his side.

"Now that's settled, you'd best prepare for their arrival," the Seer stated.

Luden, still feeling tense from the prior exchange, pointed and spoke, "You mean *we* better prepare. We'll need all hands on deck for this one."

The Seer just stared at Luden, but gave a curt nod.

"Let's see how many Lightbearers we can take down with this lot," Luden said, finally feeling his anger dissipate, replaced by anticipation for the battle.

23

F our days—Prost thought, frustrated. That's how long it had been
since they left their compound.

Watchlight had prepared and sent four companies of men to
the various awakening locations from the mass vision. Riln himself had
inspected the list of names procured from what they Saw, to ensure it was
accurate. Prost assumed Riln's extra care was because there were eight awakenings all at the exact moment. There was also the thought that if they could
take all eight, their ranks would increase very quickly. Such a gain would
definitely tip the scales in Watchlight's favor.

At the same time, Prost didn't really care. During the past month or so,
ever since his last run-in with Janis, Prost's only goal was to face the woman
again. She'd slipped from his clutches four times, each encounter validating
his fears of her powers being able to affect him. It wasn't that her powers
always affected him, but the fact that hers alone showed an impact on him
was, at the very least, distracting. That, and Riln accompanied them on this
trip.

He turned to glance back at their leader. His bone-white face was held
high and confident in the air. Many respected him, despite his temper problem, though most only feared him. Prost thought for a moment how the
mens' sentiment toward himself was founded on the same fear and how

similar that made him seem to Riln. Part of him loathed that, but the other part felt pride. In terms of raw power, it was undoubtedly Riln that came out on top, considering he had awakened into every Lightbearing power years ago. The blessing from Lanser, in Prost's opinion, could have been better founded in someone else, but he didn't think that Janis was an acceptable replacement.

No—not replacement, she's an additional Prime, he thought.

His questions about his and Riln's *Yrillnan* were brought to light even more when he thought about it all. It didn't make any sense how and why Lanser, their god, had awakened another Prime and Voidbearer. Did that mean his own Yrillnan was defunct? Did that mean he didn't need to stay with Riln? Part of him wished it was true that he could really sever his relationship with his master and escape without the annoying voices ruling his life, but the other part knew it wasn't true. Over the years he'd certainly been able to travel further and further from the man without the voices bothering him everywhere he went, but he doubted they were gone forever. Prost assumed that they weren't bothering him because he'd lost all drive and intent to get away from Riln. Though, maybe their Yrillnan really was gone and the balance taken over by another Seal.

He shook his head, pushing the wishful thoughts away. Prost felt trapped with Riln unless he truly wanted to risk letting Ugglyn free. Then again, he knew that Janis dying might also let the anti-god out, yet his drive to defeat her was stronger than any fears he had of Ugglyn, which seemed less immediate in moments when he fought against her. They'd already moved their loyalty to the anti-god for hope of domination in Lindrad, possibly even their neighboring lands. How they'd get there was still unknown, but it was clear that Ugglyn was a powerful ally. Prost privately felt uncomfortable with the dalliance and wondered if Riln really intended to give Ugglyn any sort of power at all, or if he was just using the anti-god as a means to an end.

Glancing back again, he saw Riln was now speaking quietly with Vint. Riln looked ghastly with his pale skin, almost like a moving corpse.

Prost turned to the side to see Alts, Neera, and Lathe leading their horses alongside his own. Alts's eyes met his and she pressed her lips together in a determined way. It wasn't a happy look, but there was something there. Her eyes told him that she stood with him and she would have his back. Ever since their journey and encounter with Evenir in T'Arren Vale, many of those who went with him had been more loyal. Apparently, his fight with Janis and the Evenir Mover had been somewhat of a spectacle. All those who lacked trust in Prost's ability to combat powerful Lightbearers likely now had faith that he could do so, despite him possessing no powers himself.

No, not everyone in Watchlight had seen it, but the word had gotten around and fewer people looked at him the way they used to.

Movement ahead made Prost turn his head sharply, his hand moving to his sword. The forest around them was still lit as the sun moved just to the other side of the trees. It was late afternoon, the awakenings due to happen in a few hours. Up ahead through the opening in the canopy, Prost could see the city gates. They weren't quite as large as those of the capital city, but were closed and manned by a few guards. These weren't the same trained soldiers of T'Arren Vale, so Prost wasn't overly worried about it.

A breeze blew onto the pathway, shuffling the leaves above and around them. Despite it being nearer to summer, the wind blew cool, an evidence of how far north they had to travel to get to Stilten. It wasn't cold by any means, but the air had changed significantly, becoming cooler each day they moved. Bright red orbs of Light created shadows in the trees around them. An orb had been summoned and held in front, behind, and to either side of the large group.

If we run into any Lightbearers intending to fight us, the Light from the orbs won't be bad to have at the ready, Prost thought.

Given that Lightbearing was still somewhat underground and still touted as witchcraft, Prost knew it would be best to let them fall for now.

Turning to his left, he nodded to Neera.

"Turn them off. We don't want suspicion following us through the city right now. Save your Light for actual danger."

"Of course, my lord."

Prost cocked his head at her address. She'd never called him that before now. He didn't hate the address, but at the same time, it didn't feel deserved.

Apparently, I have more sway than I thought with this crowd, Prost thought.

Neera held up her hands, palm upward and then closed her fingers, forming fists. The moment she did this, the orbs snuffed into nothing. They weren't providing much Light in the middle of the day, but the lack of the extra illumination made the forest around them seem darker and more dangerous. Prost noted a red glow still reflecting on Alts's back and turned to see a lone orb about the size of his fist floating above Riln's face.

Prost's jaw hardened when he saw this.

"Master, don't you think it would be wise to not draw attention to ourselves with your Lightbearing? We're a large enough group that attention isn't going to be hard to come by," Prost said, his words coming off a bit sharper than he intended.

Riln cocked his head slightly, wonder in his eyes.

"You dare speak to me in such a manner? Yes, I believe *I* am the ruler of Watchlight, not you. Did you forget?"

Riln's blue eyes filled with a challenge and Prost looked away.

"Do as you wish, then, but it won't make it any easier."

Prost heard a scoff behind him, but didn't turn.

"I will do as I wish. I will not hinder the progress of our entourage. Though I've not traveled with anyone in a long time, I *do* know how to take care of myself. Neera extinguished the power of her Lightbearing, and I am not convinced that we are free of an Evenir ambush, as of yet."

Prost knew there was validity to Riln's words, but he hated it. He opted not to say anything.

Alts stared at him curiously. He met her eyes and scowled, his usual reaction to making eye contact. Prost couldn't argue with their leader's logic, and by conceding, he lost ground both in the conversation and with the men and women who had heard the exchange.

The only positive thing about this whole trip is that Mert is still missing and Jord went to his hometown for the awakening there.

Prost entertained the possibility that Mert had been tortured, possibly even killed, but he knew inside that was not the case. Evenir had proven far too lenient in all their dealings with Watchlight so far. Evenir only killed when defending themselves. Prost hoped that Jord would meet some opposition as well in Wurren.

And we're about to engage in even more fighting now.

As he thought it, he moved his hand down, checking the status of the swords at his side. Prost didn't bother bringing his crossbow this time, for it was too bulky. That, and part of him wanted to best Janis without the aid of a distance weapon.

Their horses' hooves slowed down, the cacophony of sounds sucking into the empty space in the trees. Given how tightly the trees were packed on either side and how the path felt like a tunnel in the waning light, there was left an impression that the sounds of their horses should echo, though they didn't.

"We should have split up, we're too large of a group," Prost said gruffly.

Riln's smooth voice answered, high and thin. "Tut, I've got this taken care of."

Whispers sounded around them and Prost turned to see Riln's eyes glowing red for a moment before they faded.

"I've tested our alibi against the Stilten guards. They will fall for it."

Prost grit his teeth, but said nothing else. The eeriness of the glowing eyes had never left him, despite his proximity to Lightbearing for the past ten years.

"We're a band of showmen, here to take the city of Stilten with our grand performance."

The idea sounded ludicrous to Prost, but he didn't protest. Instead, he continued to lead the group at the same pace so as to not cause suspicion with the wall guards.

At length, the large entourage proceeded to the gate where one of the guards held up a hand to halt them.

"Wait right there, slowly now."

Prost led the group up to the gate and pulled the reins of his horse to slow it.

"Who here is the leader of this band?" the guard asked, eyes searching.

Prost paused, waiting for Riln to speak up. When he said nothing, he resisted the urge to look confused, knowing that it wouldn't do well in front of the guards.

Riln turned and gave a pointed look to Prost.

His confusion still ran deep, but Prost looked confidently at the guard and raised his chin. "That would be me."

"What brings such a large group as this to Stilten, especially at this hour?

I haven't seen a group this large in years, save the one that passed only thirty minutes ago."

Prost's stomach tightened, but he held his outer resolve, not letting it show.

"We're a troupe of entertainers, here to work in our humble vocation."

The guard looked curiously at the large group of men and women atop their horses behind Prost, then back at him, looking suspicious.

"That's quite a troupe you've got there. What merits such a large number of players?"

Prost paused for a moment, then opened his mouth to say something while putting his hand on his sword, but he was interrupted.

A flash of colorful fabric announced Riln flying past him on his horse. He slipped off his horse, the deep colors of his plump robe flashing in the waning sunlight.

"Why, great entertainment requires great numbers, does it not? I am surprised you have not heard of the traveling band of Yilistan! We're the most famous troupe in all of Lindrad."

The guard narrowed his eyes at Riln. It was clear he was doubting the pale man's words, but his eyes moved up and down as he inspected Riln's style of dress. Not only was it impractical, which is what Prost always thought, but it had to be extremely uncomfortable.

Riln responded to the man's gaze, "Yes, it does me well to remain in my acting state for all of our travels. You understand, I'm sure, as a man who appreciates the arts."

The comment was extremely pointed and the guard didn't know how to respond.

"Erm, yes, I suppose," he flushed, staring at Riln's lively expression. "Though I can't say I've ever spent much time watching a show of players."

Riln clicked his tongue in disapproval. "Now, my good man, is the time to remedy that problem. Let us go forth and prepare for the greatest show of all time."

Watchlight's leader bowed with exaggeration, his head dipping so low that it came almost to his bent knee.

For a moment the guard just stared at Riln, skeptical, but not willing to admit that he'd never heard of them.

"Yes, well, in you go, then. I must say, there likely won't be any room at the local inns right now. The group before you likely took all the rooms that would normally be open."

Prost nodded. "We've tents and supplies of our own. With some open space in the town center, we'll manage."

The guard waved them forward and gave the command to his fellow guards to let them through. Riln grinned at the guard and pulled himself back up onto his horse. The large company of men and women moved easily through the gates, but had to funnel down a more narrow cobbled road. As soon as they were out of earshot, Riln spoke.

"I'd have much rather just killed them, but that wouldn't do us any good," their leader said disgustedly.

Prost grunted. For once, he actually agreed with the words of his master.

"It's a good thing I saved us from whatever blunder Prost would have spat out. You really need to work on your lies and intrigue, dud," Riln said in a mocking tone.

Prost stiffened at the words, anger flaring inside of him. Part of him wanted to turn and yell at Riln, perhaps even punch the man off his horse, but that wouldn't do. Everyone would side with Riln if Prost were to harm him.

"We split from here. You've been assigned your awakening. Locate the area, and try to extract the child without consequence. If you meet opposition, you know what to do. We will secure the four new Lightbearers here in Stilten. Do not fail me as Prost has in the past."

Hearing Riln blame him and threaten the others with his name only deepened the feeling of pure hatred he held inside.

At his words, the group of black-cloaked Watchlight men and women broke into their respective groups and moved off down other alleys and roads. Some held maps up to their faces, trying to determine where they needed to go. Each person had been given a description of the teenager and where they could find them. Roughly one third of the men and women stayed with Riln and Prost.

"And now, my dear dud. This is where you come in. A Destroyer will awaken near the edge of the city. Given that you are the only one exempt from that power, it will be smoother if you retrieve the girl."

Prost figured he should be honored at such words, knowing his job was something no one else could do, yet it only angered him more. His immunity to Lightbearing made him an outcast, hated among their men, yet Riln constantly abused the ability in as many ways as possible.

"We don't have time to locate the girl, we just need to find where she *will* be and wait for her."

"Evenir is here," Prost said flatly.

Riln looked at him as if he were a mute beginning to speak. "Of course they are. It's amazing you had the ability to put that together."

The insult was likely intended to fire him up, giving Riln an excuse to leave him behind. Prost took it without displaying the rancor he so clearly felt.

"The guard mentioned not seeing any large group, save us and one other thirty minutes ago. Who else would it be?" Riln jeered.

Prost narrowed his eyes, but nodded, feeling both frustrated and embarrassed.

"Let 'em get close to 'er, then," Alts said suddenly. "'Er awakening will blast 'em all, while yous grab 'er an' go."

Alts sounded pleased at the thought of Evenir being shredded by the awakening.

"Ah, but my dear, they will have Shielders as well. A blast can be taken as such with that. We not only have Shielders of our own, but a secret weapon to be used at our disposal."

Gritting his teeth, Prost took the insult as well. How he'd put up with being called out and treated like a tool for Watchlight, Prost didn't know. It was unsurprising treatment, but still frustrating, nonetheless.

"We have to hurry," Prost said suddenly, hardness entering his voice, albeit unintentionally.

This tone awarded him a look from Riln, partially curious, partially humorous. Riln seemed to be amused at knowing that his comments were affecting Prost.

"The sun is past the rooftops now, the awakenings should happen within the hour."

"Yes, yes, the dud is right, let us move."

As Prost led the group through the cobbled streets of Stilten, the locals gave them a wide berth. The Stilten natives didn't look necessarily scared of the group of Watchlight members, but they were a bit uneasy.

In no time, Prost turned his horse around the corner to the location where the awakening was to take place. He froze, pulling on his horse's reins. Looking up, he stared right into the dark blue eyes of a woman clad all in black, a spear of blazing blue Light blossoming to life in her hand. In a flash, it was flying at him, aimed low.

Prost cursed as the pole of Light struck his horse in the chest, the creature falling to the ground with a scream.

Fog it all, of course she's here! Prost thought.

Rolling off his collapsing horse, Prost got to his feet and yanked a sword from his scabbard into his right hand.

Janis smirked at him, brandishing her own forearm-length dagger.

Let us try again then, shall we? he thought.

24

I'll have to practice Conjuring other weapons more; that didn't go as smoothly as I had hoped, Janis thought, watching Prost get up from his horse's tumble. Janis felt a little bad for the creature. She was an assassin, but unnecessary animal killings weren't something she reveled in.

Prost looked almost pleased to see her. Under other circumstances that might have seemed odd, but she had a building desire to beat him out in combat, especially since their last encounter in T'Arren Vale. She suspected he felt the same way.

The moment she'd seen him come into view on his horse, she considered throwing the javelin of Light directly at him, but she figured it wouldn't affect him. Each time she'd been able to use her Lightbearing on him, it had been random. The only other logical option was to take out his current advantage of height—due to the horse.

Tension rose in the air as Evenir men and women around her prepared for a battle. A woman to her left summoned a Shield just in front of them, the translucent wall of blue extending into the cobbled road and arching over their heads. The Shield was perfectly timed, as a ball of Destruction flew from the hand of one of Prost's companions. It slammed into the Shield with a loud crack, red Light exploding with a flash.

Janis scanned those with Prost, and her stomach flipped when her eyes met intense blue eyes set under pure white brows.

Fog it, Riln came this time.

She'd never seen the man fight in any capacity, but she knew that he had all the powers of Lightbearing at his fingertips. She supposedly had the same abilities, but she hadn't yet been able to control them. Looking around her, she saw that their numbers weren't few. Most of those with them looked to be Lightbearers as well, but Riln and Prost together tipped the balance.

A volley of normal and Light-made arrows slammed into the Shield, skittering to the side or popping into nothing like a burst of heavy rain. Magness stood next to Janis, her steel sword pulled out.

"Keep the Shield up, Gila. It's a good thing we cleared the street, this might get ugly."

Janis stared at Prost, her face full of determination. He looked equally determined, holding his sword at the ready. Smiling slightly, he reached for his other sword, pulling it into his left hand. Just then, a red Shield sprung into existence in front of Prost and the other black-cloaked Watchlight people.

Someone's got to do something, Janis thought.

"We make the first move," Janis said out loud.

Magness shook her head. "That would not be wise. As far as we can tell, the girl will come from the north side of the road, which is behind us. When one of our Seers recognizes her, we grab her and run."

Janis snorted. "Except for the fact that she's a Destroyer. How do you plan on keeping everyone safe when that happens?"

Magness pressed her lips into a thin line, her brows furrowing.

"Gila and our other Shielders will have to protect us when she arrives. We have a good vantage point—we can hold Watchlight as long as we need to," Magness replied.

"Until they send men to circle around and get behind us," Janis pointed out.

"If that happens, then we'll have to improvise. I only hope that Avryn and his group don't meet as much opposition as I think we will."

Janis thought about how Harmel had been sent with Avryn to get the set of twins and she furrowed her brow. Part of her was disappointed that Harmel, with a lot of effort, finally gave in to separate from them.

Something stirred inside her again, and she let it linger there for a moment before pushing it away. To help with that, Janis turned and inspected the road between Watchlight and Evenir.

The cobblestone road had a few shops to their left, one for travel gear and the other a brewery. A few other shops stood behind them, but the shop owners had closed up when they saw a large group of armed people setting up a defense. To their right was the city wall. It was about three times Janis's height and made from gray stone bricks, each large and sturdy. Janis eyed the wall, considering if a Destroyer could break through it easily. It was at least six feet thick, built so that a pathway could be made for the soldiers who patrolled on top of it.

Fog it, Janis thought, *we didn't account for them.*

Sure enough, soldiers, hearing the explosion and arrows bouncing off the stone, were starting to gather above them, arrows nocked and pointed down at both groups.

They have no idea who's good and bad; we're all a threat to them.

Janis could see their faces from below, a mixture of fear and wonder in their eyes at the display of Light powers.

"Look out above," Janis told the Shielder.

Gila looked up and moved her other hand to extend the Shield over and around the back of them.

"I'm stretched thin—the Shield can't hold much if I have to keep this up," the woman said.

Magness nodded and ordered another Shielder to cover the rear and the space above them. As they spoke, another orb of Destruction blasted against the Shield with a loud crack. The men on the wall gasped and shouted at the sight. They began nocking their own arrows and aiming at both the red and blue Shields.

"We don't have time for this," Janis growled.

Without much thought, she lunged forward, running through the blue wall of the Shield and barreling toward Watchlight's. Prost still stood behind it, but when he saw that she ran through, he stepped through his own Shield casually. Janis glanced above, hoping that the archers wouldn't take advantage of her exposed flesh. As far as she could tell, they were still focused on the Shields.

Lightbearers are definitely not going to be hidden any longer after all this commotion, Janis thought.

She ran directly at Prost and flicked a small dagger right at his face. He ducked deftly, the dagger spinning over his head and bouncing off the red Shield. Janis just kept running, closing the distance as fast as she could. Ten feet before she met Prost, her gut wrenched and she felt herself flying backward through the air. A faint red glow emitted from her body, and she knew that she was being Moved. Her instincts kicked in and she held out her hand. Just then, a large flash of blue announced a rough-looking cushion made of Light coming into existence just where she would slam into the stone floor. Instead of hitting the stone of the road, she slammed into it, the Conjure taking the brunt of her fall.

She hadn't needed to Conjure something in a pinch before, but it had done the job. At least she wasn't dead. Seeing how she'd managed to Conjure something successfully just now, she held out her hand and tried to create a ball of Destroying power.

Nothing happened.

Cursing, she leapt to the side as Prost came at her, sword swinging rapidly through the air. Janis spun and held her dagger up to block him, the steel of their weapons clanging as Prost's sword was pushed to the side.

He smiled evilly at her, then held both swords up high, pushing them down with heavy force. Janis saw them coming at her and knew she wouldn't be able to stop them with her one dagger. Thinking quickly, she swung with her dagger so that it caught both sword blades enough to redirect them away from her. This action backfired, as it threatened to yank her own weapon from her hand. Her wrist twinged with pain as it was pulled in an unnatural direction.

Prost didn't hesitate, but quickly spun to stab her with one of his weapons. Janis danced backward, only inches of air between the sharp of his blade and her shoulder. Suddenly, the ground next to her exploded in a flash of red Light and she was blown off her feet, rolling across the cobbles. A grunt in front of her indicated Prost was affected by the blast as well.

"Fog it, Riln! Leave her to me!"

Shaking her head to remove the dizzy feeling, Janis snagged her dagger from the ground and lunged at Prost, trying to take advantage of his distraction. It almost worked, for he gasped and barely parried her stab. Reaching out with his foot, he kicked her in the stomach and she flew backward, pain now lancing through her midsection.

Prost lunged again, but she spun out of his reach and ran to the wall. She hoped that he'd follow her, and his pounding feet proved he was. At the last moment, she turned and watched as he stabbed once more toward her. She slid to the side just enough that his sword pierced the wall with a loud crack, small pieces of rock and dust getting thrown around them. Janis feigned a swing at his face, but he easily parried that with his other sword. At the same time, she threw her elbow down onto his hand nearest her, feeling his wrist crack from the blow. He howled, letting the sword stick in the wall and pulling back.

"Ooh, that sounds broken," Janis said with mock concern.

Glaring at her, he smiled. "I'm sure your stomach will be full of great colors from that kick as well."

She didn't let her face show it, but the pain was still heavy in her gut. Instead, she tried to show that it wasn't affecting her.

"Bruises heal easily. Besides, I can be Fixed."

The comment had a much better effect than she expected, for he growled and flew at her, his blade swinging in quick blows.

Janis was able to dodge and parry each one of them, but it took every bit of her concentration. A bead of sweat dripped down her cheek and she could feel her body was heating up. Normally by this point she'd already killed the assailant or found a way to incapacitate them. As before, the two were evenly matched, even if she didn't want to admit it.

Prost side-stepped and hesitated only for a moment, but Janis lunged, trying to take advantage of the pause. He saw her move and bent his body sideways to dodge the stab. Likely her blade would have skimmed his side, but instead her dagger glowed red with Light and was pulled away from her in the opposite direction.

Janis cursed as Prost saw her disarmed and swung his blade at her. Another instinctual Conjure appeared in her hand, an exact copy of her now-missing dagger—and she raised it to block Prost's own sword. The move was impressive, but Prost's immunity to the power caused his own steel blade to pass through her Conjured one. The moment seemed to slow down, Janis seeing where she'd take the blow right in her neck. She stared at him, his own face sweating and red from exertion. Rather than feel the blow in her neck, however, she felt her body tugged heavily to the side, Prost's blade missing her by a handspan. She struggled to regain her balance.

Her body had been Moved, the blue Light fading quickly now from her skin.

Bless you, Mover, she thought, turning and nodding her thanks toward the blue Shield behind her. A man there held up his hand in a salute.

Unfortunately, the Light from the save was apparently an invitation for the men above to start firing arrows down.

I can't keep fighting with Riln interfering, Janis thought. *This better work....*

Knowing that Prost would recover in seconds, she turned and ran directly toward the Watchlight Shield. She'd hoped that her quick moves would keep them from Moving her, but that was a mistake. Her body glowed again and she was flung backward by the Moving force. As she slammed into the ground, her head flared in pain. She quickly rolled to the side, assuming that Prost was nearby. The gamble had been a good one, for his sword slammed into the cobblestones, shattering a few from the blow.

Her head was still slightly spinning as she got to her feet. She pressed her hand to her head and prayed to Lanser her Fixing would work. She then sighed as a warmth spread through her skull. She could see the blue Light of her fixing, and whispered a word of thanks.

If only I could figure out how to make this work every time.

As of now, her Lightbearing was just too unpredictable. Projectiles began flying into Evenir's Shield, which the blue Lightbearers returned in kind. Balls of Destroying power, both blue and red, flew through the air, smashing into the other sides' barriers. The sound was extremely loud. Janis had to focus her eyes on Prost to not get distracted. Prost stepped toward her, but was forced to step back as an arrow sprouted from the ground in front of him. Janis saw his jaw tighten and they both looked up, the Stilten guards taking aim at the only two people not under the Light Shields.

Janis sprung into action, jumping side to side in a serpentine nature to dodge the arrows. Prost was forced to do the same. They dodged and glanced at each other, knowing that their bout couldn't continue until the more immediate threat was neutralized.

Prost barreled toward his side's Shield, an arrow lodging in his shoulder on the same side as his broken wrist. Janis felt an arrow skim her arm as it bounced loudly off the stones next to her. She made for their own Shield, but the guards must have seen this coming, for more arrows flew between her and the Shield.

Looking up, she lobbed her Conjured dagger upward at the men with precision. A few of the soldiers yelled warning and they ducked. There was no need for that though, as her dagger puffed into nothing, having reached the conjurable limit. Janis tried creating a Destroying ball and this time a ball of blue Light appeared in her hand. She lobbed it at the wall just below the men. It flew true and smacked into the bricks near them.

Unfortunately, nothing happened.

Janis cringed as her Lightbearing failed her again.

The guards were only distracted for a moment before they started nocking arrows and pointing them at her. Just then, however, Janis heard Magness give a command and Light projectiles flew upward at the men. Some were arrows Conjured of Light, some actual arrows. A few of the men on the wall lit up with blue Light and were Moved backward off the other side of the wall, screaming. Magness herself swiftly launched a few arrows in succession. Janis had seen her spar with the sword but was equally impressed with the leader's bow skills.

Janis locked eyes with Magness, giving her a grateful look. Janis spun again and saw Riln looking at her, amused. Rather than running straight for him, she knew she had to take a gamble.

Watchlight's Shield has to come down, she thought.

She had only a few minutes to figure it out. Riln held up his hand, a ball forming there at the same time as a wicked smile. He pulled his hand back and prepared to throw it. She didn't run at the red Shield, though Riln apparently expected her to. His face turned to confusion as she dashed through the pub's door to her left.

Her eyes took a moment to adjust to the dimness of the pub, the only light coming from the front windows and some lamps hung about the room.

The bar stood opposite the door and a man jumped up, a crossbow in his hand.

"Git outta 'ere wit' all tha' witchy-craft, or I'll shoot yeh through."

Janis stopped and eyed the man. He was middle-aged and balding, a dark ring of hair surrounding his head just above his ears. Though he held a crossbow beneath his hardened face, she could see that he was shaking, the tip of his bolt dipping up and down in the air.

"I am not here to hurt you—I just need a way up to your roof," Janis spoke quickly.

When he stared at her, confused, she added, "I need it *now*. There is a man following me and he will not hesitate to kill us both."

His eyes shifted to the window behind her and his face drained of color. She couldn't see whether Prost was actually visible to him through the glass, but he hastily moved his supporting hand from his crossbow and pointed to a doorway to his left.

"Stairs—through there," was all he said, gesturing toward a door.

Janis nodded and moved quickly over to the door.

"I suggest you hide now. Unless you intend to launch that bolt directly into the man following me, you are going to want to hide. Miss or hesitate, and you are dead."

He jumped at her words, then ducked behind his bar.

Janis flew through the door, not checking to see if Prost was anywhere close behind her. She immediately spotted the set of stairs near the back, spiraling tightly in the corner. As she ran, she heard the pub door bang open. The fact that Prost was so close behind her was still in her mind. Frustration buzzed in her chest as she realized the wasted time because of the pub owner, if that's even who he was.

She deftly went up the stairs, trying to move quickly and quietly. The man wouldn't be there to tell Prost where she went, but there were only so many doors someone could go through. As she ran, she considered the danger of what she was about to try. Watchlight's Shield was the only thing keeping them from being pushed back by Evenir. Only once had she seen a Shield broken, and it was by Avryn's Destroying at the falls where Marric awakened.

Fog, that feels like forever ago. So much has changed in so little time, she thought as she passed the third landing.

Her heart pounded in her chest, sweat dripping faster down her face and neck as she rushed up the stairs. At length, she made it to a small landing, the flat of the floor only big enough for one person, blocked by a door. She gritted her teeth, hoping the door didn't have a lock on it. She released a breath of relief when it opened without trouble. Picking a lock wouldn't have been too much trouble, but she knew time wasn't in her favor with Prost close behind. The moment she thought that, loud footsteps echoed up the narrow space where the stairs cut through each landing.

Knowing she didn't have much time, Janis held out her right hand and tried to conjure something.

Blue Light flashed in the small space, causing her to wince slightly at the brightness. A small ball formed out of the Light and grew rapidly, the small object landing with a soft thunk on the top stair of the spiral staircase. Shapeless and lumpy, the Conjure grew and grew as Janis focused on making it bigger. It resembled a stone of sorts, but had pieces jutting out on all sides like spikes. Janis couldn't tell what she was going for, all she could think of was weight, making the mass heavier and heavier. At length, the spiked object grew so large that it reached her knees on the top landing, the spikes digging into the wood railing and the open space. Finally, the wood below it cracked and snapped with a loud crunch. The large spiked Conjure fell heavily to the set of stairs immediately below, breaking through. Gravity yanked the heavy object down, smashing into three more sets of spirals before disappearing into nothing. Janis cursed, but was grateful for her work.

That should stall him for some time, she thought.

There was little doubt in her mind that Prost would find a way up, despite the challenge she'd just given him. It would give her more time to figure out how to take care of the Shield. She cocked her head, the thought coming to her that the object she'd just Conjured resembled a giant puffing fish she'd seen in the markets near the sea. Shaking that away, she turned and ran through the door, throwing it closed and eyeing the other side for a lock, just in case. When she noted that a key was needed on either side, she slammed it closed and ran through the small room to the top of the roof.

Janis froze.

A dozen black-cloaked men and women stood at the edge of the roof, looking down on the scene below her. Most of them stood with one foot on the edge, bowstrings pulled back with arrows nocked there. A chill ran up her spine when she saw that the arrow tips glowed slightly silver, covered in the odd poison that had killed the boy in T'Arren Vale.

"We've precious little of the substance, so take out as many Lightbearers as you can with each shot," a man's voice said loudly.

Janis watched as the archers aimed their bows, some to the left, some to the right. Despite the Shield, Janis felt something inside warn her of the poison. She didn't have any logical reason to be concerned, but her instincts said that her allies were in danger. Without much thinking, Janis grabbed her last two small daggers and flung them at two of the archers pointing right. As the knives flew toward the men, she ran in the same direction of her throws, slipping her favorite dagger into her hand. The daggers flew true and slammed into the backs of two of the people. They crumpled to the ground, one falling back, the other tipping forward and falling off the roof. As she hoped, this caused the other three to turn back, shocked at the death of their comrades.

In a flash, Janis was among them, slashing her dagger left and right. Stabbing would be too inefficient, so Janis cut wrists and knees, thighs and stomachs. Killing wasn't her first goal, just causing chaos to keep the arrows from flying. Within seconds, the three other archers aiming at Evenir had fallen, their arrows on the ground. Attacking these archers had put her slightly closer to the roof's edge, across from where the other archers stood.

In her haste to attack, she had prevented the archers aiming at Watch-light's Shield from firing. She spun around and jumped behind the group of fallen archers, groaning from the wounds she'd cut into them so quickly. Those who remained alive were too distracted to attack her at the moment.

That mattered little, however, as Janis stared at the tips of five nocked and writhing arrowheads. In her commotion, she'd commanded the attention of the remaining archers, who now aimed at her with their arrows.

A blond man suddenly held up his hand, halting the archers from launching their arrows.

"Well, this is an unexpected appearance from the most troublesome assassin in all of Lindrad."

Janis's heart skipped a beat and she shifted her eyes to the only unhooded person on the roof. He and another man stood next to the five archers. She'd seen them earlier, but her instincts had focused on the immediate threat of the archers. Her skin tingled as if she could almost feel where the arrows were pointed and where they'd enter her if they let them loose.

She stared hard at the blond man who had just spoken, standing casually next to his kill squad.

"Luden, how unpleasant to see you here," she said shortly.

"Now, now, there isn't any need for that. After all, I didn't lose track of you after you killed my men all those months ago. I must say, in terms of a working relationship, that wasn't your wisest move."

Janis stayed crouched low, keeping her eyes flicking from archer to archer. Just in front of her on the ground, a man tried to reach for his bow and she kicked his hand away. He grunted in pain and fell back on his face, groaning.

"Despite the circumstances, I regret to say that was not my handiwork. You of all people know that I don't use crossbows. Daggers are my weapon of choice, as you can see." Janis brandished her dagger as she spoke.

She gestured grandly with the large dagger in her hand, sweeping it over the fallen men and women on the ground in front of her.

Luden pursed his lips and eyed his men. "Yes, yes, I am well aware of that. Though how am I to believe you when the boy I ordered you to kill is still alive? It seems like a rogue operation, to me."

Janis chuckled slightly. "Well, that's not to say I'm upset that I *didn't* kill your men. I wish I could take credit. Unfortunately, it's our friends on the ground with the red Light who's to blame. They slaughtered your two oafs."

Luden narrowed his eyes and shook his head slightly. "Why bother lying when I have you cornered?"

Janis shrugged, knowing her casual response would infuriate Luden.

"I've no need to lie to you now. Regardless, if you are wanting to avenge your men's deaths from all those months ago, you're looking for an ugly scar-faced man."

At that moment, the door to their left slammed open and footsteps stalked loudly around the small room behind her. Prost stopped short at the doorway behind her when he saw the other figures on the roof.

"Ah—speaking of the bloke, here he is."

The five archers spun on him, then turned back to her. Janis sensed an opening with their confusion, but didn't take it. The other hooded man next to Luden gave her pause. He hadn't said anything during the exchange or even moved, aside from turning his head side to side; but she was still somehow wary of him. A trained assassin had just downed five archers next to him and his body showed no signs of worry or shock. His lack of visible weapons was not a comforting thing to her at this moment, either.

Finally, the archers kept two of their arrow points focused on her while the other three trained on Prost.

"Why are you here, Luden? Why do you care about awakened Lightbearers?" Janis said, intentionally filling her tone with hardness.

Luden smirked at her. "Why do *I* care? Why do *you* care, my dear? I hired you because I was under the impression that you had no knowledge of it and couldn't care less about who you killed."

Janis narrowed her eyes. "I'm the one asking questions, so answer," Janis spat at him.

Her eyes flickered to Prost, who stood with one hand on his sword, the other at his belt. She assumed he'd left his crossbow somewhere, else he likely would have already taken out the archers threatening him with their bows.

Luden laughed mirthfully, causing Janis's adrenaline to spike, though no attacks came.

"Because Lightbearing is evil and should be eradicated."

Janis stayed vigilant, but cocked her head for show.

"Based on what? That your money can't control them and their powers render you worthless?"

Luden gritted his teeth at the comment. In her peripheral, she noted that Prost also stiffened at her words. She packed that away inside, knowing his lack of powers very much bothered him.

Janis glanced upward, gauging how much time she had. The sun was dipping lower now, positioned just above the wall. Once it sunk below the battlements, the girl and the other seven Lightbearers would awaken. Then things would get interesting for everyone.

As if this isn't already complicated enough.

The sounds of battle had heightened down below on the street, explosions and steel clanging loudly. Blue and red Light flashed periodically, exposing Lightbearers on each side. The wall across from them exploded with Destroying blasts, knocking more guards off or killing them instantly.

I hope that Avryn and the other companies are having more luck than we are right now.

"The blasted power killed my family and destroyed my home. It left me with nothing—no one."

Janis snorted. "Except for your parents' business and unlimited funds."

Luden growled and pulled his sword on her before retorting, "Everyone I loved was taken from me because of that fogging power. It plagues the world —kills innocent men and women every day. No one should wield such power. For years, I have plotted and planned how to eradicate it all. Then the Seer came and made it possible."

Luden gestured to the hooded man next to him, and then Janis understood. She jumped on the irony instantly.

"You loathe Lightbearing, yet you employ a man who wields the power himself? The hypocrisy is not lost on you, is it?"

Anger flashed in Luden's eyes and he moved forward, raising his sword up higher. Just before he could take any steps toward her, the hooded man stuck his arm out and blocked him.

"She isn't worth the danger. She is faster and more skilled than you. You'd be dead in an instant."

The voice came from under the hood, deep and strong. Instantly, Janis was frozen, her mind reeling and her heart speeding up, her skin clammy. A burning exploded inside her chest, filling her with a feeling of longing and confusion.

It can't be—she thought.

The voice shoved memory after memory into her mind. Nostalgia pressed its way into her, distracting her from the moment. For years she'd listened to that voice, learned from that voice, been yelled at by that voice. Part of her wanted to deny the possibility of what she'd just heard, but she knew she couldn't. Tightening her grip on her dagger, she clenched her jaw and forced down the surprised and fluttery feeling that burst within her. Janis wrapped her mind around the situation, staring hard at the hooded man.

Despite her training to keep her emotions in check, her reaction to him was obvious. It was clear that he noticed her movements, perhaps a look on her face. Still, she denied the possibility that it was him.

As if in response to her thoughts, the man lifted his hands slowly and pulled back his hood, revealing a handsome face, a chiseled jaw and nose, black tousled hair, and piercing green eyes.

Macks.

Janis's heart stopped. The world slowed and the love that she'd harbored for him filled her with a warmth of longing. Immediately, however, she felt the sting of hate. He'd abandoned her, left her for dead. She'd only narrowly escaped, injuring herself and burning her contacts here in Stilten for the foreseeable future. Her ears roared from the mixture of emotions. Then he spoke.

"Hello, Janis. How have you been?"

Something inside of her snapped. The world slowed and blurred, spinning into a mix of colors. Her eyes expanded and beams of blue Light pressed from them. Power stirred inside her, the flash of emotions transforming her into something else.

Fog it, I think I'm dying.

25

The world melted away; anger, frustration, and burning desire took control of her. She'd only seen him for moments before this vision had torn her away from the rooftop of the pub. She cringed knowing as long as she was in a vision, she was completely vulnerable.

Yet she didn't care.

For years, she'd assumed Macks was dead, captured by those who had almost ended her life in Stilten all those years ago. Now he stood before her, a Lightbearer —working for Luden, of all people.

Internally, she chuckled at the thought. Luden was a buffoon at best, yet he'd managed to capture the interest of her former mentor with money. Janis couldn't really be surprised; Macks had always taught her to work where the money was.

But then things had been different since she'd met Avryn and the others, and Janis wasn't sure if she was upset by the changes. For a moment, she thought of Evenir and Marric. Immediately, the swirling images of her vision coalesced into a view of Marric, Shrell, and the others with him. They would still be a couple days out from Wurren, but likely Watchlight and Luden's men wouldn't be far behind them.

As she watched Marric in her mind, she had the distinct feeling that there was a connection there—something that bound them in a way she couldn't explain. To validate the feeling, she noticed a thin blue line made of Light running from her to

Marric. Before she had much opportunity to observe the line, she was swept away again, the world spinning once more.

At length, the colors formed into a dark cavern, other than statues made of Light all around her. Men and women of all ages stood with serious faces, locked in time by some mystical force. One of these images began to move to her right and she spun on it, reaching for her dagger. It mattered little, however, since the person approaching her was Tryvv, the Prime who lived before Riln and herself. Janis eyed the figure of the Voidbearer behind Tryvv, but the shorter woman with cropped dark hair remained frozen like a statue.

The message was clear, no Prileen or Livella this time—this was only for her.

"So, you have finally realized your potential, Janis," Tryvv said, a smile on her face.

Janis scowled at her. "I don't have any idea what you mean."

Tryvv chuckled. "For some it comes faster than others, but you've been a stubborn one. By no means have you been the most stubborn of all T'arn Yiv'len, but it has been some time. For weeks, your powers have been held back by the only thing that could keep you from becoming what you should—from transforming into your full potential. That thing is you, Janis."

Janis furrowed her brow, confused by the words. "How the fog could I stop something like this? If I had the choice, I'd have not gotten involved with all this mess."

Tryvv looked unaffected by her words. "Now, that can't be true. What is it you just Saw before you came here?"

Janis froze, causing Tryvv to chuckle.

"No, Janis, I cannot read your mind or See what you See, but I am a good guesser. When the Prime finally reaches their transformation, one way or another, it's because their purpose has changed, their goal shifted from self-preservation to selfless preservation. I can only guess that you've found that purpose."

For the first time since her childhood, she felt embarrassed. Why, she couldn't tell, but she thought her face might have blushed if she'd had the ability. The feeling was not welcome. Yet, when she'd seen Macks, she remembered just how selfish he'd been, and how that had resulted in him abandoning her. She knew now that she didn't want to follow that same self-serving path. She could and had survived like that, but she wanted to truly live.

"I Saw someone I care about, and realized I won't abandon him, or the others."

Tryvv nodded. "Ahh, the boy. Though I don't See much, I have Seen him through you. He is quite the spectacle, isn't he? If he is truly the reason you've Transformed, then I am thankful for his influence on you."

This comment made Janis chuckle. "His influence on me is that he's needed me to save him so many times, I can't count anymore," Janis remarked.

Tryvv shrugged, then turned her back to Janis as she looked upward in thought.

"Whatever the reason, you have transformed and become what you needed to in order to restore strength to Yrillnan."

When the tall woman of Light turned again, there was something in her eyes: pain. Janis stared at her, wondering what was going on in her mind. It had taken years for her to push back all feelings of fear, insecurity, and even pain, yet this former Prime wore it on her face, unabashed.

Janis didn't understand how a leader could be so open with her emotions.

"Riln and Prost must be removed. Their decisions have tainted Lightbearing and the blessings of Lanser in Lindrad. But beware, they must die together. Lanser has invested his support in you and Livella to create a new Seal. Because of this, your powers alone can affect that of the other Voidbearer. His pact is with the other Prime, not with you. You must remove them together, and bring back their followers with Lanser's blessing. Their Light must shine blue once more."

Janis gritted her teeth, feeling conflicted and overwhelmed.

"I'm not sure if I am the right person for this."

And what about Macks? There was too much going on for her to process, but she felt strongly that Macks was the first thing she'd need to take care of. She hadn't decided what that meant, yet.

Tryvv smiled again. "Yet as you say it, you know that isn't true. You have changed, Janis, else your powers wouldn't have come to you. Now that they are here, you will lead the Lightbearers of Lindrad."

Janis's head snapped up to look at Tryvv. "I am no leader. I can't be in charge of the well-being of this many people. Sure, there are a few people who I've come to care for—"

Images of Marric, Shrell, Avryn, Magness, and others spun around her mind. Harmel's image lingered for a bit longer than the others before disappearing. The woman didn't seem to notice, so Janis assumed only she could perceive them.

"But I did not sign up to lead anyone. Magness leads them and I will not interfere."

Even as Janis said it, she had doubts that her position could remain the same.

"I know little of the woman, but I'm sure she'll step down when the time is right. Real leaders know when they need to step up—or down."

Janis glared at her, then opened her mouth to argue. Tryvv held up a hand to stop her.

"Our time is short. You must return to your body, lest you be killed. There is danger there."

Janis's skin tingled as she recalled where her body was left. How long the vision lasted was different than on the outside, but she couldn't risk being stuck for much longer.

"Farewell, Janis. This is the last of our meetings. I can rest once more."

The Light woman waved a hand before disappearing into nothingness. As she did, Janis focused on her own physical body somewhere far away, and her world quickly melted and reformed into an image of the roof. When she arrived, her vision self was in a different position. Rather than being near the roof's edge with her physical body under the archers aim, her vision self was at the door, just behind Prost. Her head snapped to the side and saw her physical body, eyes glowing fiercely with blue Light, standing there, as if mesmerized by what she saw.

Janis watched as Prost took an arrow in his arm, covered in the odd poison that no one could explain. She balked at the sight, knowing how quickly the poison could kill a person. Oddly, however, he stalked forward, slaying the archers and facing Luden.

He isn't being affected by the poison, Janis thought. How is that possible?

She tuned in her physical hearing just in time to hear Prost skewer Luden through the chest before regarding Macks, whose eyes glowed with red. Before she could wonder much about what he was Seeing, he was there, or the vision version of him, standing behind her physical body. He stared at her, eyes holding something that she couldn't explain.

Anger boiled inside her, but she focused to hold it at bay.

"You lied to me," she said harshly, "then left me for dead—and for what? Money?"

Macks grinned at her, though it wasn't a mischievous or playful smile, but rather a menacing one.

"*I warned you, Janis. Trust no one. I knew that someday I'd have to teach you that lesson myself. I must admit, we were quite productive in our years together, but then I realized that my Sight would be far more lucrative than staying with you.*"

The words stung, but Janis kept her feelings and face in check.

"*I shouldn't be surprised—that's all you taught me for all those years: go where the money goes.*"

Macks grinned at her again.

"*Yes, now you see. But it looks like you've gotten yourself wrapped up in something too big for your britches, haven't you? Why did you go about that, I wonder.*"

Janis snorted. "*You act as if you aren't wrapped up in it yourself. You've been helping Luden track and kill Lightbearers. You are as much a part of this war as I am.*"

Macks shrugged. "*I am an assassin, a paid hand of sorts. I do not consider myself a part of this war.*"

"*By even being here with Luden, you and I both know that's not true.*"

Janis regarded the dead blond man, blood pooling around him. Without being too obvious, she took stock of where Prost was. Since she'd started talking to Macks, time seemed to have frozen, even in the physical world. How the vision had stopped time like this, Janis couldn't know, but she was thankful to have some more time.

"*Looks like you'll have to find a new source of your money, anyway,*" Janis said, nodding at Luden.

Macks turned and scowled. "*An unfortunate turn of events, sure, but I'll just slip away as I always do.*"

He turned to Janis and something in his eyes shifted for just a moment. Janis glared at him, wanting to say so much more, but somehow knowing that the moment was about to end.

"*I had to leave because of you. I could see that you had become attached to me —*" Macks paused, biting his lip in frustration, "*—and I was feeling myself slipping as well.*"

Janis's chest constricted, the words carrying so much more meaning than they might under normal circumstances. She stared at him, processing the statement without really needing to. He'd started to love her. Somehow this wasn't surprising, yet at the same time, all these years she had doubted what she'd felt between them. Hearing him say it didn't make what she had to do any easier.

She would have to kill him.

"You won't slip away this time," Janis said, looking to Prost.

"Oh? I have far more tricks up my sleeves than even you can anticipate. I didn't teach you all of the things I know."

She shook her head. "Doesn't matter," Janis said, then stared Macks in the face. "I have something that you'll never understand."

Macks looked at her, confused. At that moment, she watched as his vision body fuzzed slightly at the edges before rushing back to combine with his physical body.

"How's about we take this Lightbearing for a drive?" Janis said.

Her vision body flashed backward and combined with her physical one.

26

Prost watched as Janis's eyes started to glow. He'd witnessed Riln and other Seers have visions like this, but something was different. The beams of Light protruding from her eyes were larger, longer than ones he'd seen before. His skin chilled and he felt the hair on his neck stand up. Memories of being thrown backward by her awakening stung him and he pushed them away, squeezing his fists tightly to help ward off the uncomfortable feelings of uneasiness and fear.

The odd man next to Luden had taken off his hood, a simple action, yet it appeared to make Janis catatonic. Prost considered lunging at her and stabbing her quickly, but he didn't think he'd be faster than the two archers aiming at him. Still, the oddity of the moment gave him an opening that he figured would not come up again.

Anticipating the pain, he lunged forward and pulled his sword out in a fluid motion. Both of the archers let their arrows loose, the silver glowing tips dripping liquid on the ground as they flew at him. Knowing the trajectory, he intentionally dodged the one that would have skewered his heart, but took the other in his right bicep. Pain seared into his arm. He pushed the pain down deep, focusing on the task at hand. With a quick motion, he stabbed the closest archer in the stomach, then swung his sword in an arc and cut the arm clean off the other. The archers who had been trained on

Janis now came to their companions' aid. He then kicked another archer in the chest, flinging her wide-eyed off the roof.

Prost turned to the blond man, whom Janis had called Luden just moments before, and made to kill him as well. Before he could, however, the two remaining archers had turned on him and fired their own arrows. He cursed as one took him in the left thigh, the other skimming his shoulder. More pain threatened to consume him, but he pushed it away. He felt something in his system. Training in the military had taught him to recognize when poisons were used so even if it was only moments, he could determine the best course of action to take.

This poison felt different, however. He could feel something, a tingling, coursing in his leg and up his arm, but it didn't sting, burn, or hurt as poisons often did. The feeling was almost—pleasant.

Based on the color and the consistency of the poison, he assumed it was the same that had been used on the boy in T'Arren Vale, the poison that had turned his veins black and taken him too quickly for Prost to stick around. Yet, if it could be so deadly, why did it feel this way to him?

Prost didn't have long to think about it, for the archers had nocked more arrows, these ones free of the poison. Luden stared at him, eyes shifting to each of Prost's wounds with a confused look on his face.

"It isn't killing you, but how—?" the blond man said, backing up toward his archers, positioning himself behind them. He eyed Janis, who still stood in the Seer vision, then looked back at Prost. "He said everyone, even Lightbearers would be killed by this."

Prost glared at him.

"Fog it, I'm not a Lightbearer!" Prost shouted. Hearing once again about his lack of powers caused something within him to crack.

Everything flashed in his mind: Riln constantly calling him a 'dud', the lack of respect and attitude of all others in Watchlight—Prost was tired of it all. Hearing it this time only made him see red. With a quick motion, Prost rushed forward, watching more arrows fly. This time he ducked, one arrow missing him completely, the other grazing his scalp shallowly, then pressed forward, killing the two archers with easy blows.

Luden made to swing his sword at him, but it was slow and unpracticed. Prost scoffed as he knocked the sword easily from his grip. Fear filled the blond man's eyes as he stared up at the larger man. Prost knew how off-putting his scars were, purple and gnarled, from nose to ears. They were something that he'd carry for the rest of his life as evidence of Riln's anger and lack of control. Though he'd come to terms with the scars, it still bothered him how everyone stared at him. His face, marred for eternity, caused him almost as much grief as his immunity to Lightbearing and the voices in his head.

"Wait!" Luden begged, "Please, I can pay you—!"

"Pompous rich people. You should learn that money can't buy your way out of every situation," Prost hissed at the man.

Before Luden could finish blubbering, Prost stabbed the man right in the chest before pushing him off the end of his sword with his foot.

Finally, he turned to the man nearby and paused. His eyes were glowing, Light shining brightly from them, but it wasn't blue.

Is this a man from Watchlight? Prost thought, staring at him.

He was about to kill him quickly and easily, but the redness of the Light gave him pause. Prost by no means knew every person from the compound, but he knew that only the newest of Lightbearers still had blue Light. The fact that this man's Light was red meant that he at least wasn't part of Evenir.

A gasp behind him caused him to turn quickly. The blue Light in Janis's eyes had faded and she stared at Macks, a look of resolve on her face.

Prost's gut wrenched as he noted that something had changed. His brain was screaming that he should run at her, kill her while he had the chance, but his instincts warned against this. The moment he had the thought, Janis looked at her hand, the empty one, and a blue Light blazed there, a dagger springing into existence made of blue Light and looking exactly like the one she held in her other hand.

She held out her hand toward the other man and he flew backward with a shout, body glowing blue from her power. Janis stepped forward, slowly approaching where he had landed on his back. Prost, seeing that she was moving in his direction, waited until she was within his range, then ran at her. Without even looking at him, she threw her arm outward, the steel of that dagger glinting in the setting sun. Prost felt a force slam against his sword and it was ripped from his grasp, flying over the edge of the roof.

Fear sprung inside him. He grit his teeth and forced the feeling down.

His confidence in his immunity to Lightbearing was in tatters. As of yet, there had been only minor effects of the powers on his person, but they had all been from her. He growled and pulled his other sword, running at her. She once again Moved his sword and he was forced to let it go or go flying with it.

"Fog you, woman! You can't touch me with your Lightbearing!"

Frustration had built to a peak in his chest and he ran at her at full speed, intending to tackle her, even if it meant taking a dagger to his gut. Janis suddenly turned to him and another jolt of something ran through him. Her eyes still glowed. Though her eyeballs didn't glow fully, only the pupil was glowing the same color of her Light. Without hesitation, she held her hand up to him and Prost felt as if he ran into an invisible wall.

Confused and angry, Prost was frozen a few paces from her, his hands outstretched and ready to grab her and throw her to the ground. He growled, but couldn't move. He eyed his arm and saw that he was wreathed in blue Light. He gasped to see that she hadn't summoned a Shield, she was holding him in place with her Moving.

Something inside him shattered. Panic consumed him and he thought this might be what a normal person felt like against a Lightbearer.

The corner of her mouth tugged upward in a half smile, then she let the Light dagger dissolve and flicked her wrist.

Prost felt his body fly backward, completely out of his control. Doubt had become reality. Air whistled in his ears as he flew over the edge of the roof, plummeting to the cobblestone road below.

27

Power coursed through Janis's body, a slight tingling on every inch of her skin, in every limb. The warmth that one would normally feel from a near fire or even the sunlight was blazing inside of her. The vision had come and gone so quickly, yet had been too profound for her to forget. Though she knew she was not in a vision, she somehow could See things that she normally couldn't. Images and information were flowing through her mind that couldn't be comprehended by a normal brain.

Her mind had changed. Seeing Macks again had broken her, snapped something inside of her, shifting reality in a way she didn't think possible. Her perspective had changed, and everything was different now.

Janis watched as Prost, wreathed in blue Light, flew over the edge of the roof, plummeting to his timely death. When he'd attacked her, she didn't hesitate to use her Lightbearing. All doubts she had were lost, partially because of the vision she'd just Seen, and partially because it didn't matter anymore. A mixture of love and anger had consumed her when she'd seen Macks. The feeling was still there, but it was masked by the power that she felt.

Her attention snapped back to her former mentor, now lying on the ground. He held his head where a small cut oozed blood beneath his hair.

"You betrayed me, left me for dead," she said, the words coming out slowly.

Her voice sounded different. It echoed slightly and was laced with power somehow.

"For what reason? Why did you leave me there to die?" Janis knew he'd just told her why in the vision, but she couldn't help asking. What he had done was still incomprehensible to her.

Macks coughed loudly, then pushed himself up to stand.

"Is that a rhetorical question? I just told you why."

Janis knew it was true. She'd just been there. The vision had shown how Macks had been a Seer all along. He'd awakened just months before he'd met her. How he'd been able to hide that from her, she didn't know. Though memories had flashed through so quickly that she couldn't remember them all, there had been signs she'd missed.

"You could have told me. We could have continued working together."

Macks laughed, then looked at her, disdain and pity on his face.

"Perhaps in the jobs we'd been doing, but after I left you, I took on riskier assignments which were only possible to achieve as a Seer. The number of times this wretched power saved me in the past few years proves you wouldn't have made it if you'd been there with me. You'd have died without the visions. I barely escaped hundreds of times because of them. Plus, you were getting too attached to me."

The words stung as he said them again, this time in the physical world. Janis held up her hand and created a Destroying orb. She was confident that it was correct this time. Macks furrowed his brows, looking confused. Then his eyes widened in shock as she tossed the ball at his feet. He cursed, trying to jump backward as the ball slammed into the roof at his feet, the explosion sending shingles and wood in all directions. He screamed as he fell into the hole and thudded heavily into the floor below. He had only fallen one floor, so Janis knew the damage to him couldn't have been deadly.

Dust and particles covered the air, making it so she couldn't see him. Janis tapped into the heat in her eyes, and a version of her sprung out of her normal body, a vision-self of the present, flying down into the hole and standing above her previous mentor.

He was unconscious, scrapes and cuts all along his face, each bleeding slightly. His left arm stuck out at an odd angle, proving that it must have broken his fall and snapped in the process.

The feeling of Seeing the present was an odd one, but somehow Janis knew she could control and harness it in a way she never could before. Seeing that he was unconscious, Janis focused on her body on the roof, and felt her vision body move quickly to reunite with her physical one. As she regarded her former mentor lying there, injured and unconscious, she cocked her head as she saw a small book in his belt. The book was altogether normal looking, but it pulsed with a power that intrigued her.

She held her hand out and Moved the small book into her hand. The moment it touched her, a stinging sensation sprang up her arm and she cursed, shoving it in her own belt to get it away from her skin.

I'll have to take a look at that later, she thought.

Janis turned back to Macks. Part of her knew she should kill him now, but something stopped her. Her feelings ran too deep, and she'd need to process things before she killed him.

"Stay. I've some things to take care of."

Though she meant the words, she anticipated that he wouldn't stay. He'd likely wake up and slip away before she was back. She partly hoped this would be the case, yet another part of her hoped he'd stay unconscious so she could remove him from this world when she was ready.

Janis turned and walked to the edge of the roof. As she walked, her mind shifted back to what she'd Seen only moments before. The feelings of seeing Macks again still stirred inside, but they were held back by the sheer power that she felt. For the past weeks since she and Livella had been told about the Seal, Janis had been resistant to the change. She'd pushed against the knowledge that Lanser had chosen her as the T'arn Yiv'len.

Now, she accepted it—even welcomed it.

The red Shield domed over the street below her. She looked right to see the blue Shield likewise protecting the Evenir group from most Watchlight attacks. It was flashing slightly as Destroying orbs smashed periodically against it. From afar, she couldn't see everything beyond it, but based on the flickering of the Shield, she guessed that Gila was running out of energy. Looking left again, she noted that the Watchlight Shield was still strong. Evenir didn't have as many Destroyers with them as Watchlight always had.

Avryn had gone with the group to find the twin Lightbearers who would awaken any moment, and Turrin had led the other group.

Let's even the odds, shall we? Janis thought.

Confidence swelling in her chest, she summoned a large orb of power. She knew exactly what it was. The orb, large and blue, about the size of her own head, hovered over her hand steadily as if ready to serve her. She held up her left hand, summoning another orb. This looked the same as the first, though smaller and somehow more intense.

Then she jumped.

28

Prost's entire body throbbed. He couldn't concentrate on any point of pain, as so many parts of him hurt. A man and woman groaned on the ground beneath to him. He could feel the hard and firm cobblestones beneath him, but his mind was too foggy to gather more information. Closing his mind, he focused on breathing and pushed the fear away that he'd felt consuming him moments ago.

Memories of the roof beneath his feet disappearing and being replaced by air and the roof becoming more distant flashed through his mind and he growled, shoving them away.

She can't affect me, I am immune to Lightbearing, Prost thought doggedly.

Even as the thought came, he knew it wasn't true. Not anymore, not for her, at least. A flash of blue Light behind his eyelids made him snap them open just in time to see a dagger of blue Light fly at his chest. He sucked in a breath, expecting the pain of the blade, but nothing came. The dagger flew right through him and clattered loudly on the stone behind him.

I'm still immune, I just need to stay away from her, he thought.

His mind screamed this, yet something within him pushed against it. Janis needed to die. If he didn't kill her, Riln would, and he couldn't have that. He had a score to settle with Janis, and that was only increased by her throwing him off the roof.

Looking up, he saw the Conjurer who had just tried to skewer him with a knife. Gritting his teeth, he yanked a small dagger free from his own belt and with some effort, flung the knife at her. It didn't fly perfectly true, given that he was still on the ground, but the blade slid easily into the woman's side as she turned to escape. She screamed and held her side, limping away.

It wasn't enough, she didn't die. She'll just get Fixed and be back here to get me. I need to move, to get behind the Shield, Prost thought.

Turning, he saw that the Shield was only ten paces behind him. The throw from the roof had launched him so far out that he'd landed close to the front of the Shield. Prost thanked Lanser, the irony not lost on him, for having landed on two unsuspecting battlers. Both had been knocked unconscious. He looked to the woman who was obviously from Evenir, and thought to kill her before he moved to the Shield. An arrow slamming into the ground next to him changed his mind.

With his pain now suppressed by the surge of adrenaline from his narrow miss with the arrow, he pushed himself up, grunting heavily. His wrist still ached from where Janis had broken it. Throbbing from his other arm reminded him of the arrow he'd taken there, and he looked down to see blood spilling from the wound. Staring at it, his mind focused on the immediate threat first.

The poison.

Prost took stock of the aches and pains as he stumbled toward the Shield. Oddly, he didn't feel any poisons or substances pressing their way through his body. The high command of Watchlight carried a general antivenom which wouldn't remove all poisons, but it would stop some and stall most of them.

Still, this time Prost didn't feel any poison inside of him. He could see some residue from the poison on his shirt where the arrow had pierced him, the shirt disintegrating at a slow pace, but he didn't feel alarmed.

He moved as quickly as he could, pain now lancing up his legs. Prost gritted his teeth and surged on. Arrows, Conjures, and other Moving objects slammed repeatedly into the red Shield in front of him. Through the translucent red of the wall, he could see Riln sitting calmly atop his horse, commanding those around him. If he'd seen Prost fall from the roof and hit the road below, he didn't care. Prost internally hoped that their leader hadn't seen. Even though he knew it wasn't true, it would at least indicate the smallest hint of care from Riln.

Time and time again Prost had been snubbed and rejected by Riln. The frustration had built to a peak point within the last few months, yet Prost was resolved to deal with it. Neither him nor Riln were willing to die to let Ugglyn free. Internally, Prost knew the last thing he wanted was for the anti-god to be let loose.

Shaking his head, Prost marveled for only a moment how his life had gotten so complicated so quickly. It had been over ten years since he'd trained as a soldier of T'Arren Vale with Avryn, yet there was still a small part of him that longed for it again. Life had been simpler then.

As he reached the Shield, Prost grunted as a projectile slammed into his shoulder from behind, pitching him forward through the translucent wall. He fell to his knees and rolled onto his side, breathing through the pain of the already forming bruise on his back. Prost blinked the pain away and was about to sit up, when he noticed something strange above. A figure in black flew through the air at the Shield, a flash of blue flying from her hand straight toward the blue Shield of Evenir across the way. She still held one small orb in her other hand.

Prost's body came to life, adrenaline boosting once more at the sight of the woman coming downward. He pushed up quickly and made to warn Riln, but it was too late. An extremely loud crack sounded above, causing his eardrums to throb. Riln jolted from the sound and looked upward. The Shield immediately shattered like glass, the sound similar in nature and disappeared around them. Prost saw Janis fall among their ranks, crouched like an animal.

Everyone on their side erupted in chaos.

The Shield had held back Watchlight's Lightbearers and archers, providing a sense of security. That security was all shattered with the Shield. There was a moment of pause in the Conjures and objects flying toward them, which indicated to Prost that Janis's move was unexpected to Evenir as well.

Prost spun on Evenir to see the large orb of blue shining brightly above their Shield, which was no longer flickering.

Evenir started lobbing projectiles again, though not as intensely as before. It wasn't Evenir's nature to slaughter unnecessarily. Prost found himself suddenly grateful for this. A Conjured dagger clanged to the ground next to Prost and he dodged a cart wheel that flew at his head. It smashed to the ground behind him, splinters of wood flying everywhere. The poor man behind him didn't see it coming, and was barraged by the debris.

Prost jumped backward, pain lancing everywhere in his bruised and broken body. Gasping, he turned and rushed to the doorway of the shop just next to them. An outcropping of the wall created a little nook for him to crouch in. He sagged down to his haunches and took a deep breath.

Before him was a frenzy, but not from Evenir's attacks; instead, it was from Janis. Lightbearers created their own Shields to try to ward off her blows, but she moved too quickly. Evenir had stopped their volleys suddenly, likely shocked by what they saw. Among that frenzy was a glowing blue burst of Light. That, and the soldiers had started raining down their arrows more heavily from above.

Janis flew through men and women, so quick that Prost couldn't follow her every move. Blasts of blue Light made him squint. Men and women fell as she danced through, steel dagger in her left hand, Light dagger in her right. One Destroyer threw an orb at her and it grazed her arm, cutting a fist-size chunk out of it. She yelled and threw her arm outward, the man glowing blue and flying to smack into the wall of the city. Another Conjurer made to stab her with a sword, but Janis made a Shield and then used it to bash the man in the face. He crumpled to the ground. Janis's arm Fixed itself with a bright flash.

At length, Watchlight realized that she was a force to be reckoned with and many backed away.

All of this death and chaos for a few more Lightbearers, Prost thought, rage filling him again.

Riln didn't care about loss. To be fair, Prost didn't care much about these men and women individually, but this? This was waste. Prost would have done it differently, but Riln wouldn't care.

Prost watched as an arrow pierced Riln through his stomach and he flinched, almost feeling the pain for his leader. Riln bared his teeth, eyes full of something that was not fear, but glee. He raised his hand and summoned another Shield that encompassed the company left around him, the walls forming up and blocking debris again. By now, most of the men and women in the area had run around the corner, retreating out of the way of Janis and Evenir's reach.

Janis stopped, still holding her steel dagger and her Light dagger, points downward. Blood smeared the stones below her and Prost looked to her arm where the piece had been Destroyed. There was no evidence of it ever having been gone.

Fog that Fixing, Prost thought, jealousy pinging in his chest.

"So, you have finally transformed, have you?" Riln said, staring down at her from his horse. "I so hoped that it would take much longer, you do seem so stubborn."

Janis glared at him. "What? Are you jealous that I came to my Prime powers before you did?" Janis said, smirking.

Riln looked at his hand casually. "Oh no, dear, I came to mine much quicker. I believe I only had to wait a week before I gave in to the power itself. By that definition, you were much slower."

As he spoke, Riln yanked the arrow out of his stomach with a slight grunt. Red Light glowed on his stomach and then it was gone, along with the wound as well.

"Clever trick with the Lightbearing orb," Riln remarked, pointing over his shoulder. "Their Shield was only just about to fall."

Janis smiled mischievously. "I have been known to be crafty once in a while."

Riln stared at her, unimpressed.

"Yes, you are in fact still alive. If only you'd died when we first realized you wouldn't hold up your end of the deal with Marric. Say, where is that boy? I do hope you haven't left him alone."

Janis's face flashed something that Prost hadn't ever seen from her in all their engagements: worry.

She cares about the boy—

If he'd known that, he might have used it against her.

Crashing sounds continued on the new Watchlight Shield, now behind Riln as he had turned to speak to Janis. Evenir was trying to breach the

Shield, but since most of their Destroyers were with other groups, they'd had little success.

Janis made a show of looking upward at the sun.

"As much I love this conversation, I believe the awakenings are due any moment now."

With a flash, she dashed at Riln. He nonchalantly threw his hand to the side and Janis glowed with red Light, flying sideways toward the rock wall on the other side of the road. She crashed into the wall with a shout before she was released by his power.

Riln tsked loudly with his tongue. "Far too hasty. Don't you know that I have had ten years to practice with my power? That is something you cannot replicate in a few short minutes of holding your own Prime power."

Riln Conjured a large stone, three times the size of his horse, directly over Janis. She looked upward, eyes widening as the red boulder fell downward, threatening to crush her. Janis summoned an orb of Light and blasted the wall behind her, rock debris and dust flying everywhere. Then the boulder crashed down, shattering a large dent in the cobblestones where it hit.

Riln chuckled with a dark sort of satisfaction, still sitting atop his horse.

"Well, that was short-lived."

Then he raised his hand to the sky. "With her death, Ugglyn, may our power increase!"

Prost looked to the wall where Janis had been crushed, feeling empty. All this time he had fought her, strived to be the one to best her, when in the end she'd injured him with power that he shouldn't be affected by. Now she was dead.

And Ugglyn is coming, he thought.

A chill ran up his spine.

Something caught his eye, however, and he looked up sharply. Riln hadn't dismissed the boulder, probably intending to make sure that Janis was really dead, but around the sides of the solid red Light, blue was glowing. The shining Light around the boulder intensified and the red boulder exploded into pieces. Prost flinched instinctively as red debris made of Light flew outward, but snuffed into nothing before it could hit them.

Behind the rock, a large depression had been blown in the thick city wall. Inside, Janis breathed heavily.

"Handy trick. Too bad I have some tricks of my own," she said loudly to Riln, but her eyes fell onto Prost. Their eyes met across the wide cobbled road. Electricity ran through Prost as he realized she was coming for him.

29

Janis stepped out of the crevice she'd blown into the city wall, grateful that this new power hadn't let her down as it had so many times before. Something inside of her still balked at the strangeness of it all, but it was small compared to how the feeling had ruled her even earlier that day. For years, she had only relied on her survival and assassin skills. Janis knew she couldn't keep on like that; she had to start letting people in.

Her eyes landed on a form huddled in the corner of the entryway to the shop across the street. She immediately recognized the face, but her mind took a moment to comprehend what it saw.

Prost.

The man looked small and broken in the corner, not anything like the person she'd fought more than once since she'd been pulled into all of this. His eyes met hers and there was a hardness in them—a resolve that she could understand from her own years and years of pain, suffering, and sheer willpower pushing through it all. She got the sense that he'd been through a lot over the years.

And yet, Janis didn't care. He had to die. Like the crimson-robed man who sat atop the horse.

Her eyes shifted to Riln, who was seething.

"Well, that was—disappointing. I did hope that you had been killed."

Janis didn't answer, but instead summoned and lobbed a Destroying orb at his head. He raised his hand and a smaller Shield appeared just before him, covering his body. As he did it, the large Shield around them flickered as power was diverted from it to his small one. While it flew, Janis focused on the blue orb and Moved it, pushing it with even more force at him. It struck the smaller Shield in front of Riln and exploded with a loud crack. Though the Shield blocked the blow, the force of the explosion knocked the horse over sideways, the creature screaming in fright. Riln flew from the saddle with a surprised shout and rolled onto the ground.

Then he started laughing, sending chills up Janis's whole body.

This man is far more insane than I could have anticipated, she thought.

"So, you aren't going to make this as easy as I hoped. Well, our time is short, so let us begin, shall we?"

As he said it, Janis looked to her left, realizing that at any moment the girl's and the other seven awakenings would happen. The visions weren't specific enough to really indicate the time of day, but the light from the sun above had finally reached the point where she guessed it would happen.

Let's do this then, Janis thought.

She stood sharply and Conjured her Light blade, matching the size and design of the steel one in her right hand, which she'd pulled from her side harness. Running forward, she focused on the space in front of her and summoned a Shield, a wall just her height and a few handspans wider than her body. Riln threw his hand out, apparently trying to Move her as he'd done before, but Janis remained untouched as the Shield followed her forward. He growled at his failed attempt, and summoned a sword of red Light.

Something buzzed inside of her. When she'd seen Riln the few times before, Janis had assumed that the man was incapable of physical combat, given his sickly appearance.

She bore down on him and dropped her Shield just before she swung her blades in quick succession.

Riln's speed shocked her. He parried both of her blows easily and swung his sword at her abdomen, missing her only by inches as she pulled her stomach backward to dodge. Without hesitation, he flicked his long sword in the air with such speed that Janis had to fall to the ground to avoid having her head cut off.

So fast! How is he moving that sword so quickly?

Just as before, he pulled the sword back and stabbed at her on the ground. She rolled to the side, barely being missed once again by the sharp of his Conjured red sword. Then, out of options, she put her hand out and pushed with her Moving. Riln suddenly glowed blue and was thrown backward, his next blow interrupted by the push. Instead of falling to the ground, he deftly landed on his feet, apparently practiced at being thrown about by Lightbearing.

"For years I've practiced against Lightbearers, though never another Tar'n Yiv'len. I must say, it is nice to have a challenge once again. And, once you die, Ugglyn can be free and join me in my crusade on Lindrad and the rest of the world. The king will fall and I will rule with my fellow Lightbearers."

Janis snorted. "What makes you think that Ugglyn cares even a little bit about you and the other Lightbearers? He seems the kind to use you then kill you in a flash."

Riln's face hardened at her words. "You know *nothing!*"

He then ran directly at her. She saw his arm twitch upward, and before he could throw her back with his Moving, she created the Shield again. His attempt was thwarted and he jumped sideways, his sword flicking at her from afar. As he swung the blade, it extended so far that it cut into her side. Pain shot through her body in shock, warm blood spilling from the gash Riln had made in her flesh.

Fog it, there are too many things I'm trying to concentrate on with all my new power, she thought, her hand moving to her side as she shifted her Shield between the two of them again.

The wound was bad, more than she could fight with, but Janis knew that her Fixing would work. Blue Light pooled under her fingers, glowing intensely as the pain disappeared in her side. As she worked, Riln had tried to position himself around her Shield again, but Janis focused on it quickly and turned the dome into a full globe around her, the wall extending behind her to the ground.

"You can't hide in there forever, little girl. Your death will come sooner or later."

Just then, Riln dismissed his sword and raised his right hand, Conjuring another large boulder over her. He let it fall, while at the same time creating an orb of red in his left hand and lobbing it at her. The hair on her neck tickled as she realized he meant to Destroy her Shield and crush her with the boulder at the same time. Thinking quick, Janis threw her hands outward with a shout. The Shield around her expanded quickly, slamming into the boulder above and the Destroying orb at the same time. The force of the Shield slammed into the orb, exploding outward and directly into Riln. He obviously wasn't expecting this, for he was thrown backward twenty paces, sliding on his back. The Shield disintegrated from his power, but its connection with the boulder above shifted the rock off course and it slammed heavily into the ground behind Janis.

Janis knew that she had to think differently. Lightbearers normally only used one power at a time, maybe two, but Riln was practiced at using more than one at a time. So many combinations could be used for different tactics. Despite her mind spinning through the possibilities, she couldn't think through how to combine her powers quickly enough. Riln got to his feet, stumbling just slightly before creating two identical orbs of red Light. He threw one at her and she dodged, the orb exploding on the ground, the road breaking into pieces. Riln continued to create and throw orbs, one after the other.

Though she couldn't see it, they must have been enhanced by his Moving, for his accuracy was far too on point. He barely moved his arms, yet each one flew at her with precision. Her heart thumped loudly in her chest, breath sucking in and out sharply as she jumped and weaved through the orbs. Explosions rocked around her, knocking her momentum off point each time one landed just a bit too close. Riln grinned at her evilly, apparently unfazed by the feat he was accomplishing now.

Janis knew she couldn't keep dodging; her energy would be spent too quickly. So, she threw her dagger right at his face. Riln easily Moved the dagger to the side, the steel blade clattering loudly on what remained of the cobblestones. Though he hadn't been hit, the interruption had caused a pause in his Destroying orb volleys, and Janis threw an orb of her own, the blue Light contrasting that of his red. Her orb connected with the last one he'd thrown, and the explosion flung them both backwards. Riln landed on his back, but Janis had anticipated the blow and quickly rolled to her feet.

While he was down, Janis tried to Conjure something to drop on Riln. She focused on the space above him and thought of the first thing she could think of that was heavy. A house flashed out of the air, two stories tall and looking oddly familiar to her. It hovered briefly over Riln before she let it fall. The man saw the building, and rolled quickly to his right toward the Shield that still blocked Evenir's fire. Even before he was clear of the falling Conjure, Janis felt a force tug forward heavily at her feet, and they were pulled out from under her. She fell hard on her back, cursing.

Fog it, how does he use his powers even amid a direct attack?

Janis was sure she couldn't roll while Moving something that far away. She rolled to her stomach to get up from the fall, just in time to hear the Conjured house crash to the ground with the sound of splintering and breaking wood. Riln had made it just outside of the house's reach. The Conjure disappeared to nothing.

With a slight start, Janis realized she recognized the house she'd just Conjured. It looked exactly like Marric's in Wurren.

Marric.

For a brief moment, Janis wondered what was happening with the boy, Shrell, and the others who'd been sent to Wurren. If Watchlight hadn't sent a band of their soldiers down to Wurren, she would be shocked. Riln seemed desperate to get all possible Lightbearers. Janis's side suddenly burned and she sucked in air sharply. Looking down, she saw the book she'd taken from Macks. It was vibrating. Then it stopped as soon as it had begun.

What the fog is this thing? Janis thought as her attention snapped back up to Riln.

The two stood for a moment, staring at each other, each breathing hard.

"Yes," Riln said finally, breathing as hard as Janis was, "this is proving more interesting than I thought. But in the end, you will die."

Janis smirked at him. "I'll trust my luck," was all that she said.

Movement in her peripheral vision caused her to look past the red of the Shield. Though the images were obscured, she saw a few Evenir people running toward them on the other side.

What are they doing? she thought, *Riln will just—*

Validating her thoughts instantly, Riln let one of the swords drop to the ground and threw an orb of Light through the wall, directly at the running people. Janis shouted a warning, but it was too late. The orb connected with the chest of one of the men, and then he was pieces. Janis's stomach twisted at the sight and she looked away. With a flash, Riln tossed a few other orbs and she heard explosions, glad she had stopped watching. Through the sound, she heard something—it sounded like someone was shouting her name. Her eyes flashed to Prost, who was now trying to stand. His movements were labored, but he appeared to be getting some strength. He glared at her, so much hate in his eyes.

Janis heard the shout again, though now that the explosions had faded, she knew it was from her left, through the Shields. She turned and saw Magness waving her hands at her. The image was still obscured by the Shield, but she could see that the older woman had a young girl in her arms who was curled up and crying.

They have the girl.

Janis had almost forgotten that the time was near. A little relief sprung in her chest as she realized that in her vision, the girl had come from the side Evenir was on, so she must have accidentally run into the group. That, or been found by one of the other Seers in their company.

Her relief soon vanished as a whisking sound in the air announced blades flying toward her. She spun and dodged one, though just barely, and felt her shoulder blaze from a slice as another grazed the skin there.

She turned to see Riln throwing another few Conjured daggers at her.

Janis spun and weaved through them, like with the Destroying, but this time she could feel herself slowing. This fight had been too intense and too long. Something inside her was weakening alarmingly fast. Because of this fatigue, she took a dagger in her left bicep, pain lancing in her arm.

I need to get out of here. I can't win, not today, she thought.

The idea of running frustrated her. Prost could die, right here, right now, if she could just make it to him, but he was behind Riln. Janis looked to Riln, who'd paused for a moment to observe her with an evil grin. All this fighting and she'd only managed to hurt him briefly. Janis pulled the Light dagger out of her arm and used her Fixing. As she did, more energy seeped out of her body. The Lightbearing was draining her, much faster than a normal fight would have without the powers. She looked up at Riln, who somehow looked more pale than usual.

He's drained too, I can see it in his eyes.

The look, plus the fact that he'd paused his barrage of weapons meant he was likely losing energy as well.

Janis knew that she needed to surprise him, to catch him off guard as he had done to her multiple times during the fight. Then her eyes fell on the steel dagger behind Riln and to his left. It was between him and Prost, who now stood glaring at her.

"It seems we're both running out, aren't we?" Janis said, her voice proving her point as she gasped for air.

"Perhaps you are, but I could go for hours," Riln replied, spitting on the ground.

Liar, she thought.

He was definitely intimidating, Janis had to give him that. "I think you and I both know that it isn't true. You can't keep lying to yourself."

Riln bared his teeth, fury in his eyes. He knew she saw through his words. Janis slowly moved to her left, toward his Shield. She didn't know if she could truly walk through it from this side or not, but she had to try. As she'd hoped, Riln matched her movements, walking slowly, or rather, stumbling slowly to his left, just in front of her steel dagger.

Here goes nothing.

She focused on the dagger behind him, grabbing hold of it with her Moving. Before she could pull it quickly toward her, she saw a flash of red Conjured swords in Riln's hands. He spun with a shout and threw them at her. Oddly, only one of them came directly at her, the other one angled at her feet. Then she pulled hard on the dagger. Everything slowed down momentarily as she heard Prost shout a warning to Riln, but the pale man was too focused on Moving his Conjured swords toward her. The steel dagger slammed heavily into Riln's back, sticking through him, the point of the dagger protruding from his chest. His face twisted in shock and pain.

Because she'd focused on Moving the dagger into his back, she didn't have time to turn and run at the Shield. Still, the dagger in his back had distracted him enough that the red Shield around them flashed away, the air cooling down as the fresh air of the coming night flowed in toward them.

Janis felt a bit of satisfaction as she shifted sideways, the first sword flying past her just barely. The other landed just short of her position, exploding loudly.

Shock and fear flooded her insides as she was thrown backward over the space where the Shield had only just disappeared. Her body felt light, even weightless as she flew thirty paces, rock debris stinging her arms and face where the ground had exploded. Then she fell hard on a new patch of road, the air being knocked out of her lungs. Janis felt her body panic without the air, and she fought to hold her consciousness.

Her brain fogged, but she still managed to think briefly about what had happened.

He disguised his Destroying as a sword, like a Conjure.

Riln had surprised her. If his Shield hadn't been dropped, she was sure she'd be dead, crushed between the explosion and the wall of his Shield.

Her vision spun still and she could feel her body moving backward, blue Light of the Evenir Shield passing over her until she was on the other side. Then warmth spread in her limbs and clarity filled her head. She shook the pain away, then noticed a man Fixing her body, the pulsing Light of his hands moving from one limb to another.

"Yeh righ' broke every bit of yer body, din' yeh?" he said.

She didn't recognize him, but then again she had only met a few of Evenir's Lightbearers.

Suddenly, Magness was there.

"Impressive show of power, there," the woman said, approval in her words, but apprehension in her voice.

Janis could tell the meaning behind the statement.

If you were to switch sides, we'd be in deep trouble.

Shaking her head, she stood, the pain mostly gone.

"'Ey, I'm not done wif yeh yet," the man grumbled, following her movements with his hands.

He was right; her legs, likely broken, still ached with pain in a couple places. Still, she stood and faced Riln, who was struggling to get the blade pulled from his back. Why he didn't just Move it out of his body, Janis didn't know. Perhaps he was more tired than she expected.

Satisfaction filled her as she grinned.

30

Prost stared in disbelief at the dagger poking out of Riln's stomach. It was a rare occasion where he'd seen Riln fight with full force like this, but not once had he been even close to being bested. Janis hadn't killed him, and Prost suspected that Riln would survive through this as well, but it was the gravest injury he'd ever seen his master receive.

The roadway around them was broken in so many places that carts wouldn't be able to traverse this part of the city anymore. A giant depression still showed in the wall where Janis had blasted it to pieces to dodge the falling boulder. Red blood was splattered here and there, some from Janis, some from Riln. Even now, deep red liquid was pooling at the feet of his master.

"Prost! Come here now!"

As he stepped from the entryway of the storefront, he flinched at the bright blue Light of Evenir's Shield. A red Shield suddenly materialized out of nowhere, adding a red hue to the bright Lights around them. The sun was low enough now to make the brightness of the Lightbearing even more stark in the city street.

Prost moved as quickly as he could, his walk becoming more of a shuffle due to his injuries. His own blood was still dripping from the arrow wound in his shoulder, but the bleeding had slowed just a bit. It wouldn't close anytime soon, but at least he wouldn't die from it.

Internally he laughed at the irony that the only person who could probably heal him was on the other side of the war. It also happened to be the only person who could hurt him with Lightbearing.

"Would you hurry? My Shield will fade soon if we can't get this out of me."

Prost somewhat numbly moved to Riln's side and gripped the hilt of the dagger firmly in one hand. With a swift tug, he pulled the dagger out of Riln's back with some effort. The squelching sound it made was enough to nauseate Prost. Normally such things wouldn't have affected him, but he wasn't feeling himself after falling off of a three-story building.

He watched as the hole in Riln's back started to glow red and close very quickly, the blood stopping almost instantly. Sighing, Riln tilted his head back and closed his eyes. The Shield next to them flickered as he used his powers to Fix himself, but it was soon restored to its original brightness. The glowing at Riln's stomach remained for longer than Fixing normally took, making Prost think that either the wound was much worse than expected, or his leader was growing weaker.

"There, at least the dud is good for something other than a punching bag."

He said it so lightly, so nonchalantly while he relaxed through his healing.

Something snapped within Prost.

Without thinking, he gripped the handle of Janis's steel dagger, rage consuming him. Prost's ears roared, heat collecting there, his jaw so tight he thought his teeth might break. Then he jammed the blade right through the back of Riln's neck.

Riln's eyes shot open with shock, a burst of red Light shooting from his eyes in a vision. Prost's rage shifted suddenly to a cold lack of feeling. Blood poured over his hands, dripping down his arm and onto the ground. His eyes turned and met Janis's through only one Shield now, for the red one had fallen promptly after he stabbed Riln in the neck. Her eyes filled with shock, brief apprehension, and then resolution.

Gasping and gurgling, Riln's eyes still had red beams of Light in them.

He grasped at the blade now through his neck, small bursts of red Light trying to heal the wound. For a moment, the skin started to gather, healing around the blade, but Prost held it firm until the red Light faded from Riln's eyes. He let the pale man fall to the ground, lifeless.

Prost stared at his hands, the numbness of what had just happened slowly lifting.

What did I just do? he thought.

Then the street around him started to darken, far faster than the normal waning of the sunlight. Prost looked up, the sun still visible over the wall, but only slightly. Yet silvery black smoke was coalescing around him, forming spontaneously like the fog during Isllan.

Fear struck him once again.

Janis stared across the way at the black smoke that was appearing from nowhere. Her skin chilled at the familiarity of it. Flashes of meeting Ugglyn and his unearthly creatures flew into her mind before Magness was shaking her. The shock was obvious on her face, but she didn't care. Prost had just stabbed Riln, a blow that he would not be able to heal from. Somehow, she knew that. The black-clad monster of a man she'd fought more than once had just slain the leader of Watchlight, though for what reason, she didn't know.

"Janis, we have her—we must go," Magness said.

The assassin spun on the young girl, who was breathing shallowly from shock of what was happening around her. Gila patted the girl on the back, trying to console her, though Janis couldn't quite hear what she was saying.

"Did she awaken, then? When did it happen? I thought that it was about—"

The girl doubled over suddenly, gasping for air. She threw her arms around her slight figure and held tight. Urgency flashed through every muscle in Janis's body and she shot to her feet.

"Gila! Shield us all now!"

Gila looked up, confused as the girl crumpled to the ground. She looked left and right, searching for the threat before her eyes started to widen in shock. The blue Shield disappeared around them but it was too late. The girl started to glow with blue Light and Janis shot her hands outward, forming a small Shield *around* the young girl. The blue Shield hugged tightly around her in a perfect circle just before the burst. Destroying power exploded from the girl in all directions, the walls of the Shield holding the blast, but only briefly before the Shield fell and the remaining blast threw Evenir in all directions.

Once again, Janis was flying through the air, though this time it was *toward* Prost and Riln's inevitably dead body.

She spun in the air, trying to angle herself to not land so hard on her back. The skin on her hands and parts of her face was burned. She suspected that had she not put up her Shield, she'd have been shredded to pieces like the man and woman in her vision.

And all the other Seers' visions.

The cobbled road came up at her, but she put her shoulder down, using it instead to block her fall and roll up to her feet. It wasn't a perfect maneuver, but she'd saved more bones from breaking and traded it for an inevitably large bruise on her shoulder. Taking stock of her injuries, she noted that none would be fatal, though all were as painful as serious burns. She then glanced backward, seeing that she was just outside the black smoke swirling around Prost and Riln. It was so dark that she couldn't see either of them.

Assuming Prost was busy with whatever the fog was happening near him and Riln, she looked back to the girl who'd just awakened. Rather than the lively looking young woman, she saw a burned mass of flesh. She looked away, her stomach heaving.

I contained the Destroying, but in the process—

The girl's death was Janis's fault, but at the same time, the fact that Evenir men and women had survived was her fault too. She'd saved them, but at the loss of the new Lightbearer. Never in her life had she felt guilty for a death, excepting the Fixer boy who'd died last week. Control had been her everything, her training mandated it as an assassin. One who had lack of control physically, mentally, emotionally, even situationally—often died. Lightbearing had made her lose complete control. Her newfound power had been traded for weeks of uncertainty and now an immensely strong power, but Janis still couldn't completely control it all. Not like Riln had.

Riln!

She spun on the black smoke and Conjured a dagger, an exact replica of her own. She cursed slightly as she realized her steel dagger was inside the smoke swirling in front of her.

After all this and I regret losing my dagger, Janis thought incredulously.

As much as she wanted to stay and watch what happened, she had the distinct feeling to flee. So she did, shouting to Evenir to stand and retreat to the walls and the entrance where they'd planned to rendezvous after retrieving the new Lightbearers.

Terror surged in Prost, frustrating him to no end. The number of times such fear had grabbed him and almost consumed him in the past weeks was debilitating. Scentless smoke continued to swirl around him, not like that from a fire. Its very texture and look was like the fog during Isllan, yet silvery black.

Laughter erupted in the smoke until a bit of it started shaping into a body in front of him. A man, relatively handsome with a close-cut gray beard and perfectly shaped gray hair appeared in front of him. He looked young, save for his gray hair. His eyes were dark, almost black, making them look like eyes with no iris, but instead a large black pupil.

"In the end, you couldn't take it, could you?" Ugglyn whispered to him, a wicked smile on his face.

Prost stared at him. It had been so long since they'd had an encounter from the anti-god that he'd forgotten how terrible it felt. The terror still held him, keeping him from running. That, and Prost didn't know what effect the swirling smoke might have on him if he touched it. He had almost forgotten the pain from his myriad injuries, but it came back as he stumbled away from the anti-god.

"Ah, my blessing indeed did protect you from the poison I gave that annoying little Seer. Like Lightbearing, you are immune to the Void, given that it courses through your veins."

Prost glared at him, quick to rebut, "I didn't kill Riln to release you. The Seal still holds—"

He paused, staring Ugglyn in the face, then gesturing with his head, "*Theirs* is intact."

Ugglyn smiled at him again. "Indeed their Seal holds true, holding back my true form and power, but I need only a vessel in this physical realm. I've just enough freedom for that."

The implications of the words sent lightning through his limbs and into his head. Prost's breathing increased as he stepped backward, then turned, clenching his jaw through the pain, trying to get away.

Then a force slammed into his back. Sharp pain lanced up his spine and into his head, radiating through his temples and his eyes. He screamed, the pain consuming every bit of him. Then he blacked out.

Janis ran alongside Gila, who was crying. Though most of Evenir had handled the blow from the awakening, Magness hadn't been so lucky. Not everyone knew how to break their fall like Janis, and Magness had struck the city wall just so. No Fixer could save someone who was already dead.

Janis looked away, a sadness threatening to creep into her. She wasn't glad to lose the former Evenir leader, but she also didn't have much attachment to her and didn't see a point in mourning what had already passed.

A pang of worry rocked inside her as thoughts of Marric came and went. She wasn't sure if she knew what love felt like, but she definitely felt bonded to him in a way she'd never allowed herself to feel before. At least, not since the death of her family all those years ago. Her mind flashed to Harmel and Avryn and she scanned the street ahead of them, looking for their group.

She cursed as she remembered Macks, unconscious and bleeding inside the roof of the pub back where they'd fought. Janis thought to turn back and track him down, but she decided she ought to first meet with Avryn and the other company who'd gone to get the other Lightbearers.

"You must keep up, we need to get out of here," Gila said, tugging on the hand of the woman trailing behind her. Janis looked back at Livella who was paler than she'd ever seen her before now. Apparently, they'd shoved her into the closest shop and told her to find cover. Despite that, she'd witnessed the entire fight and was in shock as a result.

Gila shot Janis a pointed look as if this was her fault.

In part it was; Livella had only been allowed to come because of her connection to Janis. Overall, she'd been quite a low-maintenance companion, but now she was catatonic, even more so than she'd been in the past.

"That smoke—it's him—" she kept saying, over and over.

When Gila had asked what the words meant, Janis just shook her head to indicate that it wasn't the time to discuss it. She'd stopped asking soon after, despite her annoyance with Livella's muttering.

At length, they rounded the last corner leading to the gates. Avryn, Turrin, Harmel, and apparently the other company were already there. Their awakenings must have been closer to the gate than Janis's own.

Avryn greeted them grimly when they arrived. "Had a run-in with more of Luden's men. They'd been equipped with the same poison that had almost killed Turrin."

He looked worse for wear, his clothes ripped and stained with blood.

Curiously, a bandage was wrapped around his left forearm. Harmel looked mostly unscathed, though his shirt was singed in a few places.

Avryn glanced down at his arm. "I Fixed the poison, but couldn't muster the strength to Fix the rest. Still, we got the boys."

"Looks like yeh've been roit through a mess yerself, no?" Harmel said, looking amused. As he said it, he reached over and grabbed her hand, squeezing it tightly. He looked relieved, as if he'd been worried about her.

She stiffened at his sudden contact, an unexpected flurry of something stirring inside her chest. Resisting the urge to lash out at the man, Janis rolled her eyes. "Says the man who looks to have gotten too close to some Destroyers."

Harmel chuckled.

Janis pulled her hand away, the feeling of Harmel's touch lingering there.

Fog it, I'm getting too fond of him.

Avryn turned and nodded to two unconscious figures, one over Turrin's shoulder, another held by two other Evenir soldiers.

"The other company lost their Lightbearer and a few of their numbers. Delegates from Watchlight and Luden's men were at both of the awakenings. Rotten luck, that's for sure."

Janis met his eyes and smiled grimly before explaining, "Luden had a Seer, that's how they knew."

Avryn pressed his lips thin and nodded with newfound understanding.

"Where is Varith?"

The long-haired man gestured back to where Varith was fussing over a bandage on someone.

"Varith is fine, just working full-time with his Fixing. Many were injured, some lost to the poison or to Watchlight," Avryn said grimly, then his eyebrows shot up. "Where is Magness?"

Janis shook her head soberly.

Sadness flashed in his eyes but he didn't say anything, tears welling up before he cleared his throat and shook his head.

"We have to leave—get as far from here as possible. Something is happening that I can't describe. We have to get far, far away, back to Terris Green," Janis said resolutely before turning back the way they'd come.

Avryn grabbed her arm. "Where in Lanser's name are you going?" he asked.

"I have to get someone. I'll catch up."

His grip on her arm tightened and he wouldn't let her go.

She glared at him, then grabbed his hand with her Moving and pushed it away. He gasped and looked up at her.

"Yes, I've got it down now."

His anger was replaced by awe, but he still spoke curtly. "Go, but get back to us as fast as you can. I feel something off about this place—"

As he said the words, a column of swirling black smoke shot toward the sky back where they'd just come from.

"What in the blazes is that—?" Avryn faltered.

"GO! Get out of here, *now!*" Janis shouted.

Evenir men and women started scrambling out of the gates, which were oddly emptied of guards. Janis was grateful for the lack of resistance as she watched her people start to leave. She turned and dashed back toward the column of silvery black smoke. She knew it was a risk, and she couldn't tell how much of her reasons for taking it were due to her love or hatred of him. Out of the heat of battle, she could feel a concern for him pushing her forward. By the time she arrived, she was huffing, her energy fading from the extended battle and her rapid run. Rounding the corner, she stopped in her tracks. The space below the column of smoke was mostly cleared, and she saw Riln's corpse on the ground, Prost standing above him.

His eyes were silvery black, a slight glow shining through the darkness of the approaching night.

The moment she saw this, she looked up to where Macks was likely still unconscious, then decided it wasn't worth it. She put her hand to her belt, where the small book was surprisingly still tightly wedged. She then pressed her lips into a thin line, worry for Macks now plaguing her mind. Her eyes met the pure black ones of Prost, and he smiled at her. A chill ran up her spine as she saw a smile that was not his own.

Janis ran, knowing escape was the only priority now. Though she knew the hope was in vain, she prayed that Marric and Shrell wouldn't meet as much resistance in Wurren.

EPILOGUE

Prost's body surged with an unfamiliar energy and a power that he had never known before in his life. The pain in his shoulder was quickly fading and he turned to see black smoke wriggling in and out of the wound as if sewing it shut. At length, the wound was closed and the pain abated. Aches and broken bones also healed.

Is this what Fixing feels like? Prost wondered.

No, this is what my *power feels like,* a voice answered in his head.

Prost went cold. The voices in his head were back. Now that he'd killed Riln, they would haunt him forever—maybe even ruin his life, just as they had all those years ago when he'd had to leave the army. He glanced up to see Janis standing at the corner of the street. Her eyes widened and then he smiled. Yet, Prost hadn't intended to smile. Anxiety still gripped him to the point that he wouldn't have smiled—possibly couldn't have even in this moment. Yet his mouth moved, involuntarily, as if someone was Moving his mouth for him. His brain was very clear and sharp, but he realized with shock that he couldn't move any of his limbs—something was stopping him.

"Yes," Prost said, though not of his own accord, "your connection with the Void has allowed us to bond. I am reborn in part into the world again."

The implication of the words was lost on Prost for a moment, until he remembered that only moments before, Ugglyn had appeared. Prost had tried to flee from the smiling anti-god, just before being slammed into by a great force, a stinging coolness spreading throughout his insides.

No, no, this can't be, Prost thought frantically. His body no longer ached, every part of him healed from some strange power or force he felt from within. He resolved to push back against the power that held him, and he met resistance. Pain lanced in his head and his body growled, his ears hearing the strain that he felt as he pushed against the power.

"No! Don't fight it, you—urgh!" Prost heard himself say.

Then the voice was back in his head. *If you resist me, then we could both die. Let me in. Let me take control!*

Fog you, Ugglyn, I don't let anyone control me, Prost thought back.

He reached to move his hand and felt a tingle as he did, the feeling returning there. Prost pushed back against the force inside, his body coming back to him.

Then the force stopped pushing.

Coexistence is all that I can afford at this time. It appears it's all you can afford as well.

Even as the words were said, he knew it was true. Though the strange black smoke had healed his body, he felt mentally tired, taxed to a degree never before reached.

There is so much we can do together, my little Voidbearer. Rest, then we can begin.

Suddenly, Prost lost complete control of his body. Panic surged in his chest as his body moved without his volition. He eventually turned and was moving down the street where Watchlight had taken cover. Many lay dead from the battle and Janis's wild attack.

We'll kill her, don't you worry. Then I'll be free from these chains completely.

Get out of me, now! Prost yelled internally.

Ugglyn just laughed inside.

Suddenly, Vint was there.

"Where is Riln? What happened with that crazy Lightbearer woman?"

Prost pushed against the force again, gaining enough control to turn his head to glare at Vint.

"Riln is dead, and I have taken his place as leader."

Vint rolled his eyes in mocking disbelief, then started to turn back down the road toward the group.

Prost moved his right hand, which he still controlled, grabbing Vint on the shoulder.

"The assassin overpowered him. Riln put me in charge."

Ooh, nice lie, best conceal the truth just to be safe.

Prost tried not to flinch at Ugglyn's voice in his head as he stared at Vint.

"How am I supposed to believe that? Riln can't be dead."

Prost's jaw hardened and he pulled Vint back, the force stronger than he expected. Vint stumbled back and pulled his sword out, a few other Lightbearers around them arming themselves with weapons.

Prost felt his left hand raise, once again the oddity of not being able to control it not lost on him. Then a sword appeared, not made from Light, but instead darkness, from the same silver-black of the smoke that had formed around him.

A stab of fear rocked his chest at the sight of the strange weapon, and the members of Watchlight gasped around him.

Tell them you've finally accepted Ugglyn's blessing and that any who defy you will die.

Prost paused, not wanting to concede. The stares eventually got to him. Out of sheer stubbornness, he didn't say exactly what Ugglyn commanded, instead choosing his own words.

"Riln trusted me to make me his second. Ugglyn has granted me the power to lead Watchlight to victory. Any who don't accept my leadership will be terminated."

To prove his point, Prost felt a surge of power in his right hand and as he lifted it, an orb of deep black smoke appeared there. He looked at it, fear and wonder coursing through him. Then he threw it at a trader's cart sitting there. It exploded, wood splintering everywhere.

Vint stepped back, shock on his face. Then he turned and bowed submissively.

"What should we do then, Master?"

Prost's dread still buzzed inside, but a thrill grew there at the sight of Vint's reaction.

"Rest, then we take down Evenir."

Then I can finally kill Janis—and be free.

Prost grinned then, realizing they could both get what they wanted.

LIKED IT? Hated it? Leave a review!

ASCENDED: THE LIGHTBEARER CHRONICLES BOOK 3: PROLOGUE AND CHAPTER 1

Read the final book in The Lightbearer Chronicles!

Order NOW!!
https://dankenner.com/ascended

PROLOGUE

Dust continued to settle from the shattered ceiling above him. He tried to focus on what had just happened. Yet his mind still couldn't grasp anything besides the pain he felt throughout his entire body. As he tried to sit up, his chest throbbed and he couldn't breathe.

Fog it, how did she of all people become a Lightbearer? he thought.

Until now, Macks hadn't considered where his previous ward had gone. He'd heard rumblings of an assassin woman who caused trouble for some of their allies, but Luden hadn't ever mentioned who it was.

In truth, he hadn't cared.

Sure, he'd suspected it was Janis they spoke of, but he never expected to cross paths with her again. In fact, his Seeing had been handy in keeping it that way. Now, not only did she know he worked for Luden but she'd aligned herself with one of the groups in this ridiculous power war between Watchlight and Evenir.

Macks closed his eyes, trying once again to breathe deeply. This time, his lungs complied, though the thick dust in the air made him choke. He coughed, his throat rejecting the debris it brought in. Everything hurt, so he couldn't pinpoint exactly what was wrong with his body.

Opening his eyes once more, he looked up through the massive hole in the roof. He didn't know how long he'd been unconscious. An explosion sounded from somewhere outside, causing his body to tense. There were other sounds, men shouting, bowstrings swishing, and other signs of a fight. He also noticed how the sun still hadn't set. Macks knew then that he must have only been unconscious for a short time.

He clenched his teeth and focused on rising. Given that he'd already been able to roll over, albeit slowly, he hoped that he'd have enough in him to at least sit up.

He was disappointed in that assumption. His body didn't respond favorably.

I have to try something. Janis probably knows that I'm not dead. She'll be back for me, he thought, frustrated.

This made everything become more urgent. Instead of focusing on moving his whole body, he moved his right arm over himself, pleased that it didn't ache too badly. Whether it was because the heavy pain in the rest of him drowned out this pain or because his arm was unhurt, he didn't know. Still, he positioned the hand over his chest, trying to breathe gently. To his relief, he felt his chest, which was likely broken in a few places, suck in air.

His lungs filled with air and he couldn't help but sigh in relief, despite the pain. Macks still knew little of Lightbearing, but based on what he'd been able to learn, every Lightbearer had the potential to develop a second power. He'd been a Seer for years with only the minor appearance of other powers but recently learned that he now had the ability to Shield. His skills still hadn't advanced much, but they'd been enough to hide him from other Seers.

Flexing his abdominal muscles, he pulled himself upward, surprised that he could do so. His body still hurt in most places, but he was able to move with quick and painful jolts.

Another explosion cracked through the hole in the roof and Macks tensed, his eyes shifting up. He expected to see Janis there, or another Lightbearer, but the space was empty. His employer, Luden, had dragged him into this mess. If it weren't for the fool's blind rage, Macks would have been paid and far away from the whole conflict. That was how he worked, after all. Now he was beaten in the middle of Stilten, a place he'd avoided for so many years.

As the sounds of fighting continued, Macks worked on inspecting his other injuries. Though there were many, he didn't feel that any were fatal. He knew he'd have to be careful with that. Sometimes the most serious injuries were those hidden from plain sight. Once he had the major breaks and cuts accounted for, Macks stopped. His breathing still labored, he felt that he could drift off to sleep. Instead, he let the pain in the various parts of his body keep his mind aware.

Just as he got to his feet, a loud crack rang through the air. Macks jumped to the side of the room he'd been lying in, causing his injuries to twinge in pain. He sucked in a breath but didn't have time to recover before shouting from the road put him on alert once more.

I need to get out of here, he thought.

Peering upward, he noted that he couldn't make the leap back up to the roof. Not without his full strength. Instead, he searched the dim room. The only light filtering in came from the setting sun through the broken ceiling. Macks opted to use one of the other abilities he still knew little about. Holding out his hand, he summoned a small ball of red. Though minuscule, it pierced the darkness of the room with ease.

He'd fallen into a bedroom of sorts, though it was bare save for a bed and a set of drawers. He remembered Luden had strong-armed the owner of the bar below to let them enter. It wasn't uncommon for bars to have a set of rooms for guests to quarter. Macks was glad his fall hadn't been farther. Noticing a door for the first time, he angled toward it and slowly cracked it open. Just beyond, a short hallway ended at a set of stairs. He moved toward it, keeping his Light illuminated.

Inspecting the stairs, Macks paused. It appeared as if something heavy had dropped from above, shattering the steps in a direct line to the bottom of the spirals. Adrenaline coursed through his body and he shifted his eyes around, expecting to see an enemy somewhere.

For a moment, Macks thought to go back to the room to think, but the shouting outside intensified, and he feared what would happen if one of the groups decided to enter the building. They might not be searching for him, but if they found him, he didn't expect it would be good.

The moment I get somewhere quiet, I'll need to summon—him, Macks thought. For the past year, the anti-god had visited Macks. He shuddered, trying not to think or say his name out loud. It never felt right, but Macks didn't regret what he'd learned. Reaching down to his belt, he tried to grab the small book he used to say the right words.

He froze. Empty.

Resisting the urge to erupt in loud cursing, Macks shuffled back to the room, holding the Light aloft to search for the small book. The simple room bore no true hiding places where the small text could have fallen. His chest filled with dread. If it wasn't here, then it meant something worse.

Janis, he thought.

Part of him felt that her taking it from him was deserved, so to speak, for his betrayal. Did he deserve this though? That book had become his everything. It was how he could manipulate Luden; it was how he could tempt the anti-god into helping him. Ugglyn had mentioned that his limited power was waning, but Macks guessed it was just a lie. He believed he could get more from the being.

Macks shook his head and moved as quickly as he could back to the stairs. He gripped the wood railing and deliberately made his way down the spirals. Meanwhile, he noticed the sounds outside had become quieter. Where there were explosions and shouting before, now there was only distant yelling and clashing metal.

But something wasn't right.

Trying to move more quickly, he breathed through the pain and made it to the ground level. There he cautiously moved into the main bar. It was empty. Before, the bartender had been hiding with his crossbow. Macks was relieved that this obstacle wasn't a problem. He moved to the door, exiting onto the street, but froze.

A column of swirling clouds spun upward into the darkening sky. His eyes widened as he followed the trail with his gaze. It extended far enough that he couldn't see the end. Something ran through the air, an energy that made his hairs stand. He recognized the feeling. It was the same he would get every time he summoned Ugglyn. His body started quivering in fright and he felt locked in position.

No, no, it can't be. He was supposed to be sealed by Yrillnan. He can't be free, Macks thought.

Until a year ago, Macks had no idea that his Awakening as a Lightbearer was part of something larger. The anti-god had explained it all to him. The being told him that Macks was the way out. It was then that he noticed his Light turning red. That part hadn't been explained to him, but Macks guessed it had something to do with Ugglyn's influence.

Macks knew something was wrong. He tried to step backward, to retreat somewhere until this passed, but part of him knew he couldn't get away. If Ugglyn was free, he would find him.

Cursing, Macks instinctively reached to where the book should be. He suspected the anti-god would be very displeased with his loss of the book. If Ugglyn knew Janis had taken it, Macks assumed the anger would be far more severe.

After a few moments, the smoke cleared, two forms appearing within the torrent.

Prost, the very man Macks had seen before Janis blasted him through the roof, stood rigidly in the road, a look of shock on his face. A pale corpse lay on the road before him. Macks realized it was the one who headed up the red-Light crew. Riln. Blood pooled outward from the body. It was obvious he was dead. Macks knew their names only from Luden's insistence that he learned of Watchlight and their leaders.

One thing he'd learned: these two men were the Yrillnan. At least, before his former ward had become involved. Macks stood there, unsure of what to do. Prost turned his direction, his eyes filled with silvery smoke.

Macks fell backward, hiding himself behind the wall beneath the window. Panting, he counted to twenty before peeking back over the sill. The larger man was gone, likely run away from the corpse of his master. A glint of something caught Macks's attention near the ground, and he squinted to see a dark pommel protruding from the man's neck. Even from here, the weapon was unmistakable.

Janis's favorite dagger. Though his gut wrenched at the thought of rushing into the open, commotion on the city wall suggested the retreating Lightbearers were distracting the city guard. Gritting his teeth, he slipped along the wall to the doorway, readying himself there. With a determined breath, Macks burst through the door, dashing across the now empty street to stand over the body. Grimacing at the mess there, he reached down and grabbed the handle, yanking it free. He winced at the sound it made as it was withdrawn.

"Hey! You there! Stop!" a voice rang out from the wall above.

Cursing, Macks dashed back to the entrance to the bar, pushing through the doors and diving behind the sill. He could hear other guards shouting about what they'd seen. Some had been ordered to come fetch him.

Muttering various curses, he crawled away from the window to the rear of the bar. He'd been to bars like this before, and if he was right, then there should be a way out the back.

There.

Macks saw through the portal to the stairs that another door led somewhere else. Based on what he'd remembered, that should lead to a stable. That meant horses he could take. Wiping Janis's weapon on the leg of his pants, he slipped the dagger into his belt to keep it out of the way.

When he reached a safe distance from the window, he got up and shuffled quickly to the door. He breathed out a sigh of relief when he saw three horses tied there. The animals were agitated, so he moved slowly toward the beasts. Knowing his time was short, he sized up the horses and selected the mid-sized one. He may have gone for the larger, expecting it to run faster, but there was a nervous energy from the creature. Macks guessed he'd have a rough time taming the beast.

Despite the lack of saddle, Macks hefted himself onto the animal and used its mane to direct it toward the stall door.

With a kick to the side, he urged the horse out into the back alley.

Macks didn't know where he was supposed to go or what he should do. He'd never received his last payment from Luden. A loss for sure, but he'd just seen his former employer skewered on a sword. His only choice was to collect what he could and get as far from Stilten as possible.

Part of him knew he needed to get away. If Ugglyn truly was free, Macks needed to leave. He hadn't ventured out of Lindrad yet, but now was looking like a good time to try.

Then again, if Ugglyn was free, he doubted he could escape, and without the book—Macks knew his death was imminent.

CHAPTER 1

Stepping into Wurren was nothing like Marric would have expected. When he'd last been here, three men had been searching for him. He remembered how terrified he'd been, waiting for the men to find out who he was and do something terrible. All because Jord had been kidnapped years before, never to be seen again.

Except he had seen him, standing with Watchlight, his hands bearing the destructive red Light that could deteriorate anything, living or not.

Marric's mind spiraled through all the things that had happened since he'd last left his little town. He might have expected the memories to flow in some semblance of order, but they came in waves with no organization at all.

He recalled seeing himself kneel on the ground next to Arrant Falls, pain exploding from inside as he awakened into a Lightbearer. Then he was in his home in Wurren, watching as Janis's dagger slammed into Tins's gut. He recalled the blood on the floor making him ill.

Seeing blood didn't affect him anymore.

A flashback brought him to Terris Green, where Janis blew up her quarters, demolishing a stone wall and almost killing herself.

I wonder how they are doing with their journey, Marric thought.

"'Ey, Mar, ya all right there? Ye've been Seeing a bunch fer the last bit," Shrell said next to him.

Marric jumped at the voice and let himself fall back into reality. They'd only spotted the distant borders of Wurren moments ago, and he'd already slipped back into reliving the past few months through his Seer visions.

"Yeah, sorry, I don't mean to be rude. Seeing my old town again distracted me," Marric replied.

Shrell cocked his head, though his face held a smile. His wavy hair now hung down to his shoulders. Apparently, he wasn't in any hurry to cut it.

"No worries, I can' imagine 'avin all tha' 'appen in a short bit o' time." Shrell glanced behind him, sizing up the group that had come with them. "Best keep them eyes dim, though, once we get into town. We don' wanna bring too much attention to us."

Marric nodded, but his thoughts once again drifted to Janis and the others. He couldn't help but wonder how their journeys were going. He knew they had further to go to get to his town, but he knew they hadn't missed the Awakening. The first day or two they'd had to push their horses to the maximum to have the chance of making it.

Just to be sure, Marric eyed his companion apologetically, then allowed his mind to slip into a vision. He opened up his mind's eye and felt his physical eyes stretch open, the blue Light likely filling them.

Shrell sighed next to him.

"An' 'ere 'e goes again. No worries, I like talkin' to myself," Shrell commented.

Marric chuckled and he would have rolled his eyes if he weren't preoccupied.

"I'm just checking up on Janis. Give me a moment."

He turned off his hearing for a moment and allowed his consciousness to materialize next to Janis. She sat atop a horse, looking displeased. All around her were men and women dressed in Evenir clothing. Magness sat regally atop her own horse in front.

"Speak of Ugglyn himself, there they are," Magness said. Her jaw hardened.

Marric shifted his vision gaze forward, following the direction the Evenir leaders looked. There, a few dozen black-clad people stood down the street.

He didn't recognize the place but could only assume it was Stilten, knowing that was where they were headed for their Awakening.

Watchlight is already there? Marric thought.

He did a quick internal check to verify that what he was Seeing was the present.

It was.

A flash of blue to his left startled him. He could feel his physical body far away flinching in surprise.

He watched as a spear of blue Light flew toward Prost, skewering the horse he was riding. The creature crumpled to the ground, its rider almost getting caught beneath it.

"By Lanser's name, Janis! Did you have to just go at it?!" Magness said, clearly as shocked as he was.

Janis didn't answer. Marric's vision eyes trained on her face and all he could see was determination. She dismounted and barreled toward the group of Watchlight men and women.

Magness ordered a Shield raised, and the blue wall sprung up just behind Janis. A red one covered Watchlight at the same moment.

The world spun again, leaving Marric reeling. He didn't want to pull away, but a thought jolted him back to reality.

"Watchlight is there already," he said with no context.

"*Wha*?!" Shrell's head spun right and left as he scanned the town border just ahead.

Nostalgia for the street entrance pushed its way into Marric's chest and he sucked in a breath.

He realized he was trying to cope with coming back to this place by losing himself in visions.

Shaking his head, Marric turned toward Shrell.

"No, Watchlight is already in Stilten. Janis just rushed their group as if it was nothing," he explained.

Shrell relaxed a little, then nodded.

"Let's 'ope they can deal wif 'em right quickly, then. Fer now, we better be ready fer anythin'," Shrell said, narrowing his eyes forward.

Just then, they entered the town border, wooden houses and shops on both sides. After Seeing what he just had, Marric expected black-dressed men and women to appear around them. His memory flashed again to when they'd been trying to leave Wurren months ago and were ambushed by others then. Movement to his right made him jump. He breathed out when he realized it was just a boy running down the street.

Marric scanned the surrounding area, two-story wood buildings on either side. The street wasn't overly populated, given that it wasn't a market day, but there were people about. Despite the impending sunset, Isllan was still far away, so there would be citizens on the streets for longer. The hooves of their horses clacked noisily on the road, the sound echoing off of the close buildings on either side. As they approached, people stared in awe at them and backed away. These people were likely astounded by the horses and the size of the group.

Was that truly so long ago? Marric thought.

Now he was with the men he formerly feared, going to retrieve his friend Crents.

"So 'ow close are yeh to this fellow? Right lucky tha' yeh get to see 'is Awakening 'f 'yeh ask me," Shrell commented.

Marric smiled, thinking about seeing Crents again.

"Crents is like a brother to me. We worked together for so long, and I was stealing money for—" Marric stopped, gritting his teeth.

Shrell perked up at the words.

"Wait, did yeh just say tha'—" Shrell cut off when they heard a scream down the street.

Marric might have blushed at his admission of stealing for Crents and his family, but the high-pitched sound set everyone in motion.

"This way!" Marric shouted, pushing his horse forward toward Crents's home. Normally, Crents would be working at this time, but with Narim gone and the shop burned, Marric wasn't sure the boy had work to be done.

Marric shook his head, not wanting to remember the loss of his home.

Dust sprang up everywhere as the pack of Evenir people pushed their horses forward. More shouts came from the locals as they dove out of the way, Shrell yelling at them to move.

Marric's heart raced, the energy clearing his mind. He didn't remember when he'd gained the ability to focus more in stressful situations, but he was grateful. As the corner approached, Marric yanked on the reins of his horse, causing it to neigh restlessly. The animal reacted and turned sharply to the right.

There, ahead, he saw Crents's home, and a handful of black-cloaked people facing them.

Marric didn't think; instead, he rushed his horse forward and threw his hands outward, scattering the men and women, their bodies glowing blue from his Lightbearing.

"Shrell! Check above!" Marric yelled, pulling his horse to a stop and Conjuring a bow, an arrow already nocked.

"Shield! Watch th' roofs!" Shrell commanded.

A blue translucent Shield appeared above them just as arrows descended from the rooftops, each clattered harmlessly against the surface. Marric could hear shouting from above as they realized they couldn't get their arrows through the Shield.

"This can' be Watchligh', I don' see any red Light. Mus' be th' others, then," Shrell said, pulling his horse up to Marric.

Dread set into Marric's chest at the words.

If they aren't Riln's people, then— Marric thought.

An image of Turrin writhing in pain, dark veins full of poison, forced its way into his mind. Just before he could shout out a warning, more arrows rained from above. Instead of clattering on the Shield, they pierced through, the tips glowing with a silver hue.

Men and women cursed as the arrows struck half a dozen down, the arrows taking them off their horses.

"Take cover! Stay close t' the 'ouses!" Shrell yelled.

The Shield repaired itself, but the Evenir men and women pushed up against the buildings to either side. Without line of sight, the archers couldn't hit them. Still, they tried, the silver-tipped arrows bouncing off the road.

"I need to get in there," Marric said through gritted teeth.

"Mar, yeh can' jus'—"

Before Shrell could continue, Marric jumped from his horse and ran full force at the door to Crents's home. Shrell cursed. Marric hoped his mad rush took their enemy by surprise, keeping his head down as he sprinted.

Many still recovered from his Lightbearing shove moments ago, but a few were up, their eyes trained on him.

To his left, he could see two figures intending to cut off his entry to the house. One of his Light arrows pierced one woman in the chest. Her falling body tripped her companion, whose shout cut short as his face slammed into the ground. Three others approached from the right, but Marric threw his hand out, Moving them into the building behind.

Air whisked past his ear as an arrow almost found its way into his head. Marric gritted his teeth, determined to make it. Without hesitation, he threw his body weight into the door, the wood shattering. Pain erupted in his shoulder from the contact, but he ignored it.

Gasping from exertion, Marric thanked Lanser that the door gave as easily as he'd thought it would.

Shrell and a couple other Lightbearers flew through the opening after him.

"Mar! Yeh can' jus' run off like tha'! If I don' get yeh back to Terris Green safely, Avryn'll kill me right good," Shrell complained. "Not to mention Janis."

Shrell shivered then.

Though he heard the words, Marric ignored them. Adrenaline still coursed through him. The urgency of knowing they hadn't found Crents before the others kept him going.

The front hallway into the home was narrow and long. Wood slats decayed on either side, the structure not well-kept. Sounds of fighting and flashes of blue Light carried on in the street behind them. Marric cautiously walked forward, seeing an empty armchair by the hearth. The red upholstery was torn in numerous places, and it held stains everywhere.

Marric knew this was where Crents's father normally sat. Stuck in his alcoholism, there wasn't a time he remembered Crents's father not sitting there.

Voices further in the home prompted Marric to hurry in that direction. As he rounded the corner, he gasped as he tripped on something heavy on the ground. Tumbling forward, Marric saw the ground rush up to his face, then pain lanced up his wrist.

"Fog it, what the—" Marric said, rolling over to see what he'd tripped on.

His stomach turned.

It was a body. The body of Crents's father.

"Mar, yeh all right?" Shrell whispered, eyeing the corpse.

Marric nodded, then rose quickly. He could still hear the voices in the next room. It sounded like two men were arguing. Then a younger voice pleaded.

That's him, Marric thought.

As they moved closer, Marric could make out the words.

"Just kill him and get out of here! Why are you—"

Crashing from behind made Marric spin. Two figures ran at them, shouting in anger. One of the Evenir companions threw up a Shield, the enemy skittering to a stop just before the barrier.

Shrell cursed at the noise, knowing that they'd be discovered. The door they'd just been about to enter casually opened, the hinges creaking.

"Well, well, here they are now," an evil-looking man said. "Told you they would get here soon."

The man's black hood was back, showing strawberry-blond hair cropped close to his head. His wicked grin sat below a sharp nose and wide eyes.

"Luden did say to take as many of you as we could, so let's get started," he said, holding up his sword.

The hair rose on Marric's neck as he saw the blade laced with the mercuric poison that had almost killed Turrin.

"Shrell, that's what they got Turrin with. The Shield won't work—"

Before he could continue, the two men behind them slashed with their swords, the blades cutting through the blue Shield easily. The Shielder gasped in shock as he was cut down with the sword. Shrell was there at once, slashing swiftly as he killed one of the men. The other engaged him in battle. The woman who had accompanied Marric came and stood next to him, her back straight, a short sword stretched outward.

Marric glanced at her, realizing it was Narinda, one of the Lighters who kept Terris Green lit. Even with her large spectacles and the memory of her poring over a large book, she looked far more imposing than she had the first time Marric met her.

"Give us the boy," she said, her voice firm.

The man chuckled, holding his sword up higher.

"You think we'll just listen to you? No, I think we'll just kill the lot of you," he said.

"Have it your way," Narinda said. She flipped her sword forward, her blade clanging into his. He cursed, not prepared for her speed.

Narinda pushed into the sword, knocking the man off balance. He apparently expected this, as he leaned into it, crouched down, and spun around to face them again.

"A wench with parlor tricks. Lucky me," he said.

Narinda scoffed, then spoke to Marric.

"Get the boy," she said, still looking at the man in front of her.

Marric heard Crents's whimper again in the other room, but he didn't move immediately.

"*Go*," Narinda said, more forcefully.

Marric jumped into motion, pressing himself against the wall, away from the man.

"You won't get him!" the man said, jumping toward Marric. Narinda slid between them and held up her hand. A flash of Light made the man scream in confusion. He backed up against the wall, his hand covering his eyes. The other hand flipped his sword back and forth in a frenzy, causing Marric and Narinda to jump backward.

Instinctively, Marric pushed his hand outward, Moving the man's sword until it smashed into the wall, where it wedged itself. Their assailant cursed, yanking as hard as he could on the sword, to no avail.

A curse from Shrell behind made Marric tense. He pushed both hands out this time, and the man in front of him glowed blue before being slammed into the wall. He fell forward and lay still.

"Help Shrell!" Marric yelled to Narinda, who turned and engaged the black-clad figures there. By now, a few more had shown up. Seeing her short sword parry a few blows from the pursuers, Marric Conjured his bow, aiming the Light-created arrow at one of the figures. His arm held taut, he tried to aim around Narinda and the others' moving forms, but he didn't trust himself to not hit his ally.

For a moment, he stood in awe, watching as the woman who he'd thought was a harmless Lighter fly through the enemies like a storm. Movement to her left made Marric shift his gaze there, where Shrell nursed his arm. Blood trickled from a wound under his sleeve. One of the black-clad figures had slipped past Narinda and was about to drop his sword over Shrell's neck. Before he could, Marric let his arrow fly, the tip piercing through their stomach.

A woman's voice cursed before Shrell thrust his sword upward, finishing her off.

"Go! I can Fix him in a moment," Narinda yelled, her voice masked slightly by the clanging of the swords and the grunting of the fighters.

Nodding resolutely, Marric spun around and pushed through the decaying door. Dark lines ran from the top to the bottom, showing where a leak in the roof must have allowed rainwater to drip.

Marric froze as his eyes adjusted. The Light from his bow illuminated the surrounding area, but it was dark in the room. A slight sound from his right made him tense before his reflexes pushed him to the left. Air whooshed past his ear, followed closely by the thunking of a blade in the door behind him.

Rolling onto his knees, Marric let an arrow fly back to where he came from. It thudded into the wall.

"Blast yeh foggin' Lightbearers. We'll kill the lot of yeh!"

The voice was husky and came from the dark of the room to his left. Squinting his eyes, Marric could barely make out a form in the dim Light from his bow.

"'Elp! Summon 'elp! They'll kill me—" Crents's voice was muffled by something being shoved over his mouth.

Marric heard heavy breathing to his front right, but Crents's voice had come from the left. That meant—

Stinging pain erupted in Marric's side as a knife sliced through his tunic and cut open his flesh.

Cursing, he shot another arrow right at the first person who attacked him, causing the man to yell and duck out of the way.

"Git 'im, yeh idiot! The poison will kill 'em all!"

The poison— Marric's stomach rolled, images of the thick veins on Turrin's legs forcing into his mind once more.

"'E's a crafty git! I'm tryin'!"

Marric launched a few arrows toward the right again. A squelching sound was followed by a howl of pain. His body was sweating profusely, and the musty smell of the room overwhelmed him. Another knife flew from the darkness, this one just between his legs. Gasping, Marric dropped his bow, plunging the room into darkness once more.

"Think yeh can hide, huh?" the voice from the left growled.

The sounds of the man he struck with his knife disappeared as the man died. Marric stood there, afraid to move for fear they would hear him. Crents screamed, his voice muffled by what sounded like cloth over his mouth.

Reaching right, Marric imagined the hilt of the short sword he'd tried to fight with at Terris Green. He knew his skill wasn't great, but he also knew he couldn't use his Conjured bow. He could guess the size of the room only by how far away Crents's crying was. The whimpering came from the floor, perhaps ten paces in front of him. Marric couldn't tell if the man was still there, but he knew he had to act fast.

Knowing the man's eyes would adjust soon, Marric sucked in a deep breath and jumped forward. Just before he got to where Crents was, he summoned a ball of Light, putting everything he could into it to make it bright.

The ball itself was small, only the size of his thumbnail, but in the dimness of the room, it made him squint. A man shouted from his right, and Marric tossed the Light that way. He swung his arm, Conjuring a short sword while he moved. The blade whisked in the air, but the man was too far away.

Turning his body, Marric dropped his sword and Conjured his bow, an arrow already nocked. Just as he let his arrow fly, he felt a sharp pain in his upper leg as a knife slid inward.

His arrow flew true, however, piercing the man's chest. He fell to the ground, lifeless.

Gasping in pain, Marric reached down and looked at the knife sticking from his leg. His stomach turned as the red blood bubbled from the wound. Gritting his teeth, he yanked it out. The pain made his vision blur and his Conjured weapons had snuffed out, but his Light ball remained, giving him just enough visibility to work. Placing his hand over his leg, he focused, trying not to pass out.

A slight blue glow pulsed under his palm. Though the pain didn't subside, the bleeding did. Marric moved his hand to inspect the wound, fearing the worst. He sighed in relief when he saw no signs of poison.

Fighting continued out in the hallway, blue Light flashing here and there. Marric could hear Narinda and Shrell shouting to each other between the flashes.

Marric thought for a moment to go out and help them, but Crents's muffled scream reminded him of their goal. He crawled over to where he could see his friend cowering on the ground. Adrenaline still coursed through his veins, and he breathed hard, trying to ward off the pain of the internal bleeding that remained.

"Crents, are you ok?" Marric said through his haggard breaths.

His friend stared at him, confused.

Crents said something that sounded like his name, but Marric couldn't be sure. He reached for his sword and realized he, like other Conjurers, didn't carry a steel sword.

"Foggin' Light, can you just come over here?" Marric said, mostly to himself.

When the Light ball didn't move, Marric just let it snuff into nothing, awarding him with another small squeal from his friend. He held up his hand again, another ball forming there.

Marric's body was getting cold, but he didn't know if it was from the blood loss or from coming off the intense fight. It felt strange, considering that the air was still and stuffy, the heat from the day caught inside. He gritted his teeth, wondering why this room didn't have a window.

"Don't panic. It's me, Marric. I'm going to do something that might seem scary, but I won't hurt you," he said.

Crents nodded, though Marric knew his words were ironic considering what his friend must be thinking about what he'd just seen.

Marric focused again and Conjured a dagger. As he moved it closer to his friend, Crents flinched.

"I won't hurt you, just—" Marric slipped the dagger along the cloth covering Crents's mouth and pushed upward. As the cloth fell away, Crents started speaking.

"They jus' came in 'ere an' grabbed me. My da', is 'e aight? Wha' is 'appenin'?"

Just before Marric could answer, the door behind them slammed open, someone breathing hard.

"Watchligh' is 'ere! We need t'get outta 'ere *now*," Shrell said.

Marric was relieved to see his friend standing there. His arm didn't look injured at all. As if to confirm his words, flashes of red Light illuminated Shrell's form.

"Ah, Mar, yeh're all hurt. Narinda will 'ave to fix yeh up, come on!"

Shrell gestured to the two boys. Crents looked back and forth between Marric and Shrell, fear clear on his face.

"We can trust him, we just need to get out of here before we're caught. I'll have to explain later, but you—" Marric was saying when Crents fell to the ground.

Oh no, Marric thought.

Shrell's eyes widened, and he shouted for Marric to back away. Everything slowed down then. Even though he knew what was happening, his stomach clenched in terror. Turning sharply, Marric tried to run through the door. Shrell held out his hand, trying to reach him. Before he could grab the hand, a force of blue Light slammed into his back.

Marric smashed into Shrell, who also was thrown backward. The two hit the wall outside of the room and crumpled to the ground. Pain erupted in Marric's head and on his right shoulder. Shrell groaned on the ground next to him.

Knowing it was coming again, Marric Moved the door, which had been blown off the hinges, and positioned it in front of them. Another blast of force hit the object, and it flew toward them. Marric pushed outward to keep it from connecting.

A third blast of the power rocked the walls of the house, one of the inner walls breaking outward, the wood splintering.

Dust thickened the surrounding air. Splintered wood covered both Marric and Shrell everywhere.

It took each of them a few moments to get their bearings. There wasn't anyone else in the room, except for the bodies of the men they'd fought just before. Marric could hear Narinda shouting from down the hall, where she must have retreated when Crents Awakened.

"Mar, yeh all right?" Shrell asked before trying to stand. He groaned in pain.

"I'm fine, but Crents—" Marric couldn't see or hear his friend. He stood, pain lancing down his arm. He felt his shoulder and realized it had been dislocated in the blow.

Marric pushed back into the room and found Crents unconscious on the floor. Kneeling by the boy, Marric summoned his ball of light once more. He sighed in relief when he could see the boy's chest rising and falling.

"Oh, fog it," Shrell cried out behind him. Marric turned to see a sword through Shrell's chest, the metal of the blade writhing with a mercuric liquid.

Marric heard himself scream, the sound inhuman and full of grief. Shrell fell to his knees, the blade sliding out of him. Behind him stood the man Marric had Moved into the wall.

Rage filled him, and Marric pushed outward with all his might. The man's eyes widened as he was thrown backward, crashing into the wall. Without hesitation, Marric Conjured his bow and shot an arrow into the fallen man's back.

He lay still.

Marric fell to his knees, tears streaming. He could hear himself yelling for help, but he sounded muffled, even to himself. Narinda appeared, worry in her eyes. She looked rough, having been engaged in battle herself.

They both watched, hopeless, as Shrell stopped moving.

ALSO BY DAN KENNER

www.dankenner.com/books

Epic Fantasy

Shielded: A Prequel to The Lightbearer Chronicles - Get the Ebook **FREE** at www.dankenner.com/free

Awakened: The Lightbearer Chronicles Book One

Transformed: The Lightbearer Chronicles Book Two

Ascended: The Lightbearer Chronicles Book Three

Young Adult

Sunfire

Middle Grade

The Search for Silence

A Voice in The Noise

The Thundering Echo

ACKNOWLEDGMENTS

I want to thank my amazing wife for all of her support during my writing and editing of this book. She has always been my number one fan, even when I had to spend late nights and early mornings working on writing and editing.

Thank you as well to my awesome editor, Rachel Harris. I am grateful that I found someone with excellent skills and insight that I can rely on to polish not only this book, but all my future books.

Also, thank you to my wonderful kiddos and the love that they have for reading. It always inspires me to build worlds and write amazing stories that someday they can enjoy.

Lastly, I wanted to thank my Heavenly Father for his continual blessings to me and my family.

ABOUT THE AUTHOR

Dan lives in rural Idaho where he happily lives with his wife, six children and numerous goats, chickens and a cat named Wilma. Aside from writing, which he'd happily do full time, Dan spends most of his time outside in the homestead he built with his wife. When he's not writing, he spends his time with his nose in a fantasy or sci-fi book.

You can connect with me at https://www.dankenner.com